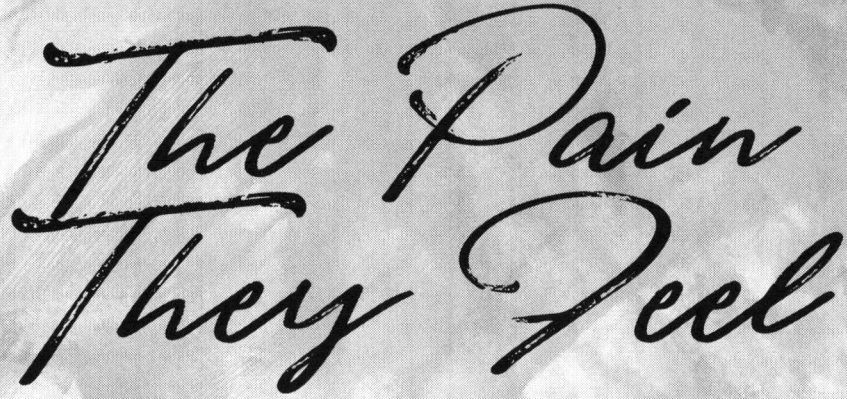

The Pain They Feel

BOOK 1 - THE PAIN SERIES

LYNDA THROSBY

Cover photograph by Stuart Reardon @Stuart Reardon Productions
Featuring Stuart Reardon
Cover design by Sybil @Popkitty
Formatted by Champagne Book Design

ISBN: 978-1-9993150-6-1
Lynda Throsby Publishing
Email ljtpublishing@gmail.com

Warning

This book is not intended for anyone under the age of 18.

This is for adult reading only and contains counts of violence and sexual content.

To everyone that picks up one of my books to read.
Thank you.

The Pain They Feel

Much love
Lynda
xx

PART I

Blaine

One

Blaine—Age 10

I'M STANDING ON THE SIDE OF THE ROAD, THERE IS NO SIDEWALK here, it's up in the hills of LA. They don't have sidewalks up here, just little tracks that people have formed over the years walking along the grass verge. I've just been playing with a bird. Well, I call it playing, it's dead now. I've just thrown its dismembered body into the road to watch a car or truck run over it. I stand, thinking what it would be like for a person to suffer, what pain would they feel?. I don't feel any pain, my mama says I'm not right in the head, she calls me a retard, a freak. What does she know?

My earliest memory, I was about five years old. I was in the back yard playing on the grass with my cars and a bug climbed onto my leg. I watched it scurry around, making its way up my leg. I don't know what it was, but it was like a beetle. I stayed so still, watching it, fascinated by it. As it got closer, I lifted my hand very slowly so as not to scare it and I let it crawl into my palm. I brought my hand up to my face to look at it closer. It was black and it had a pair of antennae and six legs. I pinched it between my fingers and turned it over so I could see its belly. One by one, I pulled its legs off, watching it squirm in my pinched fingers. Then I pulled each of its antennae off. It was now just a little black blob with no legs or anything protruding from it. It couldn't squirm now, but it was still alive. I was fascinated by it. How it was still alive and probably screaming in its little beetle language. I put it to my ear to see if I could hear any noise from it. There was nothing. I remember being disappointed. I wanted to hear it scream in agony. I wanted to *see* its agony. My mama startled me, shouting my name, I threw it on the grass and left it there to die and went to see what Mama wanted.

A little while later, after my lunch, I went back out to the yard. I looked for the beetle to see if it was still alive. I found it, right where I left it, but I couldn't tell if it was alive or dead. I remember thinking this was stupid, I need to find something else I could do this to, but it needed to be something where I could tell if it was still alive or dead afterward. I threw the beetle back on the grass and rolled my toy cars over it a few times. I think I splattered it some.

A few months later, I was in the park with my mama and papa. We had been on the swings and now I was on the grass and they were on a bench talking and watching me. I had moved away from them a little bit, but they could still see me. I was sitting near some bushes when I heard a rustle. I watched and I could make out a little bird, it looked like a baby. There was a tree above, so maybe it fell out of the tree. It was chirping away, very annoyingly, at me. I grabbed hold of it and held it in my hands. Still chirping, I held it close to my face. I examined it closely, it was very ugly and mostly bald. I turned my back so my mama and papa couldn't see what I was doing, and I started to squeeze the little bird tight in my hands. I only had little hands, but I was still hurting it, I think. It was still chirping as I was squeezing, its little eyes bulging and its beak open.

I looked around at my mama to see if she was watching me but she was just talking to my papa, holding his hands, but she looked sad. My papa looked a bit sad as well, with his head down, looking at their hands. I turned my attention back to the bird. I pinched its beak together to stop it chirping because I didn't want my mama or papa to come over. I squeezed it tight. Then I looked at its legs and started to play with them, they were like sticks, with little claws on the end. I snapped one, it was an accident, then I snapped the other, on purpose. I still had its beak shut and was squeezing. I was wondering how long it would live like this. I lifted a wing, it was so tiny and horrible to touch with the odd little feathers trying to grow. I started to take out the rest of its little feathers that were sticking out. Pulling them out one by one. I was purposely hurting this little bird, but I was fascinated by it. I wanted to know what it would do. I then squeezed its tiny neck, putting more and more pressure on it. I put its face right up to mine so I could see what happened as I squeezed. I let go of its beak, there was no chirping now as I squeezed, its little bulging eyes started to pop out of its head. One by one, they popped right out as I squeezed as hard as my little hands would let me. It went limp in my hand. I stopped squeezing and its head flopped backward. It was dead. I killed it, but I didn't care.

My mama called me and I looked around, she was just starting to walk toward me. My papa wasn't there. He was gone. I threw the little bird into the bushes just before she reached me.

My papa had left my mama that day in the park. I don't know if it was something I had done but my mama was angry with me for a long time and she was very sad. I heard her crying all the time in her bedroom. She didn't bother with me, just leaving me to do what I wanted. I ended up burning myself because I used to play with the matches she had laying around. I liked to try to burn any insects I could find in the yard. I liked to watch them squirm as I held the match to them.

One time I had caught another of those black beetles and I wanted to see it squirm as I put the lit match to it. I leaned in really close to examine it, only I was a little bit too close and my hair caught on fire. I went into a panic, trying to put it out with my hands, and burned them, but I didn't feel a thing. I ran into the house and shouted for my mama, I just stood there with my head in flames as she came sauntering into the kitchen. She screamed and grabbed a towel, soaked it in water and threw it on my head. I felt nothing. No pain, but I remember being a little excited at burning my hair and flesh, I liked the smell of it. I could see the flesh on my hand was all wrinkly and blistering and I started to play with it. My mama screamed at me to leave it alone. She was shouting all kinds of stuff at me 'about not being normal, no wonder your father left us. He was right, there is something wrong with you. It's all your fault, you little retard shit.'

It was me. I was the reason he left, but I was confused as to why. What had I done wrong?

I've been standing here on the side of this road for ages now. Some cars have gone past but no trucks yet and no one has run over the bird. I sit for a bit, I'm tired and thirsty. I should have brought some water with me but I didn't think about it as I stormed out of the house after my mama was laying into me, yet again. She found me in the kitchen with another bird. I set a net up to catch birds, bats or anything that flies, and some traps to catch squirrels or whatever else gets caught in there. I then like to dissect them alive and see how each one squirms, wondering what they are feeling.

I sit here just waiting for the bird to get squashed, but also I don't want to go back home, I'm thinking about what things must feel like. I don't feel anything, meaning any actual pain. My mama must be right, there is something wrong with me. I wonder if I was to get hit by something big like a car, would I feel anything then? I wonder what people actually feel. I think that's why I do this with animals, to see how they react. I think, what if I could do this with a person? Would I be allowed to do that? Would Mama get upset? Maybe if I tried it on her first? Maybe I could cut a finger off or a toe, but no, she would just lay into me like normal, screaming and shouting at me.

I look up as I hear a truck coming down the road. The first one today. Please go over the bird, please go over the bird, I want to see it get squashed. Just then I hear a rustling from the trees behind me and I turn to see what's making the trees move. The truck barrels past me so fast, all the dust spews into my face and I start choking and coughing from it.

The rustle has stopped. I stop coughing and stay still, I want to see what it is, my mama is always saying be careful when I'm out and about because there are mountain lions and bears. Where we live is in the middle of nowhere, there are no other houses for a long way away from us, we are just surrounded by forests. We didn't always live here, I remember when my papa lived with us we lived in a place with lots of houses and lots of shops and people around us. Then not long after that, we moved here, to nowhere. My mama said it was her cabin, that her mama had left it to her. I remember it being a mess when we got here. The windows were broken, there were floorboards missing, and weeds growing everywhere, even inside the house. She said it was all we could afford now Papa that had gone, and it was all my fault.

The rustling starts again. I turn so I can watch to see what it is. I want it to be a mountain lion, I would like to see one. I see ears appear then I watch as a deer walks out very gingerly, listening as it does. I don't move. I want to see it up close. I wonder if I could catch it? I hear a car approaching. I watch the deer as it's trying to figure out the noise. The car gets closer and the deer starts to panic, I see its nostrils flaring, I still don't move. The car gets closer still, and the deer startles and doesn't know which way to go, so he dives forward, straight into the road and right in front of the car. The car tries to swerve to avoid it, but it catches the back of the deer. It still runs off on the other side of the road and the car skids but doesn't stop. It just keeps going. Wow, that was so much fun, I got so excited, I wanted the deer to go through the window and for the car to crash so I could see what happens. That gives me an idea.

I sit for a little while playing in the dirt, I can do this, but what if it hits me? What if I go through the window and it kills me? I let a few cars go past, then I slowly get up. I wait for the next car, I'm going to do it. I'm going to see what happens. I feel funny, I've never felt anything before and it's strange, I feel strange. I don't know what it is but I kind of like it. I can feel my heart pounding faster and faster as the next car approaches. I see it coming over the top of the hill, there's nothing else around, just this one car and me. I'm clenching my fists, I feel my heart beating out of my chest, this is it. Just as the car gets closer to me I step out, right in its path. What happens next happens so fast but in slow motion all at the same time.

I stand and turn my head to look straight into the eyes of the driver. I see his eyes go wide. I see him grip the steering wheel and push himself back in his seat. I see him move his arms quickly, turning the steering wheel. I see the lady sitting next to him, her mouth opening wide to scream, her eyes popping out of her head and her hands flying to the roof of the car for support. I don't hear the screams, all I can hear is the screeching of the car as the man tries to stop it from hitting me. I just stand, watching it play out. The car misses me, only just. I feel the whoosh from it passing me so close, I feel the breeze on my face, it's that close. He managed to turn it just in time, in doing so, the car flips, it rolls and rolls on the road for a little bit, glass is flying everywhere, each turn I hear cracks, and crunching and scraping, the metal of the car being obliterated, and on each turn, the car gets more and more damaged, like it's being squashed by a giant's hand. I hear screaming now. I just stand, watching it roll and roll, it rolls over the other side of the road and down the embankment into the forest. It disappears from my view but I hear a loud crash and the screaming stops. I suddenly feel deaf because there is no noise now.

WOW. My heart is beating like it's trying to get out of my chest, I look down at my dirty gray t-shirt and I can see it moving where my heart is. I notice I'm digging my nails into the palms of my hand. That was amazing.

I kick into action, and I run over to where the car disappeared. I see it down the embankment against a tree. I see smoke coming from it and a wheel is still turning. It's on its roof. I start clambering down toward it quickly, slipping as I do, all the dirt is being kicked up from me skidding down. I stop at the car and fall to my hands and knees to look inside. I don't want to miss anything if they are still alive. I want to see the look in their eyes. I crouch down to look inside. I'm at the side where the lady was. She's not moving, her body is all twisted, her head is at a funny angle, there's a lot of blood coming from her mouth and her nose, her eyes are open but they are lifeless. Her arms are at funny angles, they must be broken. I think her neck is broken as well. I look past her and I see the man is also in a funny position, he's facing the other way. I get up and scurry around to his side so I can see his face, I'm getting no joy here. I'm getting angry because if he's dead, it will have all been for nothing.

I bend to look in. He's not dead. He blinks when he sees me. He tries to say something, but I don't know what he's saying. It's all a gurgle, with blood being spewed out as he tries to speak. I see lots of blood from his head as well. I get on my hands and knees so I can get closer to him. I see in his eyes there is so much fear, he blinks again then opens his mouth. I hear him ask, "Why?"

I just shrug but don't speak. He coughs, blood splattering everywhere and I can see he's in a lot of pain. This is so much better than with the birds or bugs. I can see the terror here, and hear it. My heart is still beating fast, I hear another sound but it's not from him. I look past him and there's someone in the back of the car. I didn't realize anyone else was in it. The man looks at me again and I just about hear him say 'help her.' I look past him again. I can just make out someone in pink. I can't see properly from this side, the tree is blocking the rear door, I need to get back around the other side. I get up and run around quickly. I crouch down at the rear door and I see a girl in there. She's awake, there is no blood, she looks fine, how can that be?

I drop to my knees. I want to get closer. I get on my belly and crawl in because the car is so squashed. I see the look of terror on her face. I don't know how old she is, but she looks younger than me. She has blonde hair, it's in those pigtails with big pink ribbons, but they are all dirty now. She's not crying. Why? She's being held in by her seatbelt upside down, she's clinging to a doll, holding it tight to her chest, and she's just staring at me.

"Hey, you okay?" I ask, but she doesn't answer.

Maybe she can't speak. She does look a few years younger close up. Maybe she's five or six, but how can she not be hurt? I don't get it. She hasn't said anything yet, she's just staring at me with the biggest, bluest eyes I have ever seen. I hear the man trying to speak again, but I don't know what he's saying. I look to her then look in his direction. She's not suffering, and I don't want to miss him suffering, so I back out of the car and run around to him. It was more interesting watching him.

I drop to my knees again and crawl in as far as I can, to get as close to him as I can. I want to see the fear in his eyes. I want to try to understand the pain he is suffering. He opens his eyes as he hears me. I see the light is leaving them. He's going to die, I want him to tell me how it feels.

"Hey mister, are you scared?"

He looks me straight in the eyes. "Help us," he whispers. He struggled with getting that out, I need to know how it feels, now.

"What's the pain like? Are you scared because you're dying? Tell me what you're thinking, mister."

I don't think he understands me. He's looking at me like Mama does when I ask her questions.

"Help us," he splutters again.

"Tell me how it feels. I need to know, the birds and bugs can't tell me. You can speak, TELL ME!" I shout in his face.

He squirms, trying to back into the seat. He's resting on the roof of the car. Looking at him, his body is being crushed by the steering wheel, it's nearly buried into his chest, that must have done some damage to him, maybe his organs are all damaged. He's looking at me like I'm insane.

"Get help," he whispers, trying to take a breath between words.

Is he crazy? There's no help around here unless a car sees us and stops. I don't have a cell, my mama used to have one of those. Oh, wait, maybe he has a cell. I try to reach into his pockets, but there's not much room. I feel his phone and managed to pry it from his pocket. It's cracked, probably no good, but I'll keep it anyway.

"Get… help," he says again, taking a breath between each word.

I look at him and think for a minute. "Only if you tell me what you're thinking and how it feels. I want to know what the pain feels like. Are you scared of dying? Is it terrifying you?"

He tries to turn his head slightly toward the back seat.

Ah, right. "Answer me and I'll get her out and get some help."

I can see the stunned expression on his face. "Is she alive?"

I nod. "She's fine, not a scratch on her. How weird is that, mister?"

He sighs with relief. He tries to turn his head in the direction of the back seat. "Primrose, y… you okay…" He can't get his words out. He's struggling to breathe and he can't move, so I don't know why he's trying.

"Answer my questions while you still can, mister, or I leave her to die here."

He looks into my eyes. "Hurts so b… bad, scar… scared."

"Come on, that's nothing. Tell me or all this would have been for nothing."

His eyes fly open wide. His face is full of blood, but I can tell he's angry with me.

"Why? You mean… meant to do thi…?"

I nod at him and give him my biggest smile. My achievement smile. "Tell me more."

"Scared for my fam…"

This is going to take too long, I pull back out of the car and sit on the ground cross-legged. I can still see his face from here. "Tell me, mister, or I will just sit here and watch you die and leave her. The lady's already dead."

I nod behind him, and I shrug. I see tears at the corner of his eyes and they roll down into his hair. I get closer again. I want to watch. "Tell me. I've got all day to wait for you to die."

"I'm scared, can't brea… I don't want to di… I want my fami… safe, I want to liv… I'm so scared."

His breaths are getting harder between his words and they are barely a whisper, but I want to know more.

"Pappy."

I jump as the little girl speaks behind him. I look to her and see the terror in her eyes as she registers me. I think she's only just realizing what's happening.

She starts to cry. "Pappy, Mama."

I see tears forcing themselves out of his swollen clenched eyes.

"Pappy, Pappy."

She sounds funny and I just stare at her and she stares right back at me, it's like we have some kind of connection. It's strange, she's not scared of me.

I put my finger to my mouth. "Ssshhh," I say to quiet her.

I turn my attention back to him. He's opened his eyes and is watching me. His breathing is getting shallower. "Tell me what the pain is like. Describe it to me." I say this very calmly to him, I know he doesn't have long left, so staying calm and not losing it with him will maybe put him more at ease. He closes his eyes for a second. I'm watching closely, I move in closer, then he opens them and looks me straight in the eye.

"It's like eve… breath is someo… with a hand squeezi… squeezing my lungs… hard, twisting them… each time get… more painful." He closes his eyes again while trying to take a breath and winces.

"Tell me more," I demand, making him startle at my voice.

He winces again. So much for staying calm.

"Never… felt pain… like this before. My bod… feels like… it's on fire, but I'm so… cold. My chest is… burnin…" He stops again and closes his eyes.

I try to see if his chest is moving, but I can't tell, I need to get closer. I move in, as close as I can squeeze into the small space, I need to feel if he's still breathing. I reach to his mouth to see if I can feel the breath, but I don't, I start to panic, is he dead already? I reach for his nose and I sigh with relief, he is breathing.

He feels me close to him and half-opens his eyes.

"Tell me more or she gets it," I whisper, diverting my eyes behind him.

I look back at him and see the panic. I smile and run my finger along his cheek, there's a big cut running down it and it's wide open, it looks nasty and deep. He flinches at my touch, but I continue on. I want to see his fear. I want to try to understand the pain. I start to push my finger into the gash. It's not hard, it's all soft and squishy. He squeezes his eyes shut and tries to take in a sharp breath as my finger goes deeper inside. I add another finger. The blood is pouring out of it now even more and running down my fingers to my hand and arm. I watch it flowing like the creek I sometimes go to. I lean in and stick the tip of my tongue on the little trickle of blood. It tastes weird, I don't know the taste, I've never tasted blood before but it's not a bad taste, just weird. I start to wiggle my fingers inside his gash, spreading it open even more.

Suddenly he screams out. I must be hurting him and it's making me happy, at least I think it's happiness I'm feeling. I'm smiling at the anguish on his face. I'm enjoying this far too much. I start to spread my two fingers wider, to open it up even farther so I can see inside more. I see the flesh is all gooey, and what looks like it might be bone. I scrape my nail along and it's hard, it must be the bone in his cheek, wow. I remove my fingers and start to pick at the gooey flesh, pulling it away from him then letting it go, watching it slowly retract back. I pull it again, only this time I pull harder with my fingers and thumb. He screams out as I pull and pull and I watch the flesh tear away from his face. It's a big chunk, I'm gonna keep this for later.

He has tears coming out of his swollen eyes and they're running down his face. He looks at me. "Why, why are yo… doin'… this? Help us. Help Prim… Prim… please help Primrose."

I look to her and I see she's crying, but silently. She looks afraid, but not of me. She smiles at me. I find this strange. Can't she hear what I'm doing to her father? She can hear him cry out, so why is she smiling at me? I tilt my head to the side, trying to understand her. I smile back. She wipes the tears away with her fingers. She watches me closely, her big blue eyes fascinate me, and her hair is blonder than I've ever seen. I stare, trying to figure out how old she is. To be honest, I have no idea. I'm ten, that's the only age I know. I don't spend any time with any other kids. She has to be a bit younger than me but her pigtails make her look even younger, I think. Maybe she's eight or something. I think she is older than six now that I've looked at her closely.

Just then he takes in a sharp breath. I turn my attention back to him. Stupid me, paying attention to her when she isn't suffering. Now I've wasted that time. I watch closely to see if he breathes out. Shit. No. I prod his cheek where the gash is, but he doesn't move. He has one eye open, the other is closed permanently, I think because of the swelling, but his eye isn't moving, it's dull, there is no light in it now. Shit. I poke his cheek harder, putting my fingers back in his gash, but there's nothing. No response. Fuck. He's dead. He died on me, the fucker, and I wanted to know more. I wanted to hear him tell me more, to try and understand.

Now I'm angry, really angry and pissed off. It's her fault I missed the last few minutes. She distracted me. I missed the very second he died. I missed it because of her. I crawl out of the space flat on my belly until I'm far enough out that I can stand up. I head around to her side of the car and I try and yank the door open but it's stuck. The window is not there anymore, in fact, there are no windows on the car now, they all blew out as it rolled down the embankment. I want to get her out and see if I can make her suffer a bit and maybe she can tell me what it feels like, maybe I can torture her.

Yeah, what a fantastic idea. I'm a fucking ten-year-old genius.

I crawl inside where the window was and I watch those blue eyes follow my every move. I search for the fastener on the seatbelt to see if I can release it. She doesn't speak, she doesn't move, apart from her head to watch me. I stop and stare into those eyes. They mesmerize me. I've never seen eyes like them. I fumble with the catch and I finally release the belt. She falls on her head to the roof of the car. I try to break her fall, but it's so tight in this space. She lands awkwardly, but she doesn't make a sound. She wriggles and falls away from me in the opposite direction, but when she looks toward me, I see blood on her face. I move my hand to her forehead to wipe it away. She flinches at my touch. It's just a small cut, nothing bad. She starts to move and tries to crawl toward me. I grab her arms and start to pull her in my direction as I wriggle out of the car. I suddenly notice there are flames at the front of the car. I know we need to get away and quick. I pull her hard. I start to panic and all the anger has now vanished. I just need to get her out. I want her safe. I don't want her to die.

I suddenly stop moving. Did I just think that? I do want her to die. I do want to see her in pain, don't I? I hear the crackle of flames and I yank her out hard. She's out and I pull her up and make her run with me. We run far away from the car and then start to head up the embankment.

"Go, go up there," I say, pointing up toward the road, shooing her in that direction. I fall, she looks back at me. "Run, Primrose, run," I scream at her, gesturing with my hands.

I know I've done something to my leg, I can see blood, I try to get up, but it's no use, my leg won't move. I watch her scramble up the embankment. She stumbles a few times, but just as she reaches the top, it all goes black.

Two

Blaine—Age 14

"BLAINE, BLAINE, WHERE ARE YOU? I NEED YOU."

When doesn't she need me? My mother is the bane of my life, I wish she would die. I wish she would just leave me the fuck alone. Doesn't she know by now not to harass me? It's the same every day.

'Blaine, go get me this from the store, go chop some wood, go get some water, where's my food? Where's my drink? I need to pee.'

On and on while she sits on her fat ass all day doing nothing. My mama used to be a real slender woman, but she has just let herself go over the years and now she is so heavy that I have to help her most of the time to get around the place. The bed even collapsed one time when I helped her onto it. She ended up sleeping on the couch all the time because she couldn't get up and down off the floor.

I learned how to use tools with having to go chop wood a lot, so I made a bed frame out of some trees down by the creek and put her mattress on it. I made it higher than her last bed frame so she could get in and out easier.

She loved it, I saw the surprise and joy on her face but all she said to me was, "About time, you lazy fuck, that couch has been killing my back."

The ungrateful bitch. It's so remote where we are, we don't have electricity and we don't have water, which is why she is always telling me to fetch water from the stream. We have a log burner as it gets so cold up in the hills during the winter, and I use it to heat water to help wash Mama and myself, yet in the summer, it's hot as hell and you sweat as soon as you step out. We don't have AC because we don't have electricity. This place stinks like shit in the summer and I hate living here but at the same time, I love the solitude of it. I barely remember living in the suburbs with my mama and papa before he left us.

I've never had much to do with anyone else with living here. It's so isolated and it takes me an hour to walk to the nearest store. I took a bike that was just lying outside the store one day and I rode home in record time. It made life a bit easier with the bike. It also meant I could wander farther away from home and still be back before she missed me. It also made it easier for me to steal clothes from back yards, I was desperate, nothing fit me anymore, I was growing so fast. With the bike it meant I had a quick getaway. I used to ride and ride, loving the freedom. It's been my way to escape her, and I think without that bike, I would have done something to her by now.

She's been at me again this morning telling me how useless I am and what a fucking retard I am. I just need to get away from her. I grab my bike and head out to a school I came across about two weeks ago when I rode into a town, I don't know what the town's called, I can't read. I remember throwing my bike down and standing at the school fence watching. It was older kids, maybe my age and older. I have never been to a school, my mama says I'm too thick for school and they wouldn't be able to teach me anything, plus I'm not normal. I've been back here every day since I found it. I'm fascinated by it and all these kids. I've never seen so many people before.

There's no one around as I arrive, but I'm earlier than usual. Just then a bell sounds and they are like ants all marching and running out of the buildings and pile out onto the field or sit on the seats around the field. I stand watching, fascinated by them all, there are so many to watch, my head moves back and forth and my eyes are darting all over the place. There are little huddles of girls eating and whispering and pointing at the groups of boys. Some groups are quiet and don't say too much, but others are so loud. Some of the boys are throwing a ball around in the football stands. Suddenly someone speaks to me and I snap my head around to see who it is. I was so engrossed by everything, I didn't hear anyone come up behind me.

"Hey, what the fuck are you doing peeping at all the girls, you pervert?"

I turn around to face the voice. There are about six older boys standing surrounding me. I look to each of them but I don't speak. One of them approaches me and pushes me back against the fence. I don't fall to the ground but fall into the fence. Another one grabs my t-shirt and pulls me forward. He drags me away from the fence and the others surround me. They start to push me from one to the other as they form a circle around me. I still don't speak. One of them grabs my shoulder and spins me around to him.

"I said, what the fuck you doin' peeping on the girls, you fucking pussy?"

I just look at him and cock my head to the side trying to gauge him, he's afraid, he doesn't know me or how I will act but he has his friends to back him up if I attack, he's also afraid they will think he's the pussy for not doing anything. I smile at him, that just pisses him off and he punches me in the face. My head snaps back from the force of the punch and I fall backward, but I don't hit the ground as two of them stop me from falling by grabbing my arms. They hold on to me tight, the rest of them start to goad the one who punched me to do it again. He does. Hard, again and again. My head just keeps snapping back with each punch but because I don't feel any pain, I just smile with every punch. I hear my nose break after about the fourth punch and I feel the blood trickle down and into my mouth.

It's then I remember the car wreck and Primrose. It's the taste of the blood. I remember tasting her papa's blood on my hand when I licked it to see what it was like. But it's her eyes I remember and I'm smiling.

"What the fuck is wrong with you? You crazy son of a bitch."

I'm pushed to my knees, then I'm kicked in the chest and I fall back onto the ground. Then I'm being kicked repeatedly by many feet. I just lay there doing and saying nothing.

"Stop this now. Jenson, Taylor, Dwayne, Conrad, to my office immediately."

I hear the footsteps getting farther away from me, and I just lay there with a picture of the bluest eyes in my head. I must have looked like a retard to them, smiling while they kicked the shit out of me. I feel two sets of hands help me up, my eyes are closed so I don't know who it is but the kicks have stopped now. I stand and slowly open my eyes. I look to each of the men's that have hold of me. I turn to each of them with half-open eyes. They must be swollen, but I can't tell. That reminds me of Primrose's dad and his swollen eyes. I don't remember if his were the same color as Primrose's.

"Are you okay, son? Why are you not in school? Let's get you to the hospital. You have some nasty injuries there," one of them is saying to me.

Shit. I need to get away from here. I don't want them calling anyone.

"Come on, son, come with us."

I look at them both in turn. They don't have my arms now. I nod, hoping they will leave.

"Can you walk? Do you need me to get an ambulance for you?"

I nod again, hoping this will make them walk away to get help. It doesn't.

One of them walks off to the side and starts talking, to whom I have no idea, he's on his own. The other one stands with me. He hasn't spoken yet. I look around to see where my bike is, to see if I can make a move for it and ride away from here. I still haven't spoken to them. The only person I ever speak to is my mama. I don't want everyone to call me a retard like she does. The other one talking turns to look at me and he gestures to the other man who moves over to him. That's exactly what I need. I edge toward my bike slowly, trying not to make a noise so they don't turn around to look at me. I pick the bike up as quietly as I can, luckily it's a bit away from where they have moved to talk. They are talking to each other. I can't make sense of what they are saying. As fast as I can, I jump onto my bike and I ride in the opposite direction from where they are standing so they can't grab me.

I ride and ride with no idea where I'm going. I just need to get away from them. I head in the direction of the hills eventually and find my way home much later than I wanted to. I know she will have a fit when I get there and I can't be dealing with her fucking shit right now. I head to the creek first to clean my face. I know it will be a mess with the blood and my eyes are half-shut from the swelling. I need to try and avoid her as much as I can and just pass her what she needs from behind.

"Where the fuck have you been? I've been dying of thirst sitting here, you lazy fuck. Get me some water and make me something to eat. I could die here waiting for you."

I wish she fucking would. I fetch her some water and fix a sandwich for her, then I go to my room to think. She didn't see the state I'm in, so I head to the bathroom first to look in the mirror. What I see staring back at me does not resemble me at all. I touch my eyes. They are huge, all puffy and swollen, I'm used to seeing green eyes staring back at me. I prod and push at the puffiness, I don't feel anything. I can feel the pressure of touching, but no pain. My nose is bent to the right slightly. There is dried blood in my nostrils so I press one nostril at a time and blow out the open one to release what I can. I then get some toilet tissue and blow as much of the dried blood out as I can. My nose feels weird to the touch, weird in the way it's not straight now. I try to straighten it as much as I can, I hear it click in my head as I'm yanking on it. It's a little straighter at least. I have cuts and bruises all over my face. I wash it properly this time.

I'm standing, staring into the mirror at my disfigured face, but all I see staring back at me are the bluest eyes, I haven't thought about them for a long time. I think back to that day and how it played out. I remember watching her papa dying, wanting to know what he was feeling, but that she distracted me right as he took his last breath. I remember being angry with her, but then I saw the flames and my only thought was to get her out before the car exploded, then as I was scrambling up the embankment and I fell and told her to run. I must have blacked out as the car exploded. I came to when I heard voices and sirens. I freaked, I didn't want anyone to find me, to know what I had done. I killed two people for my satisfaction and curiosity. I remember trying to get up, but I couldn't. When I looked at myself I saw my leg looked all out of shape, my foot was facing the wrong way. I saw a piece of metal stuck in my arm, which was why I couldn't use it to push myself up. I had one good arm and one good leg. I felt nothing. I didn't even know I was hurt until I tried to move. I heard the voices getting louder. I dragged myself with my good arm and leg farther away before they spotted me and I hid behind a huge tree. Luckily we had run quite a distance away from the car, so hopefully, they wouldn't find me. I had to stay really quiet and just wait and wait.

I must have waited for ages when fear grabbed me and I decided I had to make a move. I was sure they would search the area and come looking for me once Primrose told them about me. I managed to drag myself farther away, always trying to take cover behind trees and making sure I didn't run into any snakes. I dragged myself up the embankment. It took every ounce of strength I had for a ten-year-old. It also took me forever and drained me. It was starting to get dark by this point and I needed to get back home before it got too dark. I knew I would have to watch for the bears and cougars. My blood might have attracted them.

At the top of the embankment, I looked down the road to where the flashing lights were. There were firetrucks, troopers, and ambulances. So many of them and so many people. I scanned the area, looking for her, for Primrose, maybe they had taken her away already, maybe she was in one of the ambulances, I didn't even know at that point if she was alive or dead. The blast could have killed her for all I knew. I remember feeling sad at that thought. I sat there hidden from sight and pictured her perfect white skin, blonde hair, and stunning blue eyes, only the eyes had no light in them. They weren't the blue eyes I remembered. They were dull, lifeless, and very dark.

I managed to scramble across the road, keeping low to the ground and listening for any vehicles approaching or leaving the scene down the road. I was safe on the other side. I started the journey home. I eventually got back when it was dark, only dark in the hills where we lived was black, there were no streetlights to light my way, I was on high alert the entire time. I only encountered a small startled deer that scared the crap out of me.

Once home, my mama started to give me shit as she heard the door open. She wasn't quite the lazy fat bitch at this stage, so she started toward the door when she heard it. She was calling me a good for nothing retard when she suddenly stopped in front of me. I was on the ground. I had crawled the entire way. She looked at me like I was some piece of shit that just came crawling through the door.

When she realized I was badly hurt, she went into a panic. It's the first and last time I remember my mama ever being concerned about me. She rushed to me and tried to help me up, I couldn't feel the pain I was in, so I let her help me to my room. She rushed out and came back sometime later with a bowl of hot water and some towels. I saw she also put a needle and thread on the table along with some rags and some wood. She set about taking my clothes off me and I lay in just my underwear on top of my bed. She cleaned up my face and body first, then got fresh hot water to start on my arm and leg. She pulled the metal out of my arm and also some other glass shards which I hadn't noticed.

She didn't speak the entire time. She cleaned up the wounds and then stitched up the holes that needed stitching. She moved onto my leg which was still at a funny angle and I could see a bone sticking out of the side. She set about opening the wound and straightening the bone, she didn't have to be careful. That was one good thing about me, not feeling any pain. I didn't see what she held the bone together with, but watched as she stitched the wound up and then put the wood along my leg, tying it with the rags to make a splint. She never once asked me what I had done or how I got into the state I was in. I never told her how I got like that.

It took a while for me to recover from the broken leg. Two days later, I tried to get out of bed on my own and I fell, snapping my bone again. Mama was angry that she had to straighten it out, tie it together and splint it for a second time. I was to remain in bed no matter what. It was a change that she was looking after me for the first time that I could remember. I was bored stupid the six weeks I lay in my bed. I didn't have anything to do. She did surprise me a few times and tried to teach me to read some days. But most of the time, I ended up with a slap on the head because she got so frustrated with me. I learned far more in those six weeks than I ever had in my life. I still couldn't read though, but I learned some letters. I was still the retard she kept in solitude.

I'm lying on my bed and wondering what ever happened to Primrose. I suddenly have a moment. I saved her fucking life. Okay, I may have killed her parents, but if she's still alive, I actually saved her life. If I hadn't gotten her out of the car she would have blown up with it. I feel quite proud of myself, for once, instead of killing, I saved someone.

Since that day, I have escalated with wanting to know more about pain and moved on to larger animals. I've set traps and I've caught a few deer, a bobcat, and a few gray foxes. I've tortured them until they squealed, doing unthinkable things to them, but none of it has been as satisfying as doing it to Primrose's papa. He was able to talk and tell me what he was feeling, well to some degree, I do feel some of it was a waste of time because I didn't really get anything from it. The one thing with the animals though is after I've tortured them alive and dismembered them once they finally die, I've used their meat for food for Mama and me, so it's never been for nothing. It's just the death they endure that is not normal, and I know that, I truly do, but I want to see the pain they all feel. I want to try to understand.

I suppose people would say what I have is a gift, never feeling any pain at all. Maybe it could be seen as that until you look down and see your foot is bleeding badly because you stood on a nail. That nail was rusty and caused me to have a really bad infection. My mama had to take me to a Medicare center for the first time ever, she feared I was going to lose my foot. I was oozing this horrible green smelly pus, and I was having trouble walking. The doctor said if we had waited any longer, I would have lost my foot and maybe my leg. All because I didn't feel the nail go into my foot.

Then there have been times I've spilled the scalding water on me from the log burner. I never felt the pain which my mama said was lucky because burns are horrendous, but my hand blistered up so bad I couldn't use it for weeks under Mama's instructions, so the blisters could heal. Or the numerous times I've cut myself and not realized. It becomes a nightmare, so no, it's not a gift and always being told what a retard you are by your mama, that I'm abnormal and the Devil's son. Yeah, that is soul-destroying and you start to believe it.

I wake up and can't open my eyes. Shit, now what? I go to the bathroom, bumping into things as I do, and I wet my eyes then try to pry them open.

"Blaine, Blaine, get your ass in here now. Didn't you hear me shouting for you? I need a drink and something to eat."

I can't fucking see. What the hell am I supposed to do now?

"Blaine, did you hear me, you retard?"

I can just about open my eyes to try to get around without bumping into anything. I head to where she is and I wait for her to notice me. I'm standing by the couch and I wait and wait. The bitch doesn't even look at me.

"I want coffee, bread, and whatever meat you have left from your last kill. Hurry up. I've been waiting for ages, I'm starving."

When isn't she fucking starving? I start to move toward the kitchen side of the room to get what she wants. I've had enough of her. She doesn't give a shit about me.

No, fuck her, she will have to starve or get off her fat ass and get it herself. That gives me an idea. One I like, I like a lot. I need to think about this.

Three

Blaine–Age 18

I DON'T KNOW WHAT'S WRONG WITH ME. FOR THE LAST FOUR YEARS, I've thought about Primrose almost every day. I've thought about her blue eyes and blonde hair, wondering what she's like now, if she's alive. I reckon she will be about fifteen or sixteen now. Growing up. I wonder if she's as beautiful. I would love to see her again.

I've been venturing out into the closest town to us for a while now. I mill around watching people go about their business and try to imitate what they do. I see them at shops, drinking coffee, walking around talking into small things. These are cells, I vaguely remember Mama having one when I was little, I also remembered Primrose's pappy having one that was smashed. I've been hanging around a bar for the last few weeks, watching what people do there. I've seen a few women with men getting very close to each other and ending up almost naked. What's that all about? I'm sitting outside the bar on the fence watching people coming and going. It's late because it's dark out and I can hear the crickets in the bushes. I've never been here when it's late before, it's always been in the afternoon. I don't like being out when it's dark because of getting back home.

The bar is very noisy tonight and there are a lot of bikers here. All the bikes are lined up outside the entrance. I've seen a lot of women with hardly any clothes on, coming and going a lot. They mostly enter alone but leave with someone else. Is this what people do? I'm sitting, watching, I'm in my jeans and a black wife beater, ones I stole form a store this time not a back yard, it's getting easy to steal from stores now and I take more and more.

I watch as a woman comes out of the bar alone. She looks upset and takes out a smoke. I see her searching for something on her, but to be honest, there aren't many places she can search on herself with the little she's wearing. She looks around as though looking for someone or something. There isn't anyone else around. She's scanning the lot out front, she doesn't see me at first until she scans back again and suddenly her eyes land on me. I see her face light up and she takes the unlit smoke out of her mouth and puts it behind her ear. I just watch her, fascinated. I wonder how she would react to pain. I wonder if she'd be a screamer or if she would just cry like a baby. I would love to find out.

I'm thinking these things when she starts to saunter over to me, she's walking funny. If she's not careful, she'll fall in the dirt. She's walking like she has a stick stuck up her ass, I wonder what that would feel like to her? I see the shoes she has on and how the fuck she can even walk in them is beyond me, they are so high. As she approaches me, she licks her lips and eyes me up and down. I don't move, I just stay sitting on the fence watching her, thinking of ways to hurt her.

"Hey handsome, whatcha doin' sitting out here all on your own?"

Holy fuck, I've never had a woman speak to me before, I'm a little nervous, I rub my palms on my thighs. She watches my every move and keeps licking her lips. She moves closer still.

"Well, aren't you a pretty boy? I've never seen you here before. Do you live around here?"

I nod and keep rubbing my palms up and down my thighs.

She's very pretty with her long wavy blonde hair, I can't make out her eye color but I instantly think of Primrose because of her hair. I rub my hand over my face. I have stubble, quite a lot of stubble now. I think it makes me look older than I am.

She gets closer still and manages to place herself between my open legs. Holy fuck, she is so pretty. She has the biggest red lips. The biggest I've ever seen and she keeps running her tongue along the bottom one. She suddenly puts her hands on top of mine. I freeze.

"Hey, big boy." She looks to my crotch area as she says this then looks back at my face. "You new around here? I would know if I'd seen you before."

I just nod. I can't speak. I start to slide my palms up and down my thighs again, only this time hers are on top of mine. She's watching as I inch closer to my crotch area then back down again. Her eyes go wide each time I rub up and I feel her push down on my hands to try to get me to rub nearer my cock. I stop.

"What you doin'?" I ask her.

She looks up at me as though she's shy, she looks at me through her very long eyelashes. Fuck, how do women get big lips and long eyelashes like that? I'm a little fascinated with her. I would love to see how far I can push her pain threshold, to maybe torture her. To hear her scream and find out how the pain feels.

I'm lost in thought again when I feel her hand on my cock. She's squeezing and suddenly my jeans get so fucking tight in that area. I feel all these strange but nice sensations. I didn't know I could feel anything like this. I want her to carry on rubbing and squeezing my cock, so I don't stop her. She gets even closer to me and one of her hands starts to move under my shirt and she starts to caress my chest.

Holy cow. What is she doing? Why is she doing this? I don't even know her. Is this how people are supposed to be with each other?

"Wow, you must work out a lot, huh, those abs and pecs are to die for."

Well if that's what she wants, who am I to stop her? I'm enjoying the closeness of her. I've never had anything like this in my life, I've never had any kind of intimacy with anyone.

Before I know what's happening, she has the fly of my jeans undone and she has my cock free in her hand. I nearly fall backward off the fence. I feel like I'm in a different place. This is way out of my comfort zone. No one has ever touched me. She grabs one of my arms to steady me, while still holding my cock with the other hand. Cars and bikes are coming and going into the parking lot, but they can't see us. I sat here on purpose because it was dark. I'm surprised she saw me. I'm steady on the fence now, gripping it on both sides of me with everything I have. She smiles a great big smile at me and licks her lips. She bends her head down toward my cock and she suddenly has it in her mouth, swirling her tongue around it and sucking hard. I straighten up like a pole. I don't know what to do. I don't know what she's doing to me, but it feels fucking amazing. It's so strange that I can actually feel what she's doing, it's not that so much, but that the sensations running through my body, it feels like I'm floating on air. I'm amazed at these new sensations.

I start to breathe heavy, I feel like I want to thrust my hips up the more she's sucking and licking me. I start to do just that, holding on to the fence. Then I grab the back of her head with one hand to help steady me while I thrust up. She's taking nearly all my cock into her mouth and I can feel it hitting the back of her throat.

Fucking A, how is she doing that?

She takes her other hand and slides it into my jeans at the back, I can feel the pressure from her fingers on my ass. She's digging in, then suddenly I feel a finger in my asshole. I nearly fly off the fence but she holds me down with her body, I feel liquid spurting out of my cock and down her throat. I feel funny sensations all over my body. It feels nice, I'm panting hard as I thrust and thrust into her throat. I feel like I don't weigh anything, like funny things are all over my body. I think I actually feel happy. I don't ever remember being happy. I just can't describe these feelings because it's all new to me, but I would like to feel them again and again. This is fucking amazing. I'm so glad there is music blaring from the bar, I want to roar out loud. I do just that.

She pulls away from me and looks me right in the eye. She wipes her mouth with the back of her hand.

"So what's your name, big boy?"

I just stare at her. She does that to me, with my cock, and then asks my name? She takes the smoke from behind her ear.

"Do you have a light?"

I shake my head. I jump off the fence and put my cock away and do myself up.

"You not one for speaking or what?"

I just look at her again. I start to walk away, I need to process what I just felt and what the fuck just happened. I must look like a stupid retard at this point, my mouth hanging open trying to work it all out.

"Hey big boy, don't leave, we can do more, if you know what I mean."

No, I don't know what she means.

I head home. I still have all these mixed feelings inside me, and I try to understand them as I walk. I'm hungry now and no doubt my mama will be going mad because I didn't come home earlier. She's worse than ever now. She can barely move because she has been so inactive for years. I have to do everything for her and I fucking hate it. I have to wash her fat fucking body each morning or she gets sores and infections. We don't have the money for creams or lotions, so I've taken to stealing what I can from different stores. If I get caught, she will be screwed. I have to wipe her fat ass each time she shits. She makes a mess all the time and trying to roll her to clean her is a fucking nightmare. That woman back there said I must work out, well, you try rolling your four hundred pound mama around a few times a day and see the muscles you get from that. I've grown so tall now and I have muscles everywhere. With the food I catch, we eat good and I even bake bread in the log burner. She told me how to do it, watching me all the time.

I make good meals from her instructions. She lies on the couch which now has no legs on it and watches me in the kitchen, telling me what to do. I suppose she must have cooked and baked when I was younger, I just don't remember.

As I approach home, it's dark. I hear a noise coming from one of the traps I set, it's like a grunting sound. I have a few traps set around the land. I head to see what I've caught. I pick the lantern up from the porch first and light the candle inside then head to the trap. This trap was a hole I dug in the ground and covered with tree branches so anything that stood on it would just fall through. When I've caught them this way before I've just put a rope around their necks to haul them out of the hole. I'm surprised when I get to the hole and hold the lantern out and see a bear staring up at me. It suddenly jumps up the side of the hole, trying to get out but the hole is too deep, I'm really fucking tall and when I stand in it the edge is way above my head. The bear is grunting and snorting, it looks exhausted. I hear movement to the side of me and swing the lantern to see what it is. I see two small cubs hiding by the trees trying to get out of sight from me. This must be the mother, she must be frantic, no wonder she is worn out trying to get back to her babies. These three would give us a lot of food. But then it would be too much and some would go to waste because it would rot. We don't have a fridge because we don't have electricity still.

I'm still on a high from what that lady did to me and still trying to fathom what exactly that was. I kinda feel sorry for this mama bear. She only wants to protect her babies. She's out looking for food for them and ended up in my hole. Shit, when did I start feeling sorry for animals? They don't fucking talk. The bear is still trying to climb out. I watch as she digs her claws into the sides but the dirt just gives way under her weight and she keeps falling back. If she carries on like this she'll have pulled enough dirt from the walls to build up the bottom, making the top nearer for her. Do I leave her and see if the cubs follow her in or see if she gets out? Do I just kill her and the cubs for the meat and fur? It's not like it's cold right now, it's summer. There will be more bears without cubs coming along, they usually stumble in here foraging to get ready for the winter months to hibernate. It's too early for that yet.

Because of being in a good mood which is unusual for me, I decide to let them go. I head back toward the house where I have some long thin tree trunks I haven't cut up yet. If I put a couple of them in the hole, maybe she can climb up and out that way. I grab two that aren't that heavy, and some rope. I tie the rope around the top and bottom to make it a little thicker for her. I then head back to the hole, I see the cubs scurry back to hide as I approach. I slowly lower the tree trunks into the hole then let them drop quickly but stand up, leaning on the side of the hole and I run away so she doesn't attack me when she gets out.

I take cover behind a big tree and just peek out as I see her come out the top of the hole. I see the steam coming from her mouth as she stands, panting. She's looking around making sure the coast is clear and she grunts. The cubs come bounding out from cover toward her and she nuzzles them both. She starts to head where they were hiding and they follow behind her. I watch as they head toward the trees, but before they disappear she looks back in my direction, I think she's saying thank you.

I feel kind of good. I stand, smiling to myself while I wait to make sure she's left with her cubs. Fuck, I feel like a pussy now.

I head into the cabin, waiting for the wrath of my mama. It doesn't happen. I still have the lantern lit and I raise it so I can see her. She's rolled off the couch and is on the floor. I move closer, it doesn't look like she's breathing. I kneel in front of her and put my hand to her mouth, she's breathing. Fuck. I start to get up and in doing so, I must nudge her with my knee.

She grunts and startles awake. "What the fuck are you doing, you fucking retard?"

And she's back. "Nothing, I've just come in and you were on the floor. I was just seeing if you were breathing."

She looks around and it registers she's not on the couch. "Get me back on there. My back is killing me."

Great. "I'm not that fucking strong. I'll have to try and roll you back on." I try to get her back on, but it proves difficult. She's ranting and raving at me the whole time I'm trying. I get behind the couch and try pulling her back that way. I do her top half then her bottom half, alternating inch by inch each end. It's like I've done a full fucking workout by the time I've finished.

"Get me something to eat and drink now that you've woken me up. You've been gone for ages. I haven't had anything all day."

That's it. The ungrateful bitch. I had a thought a few years back about not feeding her and letting her die a slow death. I decide now is the time. I can't take any more of this shit from her. I hate her fucking guts. I get her some oats in water, leave it on the floor next to her just slightly farther away than normal. If she rolls off the couch again she can go to Hell. I walk into my room, shutting the door so I don't have to hear her moaning at me again. That will be her last meal.

Four

Blaine–Age 22

IT'S BEEN A COUPLE OF YEARS NOW SINCE MY MAMA DIED, A VERY slow death. I decided she made me suffer all those years, always blaming me for Papa leaving, always telling me what a pathetic retard I was. I snapped one night and decided to not feed her anymore. I left her the oats that night and that was her last meal. I went into the room the next day and saw she'd managed to pull the bowl near her but that she spilled the oats out of it onto the floor where she managed to scoop most of them up to eat. She disgusted me. I'd had funny but strange feelings that night from what that lady did to me in the car lot and I was in a good mood until I got home and saw her there, I just snapped.

It took a long time for her to die. I stopped cleaning her, which was one of the worst things to do because the smell was horrendous. She just seemed to carry on as normal for the most part at first and I endured the earache from her for a while. She begged and begged for food and water, she begged for me to help her and clean her. I ignored her pleas. I used to just stand over her watching how pathetic she was. I had no love for her, in fact, I don't ever remember a time I thought of her as a mama. She never looked after me, it turned into me looking after her. She needed me a lot more than I ever needed her.

The first week was the hardest for me. I wanted to help her some-times, when she looked so pathetic just lying there. She was this huge body mass with a little head, lifeless a lot of the time, and rancid. I stayed out as much as I could, but when I returned, she would cry and beg. I didn't give in. I never gave her anything to eat or drink. She was getting weaker by the end of that first week, but I thought it would have happened sooner.

Later on that second week, I could see how sallow her face was becoming, her skin was starting to droop which meant she was losing weight. This to me was a good thing and maybe something I should have done long ago. She still begged me to help her, one day in the second week, I could see how weak she was. I stuffed tissue up my nose because the smell was vile, I sat cross-legged at her side, facing her. I sat examining her closely. She looked at me as though pleading for me to help her, her lips were dry and cracked, I could see her skin on her face was all dry and cracking, it was peeling off her forehead. Her hair was starting to fall out, it was all over the couch. She actually looked smaller to me. I reckoned this would take weeks because of all the fat she had in her body.

She tried to reach out to me with her hands but she was too weak to lift her huge arms. Her fingers were all wrinkly, her nails looked like they were going to fall off, they were always filthy anyway, her arms had so much saggy skin. The blanket she had over her was smelly and seemed to be rotting, probably from the pee and shit. I pulled the cover back to look at her body and was shocked at how much it looked like it was decaying. The heat didn't help, her sweating and not drinking is the thing I think will kill her quicker than not eating.

"Mama, tell me what you're feeling?" I asked her.

She stared at me like I was stupid, the retard she always called me.

"Tell me, Mama, I want to know what you feel. Is it painful here?" I asked, poking her in the ribs, she flinched.

I lifted her tummy apron which wasn't as heavy as usual but I was sorry I did, the smell, even with tissue up my nose, nearly knocked me out. She screamed out as the skin under the apron started to tear as I lifted it. The skin there was all red-raw, with what looked like a rash and all blistered, it was like tissue paper, just tearing as I lifted it. I saw the blood start to ooze out, it was very weak looking blood, kind of watery. I looked at the agony on her face and I let the apron drop with a thud. I saw the tears flowing down her cheeks that had leaked out the sides of her scrunched-up eyes.

"Tell me what it feels like? You know I never feel pain, but I want to know. I need to know."

She opened her beady little eyes and stared at me. "You fucking retard, it fucking hurts so bad. Why would you do this to me, I'm your mama. Why would you do this to your mama?"

She couldn't shout, her mouth was so dry and she was so weak. She looked pathetic actually, lying there and not being able to abuse me like she was used to. She closed her eyes. I could see breathing was getting harder for her. It was shallow breaths. I didn't think she would last much longer.

I stayed in each day after that, to watch as she got weaker and weaker, dying a slow death. I kept asking her to describe how she was feeling. To explain what the pain felt like.

One day she started to tell me. "Each breath feels like my last, each breath is getting harder and harder to take. It's like someone has hold of my lungs, gripping them tightly and they just let go inch by inch until they grip tighter again. It burns, I feel pain down my sides toward the back. If I had to guess, I would say it's my kidneys failing. I can feel all the sores if I try to move, I feel like screaming, but I don't have the energy to scream. I feel so lethargic, I just want to sleep all the time. I know my time is running out." She looked me right in the eyes. "Tell me, son, why are you doing this to me? Why would you treat your mama like this? What did I ever do to you to make you hate me so much?"

I was astounded she asked me that. I got up and walked to my room, slammed my door, and laid on my bed. She had me thinking. Why did I hate her so much, was it my imagination? No, it's simple, she never loved me, she never cared about me, she blamed me for my papa leaving and has taken it out on me ever since. I turned into her caretaker, she never did anything for me. I don't love her, I never have.

I got so riled up lying on my bed, thinking, I stormed back to her. "Son? You never once treated me like a fucking son. You never loved me, always calling me a retard and blaming me for everything. You never loved me, you just used me to care for you. Now tell me more, I want to know everything you're feeling. If you don't, I'll just prolong your suffering for as long as I can."

She sighed and closed her eyes. I didn't think she was going to speak again. I just sat on the floor next to the couch with my legs crossed and my head perched on my hands, waiting. She went to sleep. I stayed like that for a while listening for her breaths, seeing if she was going to take her last one. I then decided to go outside to see if I had anything in my traps. I would cook some food and let the smell wake her, thinking she was getting something to eat.

I had nothing in the traps. I went back and decided to make some bread in the log burner. The smell of it cooking must have woken her up.

I barely heard her as she whispered to me. "Son, I do love you. I always have. It's just you're, you know, different. That's why I kept you here all these years. I didn't want anyone to take you away, I couldn't bear to lose you as well. I didn't want that to happen, so I kept you here."

I stand looking at her. Does she actually love me or is she just saying what she thinks I want to hear, so I will give her food and water? Does she think I'm totally stupid? Oh yeah, of course she does, I'm the retard, according to her. It's her fault I'm like this. It's her fault I'm a retard, that I can't read or write because she kept me here and didn't teach me. I got angrier the longer I stood there.

"You fucking lying bitch. You don't love me, and you never have. I'm stupid because you didn't teach me how to read and write, you kept me here and didn't let me go to school. The fact I can't feel pain doesn't make me a retard. It's you who made me a retard. Enough of all this bullshit, tell me what pain you're feeling, describe it to me. I want to know. Why do you think I kill animals as I do? It's not because I don't have feelings, because I do, in here," I say, banging on my heart then my head. "It's because I'm curious about pain. I want to know what it's like. Why do you think I killed those people? I wanted to know what they felt as they died. But she died right away and he couldn't tell me too much. It was a waste of fucking time. The little girl wasn't hurt though, there is that, but he wouldn't speak, he wouldn't tell me how it felt."

It wasn't a waste really, because of her, because of Primrose.

I see the shock on her face. I never told her about the car accident I caused. What did it matter? She was dying anyway.

"You killed people? When did you do that? You fucking monster."

I laughed. I stood there and laughed so hard at her. I couldn't help it. She called ME the monster. "You need to look at yourself before you call me a monster, mother dearest. The way you've treated me all these years. You're the fucking monster here. The monster created a monster. Now enough of all this crap and tell me what it really feels like," I screamed, getting right up into her face. She flinched and screwed her eyes closed.

"My lips are cracked and keep bleeding. I taste the copper of the blood each time they crack, I'm beginning to like the taste of it," she started to say and smiled as she said it. "Sometimes, although it hurts, I make them crack by stretching my lips just so I can taste the blood. My arms feel like they are dead. If I try to lift them, they feel like they weigh a hundred pounds each and the pain shoots right up my arms to my shoulder and neck. It's like fire and ice all at once, hot and cold, running through my body. The pain is excruciating, but I kind of like it, it tells me I'm still alive, although right now I wish I wasn't." She stops and catches her breath.

I still don't know what the pain is like. I don't feel burning hot or ice cold. I can feel some warm and some cold, but it's not pain. I could put red hot needles in my arm and wouldn't feel anything. I know she's right when she says I'm different but she could have let me go to school and learn.

"I don't know how to describe the pain to you when you can't feel any pain. I feel like I want to just die now. I feel like I've suffered enough and you should just finish me off. I know I'm rotting, I can smell my flesh rotting, I also know it will take longer because of how fat I am." She looks me in the eyes, hers suddenly turn evil. "Either give me some water and food, or kill me, you fucking pathetic retard. This is cruel to do this, but then I've seen you torture those animals. You can pretend all you like it was for food. You could kill them humanely, you don't have to torture them. I knew when you were little and so did your papa. He often watched you with the insects. He said you would grow up to be a killer unless I did something about it. I refused to have you put in a home for retards, that's why he left. He didn't want to be a part of what you would become."

That was the first time she ever said anything like that to me. She always blamed me. Now I know why. Or is she just making this up?

"I don't believe a fucking word you say. He left because he didn't love you. I remember seeing him with another woman. He didn't want you. But somehow you put all the blame on me because you couldn't bear the thought of him wanting someone else. It's a good thing he did find someone else. Look at you, you fat bitch, who would want you?" I storm out of the cabin, I'm not going back for a few days.

I camped out away from the cabin, I built myself fires to prepare the food I caught, I even fished and cooked that. I boiled the water for me to drink. I just wanted to be alone. I was so angry with her. I think I was away for four days in total before I decided to go back. I thought she was going to be dead, what I walked in on I will never forget and it fascinated me. She was still alive, barely, I couldn't believe it. I didn't think it was possible. With no water for two weeks, she should be dead. What I didn't count on were the rats. I saw one on her chest that was dead. It looked like she had been eating it. She had blood on her face and the rat was half-eaten with its guts hanging out. I didn't know if it was her or the other rats that had eaten it.

There were about ten rats or so on her. They were on her face, her body, and they were all gnawing at her. She was barely breathing and her eyes were open and glazed over. She was lifeless. I did think she was dead at first but after standing there watching her for a few minutes, I could see her chest going up and down, slowly. The rats just carried on, oblivious to me standing there. She was out of it, not responding, even though she was breathing. I stood watching, fascinated by the rats and the survival instincts that kick in with them. Where there is food to be had, you will find rats. I could see the covers on the floor exposing her body. It was a mess with the rats gnawing away on the flesh, there were holes all over her body, there were sores all over and the skin was all loose and just hanging. One rat was on the floor, standing up, gnawing on the hanging flesh of her tummy apron. Another was gnawing on the flesh of her arms that were just hanging off the couch. I sat on the floor crossed legged and watched them all scurrying around her.

I wondered if she could feel any of it? I wondered if she even knew what was happening to her at this moment in time or if she even knew I was there. I stayed there, watching in amazement. I relished the silence, no ranting at me and calling me names. Sitting there, I realized her silence was my new favorite sound.

I'm not sure how long I stayed watching those rats eat her alive but when I decided enough was enough, I got a pitcher and one by one took the rats off of her body and put them in the pitcher. I took it outside and emptied it, watching them all scurry away. Except for one. He stood on his hind legs and watched me. I watched him closely, seeing his whiskers and nose twitching. I bent down in front of him and he still didn't move. I reached out to him, he still didn't move, I moved quickly, and I grabbed him. I had him gripped around the neck tight and started to squeeze. He was wriggling at first, but the more pressure I put on him, the less he moved. His little eyes that already bulged out of his head were starting to stick out more. I threw him to the ground. He lay there. I thought he was dead, he didn't move at all. As I was turning, I caught the movement, he got up quickly and ran off in the direction of the other rats. The little fucker fooled me, playing dead.

That night I sat watching my mama slowly dying. I didn't touch her, she was still covered in blood. I sat watching each rise of her chest as she took each breath, waiting in anticipation to see if it was her last. In the end, I got fed up and annoyed she was lasting so long. I took my lantern and I went out into the trees and started to dig a grave for her. I knew it wouldn't be long, but the smell was making me sick every time I entered the cabin and I was sick of seeing her there. I finished digging the hole a few hours later, it was a deep hole. I wanted to make sure she was buried deep down, I headed back, hoping she had died. I stood over her and couldn't believe my fucking eyes. She was still breathing, for fuck's sake. I didn't care now. She was going in that hole dead or alive. I took her covers that were on the floor and spread them out so I could roll her off the couch easily. Then I wrapped her in the covers, tied each end and dragged her ass out of the cabin to the hole. There I shoved her body in and I buried her. I didn't know if she was dead or alive at this point, but so fucking what.

That was two years ago now. I've been on my own since then and to be honest, I've loved it. Not a care in the world. The only problem I've had is when I've hurt myself but not realized and not had anyone around to tell me. I've found blood a few times in the cabin and not realized it's been from me until I've searched myself and found a cut of some sort.

I cleared out all Mama's stuff and burned it. I found some jewelry she had that I don't ever remember seeing before. I took the couch out to burn because it was no use to me, it was that worn and soiled. I found a loose floorboard and decided to pull it up so I could nail it down properly. I found a tin in the hole. When I opened the tin there were photos of my papa holding me as a baby and there was a lot of money in there. I don't know how much because I couldn't count, only up to twenty and there was way more than twenty bills in that tin. Way, way more.

I have still been catching animals and feeding off them. I will one day, when I feel I can do it, go into the bar and get myself a drink and something to eat there and see what that's like. I haven't been torturing the animals I catch anymore. I felt there's no need. They can't tell me anything. I need to find someone that can tell me what it's like. I want to know. I've been back to that bar and sat on the fence watching the people come and go. I've never seen that lady since that time in the parking lot. I look out for her every time I go, but she's never been there when I have. I wonder if she's moved away. I've seen plenty of others like her, not much in the way of clothes and all done up with makeup, but none of them have ever noticed me. I've been studying the people coming and going, trying to learn from them, trying to learn how to react with other people. I have no social skills at all and to be honest, even as tall as I am and full of muscles, I feel intimidated by other people. My mama is the only person I've ever really had a conversation with in my life.

I need to do it. I need to interact with people. I need to go into that bar and order a drink.

Five

Blaine Age–24

I DID IT, AFTER TWO YEARS I WALKED INTO THE BAR AND ORDERED myself a beer. The place was empty. It was still early, I'm so glad it's empty, my head is all over the place. I asked for a beer then sat on the barstool. The bartender tried to talk to me but I just wasn't having any of it and just nodded as she spoke. Most of the time I didn't even hear what she said, I didn't even make eye contact with her. I just kept my head down and peeled the label off the bottle in my hands. I've never had alcohol before, but I needed this. I just got back yesterday after traveling around from town to town for some months, I'd needed to leave the cabin for a while, I was starting to go crazy there on my own. Also, I needed to get out and to try and socialize. Then after what happened with Daisy, well I just felt I needed to try a beer.

I stayed in run-down motels on the edge of the towns I traveled to. They were cheap, I used the money I found in the tin. I stopped at a truck stop yesterday on my way back home and walked in and ordered a soda. I was so nervous and couldn't make eye contact with the waitress. I stood with sweat pouring from my brow as she handed me the soda and I laid some money on the countertop. I sat in a booth by the window to drink my soda. I was sweating with anxiety, my legs were all jittery as I sat there. I started to calm as I watched the trucks coming and going and watched as cars pulled in for gas.

I watched this one lady who pulled in with steam pouring out from under her hood. She got out of her car and lifted the hood and leaned over the motor. I thought she had better be careful, the steam could burn her. Ding, light bulb moment. I would like to see that, boiling water scalding someone.

The radiator just needed some water, I think. I finished my soda and headed out. I noticed she was still standing, looking under the hood. She looked up as I passed, but I didn't look at her, no eye contact for me.

"Excuse me, sir," she said.

Was she talking to me? Shit, now I had to look at her. I looked up and saw her looking at me. I turned to see if there was anyone around me, but there was no one. I looked at the car but didn't speak.

She had on sunglasses and she lowered them down her nose to look over the rim at me. "Do you know anything about cars?"

I pointed to my chest. "Are you talking to me?"

She smiled and nodded. "Do you know anything? I was driving along and all this smoke or steam started to come from the hood."

I ignored her and carried on walking. I walked over to where there was a pitcher and I filled it up with water from the faucet. There was a funnel, so I took that with me. I headed back to her.

She smiled as I approached. "Oh, I thought you were just ignoring me."

I still didn't speak to her. Luckily it was an old car. I'd messed around with old cars before, ones that had been abandoned in the hills, stolen, or crashed and left there. I found the radiator and unscrewed the cap and poured in the water. She was talking to me as I was doing this, but I didn't acknowledge her, and I had no idea what she was talking about. I watched her out of the corner of my eye as I was pouring the water in and she was being all nice and sweet, trying to get me to talk to her. She was getting closer and closer to me until she was leaning on the edge of the car touching my arm as it rested holding the pitcher. I turned my head slightly and I could see right down her top, her tits were nearly falling out of it. I was fascinated, I turned my head more, just staring. They looked big and squishy, I wanted to prod them with my finger to see how bouncy they were. My mama's were all droopy and saggy but these looked so inviting.

"Like whatcha see, honey?"

I looked up at her face and I must have gone red with being caught, she smiled and winked at me with her sunglasses at the end of her nose. She licked her lips slowly then flicked her tongue slightly. It was only a small movement, but I caught it.

I turned my head quickly back to look at the pitcher which was now empty. "That should do it. You just needed water," I said to her as I got up, she followed me, and I closed the hood with a thud making sure the latch caught. "There you go, ma'am." I turned to walk away and put the pitcher back where I found it. I grabbed my bag as I left.

"Hey, mister?" she shouted at my back, but I didn't turn. I felt embarrassed, I think. "Hey, don't go. Look, I'm sorry."

What is she apologizing for? I turned in her direction but I didn't look at her.

"Hey, look, thank you for helping a damsel in distress."

What the hell is she talking about? She was pouting and sticking out those tits of hers as if I could miss them anyway. I couldn't stop staring at them. They were huge. I've never really thought about tits or anything about females, for that matter. It never interested me, maybe all the years of cleaning Mama made me immune to it but hers are just there in my face and I want to taste them and feel them. I hear her laugh. I'm so wrapped up in my thoughts and staring at her tits I didn't hear her say anything.

I just turn and head for the highway to carry on with the walk home. It should only take me three or four hours from here. Give me enough time to calm down. I feel uncomfortable with myself and in my jeans. I feel embarrassed. I'm walking fast along the dirt path just thinking of her tits when a car crawls slowly along beside me. I don't look, I just pick up my pace.

"Hey, mister. Can I give you a lift anywhere?"

It's her. The lady with the big tits. Fuck. I can't look at her or I'll just look at her tits. Fuck.

"I just want to say thank you for helping me back there. I can drive you wherever you need. I'm heading in this direction. Come on, hop in." She stops the car ahead of me and opens the passenger door in front of me so I either have to go around her car to pass or into the field. I stop at the door but I don't look at her. "Come on, hop in. It's the least I can do to thank you for helping me out."

I turn my head to look at her and she's licking those fucking lips again. Her sunglasses are back on the tip of her nose so she can see me. She smiles and winks. She then looks down my body to my crotch and back up slowly taking in the length of me.

"You seem happy to see me," she says, winking again. I have no idea what she is talking about. "Come on, hop in and I'll drive you."

I stand contemplating. Then I think back to the lightbulb moment, that's what Mama used to say when she had an idea, it was a lightbulb moment. I shrug and get in the car. She giggles as I get in and bounces in her seat as she starts driving.

"Where you heading to, honey?"

I turn my head to look at her and see she's looking at me. The next thing I know, a horn blows and we both look out the front window and see she's drifted out of her lane and is facing an oncoming truck.

"Shit," she screams as we both grab the wheel to turn us back into our lane.

"Keep your fucking eyes on the road," I shout at her, the stupid bitch nearly got us killed.

"Hey, don't shout at me. I'm doing you a favor giving you a ride here," she shouts back.

"What, like I did you a favor and fixed this fucking piece of junk. I didn't ask for the ride," I shout back.

We both sit in silence for a while.

"My name's Daisy, what's yours?" she whispers to me.

Shit, I don't want to make small talk. "It's Clarke."

She giggles and I turn to look at her. "Like Clark Kent?"

I scowl at her, not having a clue what she's talking about.

"You know, Clark Kent, as in Superman's alter ego." I still look puzzled. "OMG, you don't know who Superman is? How is that possible? Everyone on the planet knows who Superman is. You been hiding under a rock, honey?"

I'm still clueless so I just look out the window.

"Where we heading? Where do you want me to take you?"

I'm gonna take this one home and see what I can do with a bowl of scalding water. "Keep drivin' and I'll tell you where to turn. Where were you heading?"

She doesn't say anything for a little bit. "Nowhere in particular. Just drivin' till I get bored."

Suits me. It tells me she's not gonna be missed. We drive for a while and she doesn't shut up, I just don't talk.

"Turn up here on the left, then keep going until I tell you."

She turns onto the road. It narrows a bit and the surroundings get denser with trees. It stays a proper road for a while. We pass the ridge where I'd caused the wreck and made the car crash down the embankment. It's not there now, they towed it not long after the accident. It always reminds me of her whenever I pass this point. Usually, I'm on foot and I always stop, close my eyes and watch it all play out over and over again in my head. It was one of the best days of my life. Those eyes of hers come back to me now. I turn and look at Daisy, she's nothing like my angel.

"Turn left just up here. Then we take the second right." She does as I say. "Then take the next left."

She does and stops the car. "Where are we going?"

I look at her worried face. I can see why she stopped the car as this just looks like a dirt road, which it is. "It's not far now to my house."

She sits, contemplating. "No, you can walk the rest of the way if it's not far. I appreciate your help back there, but this is as far as I go." She waits for me to get out, but I don't.

"Hey, it's okay, my mama is at home with my sister waiting for me. I can walk from here. Thank you for the ride." I put on a sad timid voice so she doesn't feel threatened in any way and I start to open the door to get out.

"Wait," she says. I see her looking around. "I'm sorry, let me take you the rest of the way. I just got a little spooked with there not being a road. But I will take you." She starts the car moving again.

The dirt road is bumpy, she moves slowly, it's only wide enough for one vehicle at a time but no one else uses it which is why it's so bumpy and uneven.

"Just up here there is a little turn, just here see, through the trees." I point at the turn so she doesn't miss it.

This road is worse than the other one and leads to my cabin through the trees. There are holes and bumps all along this track and we are thrown all over the more gas she gives it so she slows to a crawl. I see the startled look on her face as we clear the trees and my cabin comes into view. It's getting dark now and I see the worry on her face.

She pulls up outside the cabin. She leans forward on the wheel to look around out front. "Is this where you live?"

I don't say anything, I open the door and get out. I open the back door to get my bag out. "Do you want to take off before it gets too dark or would you like a drink first?"

She looks back through the front window up to the sky and sees how dark it is now. "Did you say your mama and sister were home? Maybe a quick drink then I will take off if you give me directions."

Perfect. I grab my bag and shut the door. I head to the cabin and just walk straight in. There is no lock, who needs one out here? It's not like anyone knows I'm here and besides, there's nothing to take anyway.

"Hey Mama, I'm home," I shout out, loud enough that Daisy hears me.

I head to the lamp and light the wick. I hear the car door shut and listen as she walks toward the cabin. I hear the wood creak under her foot as she steps onto the porch. I open the door and I stand there leaning on the doorjamb with my arms folded across my chest.

I see the way she looks at me and licks her lips. All fear vanishes from her face as she looks me up and down. I can't stop staring at her tits. She stops in front of me.

"Like what you see, honey?"

She runs a finger down my chest, over my abs, from my tummy to my belt. She tucks her finger into the belt loop and tries to pull me forward. I'm no match for her slight frame.

"Is your mama home?" she asks me in her sweet voice.

I shake my head no. "She must be at her sister's with my sister," I lie.

She smiles and licks her lips again. She starts to pull my plaid shirt out of my jeans and unbuttons it. I just let her do it. I find I'm enjoying this. But I still can't take my eyes off her tits. I have a t-shirt on under my shirt, so she pulls that out of my jeans also. Her hands then both go under my t-shirt and she starts to feel her way all over my body.

I figure if she's going there then I'm doing the same. I stand up straight and I tower over her. I take both her tits in my hands and I start to squeeze them and rub them. Her nipples instantly go rock hard, like stones. I pinch them and she yelps but when I look at her face it's not in pain, but with pleasure, I think. I do it again. I rub her tits together, up and down and around. They feel fantastic in my hands. I take her top and I tear it open revealing a barely-there bra. How her tits stay in that thing, I will never know. I yank it down and I bend down and take a tit in my mouth and I bite the nipple hard. I then suck it, alternating between biting and sucking. I switch tits and I do the same with the other one. This feels fantastic, sucking these big juicy tits. She moans as I do this which spurs me on more. I bite harder and make her wince a little but then when I suck hard she starts to squirm and moan loud.

I feel her hands moving at my crotch. I didn't even realize she had my belt and buttons undone on my jeans and she was trying to yank them down with one hand while the other was inside pulling my cock hard. The sensations running through my body at what she's doing are very strange. This is similar to when that other woman put my cock in her mouth at the bar that time. I feel good for once, my body is starting to tingle. She pulls away from me and her tit pops out of my mouth. I look at her to try to gauge what she's thinking. The next thing I know, she's undoing her shorts and pushing them down. Then she pulls my jeans down so we are both standing naked on my porch.

"You sure no one is gonna come home, honey?"

I shake my head. I know no one is going to come home.

She comes up to me and stands on her tiptoes to try to reach my lips. I'm not quite sure what she's doing, so I bend to make it easier for her. I just need to let her lead the way. She kisses me and coaxes my mouth open with her tongue. The next thing I know, her tongue is rammed into my mouth and she duels with my tongue. I kinda like this but I don't feel anything inside from this.

She grabs hold of one of my limp hands as they dangle at my sides. She puts it on her tit, making circular motions, then let's go, leaving my hand there. I take it this is what she wants so I continue to squeeze and knead her tit. She then takes my other hand and pulls it forward, she moves slightly, not breaking contact with my mouth and she starts to rub my hand on her down below. Fucking hell. I've never touched a woman there apart from cleaning my mama, but that was nothing like this and was vile, the thought makes me shudder. She starts to move on my hand and moans into my mouth. I pull away from her so I can see the expressions on her face. She opens her eyes and smiles at me. She then takes two of my fingers on that hand and starts to put them in a hole down there. Fucking hell, what's she doing? She starts jumping up and down on my fingers, all the while keeping hold of them. She then takes her thumb and starts to rub herself near my fingers. She's panting hard, her head rolls back, and she moans aloud. The moans get louder and louder. She takes my other hand off her tit and places that on her pussy. She takes a finger and starts rubbing it on a bit that sticks out of her. This must be what she was touching on herself. I get it. She wants me to rub the nub while sticking fingers inside her hole. Fuck, this is hot. She gyrates more and more and screams out, she starts shaking. Then she stops but I carry on. She responds and starts gyrating again.

This time she watches me and she takes my cock in both her hands and she starts stroking it hand over hand. She starts to squeeze it tighter and tighter and I fucking love the sensations I feel from it. Just like that one other time. I feel all tingly as she pulls harder and harder. It takes both her hands to do this, he has grown enormous. I see the glint in her eye and she licks her lips.

She stops and pulls my hands from her hole. "Sit down, honey."

She pushes my chest slightly then grabs both my shoulders, pushing them down to make me sit on the porch. I sit on my ass and watch her in her high heels saunter over to me. She steps on either side of my legs and looks at my cock, licking her lips. She turns and faces away from me but edges back so her ass is literally in my face. She bends down and spreads her ass cheeks wide open.

"Lick," she says.

Holy fucking shit. She wants me to lick her ass. She takes a finger and runs it down her ass to her hole.

"Follow my finger with your tongue, I want you to lick from my ass-hole to my pussy hole."

I take both my hands and I spread her ass cheeks then I lean in and using my tongue, I do as she said. I slowly run my tongue from her ass hole to her pussy hole where my fingers were. I go back up then down again.

"Stick it back inside my pussy, I enjoy it more in there." she whispers all breathy.

I stick it in her ass hole first then run it down to her pussy and I insert my tongue where my fingers were before. She wiggles around on my tongue. She reaches through her legs and grabs one of my hands. She takes my fingers and starts rubbing her nub with them. She lets go and I continue to do this. Running my tongue in and out around her ass and pussy and rubbing her nub. She bends right over, even farther, giving me better access but then she grabs my cock and starts pumping up and down with her hands. I start thrusting up and down as she does this.

The next thing I know, she has my cock in her mouth. She's using one hand to squeeze and play with my balls, the other hand is at the base of my cock pumping hard and my cock is being sucked like a popsicle. She's swirling her tongue all around the tip sucking as juice comes out. The feelings I have are sensational. I'm panting hard as I stick my tongue as far as I can up her pussy. I take my other hand and I insert two fingers into her asshole so my tongue can stay in her pussy. Fucking hell, this is heaven. I can't get enough of the taste of her. She's gyrating harder onto my face as I'm thrusting into her mouth. She is so wet, all her juice is running down my chin and dripping onto my chest. I feel my cock get harder and my balls seem to tighten up while all this is going on. I'm panting harder and harder as she starts to scream around my cock. She explodes and squirts juice all over my tongue, mouth, and face. I suck as fast as I can, swirling my tongue all around her pussy.

I suddenly stop what I'm doing to her, keeping my tongue in place as all these feelings rush all over my body and I explode. My juice squirts up and into her throat. I thrust and thrust hard into her mouth. I don't want her to stop sucking, I don't want her to spit my cock out. I have never felt anything like this. I don't know what it is, but it feels fantastic. These feelings are so alien to me. I can't feel pain, but I can feel this, is it pleasure? It sure as fuck feels good. I thrust more and more.

My head goes back and I scream out. "Don't fucking stop. Suck with everything you have."

She does. I slowly move to lay on my back bringing her ass with me.

"Don't stop," I shout just as she sits on my face.

I insert my tongue into her pussy again, lapping up all her juices. She's sucking and sucking my cock. This is euphoric. If I can feel these feelings, I never want this to stop. I want to keep doing this for as long as I can.

We both come down from the high we were on. She is now lying with her front along my front with her ass still in my face, but I don't give a fuck. I just want to lie like this for a while and try to take in what I just felt. I'm all confused. I can feel pleasure, obviously from that, but I can't feel any pain? She could bite my cock off for all I know and I don't think I would feel it. But suck it and I fucking feel everything. I need to learn to read. I need to learn about what is wrong with me. Mama called me a retard all these years. What if it's something a lot of people have and I'm not actually a retard?

Daisy starts to get up. I just lie there trying to work out what I just felt. I don't feel anything right now. I put my arm under my head and I watch her. She looks around for her clothes. The t-shirt is useless as it's ripped.

"Well, that's no good. Not to worry, I have plenty in the car."

I stay where I am, naked on the porch. She starts to wander into the cabin and I let her. I stay like this for a few more minutes. She comes back out.

"Don't you have electricity here? I can't find any switch?"

I shake my head, no, not bothering to look at her.

"Shit, I need to clean up. Where's the bathroom? It's too dark in here."

She's annoying me now. It's like having Mama back. I slowly get up, not caring I'm naked, and I watch her watching me. I tower above her and as I try to pass her, she licks my chest. What the fuck. I move away from her and I head to the kitchen side of the cabin, I root under the sink feeling my way around until I find what I'm looking for. The rope. Daisy's not going anywhere anytime soon.

I saunter back to the cabin door where she's standing trying to focus on what I'm doing. I did light the oil lamp when I arrived but I guess it must have burned out which is why it's so dark in here. I step up to Daisy and I take her hand with my free hand. She hasn't seen the rope. I lead her to one of the two chairs I have in the kitchen and sit her down.

"Stay here a minute while I light up the place for you."

She just does it. Stupid woman. I go behind her chair and quickly wrap the rope around her torso binding it around a couple of times, pinning both her arms to her sides.

"What the fuck are you doing?" she shouts, the tighter I tie it.

I then move and light a lantern and get some more rope, I tie her legs to the legs of the chair. She's helpless to do anything now. She struggles and tries to stand up but I push her down. I don't speak, but she's screaming at me. I just stand in front of her watching her tits bounce as she exhausts herself fighting. They are tied with the rope around her body but I look at the flesh between the ropes and I see her nipples are rock hard.

I start to stroke my cock, mimicking what she was doing to me earlier and I find I like it. She stops struggling and watches me. She licks her lips.

"So this is some game you like to play, eh honey? Well, I'm all for that. If you want the power, I can play along with that."

She has no fucking idea. I don't want power, I'm just curious. But as she's happy to play along, maybe I can use that to my advantage.

I move closer to her, still stroking my cock and pulling as I do. I straddle her on the chair and start to rub my cock over her face and mouth. Her tongue darts out each time it passes over her lips to try and take it in her mouth.

"Untie my legs," she says all breathy. "You can keep the rest of me tied but I need to spread my legs for you to thrust that cock inside me. I can't do that while they are tied up. I want that big cock inside me, ramming me hard."

Fuck, I never thought of putting my cock where my fingers and tongue had been.

I untie her legs and as soon as I do, she spreads them as wide as she can and tries to shuffle her ass to the edge of the seat. I kneel on the floor in front of her and I grab her thighs, spreading them as far as I can. I put my face near her pussy and I inhale the smell of her. I lick her pussy lips then stick my tongue on her nub and flick it. She tries to lift her ass off the chair to get closer to me. I keep my hands on her thighs, spreading her legs.

"I want your cock in me now," she shouts at me, she's getting frustrated. I push her thighs farther apart, she screams. "Watch it, that fucking hurts."

Pain. She feels pain when I do that. I do it again, pushing farther and harder. I don't know my own strength and she screams out. I stop.

"You're gonna rip me apart if you keep doing that. Now bring that cock here and stick it in."

I take my cock and I play with it on her pussy. Rubbing it around and around the nub. It's rock hard and I'm getting all those sensations again. I fucking love it. The fact I can feel them.

She's panting and trying to thrust up off the chair, but she's tied too tight. I rub more, then find her hole. I push a finger inside first and feel around, I scrape my nail along her insides and she takes in a sharp breath. I watch her face. She's wincing, but she looks like she's enjoying it. I stick another two fingers in and do the same. It's so soft and wet in there. It's like sticking your fingers into a rotten pumpkin, so squishy.

"Please, I want more," she says with stuttered words.

I pull my fingers out and I lick them. I love the taste and smell. I still have my cock in my hand, yanking it hard. It's grown so big, I rub it in her folds then find her hole and I shove it inside so hard the chair slides back and I fall out of her. I push the chair back against the wall so it won't move again and I get right in there and stick my cock in again so hard. I don't move. It feels strange but I can't explain why.

"Move, push it in and out hard," she shouts.

I start to move my hips in a circular motion then I pull out so the tip is still barely inside then I slam it back in as hard as I can. This feels fantastic. The sensations running through my body are bliss. I put my hands on her ass and try to pull her toward me so I can get deeper. She's tied so tight to the chair, but it helps.

I repeat this over and over. She screams with each thrust into her. I circle, pull out and push, circle, pull out and push. I get faster and faster, not wanting it to stop. I lean down and through the rope, I bite her nipple hard. She screams but I continue my onslaught. I grab the back of the chair on each side of her head for support and I ram and ram until I explode. I stop pushing and twitch hard with each small thrust of juice coming out of my cock. It keeps coming and coming. I see it dripping out of her pussy and down the crack of her ass. I take my finger and wipe it up and put my finger in her mouth.

She moans at the taste. "I want more. Don't stop."

I swivel my hips, still pumping juice into her.

"Harder, I haven't come yet, harder."

I have no idea what she means but I start to pick up the pace again. I want to see pain and pleasure on her face. I start to spread her thighs farther apart again, they are so far apart she screams out. It's hurting her. I can see the pain. I slam into her harder and harder. My cock had gone limp after all my juices but now it's rock hard again. I stop spreading one of her thighs and I feel her ass and stick my fingers inside. I move them around, it's not as fleshy in her ass but she enjoys this from her moans. I pump away with my cock and my fingers, hard, I'm still spreading one of her inner thighs.

Suddenly I feel something strange in her leg, like elastic snapping, and she screams out so loud. This is a bloodcurdling scream, I shoot out juice again from my cock just as she does the same. She's crying but she's thrusting, it's so wet in and around her pussy from her juice and mine. Her leg I was pushing is limp. She stops moving. She's crying hard. She moves her other leg against my side, but the limp one won't move.

"I think you broke my leg, you fucking asshole," she screams at me.

I take my cock out of her and I shuffle back, I then grab the limp leg and move it around to the front of the chair to rest with the other one. She screams as I do this. Her leg is so limp there is no stiffness to it at all. I think I tore something at the top of her inner thigh or in her groin. She's crying hysterically now, her chin is on her chest, I sit back on my heels. I see blood all over her tit from where I bit her.

"How do you feel?" I ask her. I want to know what she's feeling. I feel fantastic after all that. I actually feel happy and joyful. She slowly lifts her head and looks at me through her sweat-drenched hair that is now plastered to her face.

"You broke me. I can't move my leg. You made me come so hard and you broke me at the same time."

She's not shouting. "What do you mean I made you come?"

She looks at me like I'm a retard. Just like my mother used to.

"You made me come, how else do I say it?"

I shrug, not understanding.

"Holy shit, you don't know?"

"Know what?"

She starts to laugh hysterically. She's crying and laughing at the same time. She's tied here to my chair, naked, covered in blood with a broken leg and soaking wet all over from what I just did to her and she's hysterical. I slap her face to shock her. I remember doing that to Mama once when she was crying and laughing over me hurting myself. She glares at me.

"Have you ever had sex before?"

I shake my head.

"Holy fuck, you were a virgin. I just popped your cherry." She laughs again. "You just came so hard twice, that's where all your spunk comes out of your cock. Then you made me come twice, not that you noticed the first time. That's where all my woman juice comes flowing out. It's how babies are made, but lucky for you, I'm on the pill because you didn't use a condom."

I look at my cock. Spunk. Is that what it's called? Okay, well, I liked it, I don't give a shit what it was. I look at her pussy but her legs are closed. I want to taste our cum mixed. I spread her legs, not caring, and I yank them apart. She screams out in pain and I watch her face, I want to see the pain. Her mouth twists and she scrunches up her eyes. There are tears seeping through her clenched eyes. Her head goes back and her mouth is open but a little contorted with the pain.

"I'm going to taste our cum mixed and while I'm doing that I want you to tell me exactly what the pain feels like. I want you to describe it as best as you can. I need to know what it feels like."

She looks at me like I'm insane, with tears flowing down her face. "Are you for real right now? You sound crazy, you son of a bitch!"

I lean down, watching her face the whole time. With my tongue, I take a swipe at her soaking wet pussy. I lap at it, taking in all the cum. I could feed off this and be very happy. She just watches me and squirms in her seat. She's loving it but she isn't talking.

"Tell me now?" I say on her pussy as I bite down on her nub hard.

She screams out. I stick my tongue inside and try to lap the cum from in there. She squirts in my face. She's fucking coming again. My cock is now rock hard and I want to go again, but I want to know what she's feeling more. I take my tongue out and bite hard again.

"Tell me in detail what you are feeling. Describe the pain."

She screams out in pain and pleasure again. "I don't know what to tell you. It fucking hurts. When you bite me, it's so much pain but the pleasure takes over. The pain is like something scalding me, like burning me but the pleasure takes over from the pain and that's like electricity running all through my body. It makes my body tingle all over like pinpricks. I feel amazing and it gives me palpitations. My heart beats so fast I feel like it's going to beat out of my chest. My leg hurts, it felt like something snapped inside and each time you push it, the pain intensifies. I don't know how to explain the pain. You need to experience it to understand how it feels."

"Fuck," I shout, frustrated. "When I was coming, I felt things I have never felt before. Little tingles all over my body. My heart was beating so fast, like you said, I just felt so overwhelmed with everything I was feeling. I felt happy. My mama never said I needed to experience pain to know how it felt."

I get up and walk away from her. I'm not worried, she can't exactly go anywhere with a snapped leg. I now feel frustrated and start pulling on my hair. I have long curly black hair and I hadn't realized I pulled a big chunk out with frustration until I turned and saw her looking at my hand.

"Shit, you just pulled all your hair out."

I look and see a big mass of hair in my hand.

"Are you going to untie me now? I need you to take me to the hospital to get my leg checked out."

Is she for real? I'm not taking her anywhere. I'm going to use her and experiment. She said the pain was like being burned. I get some water and light the log burner, placing the pan of water on there. I stand watching it until it boils away. She's been shouting at me all the time I've been standing here and started to sound like Mama calling me names, but I just ignored her. I did turn once when she cried out. She was trying to stand up while tied to the chair but she couldn't move her snapped leg. I smiled and looked back to the water.

Once it was boiling, I took the pan from the burner and walked over to her.

"Now, I know you will scream at this, but I want you to describe the pain you feel. Okay?"

Her eyes go wide as she looks from me to the pan of steaming water and back to me again. "What are you doing? What are you talking about?"

I place the pan on the floor near her feet. With her good foot, she lashes out and kicks me in the chest. I spill a little of the water onto my hand and I just watch as the skin goes red. I didn't feel a thing. I take the rope and tie her legs at the calf to the chair so she can't kick out. I then lift her good foot and place it over the boiling water. She's begging me not to do it but I slowly lower her foot into the pan, watching her face as I do this. She screams out with another bloodcurdling scream and then stops suddenly. Her head flops forward, she's passed out.

Fuck, I wanted her to tell me how it felt, not fucking pass out on me. I get up and get some cold water and throw it in her face. She startles awake. She looks shocked, trying to remember where she is. Then it dawns on her. She screws her lips tightly shut. I see the tears run down her face. I kneel and take her good foot out of the pan then I put the other foot in. The water's cooled a little now, there isn't as much steam coming from it. I watch her face as I slowly lower the not so good foot. I want to see if the snap has damaged her nerves or if she still feels the pain. She screams again. She feels the pain.

"Tell me, quick, how does it feel? What's it like?"

She screams and starts to tremble. "You fucking psycho, it burns, you're burning me. How else can I tell you that it fucking burns? It hurts so bad!"

I look at her other foot and see how red-raw it has gone. I can see white patches appearing that look like blisters all over her foot. I look at my hand where I got wet and my skin has done the same. I prod it and it's a blister full of fluid. I press her blisters and she screams again. She's crying hysterically, her eyes start to roll back in her head and her body trembles uncontrollably. Shit, I don't know what's happening to her. Is she gonna fucking die before I find out what the pain is like? She stops suddenly and goes still. I stand over her and lift her head. She doesn't respond. Her eyes are closed, I feel for a pulse, she has one, thank fuck she isn't dead yet. I drop her head and leave her. I go have a cold wash, I'm all sticky and for the first time ever, I want to go to the bar and get a beer.

———

I'm sitting in the bar and I've ended up with four beers. It didn't taste nice at first, I wondered what all the fuss was about, but on my third one, I kinda got used to the taste. I've watched as people have come and gone, just wondering what they were all up to. Did they have someone tied up in their cabin like I do? I bet not. I decide to get back to Daisy and see if she's come around. I blew the lantern out when I left, so she couldn't try to knock it over so she'll be in complete darkness.

I wobble a little as I leave the bar, I'm a bit confused as to why I can't walk properly but I manage to get down the steps and walk home. I seem to stumble a lot and at one point I fall, when I look at the palms of my hands I can see scrapes and blood, great. I make it to the cabin and I sit on the porch for a while. As I sit, I hear Daisy shouting for help, asking who's there, but I just ignore her. I need to clear my head for a little bit. It's so dark out, I lay back on the porch. There's a hole in the roof and I watch the stars through it. I find this peaceful and something I do quite often. I think back to what Daisy was saying, and it kinda makes sense. How can you describe pain unless you can feel it? I don't suppose there are any words to describe it, if you can't feel it. Telling me it burns means nothing because I can't feel burning. How am I gonna find out? Maybe I need to cut her and see if she can tell me that way.

I must have fallen asleep on the porch as I wake up to a grunting sound not too far from me. A bear. I'm sure of it. I stay still and I listen. It's not getting any closer. I figure it's looking for food and can either smell myself or Daisy. I just hope she stays quiet and doesn't start shouting when she hears the noise. I can hear it foraging in the bushes, but it seems to be moving farther away. I slowly lift myself, not making a sound so I can see how far away it is. I can just make it out near the trees. If it goes any farther, it will fall into one of my traps. Just then I hear the sound of the twigs snapping and I know it has fallen into one of my holes. I get up quickly and run over. I knock the chair as I do and must have woken Daisy up as she starts shouting for help. I look into the hole and see the bear, it looks okay to me. I need some fresh meat, I've been away for a while and didn't have anything in the cabin. I'll sort it out later on.

As I open the door, Daisy hurls abuse at me, calling me a psycho, sicko, insane, anything she can think of. I light the lantern and take it toward her so I can see her in the light. She looks a mess.

"Are you in pain?" I ask her.

"What do you fucking think leaving me scalding in boiling water?"

I look at her bad foot that's still in the pan, but the water will be freezing now. I take the pan away and get some more water to put on to boil. I need some coffee. As I move around the kitchen, I get the scissors from the drawer, I'm gonna see what else I can do and find out if she can describe the pain to me. I walk over, scissors in hand, and I see the look of horror on her face.

"What are you doing, please don't hurt me any more. I'll tell you what you want to know. Please don't hurt me!"

I look at her pathetic face. She's still naked and shivering from the cold. I reach out to her erect nipple sticking out between the pieces of rope wrapped around her, the one I bit hard earlier and I can see the teeth marks around her nipple, I pull on it hard. She winces.

"What do you feel?"

She looks at me, terrified. "It feels like sticking a knife in me when you pull like that. It's still sore from you nearly biting it off."

That doesn't help me. "How do you know what it feels like to have a knife stuck in you? How can you say that it feels like that? Let's see if you're right."

I take the scissors and I stick them into her tummy. She screams out in pain and shock.

"Well, does it feel the same? Me pulling your nipple as sticking scissors into you? Does it feel like the same thing now?" I spit out.

She coughs and blood comes from her mouth. She shakes her head as she's trying to bend forward. I yank her head back by the hair. "Tell me, does it feel the same as this?" I then twist her nipple hard again.

"NO," she screams at me. "It feels fucking different. Please let me go. Please."

Does she not get it? She's not going anywhere.

"Tell me what the pain feels like now." I get right into her face and spit the words at her. She tries to recoil but I still have her by the hair.

"I don't know how to tell you. It hurts so bad. Both hurt just as much. The nipple feels like you're going to rip it off and the pain is excruciating. The scissor wound hurt at first but now it just feels numb. I don't feel anything. When you stabbed me, the pain was immense. I felt like I was going to throw up and pass out all at the same time. You fucking psycho, why are you doing this?"

I twist the scissors a little before pulling them out. Blood gushes everywhere. I must have hit something important. I get a rag from the cupboard and stuff it into the hole the scissors made. I don't want her to bleed out just yet.

"I want to know what pain feels like. I don't feel it for some reason. I don't feel anything. The first time I've felt anything is having sex with you. I didn't know I could feel anything. So after feeling the pleasure, I want to know more than anything what pain feels like. Does it feel anything like pleasure?"

She shakes her head. "Pain is the complete opposite of pleasure. Pleasure and coming, or having an orgasm, releases dopamine into your body. Dopamine is a hormone your brain releases and it's responsible for the feelings of pleasure, desire, and motivation during sex. Pain is from a different area altogether, which is why you probably feel the pleasure. Pain comes from the nervous system, I've heard of that before where a person doesn't feel any pain. It's a rare congenital disease but I can't remember what it's called. If you pass me my cell, I can look it up for you if I can get internet out here."

I look at her baffled at everything she's just told me. "How do you know all this stuff?"

She shrugs. "I studied medicine for a while at med school. I was going to be a doctor but then shit happened, and well, here I am, just wandering around from town to town with nowhere to go. Now, are you going to release me? I need to get help for this wound and I've peed myself and I stink."

I can't smell anything. I walk away. I need to think about all that she has just told me. The main thing is I have some kind of disease, so I'm not a retard.

I go to my room and lay on the bed for a little while. I feel bad that I stabbed her with the scissors now. She may already be dying a slow death with the blood that was coming out of her mouth. I want her to help me find out what is wrong with me. She said she's heard of this before. That makes me feel better. There must be other people out there that are like me. So many things are running through my mind as I contemplate what I've learned.

I must have fallen asleep as it's now light outside my window. I get up and use the bathroom then wander into the kitchen. I forgot about Daisy. Shit. I think she's dead. Her head is on her chest, she's either asleep, but me moving around making noise would have woken her, or she's dead. I move over to her and lift her head. I can see the rag still stuck in the hole but it's so bloody and blood has dripped out and pooled on the floor. She moans as I hold her head. She tries to open her eyes but is struggling. She's very pale, I suppose being here naked all night she must be freezing. There are a couple of rats running around, I wonder if they've been nibbling on her as they did with Mama. I was flat out and if she made any sound during the night then I didn't hear her. Her lips are blue, just like Mama's were near the end. I start to untie her legs, then remove the rope binding her body to the chair. She flops over and falls onto the floor with a thud. I can see her feet are all blistered from the boiling water but the rats must have been gnawing on them as they are now all bloody. Shit, I never got to know what the pain's like. Too fucking late now for this one.

I hear a noise from outside. I move quickly to see what it is through the kitchen window. I don't see anything, I go to the door. Nothing there. I hear it again. Then I remember there was a bear last night that fell into one of my traps. I could always put Daisy in the hole with the bear and let him maul her, that would get rid of one problem. I move out of the cabin and head to the hole where the bear is. I look down and see him lying there. I think he must be injured, probably from the fall, he looks up at me and grunts. I'll put him out of his misery and I can use his meat to feed me for a couple of weeks, I'll just dig a hole and bury Daisy up near where Mama is buried or even in Mama's hole. That way no one will know she was here and there will only be the one grave. I'll grab her belongings from her car and burn them before I get rid of the car. I paid attention when she drove us here, I think I can do it, I'll drive the car miles from here where there's some hills and then let it roll down and crash at the bottom. I put the plan into action. I kill the bear, haul it up so I can butcher it, I dig up Mama's grave and I place Daisy in the hole. She's not dead yet but it won't be long, the earth will suffocate her in no time.

Six

Blaine—Age 28

FOR THE LAST FEW YEARS, I'VE BEEN WANDERING AROUND FROM town to town just like Daisy did, she was my first. I've had so many sexual encounters, I've become a bit of an addict, I can't get enough of the way I feel when I have an orgasm. Just to be able to feel something is amazing to me. I still torture the women, I still want to know what the pain feels like. Not one of them can describe it to me. It's all a waste of time and their lives.

I've cut fingers and toes off, I even cut one woman's ears off, that was a bit horrific. I've torn hair out by dragging them by it, and one time, while licking a pussy I bit her nub off and spat it into her face. She was so far gone with her orgasm at the time she hadn't realized what I had done until it landed on her chest, she couldn't make out what it was until she then noticed all the blood between her legs and the pain must have started. She screamed hysterically and because I wasn't at the cabin, I had to shut her up by knocking her out. We were in a cheap, dirty motel. One of those that are used for sexual encounters and no one bats an eye at anything going on. I ended up waiting till it was dark and putting her in the trunk of the old banger I was driving at the time. She stayed in there a few days until I made it back to my cabin and buried her in Mama's grave. I just thank god I dug that grave so deep for Mama.

I've been to a lot of bars on my travels. I love beer now. I can drink and drink and I only ever get a little wobbly and tired. I never take a woman from my local bar, that's too close for comfort for me. I don't want to take a local girl and have a search done on my property. I now have signs up that say trespassers will be shot, at least I hope that's what they say, the guy in the store told me they said that.

I've been doing jobs for the local garage, helping clean cars and I was also shown how to change tires, check the oil and generally how to tinker under the hood. I've then been able to do this on my travels to make sure I had some cash to live on.

I need to try to find someone that can teach me to read and write. I was talking to one woman before I hurt her and she said she worked in a library years ago, but she hated quiet. I asked what that was, and she told me it was a place full of books where people go to read and they had computers for them to use. I had no idea anything like that existed. I then killed her, she wasn't telling me anything about pain, so I slit her throat and watched the blood gush out.

I found a library in a town not far from downtown LA just this last week. I walked in and was astounded by the size of it. If I could get someone to help me out maybe I could find out what this disease is that I have. I've never forgotten what that first woman Daisy said. That she had heard of this. I want to find out, to know I'm not a retard after all, well, not in the sense there is something wrong with me, but yes, the fact I can't read or write makes me a retard. That's all Mama's fault. I wandered around that library for hours, going down each aisle, looking at all the books but not knowing what they said. I picked one out from the children's section because it had lots of pictures in it and I sat at a table flicking through that book for hours. It was all big creatures, I loved it. I then picked up other children's books with numbers and short words in them, I wondered if I could teach myself to read and write but it was no use. Mama only taught me a few numbers and letters. I needed someone to help me, to show me. I got some funny looks sitting there with children's books and I guess someone must have said something as I was asked to leave. I was so mad. I loved it there. I tried to explain I couldn't read or write and wanted to learn but the security guy escorting me out told me to go to school for that.

I found a bar not far from that library and I've been coming back to it the last few nights. I'm gonna head back home tomorrow, so I'm sitting with a beer watching everyone. I love to people watch. I learn so much from it. I learn how men and women act with their friends and with each other. I see all the flirting and I've seen so many just randomly having sex outside the bars, in alleyways or even in the bathroom stalls. I've done it a few times just to get the feelings I crave. I find it so easy to pick a woman up. They seem to just be attracted to me for some reason. I can never just sit and have a beer without countless women coming on to me.

I remember one time there were these three girls all eyeing me up as I sat drinking. They were young and were very giggly. One of them plucked up the courage to come sit with me. The other two watched. I eyed them all up, nice bunch of girls. I got the feeling it was new for them, so they either just turned twenty-one or they were using fake IDs. She started to talk to me, she was very nervous but very pretty, she had white-blonde hair, blue eyes, a little turned-up nose and nice tits under the sparkly top she had on with jean shorts. She said her name was Lou for Louise and that she and her BFFs, whatever the fuck that is, were celebrating her birthday. She didn't say how old she was though.

Her BFFs were Geo and Sandy. I motioned for them to come and join us and I bought us all a drink, not that I had much money on me, just enough to get the drinks. Sandy, whose real name was Bethany I found out later, had sandy-colored hair, hence the nickname Sandy. She had green eyes and also had nice tits, but they were smaller than Lou's. She was slightly more covered up than Lou. Now Geo had black hair and looked tanned, I figured she was Hispanic. She had brown eyes, and she had the biggest tits out of the three of them with a barely-there top on, they were trying to escape, popping out of her top. She also had a huge ass and hips, which I just wanted to grab hold of and plow into. Later.

They each bought me a drink and we chatted for a while. They were all happily drunk by the time Geo had got her round in. They asked if I wanted to join them back at their hotel which was not far from the bar. Fuck yes, there was no way I was missing out on this. We headed to their hotel, they were all sharing a room. They had wine and I found out they had drunk two bottles before they went out.

I sat on the bed and watched the three of them interact. I lay back and rested my head on the pillow. Geo climbed onto the bed and straddled my legs, sitting on my shins. She had the tightest short shorts on and her ass cheeks were sticking out. I propped myself up and grabbed her ass cheeks, pulling her forward. She put her hands on my chest. The other two stood watching, giggling. I started to feel those ass cheeks, squeezing them hard and pulling her right into my chest. My cock was rock hard in my jeans, trying to break free. I lay back down, pulling her with me so she was right over my cock. She could feel how hard he was and she started to rub her covered pussy on him, trying to gain some friction. I held out my hand and beckoned to the other two. Lou came to the side of the bed and held my hand. I beckoned with the other hand to Sandy and she mirrored Lou.

Geo was starting to get really rough on my cock. I let go of Lou and Sandy's hands and I undid the buttons on Geo's shorts and then undid the buttons on my jeans. As soon as I did this, Geo knelt up and pushed her shorts down. Fuck, she wasn't wearing any panties, she barely had any pubes, just a small strip on her pussy. I so wanted to lick it. She managed to pull her shorts off then as she was above my cock, she pulled my jeans down watching him spring free. He was standing up at attention, just waiting for a ride. Her eyes went so wide as she watched him and she licked her lips. Fuck. She grabbed him and started to rub him along her pussy and her nub, or clit as I now know it's called. I reached out for Lou and Sandy and I grabbed their pussies, rubbing them both at the same time. They all started moaning together and it was music to my ears.

I looked at Geo. "Sit up for me."

She did, I moved lower down the bed until her pussy was hovering over my face.

"I want to stick my tongue in your pussy. Lou, Sandy, strip now, everything off and take Geo's pathetic excuse of a top off her. Lou, climb up and straddle me, take my cock and play with your pussy with him. Sandy, I want you up behind my head. I want you to play with Geo's tits, and I want to finger you."

They all just did as I asked, none of them bothered by my demands. I got the feeling they liked giving me the control and being told what to do.

I grabbed Geo's ass and I palmed her cheeks, I then grabbed her hips and lowered her over my face and I stuck my tongue right up into that sweet pussy. I then moved Lou in place over my cock and I took him and stroked her pussy for a little bit then made her carry on doing it on her own. I then felt for Sandy's pussy, I stopped tonguing Geo.

"Sandy, play with Geo's tits, now" I demanded because she wasn't doing it. I had my eyes open and I watched as she reached out and a little gingerly at first, she started to rub her nipples and then knead her tits. "Harder," I said to her, I wanted to see those glorious globes being squished and pinched. I then resumed tonguing Geo and stuck my fingers into Sandy's wet pussy. Everyone was moaning. They were loving this as much as I was.

When I felt Lou take my cock near her hole, I thrust up quickly and penetrated her. She screamed out, but I carried on thrusting and thrusting as hard as I could. I held Geo down with one hand on her hip and I sucked and tongued her with everything I had. I had two fingers in Sandy but increased it to four and I pumped away into her pussy. I could feel them all nearing orgasm and I was about to shoot my load myself. I tried to hold out as long as I could. Lou was the first to go. She was riding me like a madwoman, up and down, round and round, faster and faster. She stopped suddenly and screamed out then started up again. Sandy was the next to go, she screamed out and squirted all over my hand. I wanted to taste it but waited. I was about to go and just as I did, Geo went with me. She screamed and screamed and I sucked and sucked all her cum as I squirted all mine up into Lou. We all collapsed in a pile of bodies. All trying to catch our breaths. What a fucking experience that was. One I sure as hell will be repeating.

Time passed, Lou fell asleep. Sandy asked me where I was from as I didn't tell them. I just said I traveled around. She let it slip that it was Lou's eighteenth birthday and that Lou was a virgin but wanted to lose her virginity on her birthday. She told me that no matter what, Lou was going to have me when she saw me in the bar. She said Lou thought I was an Adonis, whatever the fuck that is, and that if she was popping her cherry tonight it would be with me. Glad I didn't disappoint but looks like

I wore her out. I knew she was a virgin, there was blood on me and the bed. I've had a few virgins in my time. I love breaking them in, I see the pain and then immediate pleasure on their faces. I love the feel of tearing into them. They suddenly stop, I am never gentle, I feel they need to be broken in fast and hard not slow and easy. They stop, have horror written on their faces, then when I carry on pumping away, the horror and pain turns to pure bliss. I love a virgin for that reason.

We moved Lou out of the way onto the other bed as she was well and truly passed out from the exertion and the drinks. I made Geo get on the bed on her hands and knees, and I got behind her ready to plow into her. Sandy played with my balls and my ass, getting me ready to enter Geo. I thrust into her so hard she almost collapsed on the bed from the thrust. It was what Sandy was doing to my ass and balls that made me do that. The feelings I was getting from her doing that and thrusting into Geo was unreal. I went harder and harder, grabbing those hips of hers, and I plowed as hard as I could.

"Sandy, come here."

She moved to my side and I slowed down on Geo. I removed my cock from her and told Sandy to get in front of me so I could plow into her but I wanted Geo to get on her back and spread her legs because I wanted Sandy to finish her off and lick her pussy. I plowed into Sandy's ass, not her pussy. She froze, I could feel how rigid she was. I pulled her back to my chest and I started to play with her pussy with my fingers and rub her nub with my thumb. I started to thrust into her ass a bit more and with each thrust and me playing with her pussy, she relaxed more. She inserted her fingers into Geo as I had her sit up.

"Geo, stand up in front of us."

She got up and I continued to thrust into Sandy's ass and play with her pussy and Sandy moved Geo so her pussy was in her face and she started to lick her pussy, sticking her fingers into her ass. It wasn't long before one after the other we all reached orgasm, I'm not a screamer, I'm silent but the girls love to scream. I pulled out of Sandy and I turned her around to lick her cum off her pussy and I smeared my fingers full of Sandy's cum all over Geo's pussy. I then licked her dry as well. We all then lay down on the bed. I had Geo in front of me, I had my cock in her ass and was kneading her globes and Sandy lay behind me, spooning me, playing with my balls and ass crack. We fell asleep like that.

When I woke in the morning, it was to Lou straddling me, Geo holding my rigid cock and Sandy sitting on my face. We were all a mess by the time we finished. I took a hot shower with the girls all joining me of course then I left them all, thanking them for an amazing night. One I have repeated a few times since with other women, young and old. I don't care, and the more the merrier. All the feelings I get from it just turn me on even more. I just can't stop.

I'm sitting in this bar nursing my sixth beer or maybe the eighth, I dunno, I lost count, and shunning the women that come on to me. I think it's time to go. This bar is similar to the one near my home in that it has a porch with steps. Leaving the bar, I feel my legs wobble a little more than usual. What the fuck, I didn't think I'd drunk that much. I try to walk straight, but struggle. I grab hold of the handrail as I start to descend the steps, but it's no good, I fall down the steps, flat on my face. I feel someone trying to help me up. I turn my head and almost throw up when I see the most beautiful pair of blue eyes staring down into mine. Holy fucking shit, it's her. It's Primrose, I would know those eyes anywhere. How can this be? How the fuck is she here. She's like the angel I remember from all those years ago. I must have knocked myself out. How the fuck is this real?.

"Primrose," I mumble. She looks at me, startled.

PART II

Primrose

Seven

Primrose–Age 7

I'M SITTING IN THE BACK OF THE CAR WITH MY MAMA AND PAPPY playing with my Barbie doll, well it's not my doll, it's Poppy's doll. She's my sister. She had to stay home today with my aunt Cassy because she was sick. She was really upset 'cause she wanted to see Grandma. We both love going to Grandma's, she spoils us, that's what Pappy says. We just visited with Grandma and we are now on our way back home. Pappy says we can stop near home and get some pizza for our dinner. He says Poppy might be feeling better. I'm hungry, I feel my tummy rumbling, but I don't know if it's from all the cookies I ate at Grandma's. She always makes the best chocolate chip cookies when she knows we are visiting. It's just, I think I ate more than I should because she made them for Poppy and me. She made extra while I was there to bring back to Poppy.

I don't get to see Grandma often as we live a long way away from her. She has a dog that I love playing with. I think his name is Ruff or it might be Gruff, I don't understand Grandma that good. She tries, but it's hard for me.

I play with my Barbie and I look up and see Mama looking at Pappy and they are talking. I don't know what about. I smile and carry on playing. Suddenly the car starts to move funny and I look up from my Barbie and I see a boy standing in the road. My pappy is trying not to crash into him and is trying to move the car away. My mama looks back at me, and I see the fear on her face. I've never seen her look like that before. She's opening her mouth and saying hold on, then she looks back to the front of the car. The next thing I know, I'm upside down, then I'm not, then I am, we are turning over in the car. I grab Barbie and hold her to me, clutching her hard as I screw my eyes shut. I start to say please be okay, please be okay, over and over in my head. Suddenly the car jolts to a stop. I don't dare open my eyes. I'm scared of what I might see. I stay as still as I can with my eyes still screwed shut. I'll just wait for Mama or Pappy to get me out of here first. If I stay still, then I won't get hurt. I don't feel hurt anywhere, but I think I'm upside down. I keep hold of Barbie for comfort.

Some time passes and I still don't open my eyes, I'm scared, my head is hurting because I'm upside down, I don't feel any movement in the car. I don't know what to do. What if Mama and Pappy are hurt and I need to help them? Stupid me just hangs here upside down, scared. I grip Barbie tighter, I try to shuffle in my seat to see if I can move okay then I brace myself and open my eyes. I see the greenest eyes staring back at me that are not my pappy's. He's trying to look at me. I don't move. He moves out of the car and then appears at my side, trying to crawl through the smashed window. He just stares at me as though examining me. I stare back. Why isn't he helping? He asks me something. I see his mouth move but I can't tell what he's saying, he's mumbling, barely opening his mouth. He finishes looking at me, but he doesn't help me. He looks to Pappy and then edges out backward. He runs around to Pappy's side and I can make out that he's crawling back in. Maybe he's going to help Pappy.

I look at my mama's side. I can see her bent over all funny and weird leaning in my pappy's direction, but she isn't moving. Her long blonde hair is a tangled, dirty mess. That's not my mama, she's always so clean and dresses nicely. I love my mama. I see my pappy moving a little bit, I think he's talking, he's trying to twist around but I see he can't move.

"Pappy," I shout out.

The boy looks directly at me. We just watch each other for a few minutes. He can't be that much older than me and he looks a bit mean and he's dirty as well. We stare into each other's eyes for what feels like ages but must only be a few seconds. I'm not afraid of him, he's going to help us all. He just keeps looking at me, why isn't he helping Pappy? I start to get upset and tears flow down my cheeks.

"Pappy, Mama," I cry out.

He doesn't flinch but puts his finger to his mouth to shush me. He's not helping them, why isn't he helping them? I continue to watch him for a few more minutes and I get upset that he's still not helping them. Maybe if I'm good and nice to him, he will help. He looks at me again for a few seconds, just staring into my teary eyes, and I smile at him. It's my 'please help us' smile. He smiles back. Maybe he understands and is going to help. I wipe the tears from my eyes. When I look back, he's not looking at me anymore and I can't see his face now.

I wait and wait. It seems like forever and no one is moving, apart from the boy but only slightly. I don't know what he's doing. The next thing I know, he's back at my side and scurrying as far as he can get into the car. He frantically tries to undo my seatbelt, he's going to help after all. He's trying to get me out of here. He struggles with finding the release catch, he's staring into my eyes while fumbling to find it. He suddenly releases me and I fall to the roof of the car, on my head. I'm bent a bit awkwardly, ouch that hurt. I look to him and I see the panic on his face. Why's he looking at me like that? He reaches out and wipes at my forehead. I flinch at his touch. What's he going to do to me? I watch as he pulls his hand away and I see blood on it. Oh, is that from my head? I must be bleeding.

I need to get out of here and help Mama and Pappy. I start to move and crawl toward the boy. He starts to back out of the car to let me get out. I see him look away and then back at me with panic on his face. He then grabs my arms and pulls me hard out of the car. I don't know why he's freaking out, but he's starting to freak me out now. He pulls me up, and he starts to run, dragging me along with him, I try to resist a little. I need to help Mama and Pappy. He just drags me along, not realizing I'm trying to get out of his hold. We run for what feels like ages, far away from the car, I try to look back at it but I don't have time. He starts to pull me up the slope. He suddenly slips but manages to push me in front of him and points up the embankment. I look back toward the car and I see flames. Mama, Pappy, I need to help them. I look back at the boy.

"Run Primrose, run," he tells me.

I do, I run up that embankment as fast as I can, I'm still gripping

Barbie. I stumble slightly just as I near the top. I feel trembles all through my body and before I know it, I'm in the air and landing heavily back on the ground. I'm still gripping Barbie when I turn slightly toward the car and see there was an explosion, the car is on fire. I lay my head on the dirt and I cry and cry. The car blew up with my mama and pappy inside. I know they are gone. The boy helped me out in time. He knew it was going to blow up. He knew, and he saved my life. The boy with the greenest eyes and messiest black hair saved my life.

I think I must have fallen asleep from the exhaustion. I got up when I saw flashing lights approaching from the opposite direction, they stopped up near where the car was on fire. I limped to the edge of the road and I looked down behind me, but the boy wasn't there. I looked all around for him going in a circle, but I couldn't see him anywhere. I limped toward the flashing lights. There were now so many people and fire trucks, policemen, ambulances. Suddenly someone spotted me limping toward them. A sheriff came running to me. He bent in front of me.

"Hey little one. You're hurt. Were you in the car?"

I just nod my head at him, yes.

"I can see you have a hurt leg and a cut on your head, let's get you some medical help. Can I carry you?"

I just nod again.

He scoops me up into his arms and walks very quickly to an ambulance where the paramedic takes over and starts to clean me and examine me for injuries. I don't speak. I don't tell anyone about the boy with the greenest eyes. He's gone, so what difference does it make? I cry. I know I have no mama or pappy anymore. I know it was because of that boy they died. If he wasn't standing in the road, the accident wouldn't have happened. I also know he saved my life.

I get rushed to the hospital, I'm numb. I don't speak to anyone. I have nothing to say. I have cuts on my head and they said I had a broken leg from the explosion. It threw me in the air and I landed on my leg funny. I knew it hurt, but I didn't look at it. I just needed to get help. I remember them saying my leg was snapped and they needed to take me to surgery to have it pinned.

I wake up sometime later and my aunt Cassy and Poppy are sitting in chairs in my room. Poppy has her Barbie clutched to her chest, I can see how dirty the doll is but she doesn't care. She notices I'm awake and runs over to my bed and strangles me trying to give me love. I choke out. Aunt Cassy rushes to me and gets the water.

"Here, sweetie, take some gentle sips of water. You've had a big operation. Do you remember what happened, sweetie?"

I look at her, and I cry. She sits next to me and hugs me to her. I look up into her face.

"Mama and Pappy are gone," I say to her.

She nods as tears run down her cheeks. Poppy is sitting on the bed crying with us. We all three just cling to each other and cry for what feels like ages. I'm so tired. I yawn and lay my head back down. I keep hold of both their hands, I'm afraid if I let them go, something bad will happen. I start to fall asleep, drowsy from the surgery. As I fall asleep, I see the greenest eyes and messiest head of black hair looking right at me.

I wake up with a start. I sit up, gasping for breath. I had a dream that Mama and Pappy were now angels looking down on me. I cry and cry, my aunt Cassy has hold of me and is hugging me. I look up into her face.

"It's okay, sweetie, you had a bad dream."

I shake my head no.

"It was good, Mama and Pappy are angels now. They are watching us." She smiles and I see a tear escape the corner of her eye, I smile, rest my head on her and cry. After a few minutes, I look up.

"Where's Poppy?"

She motions to a cot in the corner and I see Poppy curled up asleep on it, she looks peaceful but I know she's not. We lost our parents and she nearly lost me. My leg is starting to hurt now, I lean forward and lift the sheet to look at it. It's in a plaster cast from my foot to just past my knee.

"It will be in that for about six weeks, sweetie. Then they will see if the bones have mended together and decide if you need a brace or not. It was a bad break you had there. The sheriff told me you were walking on it to get to them, you brave little girl." She kisses the top of my head and pulls me back to cuddle me.

I wake in the morning, and the room is empty. I start to panic. Where is everyone? What's happened to them? I can't get out of bed because of my leg which is really hurting me. I ring the bell for a nurse. Not long after a nurse comes wandering in followed by Aunt Cassy and Poppy. I sigh with relief and lean back on my pillows. "I thought you had all gone," I say to them. Aunt Cassy shakes her head no and comes to my side, grabbing my hand.

"We were just outside the door, Prim, we had some breakfast and were just on our way back in."

The nurse looks at me a bit funny. "Are you in any pain?" she asks me, pronouncing each word like I'm a foreigner.

I just nod. She gives me a shot for the pain and then brings me some breakfast. I don't want to eat. I can't stop thinking about Mama and Pappy, how Mama never moved once while I was in the back of the car, and how Pappy only moved slightly. Mama must have already been gone from the crash and Pappy not far behind her. I hope they were both gone before the blast. The only person that can tell me is that boy with the greenest eyes. I think back to him and how weird he was. He was with Pappy a while but not Mama. He then saved my life but I don't know what happened to him. Did he get injured? Did he run away? Why wouldn't he stay? All these questions I need answers to. Will I ever see those eyes of his again? I have to think that he only saved me because they were gone. I have to hope that was what happened.

I'm at my house. It's been a week since the accident and Aunt Cassy took us to her house. I wanted to come home and see our house. I wanted to get my things. Poppy hasn't spoken much about Mama or Pappy. I don't think she believes they are gone. I, on the other hand, was there and saw what happened. I think she kind of blames me for surviving and not them. She's been so mean to me when she has spoken to me. Aunt Cassy said Poppy just needed time to process it all. That I should just try and be normal.

I know Aunt Cassy cries each night. She tries to hide it from us but when I went to the bathroom one night, her door was open and I saw her crying. She's my mama's twin sister. It's hard to look at her sometimes because I think it's Mama standing there. They are identical but Aunt Cassy changed her hair to a light brown color, and that's the only difference. She helps me get what I need while Poppy is in her room getting what she needs. I'm on crutches, so I can't carry anything. I notice Poppy hasn't let Barbie out of her sight since the accident. I don't know if she thinks that's her last piece of Mama, as Mama bought it for her, but she won't let Aunt Cassy clean it up. It's still dirty from the accident. I saw Aunt Cassy on her cell yesterday, talking to someone about the funeral arrangements. They are waiting for the coroner to release the bodies. That's what she said to someone on the phone. She wants them both buried together which makes sense. I'm dreading the funeral.

Eight

Primrose—Age 14

FOR THE FIRST TIME EVER, I HAVE A BOYFRIEND. POPPY'S HAD SO many boyfriends I've lost count. She's what the boys call the school bicycle. Damon is sweet. He's nothing like the boys Poppy dates, if you can call it dating. She's a slut, that's what I call her. She will go with anyone no matter if they are freshman, sophomore, junior, or senior, even eighth graders, she has no shame. She's been a rebel ever since the accident and she treats me like a leper. She doesn't speak to me, she stays as far away from me as she can, and when we do have to communicate it usually ends up with her hurling abuse at me and blaming me for the accident. Aunt Cassy blames herself, she says she supported me too much and left Poppy out. She thinks Poppy's rebelling against everyone, that in her mind, everyone left or rejected her. I love Poppy, I just wish she would open up to me.

I have a date with Damon tonight, it's our first date. He's a nerd like me. Well, that's what the other kids call us, including Poppy. Just 'cause we are straight A students we get categorized and segregated by the others. I don't care, I love math and physics and I'm an amazing artist. My artwork has been shown on school open days and my art teacher has talked about me showing it in a small gallery in LA which would be my dream.

After the accident, all I did was draw in my sketchbook. I drew lots of pictures of the accident, especially the boy with the greenest eyes and messiest black hair. Poppy found my sketches one time last year, she demanded to know who the boy was and why I was drawing him next to the crashed car. I told her I made him up. He was no one, but she didn't believe me. I sketched him so many times over the years from memory and tried to sketch how I think he looks now, as he's grown older. I have a full book of just his images, which I hide. I don't want Poppy finding it.

We've lived with Aunt Cassy ever since the accident. It was so hard at first, getting used to not having Mama and Pappy around and with Aunt Cassy looking like Mama. Poppy has never gotten over their deaths. She hates me. I've tried so hard to be her friend and sister but she won't let me in. It got worse when Aunt Cassy started dating Trevor, who is now Uncle Trevor, and they had twins. We have two beautiful cousins who are now nearly three years old. Trixie and Pixie, yeah I thought the same when Aunt Cassy told us their names, but Aunt Cassy is a free spirit and loves nature. We had to move when they found out they were expecting which didn't bother me but Poppy kicked off.

I love Trix and Pix, my nicknames for them but Poppy barely acknowledges them. She's a bitch to all of us. I love helping Aunt Cassy with the girls and I do everything with them while Poppy goes out or stays in her room, I don't know why Aunt Cassy puts up with all her attitude and lets her get away with everything. She never comes home at curfew, it's always later. Aunt Cassy has tried to punish her by grounding her, but she would just not come home from school until later. She took her cell away from her, but Poppy didn't care and bought herself a disposable one each time she did that. She was grounded from using her laptop but she says it's fine, she has her cell to speak to friends and go on social media and that Aunt Cassy was just stopping her from getting good grades because she couldn't do her homework.

We have a good monthly allowance from our inheritance from Mama and Pappy and we get the rest when we are twenty-one, for our futures. We still own the house we lived in with them, Poppy wants it sold so she can have the money added to her inheritance but I refuse to sell it. I will live in it when I'm old enough and just pay Poppy her share so I will own it outright. I just can't bear to part with it. Because we are in a deadlock with it, Aunt Cassy who is in charge of the estate says it has to remain as is until we are twenty-one, then we can legally decide between ourselves what to do with it.

Poppy is younger than me by twelve minutes. We are identical. We look so much like Mama and Aunt Cassy and now Trix and Pix are the same. All of us have natural blonde hair, although Aunt Cassy's is still dyed a light brown and Poppy's changes all the time, it's currently purple. At least everyone can tell us apart, thankfully. She also dresses in the shortest, skimpiest clothes whereas I cover up more. I prefer not to show everyone what I have. I also walk with a limp ever since the accident. When they pinned my broken leg it made it slightly shorter than the other one. I should be the angry one here, I have all the problems while Poppy has none. She's perfectly healthy and just abuses her body. I know she's smoking, you can smell it on her all the time and I've seen her hanging out with the older juniors and seniors. Some of them do drugs which I have no doubt she's tried and they drink a lot. She's come home drunk on more than one occasion and I've covered for her, not that she ever deserves it but I feel for her. She has never gotten over losing Mama and Pappy.

The door light goes and I run to get it before Uncle Trevor has a chance to interrogate Damon.

"I'm going out, Aunt Cassy. I won't be home late. I'm going to the diner with a friend," I shout as I open the door and beam at Damon standing there all coy. "Hi," I say all coy right back.

Aunt Cassy touches my shoulder to get my attention. "Prim, make sure you have your key, sweetie. Have a good time."

I nod and smile.

"Hi Primrose, you look lovely." Damon looks me over then down to the ground, he's embarrassed.

"Thank you. Shall we head to the diner? I'm hungry."

He nods and we head out, side by side. We are walking into town as it's not too far. We talk about school at first as we know we have that in common. Then we move on to movies. We like a lot of the same movies which is great. He takes my hand in his and we hold hands all the way to the diner. We get a milkshake each and he gets a big-stack burger and I have an all-American hot dog. He sits opposite me, it's easier for me that way and we talk about films and he tells me my art is amazing. I blush.

He walks me home holding my hand. We're happily talking and just before we get to my street a car pulls up beside us, Damon nudges me and nods in the direction of the car and Poppy hangs out of the window. Great, just what I need.

"Hey big sis, what ya doin'? Where have you two lovebirds been?"

Damon stops, but I just pull his hand to let him know I want to keep walking. I ignore Poppy and the car but Damon nudges me again, I look at him.

"She's talking to you."

Great, now I have to look at her again.

"Aww big sis, what's up? Cat got your tongue or has it been shoved down lover boy's throat all night?"

I see one of her friend's faces appear and she's laughing. Then Carter Mallick, Poppy's flavor of the week, pops his head out next to Poppy's.

"Hot damn, Prim, come join us, what're you doing with that jerk when you could have me? Oomph."

"You fucking creep. What do you want her for when you have me? You asshole. Stop the car, Mickey."

I carry on walking, holding Damon's hand, pulling him along and ignoring the others, but they are crawling alongside us. I glance back over to Poppy and she's shouting.

"I said stop the fucking car, Mickey. I want out." Poppy is real mad and no doubt it will be all my fault.

Carter tries to stop her. "Babe, I was joking, kinda. I thought a nice twinny sandwich in the sack would be good, you know."

I suddenly stop and fully turn to the car. "You are sick, you pervert. You think I'd go anywhere near you? You creep," I spit out at him.

He mimics me, probably making fun of the way I speak.

The car door opens and Poppy gets out. "Same here, douchebag. You're fucking sick if you think that would ever happen. If you want her then we are so done. Take a hike." She points at me as she's saying this. Like there's something wrong with me. We're the same, apart from hair color. She storms past me and pushes me, and I lose my footing and fall back on my ass.

"Hey, what the hell was that for, Pops? I didn't do anything."

She stops and turns to me, scowling. "You just existing in the same space as me is problem enough, you parent murderer."

Whoa, parent murderer? Where's that coming from? I know she's always thought it was my fault, that it should have been me killed and not them, but I didn't kill them. I'm stunned into silence. I'm sitting on my ass on the grass verge which is not very nice, I'm looking down into my lap. I feel the tears start to roll down my face.

She kicks my foot to get my attention. "Aww poor baby, here comes the usual feel sorry for poor me tears."

I don't understand why she hates me so much. I stare at her. I don't speak, instead I sign for her to "Fuck off."

I see her laughing at me. I hang my head, not wanting to see what else she has to say. She is a grade A bitch.

I feel a hand on my arm and look up to see Damon crouching in front of me.

"Come on." He gestures for me to take his hand which I do and he helps me up. Poppy has moved on, thank goodness. He wraps his arm around my shoulder and turns my chin so I'm looking at him.

"Hey, she's a bitch, Prim. I'm sorry and I know she's your sister but she is nasty. Come on, let's get you home." I give him a small smile, but I don't say anything. It always knocks my confidence when anyone makes fun of the way I speak. For a deaf girl, I've been told I speak almost perfect, but I speak very nasally like I'm muffled and sometimes it's hard for those who are not around me a lot to understand me. My mama took me to special therapy groups to learn to lip read and speak, which I do.

Everyone knows I'm deaf but nobody treats me like I am. Well no one close to me. I have people making fun of the way I speak and they laugh at me pretending to sign when they have no idea how to sign. It's mostly boys that do this, they see me as disabled, I'm not disabled. I refuse to be categorized. I have had some mean girls at school that think it's funny to walk up behind me then suddenly jump on my shoulders to scare me, but like I said, it's mostly the boys that do that. My aunt Cassy was going to take me out of high school and send me to a specialized deaf school but I refused to go. I just want to be a normal teenager and not be treated any differently. I make sure in class I can see the teachers and they know to make sure they face forward so I can understand them. No one can complain, I'm top of most classes with my grades.

Damon walks with me slowly to my house, holding my hand. At the gate, he turns to me, making me face him.

"Hey, I had a great time tonight. I'm sorry I called Poppy a bitch, I know she's your sister but she should not treat you the way she does. I've seen it in school." He hangs his head.

"It's okay, Damon, she is a bitch. I just don't know why she is like that with me all the time." I shrug. "I had a good time tonight too. Thank you." I lean in and kiss his cheek. He turns and kisses my lips. It's just a peck but it's nice. I've never been kissed before.

Inside the house it's quiet. Aunt Cassy and Uncle Trevor usually go to bed early because of the twins. I try to be as quiet as I can as I enter the kitchen to get some water to take to my room. It's dark so I flick the light switch and I jump out of my skin when I see Poppy sitting at the island just staring at me. I go to the fridge to get some water, ignoring her. I turn and she's standing right behind me. I drop the bottle of water.

"Poppy, what the hell?"

She just stands there and stares at me. She tilts her head as though trying to work something out.

"Why?" she mouths to me.

I stare at her, confused.

"Why did you survive and they didn't? What caused the crash? Was it you acting out, being a brat?"

I've told her over and over I don't know the answers. I try to move past her to go to my room but she pushes my shoulder back against the fridge.

"You ruin everything, you survive and they die, you ruined my life, and you still keep doing it now. Look at the way Carter was. You ruined that fuck for me as well."

I'm shocked. She's blaming me for her ass of a boyfriend. It wasn't me that said anything to him.

"Maybe if you didn't act like a slut, you could keep a boyfriend, Poppy."

She slaps me across the face, hard. I hold my cheek which is burning and I have tears running down my cheeks.

"Why do you hate me, Poppy? Why?"

She just sneers at me and turns her back to walk away. I watch her disappear out of the kitchen. I wait a few minutes before I grab the bottle of water from the floor and close the fridge. I sit at the island for a while trying to figure out why she hates me so much. I try to be nice to her. I just want us to be close, all I've ever wanted was to be her best friend and for us to have that twin thing where we are inseparable and finish each other's sentences and play jokes on people. All the stories Mama used to tell us about her and Aunt Cassy. Aunt Cassy told me not so long ago that she knew immediately when Mama died, that she felt pain in her chest and had keeled over in agony, that she felt like something was being torn out of her. It was at exactly the same time Mama passed away.

I've felt little things before, like feeling sad even though I wasn't sad, and I put it down to the twin thing. I knew it was Poppy feeling sad. I wonder if she felt it when I broke my leg. I've never asked her before because she very rarely answers me when I speak to her. I head up to bed thinking it will be safe enough to go now without risking another encounter with Poppy. I feel so sad that we are like this when all we have is each other, apart from Aunt Cassy. Despite the way she is with me, I love her. I love her so much which is why it makes me so sad she is so mean to me. Maybe one day we can talk and sort this out. Until then, I will avoid her as best I can.

Nine

Primrose—Age 20

I'VE JUST COMPLETED MY FIRST YEAR AT CCA AND I'VE ENROLLED again to do another year. I finished high school with honors and after doing a four-week pre-college program at California College of the Arts where I lived on the Oakland campus while studying the various degrees of art, I knew it was the place I wanted to go after high school. I got accepted immediately but I had to defer for a year.

I attended my senior prom with Damon, who I had been going steady with since we were fourteen. You can imagine our suprise as we watched Poppy being crowned prom queen, I have no idea who whould vote for the school slut, but they did. As we were leaving I was pushed by Poppy, yet again, only this time I twisted as I fell and my bad leg that is pinned together broke, again.

I was in a long sleek emerald-green prom dress and I was trying to stop myself from falling and ruining the dress. I was in agony and couldn't move. Poppy panicked for the first time because she thought she had seriously damaged me this time. She knelt beside me and tried to help me, telling me how sorry she was. She didn't mean to hurt me, but we all knew she did. They could see the agony I was in and called 911. I was mortified and I could see Poppy felt the same. The one thing I did notice as she kneeled on the sidewalk next to me was her pain. She kept wincing as she knelt there and I knew it was the twinsie thing. I was in pain and so was she. I was glad, she deserved to feel it because she caused it. I had to have surgery that night to try and replace the plate and pins, it was a difficult operation because the pins had snapped and the plate warped. They said I might end up losing my leg.

They managed to fix my leg but I had to wear a brace for three to six months, which is why I defer going to CCA for a year. I knew it would be hard hobbling around a new college and trying to create masterpieces. Poppy couldn't do enough for me during the time I was in a brace. Aunt Cassy and I saw a new side of her, one we liked. One day I finally did ask Pops why she was so mean to me and if she felt the same pain as I did on the day of the accident that killed our parents. She ignored my question at first and just left the room, but then she later came back in and sat on my bed, she took my hand and told me yes, she felt everything. On the day of the accident she felt the fear I felt, she felt it when I snapped my leg and was walking on it trying to get to help.

She said she also knew I was lying about the sketches and the boy with the green eyes. She said she knew he had something to do with it all and she was angry at me for hiding it. She was so angry that we lost Mama and Pappy and that I was hurt and could also have been killed. That was a turning point for us. We didn't hang out with each other, and we were never best friends, but she stopped being as mean to me. That's not to say it stopped completely.

Poppy moved to San Francisco to go to college and to be honest, everyone was more relaxed now that she wasn't in the house, even though she was only like twenty minutes away. Trix and Pix are now in third grade and I love them like sisters. They are inseparable and I envy that about them. They are how I had longed for Poppy and I to be, how Mama and Aunt Cassy were. I come home on holidays and some weekends and I always take them out to the movies or the ice cream parlor, but their new favorite is the cupcake shop that opened not so long ago not far from home. I stayed friends with Damon but we are more like BFFs than anything else. He was my first boyfriend, and last. We did have a sexual relationship, which was okay, but it's all I ever knew so I have nothing to compare it to. I still love him, but as a BFF, not as a boyfriend. He has a new girlfriend now, he met her in college and she is really sweet. I don't see him as much as I did, for obvious reasons, which is why I spend most of my time with Trix and Pix and Aunt Cassy just hanging and having girly time, and Uncle Trevor when he isn't working.

I've had a few boys ask me out, but some of them run a mile when they realize I'm deaf, which I'm used to now. I did go on one date my first year at college but it was a disaster. He took me to the movies which did not offer closed captioning and it was a boring sci-fi film. I spent the whole time there trying to read the lips of the actors but missed what else was happening because of it. He just never thought about me not hearing the film. He then took me to a club to dance, although I can dance to the vibrations, it hadn't been that long since my second break and I couldn't dance yet. All in all, it was not my ideal night out. I never went out with him again.

I haven't bothered with anyone else since. I lose myself in my art. I still draw the boy with the green eyes. Each time I make him older, imagining what he's like now. I'm nearly twenty-one, so he must be about twenty-four I think. My art professor saw a couple of the images and wanted to display them but I wouldn't let him. Instead, I showed him other stuff I'd done and let him use those. Poppy, as far as I know, hasn't seen any of the sketches since that first time. I don't want anyone else to see them and ask me questions.

It will be our twenty-first birthday in a couple of weeks and I know Aunt Cassy wants to throw us a party, but I don't want one and I don't even think Poppy is coming back for our birthday. It's also the day we get our inheritance and I can officially move into our family home and buy Poppy's share if she still wants that. We haven't discussed it for a long time, but it's always been my intention. I go to the house some weekends when I tell Aunt Cassy I'm not coming home. I just like being there. We cleared it out a few years back. Me, Aunt Cassy, and Uncle Trevor. Poppy didn't want to have anything to do with it. We sorted out all of Mama's and Pappy's clothes and other stuff and we took it downtown and distributed it between the homeless charities and the youth charities. There was a lot of stuff so I know it would have helped.

While doing that, I found out about volunteering. It's something I always wanted to do but I could only do it during the daytime with being in high school and then part-time with me being in a leg brace. I also now volunteer every January for the Great Los Angeles homeless count where we scour the streets of LA and count all the homeless people we find. This increases every year, and it astounds me. I always think back to the boy with the greenest eyes, as I've often wondered if he was alone and homeless. From what I recall, he had dirty clothes and he wasn't clean. The homeless count is vital and Aunt Cassy has always done this with me. We go out in groups for three days in January and count. We also take food and essential toiletry parcels with us to hand out.

I want to move straight into our home when I can. I spoke to Aunt Cassy about it and she's fine with it. She always knew it was what I wanted. I've kept the house clean all these years even though it was never lived in and Uncle Trevor always made sure the lawn care was maintained. If he didn't do it himself, he hired a lawn maintenance service to do it.

I've been in talks with an art gallery in downtown LA about displaying my work, we've been messaging and he is interested in my work. My professor knows the gallery owner and he showed him some of my pieces. I'm going to meet him tomorrow and iron out the details. This is my dream and I can't believe it's finally happening. It's not just my pictures though. I have done some sculpting this last year and he is interested in showing those as well as the pictures. My sculptures are a little bit harrowing though. They depict my interpretation of the accident that killed my parents. I haven't done a sculpture of the boy with the greenest eyes but I have morphed him into the sculptures I've done. You wouldn't know unless I pointed him out, but he's there. One sculpture is of a crushed car on its roof. It's my abstract interpretation of it and I added green eyes into the piece. Another is of a warped tree, depicting the tree that the car was crushed against. In that one, I had his messy black hair in the branches, again, my abstract interpretation of it. Some of my art pieces are images I remembered, like standing on the road and looking in the distance at all the red and blue lights of the emergency services. Or climbing the embankment and looking back into the trees and imagining those green eyes. A lot of my work is based on the accident but most people wouldn't know that.

Other art pieces are fine art of buildings and different people. This last year, I took a few trips to Venice Beach and I used to sit and draw the life around me. It's the perfect place with such a diverse community from the homeless to the tourists to the locals. It's a scary place to be if you're there alone and it's getting dark but I never stayed there too long. I have lots of paintings of people on rollerblades, on the equipment at Muscle Beach, homeless men sitting on a couch listening to their ghetto blaster. It's an amazing place.

I want to travel in the next couple of years and paint different cultures. I would love to go to Europe and South America and the far east to see all the different buildings, especially in Singapore. I will see where the next year takes me first. I hope Poppy comes home for our birthday. I wouldn't want to celebrate it without her. I'm going to text her and see if she'll come home. I haven't heard from her for a while, she never messages me. I text her all the time and half the time she doesn't reply. I thought once we got older we would become closer but she has other ideas. I don't even know if she is still in college or where she is, and I don't think Aunt Cassy has heard from her in a while either. I just hope she's safe.

Some days I feel down for no reason and I'm sure it's because that's how Poppy's feeling. I know she's in with the wrong crowd again. Aunt Cassy was telling me she had a call from the college to let her know Poppy had not been in for a week. When Aunt Cassy finally got hold of Poppy, she fed her some story about not feeling well. If that was true, I would have felt something. I was just tired all the time while she was not in college and we think she was taking drugs or some kind of substance.

Aunt Cassy and Uncle Trevor drove to San Francisco, and I looked after the girls for them. When they found Poppy, she was not in her dorm sick, they managed to find her holed up in an apartment with about ten other people. Aunt Cassy said it was like an opium den and they pulled Poppy out and brought her home. I went back to CCA, and they made sure she was well enough before letting her go back to college. Aunt Cassy told me it was a tough few weeks, and that they had to plead with the college to let her back in as long as she promised to catch up on her missed studies. As far as I know, she has been doing well and has been clean since. Aunt Cassy makes her come home most weekends so she isn't out partying all the time, those are the weekends I either stay at CCA so I can use the facilities over the weekend for my pieces or I go and stay at our home and work there.

As much as I love Aunt Cassy, Uncle Trevor, Pixie, and Trixie, I miss my parents and Poppy so much.

Ten

Primrose–Age 25

POPPY DIDN'T COME BACK TO CELEBRATE OUR TWENTY-FIRST birthday, which I'd expected, and I didn't see her for a long time after that. She refused to come back for a visit once she found out Aunt Cassy had the estate changed so we wouldn't receive our inheritance until we were twenty-five. Aunt Cassy sat me down to tell me the day before our birthday. She explained it had nothing to do with me, but had everything to do with Poppy and that for her to make the changes it had to affect both of us, she couldn't just change the one. I was shocked, but not angry. I was upset I wouldn't be moving into my family home. When I told her this, she said I could move in any time I wanted. I just wouldn't own it personally for another four years.

The reason she changed the terms of their inheritance was because she discovered Poppy was using drugs again and had dropped out of college. Aunt Cassy believed Poppy's new boyfriend moved her in with him because he knew she was about to inherit a lot of money. She suspected he was a dealer but had no proof of that but she did a background check on him and he was a lot older than Poppy and had been arrested for possession with the intent to distribute. He managed to get off that charge and it was just dropped to possession. He also served time when he was younger for assault. He has also never been employed. All this threw up red flags and Aunt Cassy believed he would just use the inheritance money then blow Poppy off and she would be left with nothing.

As you can imagine, the shit hit the fan once Poppy found out she wasn't getting any money. This was the day of our birthday and she called Aunt Cassy to ask where her money was, why it wasn't deposited into her account. She called Aunt Cassy every name under the sun and told her she couldn't do this and she was going to fight it. The problem was, Poppy had no money to get a lawyer to help her fight it. She also brought me into the argument telling Aunt Cassy it was all my fault, I was the parent murderer, nothing I hadn't heard a thousand times from Poppy. This put a damper on our twenty-first birthday, but Aunt Cassy, Uncle Trevor, and the twins made sure I had the best time that night.

We found out that Poppy was still living with the boyfriend but that she had to work full time for him as his mule. We couldn't do anything about it. Aunt Cassy tried everything but there was no proof, and Poppy said she was happy living with her boyfriend. That all changed just after our twenty-second birthday and she came back to live with Aunt Cassy. I had moved out so I didn't have to see her until she wanted to see me. She was a mess when she came back and eventually she told Aunt Cassy everything that had happened to her. I was shocked to find out her so-called boyfriend was not only using her as his mule to distribute the drugs but that he was prostituting her out to punters and every time she tried to deny him or his punters, he would pump her with drugs and lash out at her.

When I first saw her about three weeks after she returned, I broke into tears. She was nothing like my Poppy. She was so thin, she had bones sticking out everywhere, her hair was so dull and had been hacked in places, her eyes were lifeless, there was no spark in them and the color was dull. Her skin was a mess, full of blemishes all over and so dark under her eyes. It was Uncle Trevor that went posing as a drug user and wanting sex that got her out of that mess. She has slowly come around the last couple of years and she says Aunt Cassy did the right thing with the inheritance because she would have used it all by now. She even came and visited me a couple of times with Aunt Cassy and the twins but she didn't say much to me. She's looking more and more like me again.

I've been traveling the last couple of years. I've seen all the places I wanted to see and I have an amazing job at an architect firm in the city. I love my job and it takes me all over the world. Poppy went back to college, but in LA, she wanted to go into social services to help others who got into the same situation as she did. I'm proud of her, but she still resents me.

I've had a couple of boyfriends over the last few years. I just broke up with my most recent boyfriend, Gordy. We were together for eleven months and we were getting serious, but I think it freaked him out when he saw my shrine to the boy with the greenest eyes. He had no right snooping in my house even if he more or less lived here.

He went into the attic one day, that's where all my sketches are. I have still been sketching him these last few years but not quite as much. I have an image in my head of how he looks now. He will be about twenty-eight or nine, if he's still alive. I have always secretly wished I would run into him one of these days, I still want answers. Gordy went into the attic, apparently to see what space there was up there and as no one but me usually goes up there, I didn't put all my paintings and sketches away. He came down into the kitchen with an oil painting I had done of how I think the boy now looks. In my head, he is chiseled, with high cheekbones and a strong jawline, still with the greenest eyes and messiest black hair. I painted him like a Greek Adonis, so I understand Gordy was a little perturbed by it all.

He walked in carrying that picture and threw it onto the island. I screamed at him in horror that he could damage one of my paintings. "Who the fuck is this, Prim?" he shouted across the island, I scrambled to get to the painting before it slid off to the floor.

"It's no one." I saw him laugh, so I looked down at the picture. He had moved around to me, jerking my head in his direction so I could see what he was saying to me.

"Like hell it's no one. Why are there like a million and one paintings and sketches of him in your attic if he's no one?"

I picked up the painting and walked past him and up the stairs to take it back to the attic. He followed me, I could feel him stomping up the attic stairs behind me.

I turned. "Stop, Gordy, you are not coming up here and how dare you go up there without my permission anyway."

He looked shocked that I had turned on him. "What the fuck, Prim? I practically live with you in your house. You never told me there was a no-go zone in the house, for fuck's sake."

I started up the stairs again and glanced back to see if he was still following me. "No, Gordy, you do not come up here ever again. This is my personal space, where I do all my art, it's not for anyone else."

He was livid, I could see his cheeks turning red and his eyes narrow to slits and he pursed his lips before opening them to speak. "You have a fucking studio to do all your art projects, Prim, why the hell do you have an attic full of this guy? Who the fuck is he?"

"He's none of your fucking business, Gordy, now back off and leave me alone."

"If that's what you want, Prim, I'm out of here. You have a fucking shrine up there to this so-called no one. That's creepy, Prim, very creepy." He backed down the stairs.

I tidied up the attic that day and I put most of the pictures away. I didn't want anyone else seeing them. It is kind of creepy when you think about it. This is the boy that caused the accident that killed my parents, he saved my life and I now have a shrine to him. Do I hate him or am I just fascinated by him? I still paint and sketch him to this day. I just can't help it. I think about him a lot.

Gordy left the house that day for good. I didn't see him until two weeks later. We hadn't messaged each other and if I'm honest, I think I loved him a little, but I wasn't heartbroken when I didn't hear from him and you'd think I would be after eleven months of being together. I only saw him once when he came to collect his stuff from my house. We were civil to each other but neither of us begged the other to stay. Maybe we were both just making do.

To be honest, the few relationships that I have had have only filled a void, meaning it was just like I was making do. I have never been madly in love with anyone. Even Damon, my first boyfriend, was more of a friend with benefits. But as he was the first person I slept with, it wasn't anything special. The other few I have slept with have not been anything special either. I would be quite happy just being me and being single. I have a job I love that sends me all over the world, I have my own house and a family I love.

Poppy just messaged and asked if I wanted to go get something to eat tonight after work. She's near my office and thought we could catch up. Since when did Poppy ever want to do anything with me? It makes me nervous, she never wants to just spend time with me. I agree to meet her anyway. At five-thirty p.m., I finish what I'm doing and head to the restaurant, ready to meet her. It's even a high-class restaurant, which surprises me, as she picked it. I didn't think she ever did anything like this.

I'm sitting at the bar watching the door for when she arrives. I see her and watch as she walks in and the hostess looks at her quizzically then looks to me and smiles. She just realized we're twins. I could see the confusion on her face. She brings Poppy over to where I'm sitting at the bar.

"When you are ready, ladies, your table is ready for you."

Poppy smiles then leans in to hug me. This is not the Poppy I know. She doesn't ever ask me to meet her, let alone hug me. I look at her skeptically. She just smiles. "Shall we sit and order?" she asks me, I just nod yes to her. I'm still very disillusioned where Poppy is concerned.

I know she doesn't want money, we both got our inheritance from the estate not so long ago and I bought Poppy's share of the house. I own it outright now. As far as I know, she's still living in an apartment on her own. She qualified as a social worker and now helps out around the city for those women that have been caught up in the sex trade or have had substance abuse problems. I'm amazed at her for taking the path she has. She never wanted to help anyone growing up. She was always very selfish.

We sit down and a waiter comes over to fill our water glasses as we look over the menu. To be honest, I'm not that hungry. My nerves are in turmoil sitting here.

"I'll have a white wine, please," I say to the waiter. "Poppy, do you want anything to drink?"

She looks at me, but it's a 'how dare you' look, what did I do? "Water is fine for me, thank you."

The waiter goes off to get my wine. We sit in silence going over the menu, he comes back. "Ladies, are you ready to order?"

I close the menu. "Can I have the soup of the day please in a bowl with the brown bread?"

He nods then looks to Poppy.

"I'll have the filet mignon please, medium rare with sweet potatoes and green beans." She closes the menu and hands it to the waiter who then goes off to put the order in.

We look at each other while taking a sip of our water. I have to start. "What's this about, Pops?"

She puts her glass down then clasps her hands together in front of her. "I ran into Gordy two days ago."

I roll my eyes. Great, just what I need. "And?" I say curtly.

"Well Prim, he was saying how he wished it hadn't ended between you two and he was telling me about some creepy shrine you have in the attic. I knew as soon as he said that, who it was a shrine to."

She slams her glass down hard and I see a little bit of water splash over the rim, I just glare at her, horrified that she is even here questioning my relationship or what I have in the attic. She's never taken an interest in me in twenty-five years, so why start now.

"Look, Pops, I don't know what he's filling your head with but in all honesty, my relationships or what I have in my attic has nothing to do with you or anyone else for that matter."

She picks up her water and takes another sip then puts it down a little harder, I feel the vibration on the table and water spills over the rim again.

"I know he had something to do with the accident, Prim. I know it, but you're protecting him and always have," she grits out at me and I see her clenching her teeth. I know I shouldn't be, because, well, this is Poppy but I'm a little shocked at the venom I feel radiating off her, even after all these years.

"Look, Poppy, I told you years ago he was just in my imagination and that's it. Nothing else. What you want to take from that is up to you. If you want to believe he had something to do with the accident, then that's your prerogative. You've always accused me of killing our parents. How? I have no idea, but it was always my fault to you."

I don't want to sit here arguing. I've had enough tormenting from her and her friends over the years, I don't have to put up with it anymore. "Look, I'm leaving. Gordy has nothing to do with you or me and I'm not going over old stuff again. You have your life and I have mine, so let's keep it that way. It's how you always wanted it anyway. Goodbye Poppy, I'll see you around."

She grabs her glass of water and throws it at me as I stand up to leave.

"What the hell, Poppy. I'm tired, I've endured twenty years of tantrums from you. You hate me and always have, so let's just go our separate ways and stay out of each other's lives. Okay?"

I grab the napkin to absorb some of the water she threw on me just as the waiter arrives with our food. I throw a fifty on the table and tell him to give my food to someone on the street that needs a hot meal. I start to leave, shoving my chair to the side in anger.

"That's right, run off like you always do, Primrose. I'll get the truth one day, you mark my words." I catch her saying, but ignore her, turning away from her so she knows I won't know what she's saying and I head out.

I stand on the street outside the restaurant for a minute trying to compose myself. Trying to fathom what that was about. What does she want from me? What truth? She thinks the boy with the greenest eyes killed our parents. Well, she's right. He was standing in the middle of the road from what I remember. To be honest, the story changes in my head as the years pass by. I do remember him standing in the road, but what I don't know is why. Was he just crossing the road or standing there intentionally. It changes in my memory so much. I hope I can get an answer one day, but I'm not holding my breath at ever seeing him again.

At home, I go up into the attic and gather everything I have of the boy with the greenest eyes. I have a huge chest up here so I place it all in there and lock it. Unless someone breaks the lock, no one will see any of the images again. I won't draw or paint him anymore. He needs to be dead to me from now on.

PART III

Blaine
&
Primrose

Eleven

Blaine–present

"**D**O I KNOW YOU?" SHE ASKS ME.

It's her. There is no doubt in my mind. She has the eyes of an angel and her hair is still as blonde as I remember it. Her eyes have haunted me all these years. I think I may have banged my head, not that I would know. Maybe I had more beers than I thought. I've never been drunk like this before. She's trying to help me up, but I'm a bit too big for her to lift. I turn over onto my knees and help myself up with her trying to help, but not helping that much. I can't believe it's her. Maybe if I look at her now, it will be someone else and I was just imagining Primrose. I'm fucking scared to look. I want it to be her so bad. I straighten up but don't look. I turn away from her.

"Hey, are you okay? You took quite a tumble down those steps."

I need to face her to see if it's her or if I was imagining it. I turn slowly. The anticipation is killing me, but I'm terrified it won't be her. FUCK, it's her. It's HER, fucking standing in front of me. My angel, the girl who didn't get hurt in the crash. The girl who was somehow saved, I've always believed she was saved just for me. Always hoped I would meet her again one day, but I never thought it would ever really happen, yet here she is standing in front of me asking if I'm okay. Well, fuck me.

"Fuck, it's you. Where, how, I don't fucking believe you're standing here."

She looks a bit angry, but then she notices something on my head. She runs into the bar leaving me standing, just watching her disappear. It's like she's moving in slow motion.

"Hey, where the fuck are you going? Come back. I need to talk to you." She's gone before I can even put a foot on the step to follow her.

I grip the handrail so I don't fall again. I feel okay, so I'm not sure why my legs were all wobbly. Then I try to climb the steps and my leg gives way under me and I fall backward onto my ass. Fuck, what's wrong with me? It's then I look at my legs and see my sneaker is missing and my foot and ankle are swollen. I look around for my sneaker but don't see it anywhere.

"This what you're looking for?"

She's there at the top of the stairs, holding my sneaker along with some paper napkins. She comes down the steps to me and kneels beside me. One of the napkins is wet and she starts to dab it on my head. I lean back wondering what the fuck she's doing and I see blood on the napkin. Oh, I put my hand to my forehead and look at it, it's covered in blood.

"That's a nasty cut you've got there. You may need stitches." She starts to dab my head with the dry napkins. "Maybe just a couple of butterfly bandages are all you need."

She carries on dabbing away. I just stare at her face, I memorize every detail of it that I can see in this light. I move her arm away from my head, I still don't believe this, she looks a little hurt.

"Just need a bandage and to put my sneaker back on and I'll be fine, thanks."

She grabs the sneaker and slams it onto my lap then gets up.

"Have we met?" She stands with her arms crossed over her tits, she's pissed at me. I take the sneaker and try to put it on my foot, it won't go on, it's too tight with my foot so swollen, I loosen the laces to make it bigger. Now it goes on. I look up at her and she's still standing there watching me.

"We did meet once, yes. You must have forgotten, we were both young."

She tilts her head then bends down closer to me. She's moved right into my face and I find it intimidating.

"What the fuck you doin'?" I move back on my ass and then turn over so I can lever myself off the ground. I nearly fall again, but she's at my side with her arm wrapped around my waist and she puts my arm around her shoulders. I try to walk but my foot wants to give way again. She keeps hold of me and helps me to sit on the steps.

"Does it hurt?" She motions to my foot, then moves in and dabs my forehead again. "Wait here, I'll go see if they have any dressings for your ankle."

While she's gone inside, I try to stand using the rail to lever myself up. I need to get away from her. It's making me angry knowing she doesn't remember me. The one person who I didn't hurt, and would kill if someone hurt her, doesn't even fucking remember me. Well, screw her. I need to get back to the motel and maybe rest my foot. I don't know what I did to it, but it's swollen up. That's the problem with not feeling anything. I've had so many infections from cuts I didn't know I had or bent fingers from breaking them and them not setting right, even toes. I'm a danger to myself. I manage to hobble to the outer bushes around the bar and I duck just as I see her coming back outside. She stands there looking around for me but she doesn't see me.

I see her mouth moving but can't hear her from here. I watch her, still in shock, it's her. My angel. She saved something inside me that day. I can't put a finger on what but I know she did. She stands with one hand on her hip, still searching for me. Just as she sweeps her eyes my way, I duck more to make sure she doesn't spot me. She's beautiful. I knew she was way back then, but now she's even more so. I will need to find out more about her. She's been my obsession for all these years. Her eyes are always there whenever I need them. They seem to always appear at the right time. I'm now sitting back on my ass, leaning against the bushes.

"Why the hell didn't you wait for me? I went to get stuff to help you and you do a fucking runner. Nice. Here."

I startle at the sound of her voice. I sat with my eyes closed thinking about her when we were younger. I need to know more about her and what she does now. She throws dressings at me and starts to walk away.

"Fuck, Primrose, wait, I'm sorry. I just thought I could move on my own. It seems I can't."

She stops and turns to me with a slight smirk on her face. I don't know what that's about. She saunters back to me and takes the dressings back. After dabbing my forehead with some tissue she puts a sticky bandage on my head. Then she sits on the floor next to me and lifts my foot into her lap. I watch her as she tries to slowly take the sneaker off, I think she's trying not to hurt me.

"It's okay. Just pull it off. It won't hurt."

She looks at me and shrugs. "Okay Mr. Macho, if you insist." She pulls the sneaker off and watches me as she does.

I don't move a muscle. I see her eyes widen slightly. She takes the wrap bandage and starts to wrap it around my ankle.

"What did you do to it?"

I shrug. "I don't know. I was a bit wobbly coming out of the bar and the next thing I know I'm on my ass staring up into your beautiful eyes. Maybe I twisted it when I fell down the steps."

She doesn't look away from me, instead she stares straight back into my eyes. "The boy with the greenest eyes," she whispers and I just about make it out.

She does remember me.

"There, let's see if you can stand up now. I got your sneaker on and laced it for support." I didn't realize she had finished with my ankle. I was too engrossed in her, not what she was doing. She keeps looking at me strangely. There is something different about her from what I remember. I know she was young, but I remember her eyes as clear as anything. Although they are the same shade of blue, I remember her left eye had a slight abnormality to it. It had the tiniest of black flecks on the iris. When I look into her eyes now, there is no abnormality, maybe it grew out as she grew up.

"Do you remember now?" I ask to see what she says.

"Not really. Remind me." She's playing with me. I heard her clearly say the boy with the greenest eyes. I remember that day like it was yesterday. We both stared into each other's eyes. I was as mesmerized by hers as she was by mine.

"Well, I was just sitting on the roadside when you walked past and you offered me a cookie."

She frowns at me as though trying to remember. She looks confused. "Yes, I remember now and you took the cookie from me."

It's not her. How could I have this so fucking wrong? I examine her face but it's dark out and I can't see it clearly.

"I think I need help getting back to my motel. Do you think you can help me up and I'll try to hobble there?" I want to see if she volunteers to come with me. If she thinks we know each other, she may feel safe enough to come with me. She looks at her watch.

"Are you busy? Look, it's okay if you need to go, I'll be fine getting back."

She looks back to the bar. She must be meeting someone. She takes out her cell and does something on it, I thought she was calling someone, but she puts it back into her pocket. She then moves to my side and helps me get to my feet.

"Where is your motel?"

I nod in that direction. "It's about ten minutes that way."

She puts her arm around my waist and then puts my arm around her shoulder, holding my hand for support. I'm a lot taller than she is, she's small. There is something not quite right, I know it's her, but then it's not, and I don't understand why. I'm confused as hell here. First, I fall and don't know why, then she's here, my angel, helping me but it's not her. How could I get this so wrong? I know it's been years and she's all grown up, but I remember her and those eyes and she's just playing along like she remembers me, but she doesn't. I don't get it.

She helps me to my motel. It takes longer than the ten minutes I said, with my foot being this bad. It's not that it hurts me, it's just it doesn't want to work and keeps twisting as I step on it. At this rate, I'm gonna break my ankle if I haven't already done so. Just as we approach my door at the motel, I feel her hesitate. I look down at her and she looks up at me, she stares into my eyes, I think she's trying to see if it's safe.

"Hey, it's okay, I can manage from here. Thanks for your help, but you best get going if you're meeting someone."

She gives me a stern look. "No, come on. I'll help you inside and onto the bed then I'll leave."

I open the door and she helps me to the bed where I lay and shuffle up. "Thanks, Primrose. It was nice to see you again after all these years. You're exactly how I remember you, except your hair isn't in braids like that time we met. I just wish it was under different circumstances as well and not me like this," I say, pointing to my foot. She looks at me and cocks her head to the side.

"Yeah, I haven't had it in braids in forever. Nice to see you again, erm…"

"Nick, my name is Nick, well it's Nicholas really but everyone calls me Nick." I never did tell her my name, we never spoke back then and she's lying again. Her hair was in pigtails, not braids. This is not Primrose. I don't know who she is, but it's not her, and I guess I just got it all wrong. But how could I? How could I get it so wrong when she is all I've thought about. She looks at me with a frown, I guess because I was staring at her.

"Is there anything you need before I go?"

I blink and think. "Just a glass of water if that's okay?"

She walks over to the bathroom and comes back out with a glass of water and places it on the nightstand.

"Thank you."

She turns to the door and leaves.

Well, that was a disaster but I need to know who she is and why she looks like Primrose. Could they be sisters? If they are, then Primrose might not be far, I need to know. My stupid fucking ankle is going to hinder me now. I need the swelling to go down. If I fall again, I may break it and I will be out of action for weeks. I don't want to go to a doctor and I don't have insurance for the hospital. I found that out the hard way last time I needed fixing. I've just fixed myself in the past, that's why I have disjointed fingers and toes and scars everywhere.

I try to sleep, but it's almost impossible, I can't stop thinking about Primrose and those eyes. The next thing I know, I hear a quiet tap on my door. Shit, I sit up and swing my legs around. I look at my foot. The swelling doesn't seem quite as bad as last night but it's bruised. I wonder if I can stand on it. There's a firm knock now.

"Just a minute," I shout at the door.

Who the fuck is knocking on my door? I try to stand using the bedside table to help me. The last thing I want is to collapse. I manage to walk to the door and look through the peephole to see who it is. I don't trust anyone. It's her, the girl from last night, the one I thought was Primrose. I open the door, the chain wasn't on because I didn't close it last night, I take my time not wanting to look too eager.

"Hey, thought you might need some food. I stopped by the diner down the road and picked up some bacon and toast for you with some coffee." She holds up the bag to show me.

I open the door wider for her to come in, I still have my hand on the door, she has to duck under my arm. Fuck, I don't know what to do now. I thought last night if I saw her again then I would play along with her, calling her Primrose and see if she corrects me. I'm still standing, looking out the door at the parking lot.

"Hey Nick, you want this food and coffee, or not? I can just put it here and leave so you can eat in peace. I just didn't want you going hungry if you couldn't get out."

I close the door and turn to her, I cock my head to one side looking at her. She has the same clothes on as last night, didn't she go home? Is she some kind of whore? Is that why she's playing along with me?

"Nick, you okay there? You look kinda angry."

I shake my head and give her a small smile. "No, sorry, you just woke me up." I hobble around the room using the dresser to get me to the bathroom. I need to pee bad.

She moves out of my way and watches me, then she comes toward me to help.

"No, I need to do it myself," I say, she looks hurt.

I get to the bathroom without falling. I sit down to pee because it's difficult standing as it is. My ankle just keeps giving, almost sending me flying. I'm beginning to wonder if it's broken already. It just doesn't want to take my weight. I manage to stand using the sink to help lever myself up. I head back into the bedroom and head for the bed using the wall to steady myself.

"I'll just leave this for you and go. Sorry to bother you but I felt bad leaving you when you couldn't walk last night. I didn't think about you using the bathroom. How does it feel?" She nods to my ankle as I clamber onto the bed and sit against the hard wooden headboard.

"It's okay, a little better than it was last night at least. Maybe if I rest it for the rest of the day the swelling will go down."

She comes over to the bed and sits next to where my foot is. She lifts it and watches my face as she does. I make a face and wince as though it hurts when I don't feel a fucking thing.

"It's badly bruised, I think you may have broken it. If it's not better by tomorrow, you need to go to the hospital and get it checked out just in case."

I nod, knowing full well I won't be going to no hospital. I reach for the bag she brought in and take out the plastic tray of bacon and toast.

"There's scrambled eggs in there too. I just wasn't sure what you would like. I got the eggs in case you didn't eat meat and the toast in case you didn't eat either of them." I look at her, I'm surprised she was so thoughtful and even came back to check on me.

"I'm good with it all, thank you. You didn't have to come back with this." I watch her face and see different emotions running over it. Oddly, I don't feel anything for her. Maybe because I know it's not Primrose.

"I just thought I would pop by and see how you were doing. It's no problem and it's on my way to…" She looks away from me.

What was she going to say? "Where?" I ask.

She looks at me. "Home." She doesn't say anything else.

She's obviously been out all night with being in the same clothes. Maybe it was a boyfriend she was meeting last night, and she stayed with him, I don't see a ring on her finger. I start to eat the food. It's nearly cold now, but it's better than nothing. I wolf it all down and she watches me. I then start to drink the coffee. It's black, no sugar, just how I take it. I never had this growing up, I only ever had warm water. Even with the log burner and boiling water, we never had anything to put into it. Mama used to say we only needed water to survive. Since I started going into diners I only ever have black coffee.

"I didn't know how you took it so I have sugar and milk here." She pulls out sugar and milk from her purse.

"No, this is fine just as it is, thank you." I watch her watching me as I drink my coffee. "Didn't you get yourself anything?" She shakes her head no. I raise an eyebrow. "I take it you already had your breakfast then?"

She starts to get up off the bed, I lean forward and grab her arm, maybe a little too hard because she winces and pulls away from me. I hold up my hand. "Sorry, I shouldn't have done that. It's just I didn't want you to go just yet, unless you have to." She looks at me, she's still sitting on the bed and rubbing her arm.

"I have to go, I need some sleep."

"I take it you were up all night then if you're on your way home to get some sleep?" I say as I make a show of looking at her clothes.

She looks down to see what I'm looking at. She's not dressed like a whore, in fact, she's all covered up in sensible clothes which I thought a bit odd last night, seeing as though she was going to a bar. She's in tight jeans and has on a plain white t-shirt under a zipped up hoodie. Not exactly clothes you'd wear to attract attention if you're a whore. It must have been a boyfriend then. She looks me in the eye trying to gauge what I'm thinking.

"Yes, I was up all night, it was a long night actually and not one I want to repeat any time soon, not that it's any of your business, Nick. I was only popping in to make sure you were okay and give you the food. Look, it's time for me to go. If I have time later, I will bring you some more food, do you have any preference? There's the diner that does a lot of homemade take-out food and then there's a Wendy's or a Chick-fil-A up the road I could go to."

"You don't have to do that. I will survive, thank you, Primrose. I don't want to put you out. I'm not your responsibility. You didn't do this to me," I say, pointing at my foot.

"I know, but I want to for my peace of mind."

Why is she doing this? She still hasn't denied being Primrose, what is her game? Is it her? Did the pigment grow out of her eye as she grew up? I'm so fucking confused right now. Maybe she couldn't remember how her hair was that day, she was young after all, maybe it is her. Fuck.

"I like burgers or chicken, you choose and eat with me, if you have time, of course."

She nods. "I'll see how it goes when I get up later. I don't know what time it will be but I don't think you're in any state to be going anywhere." She stands up, then suddenly she rushes out the door.

Fuck, what was that about?

She comes marching back in a few minutes later carrying a brown bag. "I forgot, I stopped at the pharmacy late last night and got a bandage and an ankle brace. Here let me put them on for you before I leave." She comes back and sits on the bed and gently bandages my foot around my ankle and up my calf then puts on an ankle brace. "There. With that on, it should help the swelling go down and give you support for getting to and from the bathroom. Let's hope it's just a sprain and not a break. How long are you staying here?" She gestures around the room.

"I'm paid up for two more days then I'm heading home. Thank you for all this. You really didn't have to do it. You don't even know me."

She smiles and shrugs. "I like helping people. It's not something I've ever been used to until recently, I find I enjoy it. Making a difference in people's lives, it gives me a sense of fulfillment."

I just stare at her. I don't know what to think. I'm so fucking confused.

"See you later." With that, she's gone, shutting the door behind her.

I lay my head back and look up to the ceiling. What the fuck is happening? My head is all over the place. I don't know if it's her or not. One minute I think it is, then the next I don't. Even if it is her, there is no connection, I don't feel anything and that's killing me. I decide to watch some TV. The only time I've ever seen anything on TV is when I'm in a motel. I remember the first time watching TV, I was amazed there were people in this box talking or singing or fucking. I had never seen a TV before my first time in a motel. I'm not in the mood for the sex they put on these motel TVs, so I just put the news on instead to see what's going on in the world. I fall asleep, it's boring.

I wake up needing to piss. I also must stink and I hate that. It's only the last couple of years I realized how bad I must have smelled growing up. I couldn't smell anything, but when I first left my home I could see the looks on people's faces as I passed or stood near them. One guy told me to take a fucking shower because the smell was going to knock him out.

He will never know, but I am grateful for him saying that to me and ever since, I have cleaned myself every day without fail. I usually stock up at home by taking the little soap bars from these motels I stay in.

I get up off the bed, I think my foot must be a little better as I seem to be able to stand on it more than I could this morning, it must be the bandage and brace she put on it. I hobble to the bathroom and sit on the toilet. I undo the bandage she put on so I don't get it wet in the shower. Luckily these motels have really low tiny baths with a shower overhead so I don't have to climb into a big bath tub. I stand under the water for what feels like ages, not that I can feel how hot it is but all the steam tells me it's hot. I soap myself and rinse off and get out. Wiping the condensation off the mirror I can see how red my skin is. Shit, it must have been too hot. I'm just wrapping the towel around my waist when I hear a knock on my door. I have no idea what the time is, not that I can tell the time, I usually judge it by the sun outside. I start to head to the door when the knock comes again.

"Okay, I'm coming," I shout. I open the door and Primrose is standing there. I don't react to her like that very first time all those years ago. I still don't think it's her. "Hey Primrose, sorry I was just taking a shower, please come in."

She has to duck under my arm again to enter the room with me holding on to the door for support.

In the light of my room, I can see she's a little embarrassed, I'm standing in a towel and nothing more. It's a small towel at that.

"Sorry, let me get some clothes on." I start to move toward the bathroom where there is a walk-in section that has my backpack with some clean clothes in it. I struggle to stand and tug out the clothes.

"Here, let me help. If I put the bag in the bathroom and you sit on the toilet, you will be able to find what you need easier." She grabs the bag and puts it next to the toilet. I hobble in and sit down. She leaves. I take out what I need and get dressed. It's much easier doing this sitting down. Then standing, I just pull up my jeans.

"Are you decent in there?" she shouts through the door.

"Yes."

She comes in. "Sit down and I'll put the bandage back on. It looks a lot better already."

I sit back on the toilet and she kneels in front of me and gently wraps it back up like she did this morning. I don't feel a thing, but she doesn't know that.

We both head back to the bedroom. I sit back on the bed and she brings me a bag. I've never had this food before but I like meat, so I know it will be okay. She also brings out bottles of water for me.

"I wasn't sure if you drank soda or not, so I thought it would be safer to go with water."

"Water's great, thank you for this. You must let me give you some money before you leave."

She sits near the window at the small table and pulls out her food and water from another bag.

"So you decided to join me for dinner then?" I ask, smiling at her.

She smiles back, nodding. It's not Primrose. I know it's not her. I pull all the shit off the burger and just eat the meat and the bread.

"I take it you don't like salad stuff or ketchup?" she asks, looking at me eating the burger.

I shake my head. We sit in silence eating. The news is still playing on the TV but I'm not listening to it. I look at her just as she finishes and she looks at her watch.

"Do you need to be somewhere?"

"Yes, sorry, I have to get going but I'll come back in the morning with some breakfast for you. I'll have some with you. Is that okay?"

"Yes, thank you."

She pulls out some painkillers from her purse. "I got these for the pain. Take them with your water, it should help you sleep better as well." With that, she's gone again.

After she left, I was bored, laying on the bed thinking about her, then and now. I needed to get out of here. I got up and tried walking around on my foot. It wasn't giving way quite as much now. I decided to try and walk to the bar, what usually takes me ten minutes, took me nearly an hour. Once or twice I nearly fell, only grabbing on to a railing or bush stopped me falling, thank fuck. I'm probably doing more damage to it by being on it. I make it to the bar and head up the steps one by one, holding on to the handrail as I go up. Once inside, I order a beer but ask them to bring it to the table I point to. I hobble over and sit. I can see what's happening around me from here and see who is coming and going. I like to sit and watch.

I'm on my third beer when the door opens and in walks Primrose. Shit. I put my head down, hoping she doesn't see me. She's with a couple of people. One male and one female, I guess they're her friends. I shuffle into the farthest corner of the booth I'm sitting at but just enough that I can still see her. I watch as the three of them get a drink and sit at a table not too far from me. She has her back to me, luckily. I can't make out what they are talking about, I'm not close enough. She isn't close to the others, in fact, I would say none of them are close friends. The guy catches my eye and gives a small smile. I look away quickly and just concentrate on the beer in my hand. I hope he doesn't say anything.

There's a small cough to the side of me. I slowly turn my head and Primrose is standing there with her arms folded over her tits, pushing them up. She has on a t-shirt with a V-neck so I can't help but look at them. Shit.

"Well, I see you managed to get here okay with your bad ankle." She looks pissed at me.

Fuck her. She doesn't own me. I don't speak, I just stare into those beautiful eyes of hers, I could stare into them all day and wouldn't get bored. Those fucking eyes will be the death of me. She stares me down. What does she want me to say? She's not my fucking keeper.

"What?" I say a bit too harshly.

"How's your ankle?" she says sarcastically.

"Great, thanks for asking," I say with sarcasm in my voice to match hers.

"How did you get here? Please tell me you didn't walk here."

I continue to stare into her eyes, neither of us has broken eye contact yet. "Yes, I did walk here and it may have taken me a little longer than usual but I'm fine." We continue to stare. I take a sip of my beer but still don't break eye contact. She moves her hands to her hips, still staring into my eyes.

"Well I guess you don't need my help anymore then if you can manage to get to the bar okay on your own. Nice to meet you, Nick. See you around." With that, she turns on her heel and heads back to her friends who are watching this play out.

The guy smiles at me again. What is it with him? I just glare at him.

"What's his problem, looks like you stuck some dynamite up his ass there, Pops. Mr. Moody, but those eyes," I hear him say, he's making a point of saying it loud enough for me to hear.

Pops. Why did he call her Pops. She taps him slightly on the arm telling him to be quiet. I stare at her back for a bit and he's staring at me. Fuck it. I need to get out of here now. I can't watch her here with another guy. The other woman keeps eyeing me slyly out the corner of her eye. I down the rest of my beer and make to get up, fuck my ankle won't work. It wants to stay on its side. I must have had it like this for a while and now it's gone dead. I sit and lift my ankle slightly stretching it out and rotating it to bring it back to life. The guy taps her and nods my way. She turns to me and watches what I'm doing with my ankle. She pushes back on her stool and stands up coming over to me.

"Here, let me help you, Nick. What's wrong?" She grabs my leg and starts doing some shit to it and my ankle. She's rotating it then pushing it up and down. "Tell me if it hurts too much."

Ha, she has no idea. I don't say a word, I just watch her, mesmerized.

"There, try that." She looks up to me. I don't move or say anything. She scowls at me. "Nick, try that. See if you can get up. If not, we have a car out front, we can drop you off on our way out."

I try to stand, hitching myself up using the table and the back of the booth. I manage to stand on two feet this time, she puts her arms around my waist like she did the night before and puts my arm over her shoulder, she helps me to try to move. The next thing I know, the guy is at my other side mimicking what Primrose's doing. I just stand there looking at him. He's touching me and seems to be enjoying it a little too much.

"Thanks, buddy, but I can manage from here," I tell him sternly.

He ignores me. What the fuck. I try to move forward and my ankle, the bastard, almost gives way again. The guy grabs me tightly so I don't go down in a heap on the floor. I can see people watching this play out. They probably think I'm a drunk, being helped. Well, screw the lot of them. Between the guy and Primrose, they manage to get me out of the bar, down the steps and into the car which is waiting just at the bottom of the steps for us. The other woman must have seen what was happening and went to get the car. I wasn't paying attention, so I didn't notice she'd gone.

Primrose tells the woman where to go and we are pulling up outside my motel a couple of minutes later. To be honest, there's no way I would have gotten back here on my own. Everyone piles out of the car and the guy who introduced himself as Don, helps me out, then they both help me inside. Don stands staring at me as Primrose busies herself around me making sure I'm comfortable and have some water. She even places a trash can beside me

"If you need to pee and can't make it to the bathroom then use this." She thinks of everything. "Nick, do not get off this bed at all. I don't care how bored you are just lying here. That foot needs to be rested and elevated. If you don't, then the chances are you will break it and that will entail a visit to the hospital which you seem to be against. I will come back in the morning on my way home and see how you are and bring breakfast like I said earlier. Please do not use your foot." She looks at me with sad eyes.

For whatever reason, she cares about me. She doesn't know me, but she cares. Fuck me.

Twelve

Blaine

FOR A WEEK SHE KEPT THE SAME ROUTINE. SHE WOULD COME IN the morning bringing me breakfast, water, and clean bandages then she would come back early evening and sit with me to eat dinner and again she would leave me water. She made sure I was paid up at the motel so they didn't try and kick me out and she even brought me newspapers to read and some magazines, as she called them, so I didn't get too bored. She didn't know I couldn't read. I flipped through the pages making them look read. I skimmed through the TV channels for days. I watched more TV this last week than I have in my entire life. It's amazing what you learn just from watching some of those daytime chat shows.

Don and Tilda, the other two who were with her that night have been with her a couple of evenings. There's not much conversation from me but I do try. After all, they're all making sure I'm cared for. I don't want to appear too rude. I think Don has a crush on me. When he comes, he's always got to be near me, fluffing up my pillows as he says, or straightening out the covers. Primrose has even brought me some used clean clothes, I think she realized I didn't have many left when she tried to take some home with her to launder and I wouldn't let her. The first couple of days she and Don helped me to the bathroom, and I managed to use the toilet, as embarrassing as it was, they stood waiting for me to finish on the other side of the door, but when a man's gotta shit, he's gotta shit.

The third day she brought Don, I decided I wanted to take a shower. They both helped me into the bathroom, I could stand on my foot at this point but Don insisted on helping me out of my clothes. I didn't give a shit if he saw me naked to be honest, so I stripped in front of him. He helped me step into the bathtub. I don't know but I think he may have had a slight feel of my ass, when I turned to look at him, he was bright red. That's what made me think he did.

"Thanks Don, I can take it from here. I'll holler when I need to get out."

He left. I stood in the shower for a while. The room was full of steam so I guess it was hot.

"Don, I'm ready to get out now," I shouted when I turned off the water. I put the towel around my waist so he didn't get another eyeful, not that I think he would mind, he got a good look when I stripped. He opens the door and comes to help me, followed by Primrose.

"Jesus Nick, how hot did you have the water? You look like a lobster standing there," Don said as he took a hand and elbow to help me out. I hate this shit, I've never not been able to take care of myself.

I just shrugged. "I like it hot." I wink at him. He goes bright red again.

It's been like this for a week. I can get off the bed on my own now and walk. My ankle doesn't give way, I feel more stable on it. It's time to head home but it's a long walk back. Maybe I can get a lift for part of the way. Primrose's coming back this evening like she has been most evenings. We talk but I still don't know what she does at night. She comes to see me on her way out then comes back in the morning on her way home. I don't ask, it's none of my business and to be honest, I don't give a fuck if she's a whore. I'm disappointed, if I'm honest. I thought seeing her after all these years I would feel different but I don't. Don and Tilda still call her Pops, so I'm still none the wiser if it is her or not. She never corrects me when I call her Primrose and the others haven't called me on it either, so it must be her.

When she arrives, I'm packed up and ready to leave. I paid the motel for the extra day to have a late check-out and I have some money ready to give to Primrose for all that she has paid out for me. I actually for the first time in my life feel like I matter to someone. I don't care if Don had a feel of my ass or not, he's helped look after me. Anyone would think I'd had major surgery, I only sprained my ankle for fuck's sake.

"Hey, are you leaving?" She notices my bag ready by the door.

"Yes, I've been here long enough, it's time for me to head back home now."

She looks at the bag in her hand then shoves it into my chest. What the fuck. I scowl at her, but she isn't looking at me.

"What was that for?" I ask harshly. She looks at me and just like the night in the bar, she folds her arms over her tits and scowls at me.

"You didn't say this morning you were thinking of leaving. You could have given me some warning. I wouldn't have bothered coming back now if I'd have known." She's mad because I'm going.

"Sorry, didn't realize I had to report all my movements to you." I stand and cross my arms over my chest to mimic her stance. She moves her arms and puts them on her hips.

"You don't have to report to me but it would have been nice to know your plans. That way I could have rearranged my plans, instead of trying to fit you in every night."

Well, that told me.

"I never asked you to do that. You took it on yourself to take control and come to visit me. You did all that, Primrose, or is it Pops? You took that on yourself, not me. So don't stand there all high and fucking mighty giving me shit because I've decided to go home." I bow down so I'm eye level with her and I lift her chin so she has to look at me.

"I'm grateful for all your help, truly I am, but I don't answer to anyone, never have and never will. I'm a lucky son of a bitch that it was you who tried to help me that night I fell. You of all people, I couldn't believe it when I saw you. I've pictured you and your eyes almost every day, since that day we met, then to have you standing above me like that, I thought I had gone to heaven. Thank you for everything you did and please thank Don and Tilda for their help too."

She looks shocked, I see her face soften as I speak to her. I lean in and I kiss her on the cheek. She jerks her head back.

"Whoa there, stud. Thank you is just fine. No need to get touchy-feely."

What a bitch. If it was anyone else, I would deal with her the best way I know. Pain. But it's her, so I can't. I step back and reach in my jeans pocket and pull out the money I had for her.

"Here, this is all I have but it should cover the motel and food you've been getting. Thanks again, Primrose, for everything." I turn and grab my bag, ready to leave. I have to ask. "Just one thing I gotta know. Why do they call you Pops?"

Her eyes go wide and she backs away. "I don't need your money. Like you said, it was my choice."

She turns as though to leave, I grab her arm. There's something she isn't telling me here. That look when I asked about the name Pops. My gut tells me there's something not quite right.

"Hey, get off me, Nick." She jerks her arm from my grasp.

I didn't mean to grab so hard. I don't know my own strength at times. I hold my hands up. "Sorry, I didn't mean to do that. But why are you not answering my fucking question? What are you not telling me?"

She looks away and sighs. She walks slowly to the door and holds the handle.

She turns her head to me. "My name is Poppy, not Primrose."

I fucking knew it wasn't her. Why did she lie to me? Why did she say she remembered me when she didn't? How can it not be her? It looks just like her. Fuck. I grab my hair and start pulling at it. I don't realize how hard I'm pulling until I feel her hand on my arm bringing it down from my head.

"You're hurting yourself, Nick." I look at the bit of hair in my hand.

"FUCK," I shout out, making her wince.

She heads back to the door. "I'm sorry I didn't tell you the truth. I wanted to find out who you were. You were convinced you knew me."

I cock my head to the side, looking at her. Really looking, now I know it's not her. That's why I didn't have the connection I had when we were younger. I knew in my head all along it wasn't her, but my eyes deceived me. They fooled me. I should finish her for lying to me. I should make her suffer, make her feel the pain I can't.

"Why didn't you tell me you didn't know me? Why string me along all this time, letting me think you were Primrose? Why not just tell me the truth? Do you get off playing with people's feelings? Is that it, Pops, you enjoyed this, didn't you?" I start to walk toward her, my bad foot forgotten. I see the look in her eyes, it's the look I've seen so many times. It's lust mixed with trepidation. It's what makes me do what I do. She hasn't opened the door to leave yet, it's like she's in a trance watching me prowl toward her ready to pounce. Maybe that's what she's wanted all along.

Once I reach her, I box her in against the back of the door, placing both my arms on the door on either side of her head. She doesn't look at me, I see her chest rising faster and faster as her breathing gets heavier and heavier. I run my nose down her cheek, then lick upward where my nose just came from. She screws her eyes shut, her body goes rigid.

"Open your fucking eyes and look at me," I whisper into her ear. I pull back to look at her face, she's looking right into my eyes.

"Is this what you want, Poppy? Is this what it's been about all along? You helping me, hoping to get my cock rammed into you?"

She inhales sharply, holding her breath, and closes her eyes again. I wait for her to exhale, I have my mouth level with hers ready to catch her breath when she finally lets it out.

It doesn't take long and she opens her eyes and watches me suck it in, I'm that close to her mouth. She licks her lips, just like all the other fucking whores, she's no different. I run my hand down her arm to her wrist, then with my fingertips, gently run them back up her arm. She inhales again at my touch. It's only now, I feel marks on her inner elbow. Track marks. I've seen whores shoot up and I found out what it was they were doing. That's the thing with being inquisitive and learning about life all the time. I grab her arm and bring it closer to my face to see the marks. I look at the other one. She's a junkie, or she was a junkie. Maybe that explains why she's out every night. Maybe she's a prostitute. Is Don her and Tilda's pimp? Fuck, how could I get them all wrong?

She pulls her arms out of my grip, she's glaring at me. She's embarrassed and ashamed, I can see it on her face, and her eyes have gone from lust and fear to shame. She pushes on my chest for me to move, which I do and she turns to face the door ready to open it. I put my hand on the door above her head to stop her leaving.

"Let me out, Nick, I need to leave."

Like fuck. I want to know why she's been so good to me this week.

"You still a junkie, Poppy?" I see the slight shake of her head telling me no. "Look at me," I demand. She doesn't move. I turn her slowly to face me and lift her chin. "Tell me," is all I say. I can see her biting the inside of her cheek, she's closed her eyes so she doesn't have to look at me.

"When are the marks from?"

She looks up, now I see fire and anger in her eyes. "Fuck you, Nick. I don't have to tell you anything. You don't know me, I'm not your precious fucking Primrose, thank god for that, she's a fucking angel. I helped you because you needed help. Nothing else. And you don't get to ask me about my past. I helped because I wanted to." I can see how angry she is, staring me down. She turns again and grabs the handle and opens the door. I let her and just before she leaves she turns her head to me,

"No, I am not a fucking junkie, I've been clean for years. There, now I'm leaving." And she's gone, slamming the door behind her, leaving me standing like an idiot.

I hear the car spin out of the parking lot. It's late, it's nearly dark out. I've paid for the night, so I may as well stay and then get an early start tomorrow. I don't have a ride now anyway, I would end up walking in darkness most of the way. She brought me food for dinner. I sit and eat that, I eat her share as well, I'm starving. I sit pondering her, and how I thought it was Primrose. I decide to walk to the bar, it's a test to see how my foot will hold out on the walk home.

I sit in a booth where I can see people coming and going, nursing my second beer. I've only been here ten minutes and chugged my first one. I think back to Poppy and how angry she got, but what's bothering me is the venom in her voice when she said she wasn't Primrose, but she also called her an angel! Why would she be so bitter about her and why call her an angel. I've never said anything to that effect, it strikes me as an odd comment to make about someone you supposedly don't know. Wait! What a fucking idiot I am. She has to fucking know her? What if they are sisters or related? The way she said it, it was like she knew who she was. Fuck, why am I only just now thinking about this? Living up to my name as a retard. How slow am I? Now I can't ask her what she meant by that comment. I throw my drink down my throat and get up. I'm so angry right now. How am I going to find Poppy and ask her what she meant? I look around to see if there is anyone in here who she spoke to. Just then my eyes land on Don sitting over on the other side of the bar with another guy.

"Hey Don, how you doing? Listen, do you know where I can find Pops? I need to give her some money I owe her before I leave, I don't have a way of contacting her."

He looks happy to see me with a big cheesy smile on his face. "Oh hey Nick, this is Tony. Tony, this is the guy I was telling you about." He tries to whisper that last bit to Tony but I still hear him.

"Hey, Nick, nice to meet you," Tony says, holding out his hand. I don't take it, I just nod at him and look back to Don. "Can you help me please, Don?"

He looks at me, he has no reason not to trust me, he's been helping look after me for a week.

"She's not working tonight, said something about seeing Prim. I found it odd because they haven't spoken for a few years now, but she was in a rush when she called me earlier."

I'm standing there staring at him, trying to wrap my head around what he's saying. She's going to see Prim as in Primrose? I need to play along here, I need to be smart.

"Ah, she said something about Primrose earlier. She laughed at me because I kept calling her Primrose."

Don laughs. "Yeah, you kept doing that this week. I just thought you couldn't tell the difference between them, we had a laugh about her playing along with it."

I laugh but inside I'm ecstatic, but so fucking angry all at the same time. My eyes were right but so was my heart. She's my way to Primrose, I need to find her. Fuck, I need to think about this. If she speaks to Don, he will tell her about this. I'm so angry at Poppy for not telling me. She pretended she knew me from years ago, but why? Why would she do that? He also said they haven't spoken for years, so is she a sister or just a relative?

"Hey Nick, you okay? You look lost there. Here, sit down, let me get you a drink."

I take the stool next to him. I need to stay calm and compose myself before he thinks I'm a retard like everyone else. I hear him speak to Tony but don't listen to what he says. The next thing I know, Tony leaves us. I think he's gone for the drinks.

"Did Poppy say when she would be back? I don't know where she or Primrose live, so I can't give her the money I owe her. I met Primrose many years ago. They look so alike I thought it was her."

He's thinking about how much he can tell me. He doesn't know if I am close to either of them.

"Primrose lives near San Francisco, Poppy lives not far from here. I think she'll be gone for a few days. She told me she would let me know when she would be back at work. I know what you mean. Being identical twins must have been a nightmare for them growing up. I haven't met Primrose and to be honest, Pops doesn't speak about her much. She showed me a picture once and I couldn't tell who was who. It's freaky."

Fuck, twins. That explains it. I knew it was her, but that it wasn't, and I couldn't wrap my head around it. She's my way to Primrose. I need to find her. I can't leave here yet. Tony arrives back with beers for us all. I nearly down it in one. Don has a cell in his hand and he turns the screen to me. It's a picture of Poppy.

"Who is this?" he says.

He gives me the cell and I squint, trying to look at it closely. He takes it back and he does some kind of magic with his fingers because when he passes it back to me, the image is of the face only and it's a big image. I freeze. Those eyes, it's Primrose, I know it is.

"That's Primrose," I say, staring at the image.

The screen goes black and I shake it. Don laughs at me and takes it back. He holds it to his face and turns it back to me and there she is again. I need a plan. I need Poppy so she can tell me where to find Primrose.

"Don, can you please ask Poppy to drop by the motel when she contacts you. Can you let her know I will hang around for a few days and wait to hear from her?"

He nods as I pass him back his cell which has gone black again anyway. Stupid fucking thing.

"Why do you have a picture of Primrose on your cell, Don?"

He looks at me and raises an eyebrow. "It's Facebook, Nick, if your profile is public anyone can see the photos you put on there." I have no idea what he just said to me so I just nod, pretending I understand. He may as well be speaking in another language to me. I finish my drink and we all head out together. They are going out dancing someplace. They asked if I wanted to join them, not a chance. Dance? Me? I just pointed to my foot and shook my head no.

I waited all day yesterday, and it's late afternoon now, and still no Poppy. I had to step out to stock up on food and water yesterday morning, I hope to God she didn't drop by then. I lie on the bed bored, flicking through the TV channels when I hear a light tap on the door. I dive off the bed, opening the door as quickly as I can. Poppy's standing there with her arms folded over her tits, and she's scowling at me.

"Well, hello to you too, Poppy," I say, laughing.

That puts her at ease a little, she pushes past me and walks into the room.

"I thought you were leaving. Don said you wanted to see me urgently. I was out of town, so what's the urgency? I cut my trip short, I thought you were hurt again, you look fine to me." She looks me up and down.

"Sorry, I just needed to ask you something and I had no way of getting in touch with you, I didn't know where you lived." I shrug.

She stares at me, waiting. "Well, what is it, Nick? I told Don I would work tonight so can we get on with it, please?"

Why is she being so hostile toward me?

"What's rattled your cage? I didn't say it was urgent, only asked if you could stop by when you were back. Did you see who you wanted to see?"

She squints her eyes at me, then she jabs me in the chest with her finger. "You know, don't you? Fucking Don, why couldn't he just keep his mouth shut."

I grab her finger to stop her jabbing me again. She tries to pull it out of my hand but I hold it tight. "Don't poke me again," I warn her and let go of her finger. "Yes, I know your twin sister is Primrose. Why the fuck couldn't you just tell me that the first time I called you by her name? Why all the pretense and secrecy?"

"I wanted to know who you were." That's it, that's all she says and shrugs.

"Did you see her? Don said you had gone to see her but that you don't usually speak to each other. Why would you take off so suddenly to see her?"

She scowls at me. "Is it any of your business what I do? I don't have to tell you where I've been or why I've been there."

She's starting to rattle me. I just want to fucking know if she told Primrose about me. I need to know. I need to see her for myself. I try to stay calm when all I want to do is hurt this bitch. She's holding out on me and it's killing me. I need to try to be smart about this though. I need to make a good friend of Poppy, not make her my enemy. If I was to hurt her in any way, I'm sure Primrose wouldn't want anything to do with me.

I hold my hands up. "Look, I'm sorry, Pops. You're right, it's none of my business. I just wanted to reconnect with Primrose after all these years. I would love to see her again. That's my only reason for asking if you saw her."

She looks at me, trying to gauge what I'm playing at. She sits on the edge of the bed so I sit next to her.

"She wasn't home. She travels a lot, I went and visited with my aunt Cassy and uncle Trevor, they raised us, they are like our parents. That's why I came back when I spoke to Don because they told me Primrose is away for a few weeks."

Fuck, I got the best lead ever and she's not even around.

"At least you got to see your aunt and uncle." I smile at her, trying so hard to keep it together when inside I just want to explode.

"Yeah, and I saw my cousins Trixie and Pixie, another set of twins. My mama and Aunt Cassy are twins as well."

She's opening up to me. I need to keep this going. "Hey, do you want a drink of anything? I have coffee or water."

"I need to get going soon, so water would be great. How's the foot now? I hear you walked to the bar."

I smile at her and get up to grab some water. "It's good, it didn't twist on me, so that's something." I sit back next to her. "Do you mind if I ask you a personal question?" I want her to tell me more. I want to find out what I can about Primrose. She shakes her head no. "Why did your aunt and uncle raise you?"

I know exactly why I was there, I fucking killed her parents, but I need to know if Primrose ever mentioned me and what happened that day.

She looks sad. "They were in a car wreck. They both died."

I look shocked. "I'm really sorry, Pops. How old were you when that happened?"

"We were seven. Primrose was with them. I wasn't feeling well that day, I stayed with Aunt Cassy."

I want her to continue. I know what happened.

"What about Primrose? Did she get hurt?"

She shakes her head no.

"That's the weirdest thing about it. She was in the same wreck and never got hurt apart from when she was getting out of the wreck. I still, to this day, have no idea how she survived when the car blew up and they died. I've never forgiven her for surviving."

She looks down at her hands. I see a tear slide down her cheek. Shit, what do I do now? I do what I think I'm supposed to, I pull her into my side and cuddle her to try and give her some comfort.

"I'm sorry you had to go through all that at such a young age."

Like fuck I am. I enjoyed it all. I even remember when I got home, I still had some of their papa's flesh in my pocket. I kept it for the longest time, I used to play with it but it started to dry out. If only she knew.

She looks up into my face. She licks her lips. Does she think I'm going to kiss her? The way she's looking at me tells me she wants me to. I can't do that. I wouldn't want to do anything with her that could jeopardize any chance with Primrose. It's Primrose I've thought about all these years. It's her I want. But then what if she's married or with someone else or doesn't want me. Isn't having Poppy the next best thing? It would be like having Primrose, only not. I'm confusing myself, looking at her looking at me. But I'm not going there. I just pull her head into my shoulder.

"Why have you blamed Primrose for surviving? Wouldn't you have been destroyed if your sister had died as well? Is that why you don't speak?"

She looks at me quizzically.

"Don said you don't talk."

She looks angry again and pulls away from me.

"Yes, maybe I would have been heartbroken if she had died but not if my parents had survived. Why was she saved and not them? I've never gotten my head around it. For that reason, we have never gotten along. She's Miss Goody-Goody, while I went off the rails."

I pull her to me again so she doesn't look at me longingly.

"Is she married now? Does she have a family herself?"

"No, she has no one, just like me. We are very alike in that respect. I did have someone a long time ago, but he was no good for me." She rubs the track marks on her arm. She had a druggie boyfriend. We sit in silence for a while. I don't want to push her too much by asking more questions, and to be honest, I'm so happy inside at the moment, knowing Primrose isn't married or with anyone else. I want to jump up and down and make Poppy take me to her.

"Right, time for me to get going. I have work to do with Don and Tilda." She gets up and heads for the door. She turns before she heads out. "Don't suppose you need me to bring you breakfast in the morning, do you?"

I smile. "I would love that, only if you join me. Maybe once you've slept, we could do something in the afternoon. Maybe show me the sights, I've been stuck here for over a week and it's making me crazy. I travel around by myself when I'm not home, so staying in one place this long is not something I'm used to."

She smiles and nods a yes. "I'll see you in the morning, then we can make plans." With that, she's gone. I stand at the door and watch her get into her car and pull out of the parking lot.

Back on my bed, I decide what needs to be done. I need to play it cool with her. Reel her in, but not close enough to get intimate. Just let her think it's heading in that direction for now. Once I get in there and find out more details on Primrose, I can decide what to do with Poppy. If I hurt her like I want to and Primrose found out, that would screw it up for me. If I get too close to her and Primrose thought we had a thing going, I'm sure she wouldn't want anything to do with me. This is going to take me being smart. I know I'm smart, I've always known, how else could I be so crafty and survive this long. How else could I do what I do, inflicting pain, and killing, and get away with it? I'm not the retard my mother always told me I was. This might take me a bit of time with Poppy, she's quite fiery and sassy. I just need to be patient with her. It will mean me sticking around here for God knows how long as well. That's gonna cost me. I need to find a garage or someplace I can do some casual labor to get some more money. Fuck, I hope it doesn't take too long but if getting to Primrose at the end is my reward then I will do what I need to do. I will have Primrose one way or another and Poppy may just be the collateral damage.

Thirteen

Blaine

POPPY AND I HAVE BEEN GOING OUT IN THE EVENINGS FOR THE past week. She's been showing me around before she goes to work. I found a garage not too far from the motel and the owner was happy for me to help out during the day. Poppy's coming to pick me up soon and we're going to the bar to meet Don and Tilda. I still haven't found out what they all do and why they work nights. I'm going to make it my mission to find out. I also need to broach the subject of Primrose. I haven't mentioned her since that day she came to see me after she went to see Primrose. I don't want her thinking this is all just to get to meet Primrose, even if it is. I'm a patient man.

Poppy looks at me longingly all the time. I hold her hand when we're out, just so she thinks it's going somewhere, but to be honest, I find even that hard to do. As each day goes by, I feel more resentment toward her, and it's getting harder to hide. I snap at her more than I should, and she doesn't put up with that shit. I need to be careful and try to be nice to her, I just need her to think it will go somewhere eventually. I've been thinking about telling her I've never had a girlfriend before, but not sure she would buy that with me being older, and I also know the way women look at me, she would find it hard to believe. She's caught on to the looks I get, and when we've been in the different bars, women, bold as brass, come up to me and flirt, trying to rub against me. Poppy soon sends them off, but for them to do it when I'm with another woman, these women have no shame and it pisses me off. It's making it worse because I could be having so much sex and inflicting so much pain on these women. It's all Poppy's fault, and for that I resent her.

In the bar, meeting up with Don and Tilda, we're all sitting around talking, well I'm listening more than I talk. Poppy's sitting right next to me with her thigh touching mine, she keeps sliding her hand up and down my thigh. I watch as she does it. Don gives her a questioning look, she just smiles at him, he gives me a stern look, and I shrug slightly. They only have the one beer as they're all heading to work.

I lean in to whisper to Poppy. "Hey, when are you going to tell me where you go every night?"

She looks at me then to Don. Fuck, maybe it is what I thought, but none of them dress as though they are prostitutes. I don't get it. Don gives her a look which I interpret as him telling her she should tell me. She looks to me and I smile and wink at her trying to be the nice guy. She sighs.

"We work on the streets." That's all she says.

I jump up out of my chair and stand there at the table glaring at Poppy then the others. "What do you mean you work on the streets? Please tell me you're not fucking prostitutes?"

Don spits out the beer he just took a swig of, and Poppy stands up and slaps my face.

"What the FUCK, what was that for, you bitch?" She's definitely just pushed my buttons. No one hits me. She goes to do it again, this time I grab her wrist to stop her. "What the fuck is that for?"

"Don't ever call me a bitch," she grits at me, clenching her teeth together. I hold her wrist tighter. "Let go of me, you're hurting me."

Good, that's what I want to do. She tries to yank her wrist from my hold, but I hold tighter still.

"Tell me what you meant by working on the streets if you're not prostitutes because I don't know of anything else you would be doing on the streets at night."

"Let go of me, before I scream loud enough for everyone in here to come and help me."

We glare at each other, but I still don't let go.

"Hey Nick, please let's sit down, I'll explain what we do. You're so wrong," Don pipes in.

I let her go and sit. She stays standing up, glaring at me.

"We help people out, Nick. We walk the streets and go to different shelters, we help anyone that needs help. Mainly young people who are new to the streets, the homeless, Nick. A lot of them fall in with the wrong people, they end up as users, we try to help prevent that. We have all been there, Nick. We were all on the streets, or in a relationship where we were controlled by drugs and other people, one way or another. We are part of a task force called A Helping Hand, see."

He unzips his hoodie and shows me the t-shirt underneath. I have no idea what it says but there is a picture of hands holding each other. I've seen the t-shirt before on one of them at the motel, I can't think who it was. It might have even been Poppy. I feel terrible now. I didn't know anything like that even existed. I look up to Poppy who is standing with her arms folded over her tits, she's glaring at me. I give her puppy dog eyes to try and soften her.

"Look, I'm sorry. I didn't know anything like that existed. The only thing that came to mind was prostitutes. I know Don likes the men, so I just assumed he was one also." I hold my hands up to say sorry. I look to Don then to Tilda. "I'm sorry," I say to them both. I see a tear fall from Tilda's eyes. I feel bad now. How could I think the worst of them when they were only doing good. To be honest, Poppy didn't strike me as a caring person at first. She was quite hard with me, but she stuck it out looking after me, so I suppose I should have given her some credit.

I'm still looking at each of them. I can see the anger on their faces, especially Poppy's. I stand and move toward her and pull her to me. "Look, I'm really sorry. I didn't know what else to think when you said you worked on the streets." I have my arms around her, holding my hands at the base of her back, gently pulling her to me, I kiss the top of her head. I feel her relax slightly. I crouch to her eye level. "Pops, please don't be angry with me. I've wondered for some time what you could all be doing each night. You come to see me in the mornings in the same clothes as the previous night. Although I wouldn't call what you all wear streetwalker clothes, I did wonder about it. Then as soon as you said you worked on the streets, I flipped. I'm sorry for jumping to that conclusion. Please forgive me, all of you." I look at the others and they nod at me.

I keep holding Poppy for a little bit longer. The last thing I want is for her to take off in a huff and not want to bother with me again. I need to stay on her side, it's killing me having to act like this when all I want to do is hurt her. The urge to squeeze her hard right now, and feel a rib or two break is killing me, but I need to be patient. I have to find out about Primrose. Just saying her name calms me. Poppy looks up into my eyes and she nods and gives me a small smile.

"Okay Nick, we have to leave now. We have to get to work."

I release my hold on her and step back. They all get up and leave saying sheepish goodbyes to me.

Fuck.

I'm so angry, I need to let off some steam, but I can't do it here. I leave the bar and start walking, heading farther away from the motel. I need to find somewhere that I haven't been to before. I walk for a long time, must be at least a good hour or more. I hear music in the distance. There are no buildings or anything around where I am. It's just roads and dirt tracks leading off the main road. I follow the sound of the music and hope it's another bar. The farther I walk, the angrier I get, and the more frustrated I become.

I turn onto one of the dirt tracks, this is where the music seems to be coming from. It's getting louder and louder the farther I walk. Just around a bend I see what looks like an old farmhouse. Fuck, I wanted a bar. I move closer to see what's going on. It's a run-down place, I look through the window, I don't see anyone inside. I move around toward the back of the house, taking care not to make any noise, although with the music coming from inside, I doubt they would hear me anyway. I gingerly move around toward the back, I pass another window on the side of the house, again I don't see anyone inside.

I keep going, there are no fences or gates to keep people away, but then there doesn't seem to be anything around for miles, I'm in the middle of nowhere. I peek around the corner to see if there is anyone at the back of the house. The last thing I want is to startle anyone or let anyone see me for that matter. The music is louder here than at the front. I suppose with no one around for miles, you can play music as loud as you like. I edge closer, peeping around but still don't see anyone. I wait to see if there's movement anywhere, or if I can hear anything other than the music, but there's nothing. I edge around more trying to keep close to the building but not too close, looking at it, all the wood slats are rotting and falling off in places. I don't want to make any drop, making a noise.

I stay low as I approach a window, I edge closer so I can look inside, there's nothing, I can see farther into the house from this window. I start to straighten up a little, to move past the window when suddenly I see someone move, it just catches my eye, I pull back. I hear a clatter then the music stops, shit, maybe they saw me. Maybe they dropped what they were holding because I scared them. I stay still trying to listen. Just then the outer screen door creaks open. I freeze, watching the door. If anyone comes out, they will no doubt see me. I watch cautiously, trying to move back toward the edge of the house.

"Hello." I hear a female voice call out. "I have a loaded gun, show yourself."

Fuck. I don't see her yet, she's still standing inside the door, I continue edging back feeling for the corner. A twig breaks under my foot making a noise, I freeze. The screen door slams shut. She let go of it, making me jump. I turn and head for the front of the house. The last thing I want is to be shot for trespassing. I'm walking quickly back toward the dirt track I came down when I hear the door open,

"Hey, you, what are you doing on my property? Be careful turning around, put yer hands up, turn slowly. I have a 12 gauge pointed at your head."

I stop dead in my tracks, I slowly hold my hands up and very tentatively turn toward the front of the house, and the woman standing there. I see the moment she can see my face. She slightly lowers her shoulders, relaxing a little and her eyes thin out slightly. I get this all the time from women. They see a pretty face and they tend to turn to mush.

"Please, lower the gun. I'm not here to harm you. I was walking down the road, I heard the music and I guess curiosity got the better of me."

She doesn't lower the gun, she relaxes a little more. "Whatcha doin' around these parts anyhow? There's nothing around for miles. Is something wrong with your car?"

Do I lie and tell her I broke down? Nah, no point.

"I don't have a car. I was out walking, clearing my head and looking for a bar, to be honest. I guess I walked farther than I realized. I heard the music and thought there was a bar here. Sorry for creeping around the back. I did look in the front window but couldn't see anyone, that's why I went around the back. I just wanted to make sure everything was okay here. That's all." I slowly lower my hands.

She's back to squinting at me, trying to work out if she can trust what I'm saying. Looking at her from here, I can only just make her out, it's difficult with the light being behind her head, and it being dark outside, but I would say she was probably in her thirties. She has dark hair, I couldn't say what color it was from here.

"Look, I'm sorry if I startled you, if you just let me be on my way, I would appreciate that. I mean no harm."

She just stands there, looking at me. Eventually, she lowers the gun and places it under her arm with the barrel down, she could still quickly take a shot if she wanted to.

"Well, there ain't no bars around here for at least ten miles in either direction up on the main road. There's nothing else along this here dirt path but my property. Not sure where you came from, but I think you should leave now." She nods her head in the direction from which I came. I think she must be alone in the house to be so on guard, plus she probably doesn't get many visitors, or strangers at least.

I start to edge backward so I can get back on the dirt track, and just head back to the motel, maybe stop at the bar on the way. I didn't realize how long I'd been walking. I can walk for hours, with walking being my way of getting around from place to place. I've backed farther away from her, all the while watching her in case she tries to take a shot when I'm suddenly on my ass. I tripped on a rock jutting out of the dirt path. She steps forward trying to check to see what I'm doing. Shit, I hope I didn't do my ankle in again. That will screw me up for walking back. I don't know if I have, I can't feel anything, I start to get up

"You okay? What did ya do?"

Well, brainiac, I fell on my ass, what a stupid fucking question.

I start to get up, not answering her, it's pretty obvious I fell on my ass. I get to my feet, gingerly putting the weight on my bad ankle. It seems okay, but I won't know until I try to walk on it.

"Hey, you okay?"

"Yeah, think so. I must have tripped on this rock," I say, putting my bad foot on it. "I'll leave you now. Won't bother you again." I turn with my back to her and start to walk, my bad ankle gives slightly but I don't fall. I guess it's okay.

"You sure you're okay? Looks like you're gonna fall again."

I stop to look at her. She's moved off the porch now and onto the ground just in front of the house, still holding the gun.

"It'll be okay, I'm just recovering from a sprained ankle so it's a little bit weak at the moment. It wasn't the ankle that made me fall, just that rock."

She's unsure, I can hear it in her voice when she speaks. "Would you like a glass of water before you leave. If you've got a long walk back, you might need a drink."

I smile at her and nod. "That would be kind of you, ma'am." And just like that, she's putty in my hands.

She heads into the house, I head back toward the house and stand at the bottom of the porch, waiting for her to come back out. The porch light suddenly comes on, the door opens and she comes walking out with a glass of water, minus the shotgun I notice. I stand, giving her my mega-watt smile, she cautiously descends the three steps and stops on the fourth one to hand me the glass. I take it from her and my fingers brush hers. I hear the sharp inhale from her when they touch. That's the sound I'm used to.

I smile internally knowing I have her. I put the glass to my mouth and very slowly drink the water, keeping my eyes on hers at all times. Now the porch light is on I can see her more clearly. She has long dark hair, her bangs are pulled to the side of her head to keep the hair out of her eyes. She's older than I first thought. I would say she was more in her late forties than thirties, maybe the California sun just hasn't been too kind to her. She has on jeans that look dirty and a tee that I think was white but has seen better days. It's low cut at the front in a V-neck and she isn't wearing a bra, I can see her nipples sticking out from the tee like stones. I see her lick her lips as she watches me drinking the water and sees me looking at her tits. My eyes meet hers again and I see the lust in them. She smiles slightly, she's acting like a teenage girl, trying to be all coy and shy.

I finish the water and I slowly lick my lips, watching her mimic my actions. I take my middle finger and wipe around my mouth with it, then I place it in my mouth and suck on it. I watch her inhale deeply, watching my actions. I watch her chest rising and her nipples getting harder, if that's possible. I watch her purse her lips and her eyes widen. She wants me. I know it. I reach out to pass the glass back to her. She takes it from me, but not before sliding her finger along the finger that was in my mouth. I smile at her.

"Thank you so much. I needed that. I was thirsty, and it's a long walk back. Listen, I'm sorry for scaring you like that. I didn't mean anything by it and thank you for not shooting me." I laugh a little, then keep a smile plastered on my face. She looks down, then back up to me.

"I'm sorry for overreacting, you just never know these days. I've had people come by in the past and they have been bad people. I think once word got around I lived alone, after my husband passed, the undesirables in the town started to snoop. I've always been on my guard. It's hard being out here all alone."

Well shit, talk about coming on to me. Letting me know she's on her own. If I play this right, I may just get what I originally went looking for, a good fuck.

"Hey, I'm sorry about your late husband. Was it recent? It must be hard for you being out here on your own." I look sympathetic, laying it on thick.

"It was eighteen months ago now. It's still hard looking after this place on my own, I do miss not having a man around the house." She looks to my lips then down to the glass then back at my eyes. "You know, to do all the manly things, like taking care of the place, the fields, and me?"

Well, fuck me, she wants me bad. I can see it on her face. She isn't half bad either for her age. In fact, she's got a nice face with high cheek-bones. To be honest, I don't care what she looks like, as long as her mouth works on my cock, and her pussy is wet for me. I'm gonna play hard to get, if she's desperate she'll invite me in.

"I'm sorry to hear that. I guess it's hard not having all those things looked after." I smile at her and lick my lips again. "Well, thanks for the water, like I said, I guess I'll be on my way now, ma'am."

I see the startled look on her face just as I start to turn to walk away. My ankle tries to give way a little, she's at my side grabbing my arm before I realize it. The glass smashes on a rock as she drops it, grabbing my arm.

"Hey, why don't you come inside, rest your ankle for a little bit before you head back. I can get you a whiskey if you like, that or some more water, and make you a snack if you're hungry."

She's mine now.

"Thank you for the offer. I don't want to put you out, you've already been real nice to me. I'll just head back now. Thank you." I see the desperation on her face.

"No, honestly, come in, a bit of company would be great."

I think about it for a minute and then nod yes to her. "Okay, thank you. I'll just rest my ankle for a little while if you're sure that's okay? I promise I'm not an ax murderer. See? No ax hidden," I say, smiling, opening my jacket to show her I don't have anything inside.

She looks me up and down, now I've shown her more of my physique, there is no mistaking the want and desire in her eyes.

She helps me up the porch and into the house. It's nicer inside than outside. I see what she means. She just needs a handyman around the place to fix things up and take care of her. Maybe I should offer my services. She takes me into the seating area and puts me on the couch. I can walk myself, I know I can, but I'm letting her help me. She's feeling my biceps with my arm draped around her shoulders, and she has her other hand on my waist. She's feeling me up, I'm just not sure she realizes what she's doing. I sit on the couch.

"Would you like the whiskey or water? I'm gonna have a whiskey myself. You gave me quite a fright," she says, smiling at me.

"Yeah, whiskey would be great thank you." I don't even know what it's like. I've only ever had a beer, fuck it, I'll try anything.

She comes back with two glasses, passing me one. She sits next to me on the couch, I don't think she believes in personal space, she's practically sitting on my lap, but hey, I'm not gonna complain. She sips away at her drink, I take a sip of mine. I start choking as it hits the back of my throat. I lean forward placing the glass on the table and I cough. She's patting my back and rubbing it at the same time.

"Did it go down the wrong hole? Are you okay?"

The wrong hole, I don't think so, it's shit.

"Yeah, something like that."

She laughs. "You've never had whiskey before?"

I shake my head no, still coughing slightly.

I lean back and rest my head on the back of the couch, looking up to the ceiling. She starts rubbing my chest, the rubbing turns to caressing my abs and then she starts to play with my nipples. I lift my head and look down at her hands, then back to her.

"I guess if you can play with mine it would be rude for me not to do the same?"

I copy what she is doing and I start to caress her tits and roll her nipples between my fingers. She starts gasping loudly, I pinch them hard. She's still caressing mine with one hand and the other is wandering down to my waist.

I lean forward and take one of her nipples into my mouth. I start to suck on it through her tee. She pushes her tits farther out to me. I start to lift her tee. I need to suck them in the flesh. She doesn't hesitate and helps me take it off. It's handy, her not wearing a bra. I pinch one tit hard and I bite down on the other. She moves to straddle me and tries to remove my tee. I have to drop her tits so she can pull it over my head.

"Wow, look at you," she says as her hands wander all over my abs and pecs.

I have a few tattoos on my torso and arms. I've had them gradually done over the years, when I've worked and got the money, I had nothing else to spend it on. Watching all the bikers in the bars full of tattoos, I wanted my own. I watch her hands move all over my chest, she leans forward and bites my nipples. I start to play with the zipper on her jeans, trying to pull it down. She follows suit and starts to do the same with mine. She pops the button, pulls the zipper down, and her hand goes straight inside. She looks at me and smiles the biggest smile.

"No undies, I like."

That's me, I never wear them. "Stand up," I say assertively, she doesn't hesitate. I like that.

She stands in front of me and I lift my ass and pull my jeans from under me, she leans down to pull them off my legs. I shuffle forward so my face is at her tummy and I slowly edge her jeans down while licking around her belly button. She steps out of them and I discard them to the side.

I pull her into me and nuzzle her tummy, lowering to her pussy. Fuck me, I've never been with a woman with such a hairy pussy before. All the ones I've had have been bare or almost bare, just a little strip of hair. I start to nuzzle in between her thighs with my nose, then I stick my tongue out and lick the top of her clit. She exhales and pushes her pussy farther into me, breathing heavily. She then grabs my head and pulls me as far into her as she can. She's gonna suffocate me in all this fucking hair if she's not careful. She starts to spread her legs voluntarily. I have to try to bend lower to reach her. She's a lot smaller than I am. I edge off the couch and sit on the floor with my back to it, this puts me just at the right height to get in there.

I look up at her. She's standing with her eyes closed, face looking up toward the ceiling. Her chest is heaving and those fucking nipples are like rock hard stones. I reach up with a hand and push and squeeze one of her tits. She looks down at me and licks her lips. I take that as a good sign. I let go of her tit and pull her pussy toward my mouth by her ass. She's almost sitting on my face. I edge down on the floor a little more so I can rest my head back onto the couch cushion. I then pull her ass and make her lower herself over my face. That fucking hair is tickling my nose. It's like a fucking stack of hay. I swipe my tongue out and flick her clit. She starts moving to try to get more friction from my tongue. If what she says is true, and she hasn't been serviced since her husband died, then she's not gonna last long.

I try to make it last. I swipe up and down along her pussy, sucking as I do, sucking the juices and her clit. I then play with her ass and spread her cheeks open wide. I place a finger at her butt hole, I start to insert it, at the same time, I insert my tongue into her pussy. I lick and lick while pumping in and out of her ass. I then move my other hand around to the front and I insert three fingers into her pussy and then flick and suck her clit. This is driving her mad. She doesn't know what to do with herself. She's up and down, round and round, gyrating all over my face. Sometimes I struggle to breathe, I can hold my breath, I suck all her juices away. She comes with such a wild scream she makes me jump. I suck and suck, and flick and pump, in and out, more and more, and let her ride it out until she collapses on top of me nearly breaking my fucking neck.

I let her catch her breath for a few minutes. I suck her tits, biting while she comes down from her high. She slides down my body and sits on my lap looking at me.

"Wow, I have never come like that in my life. My husband was just plain vanilla. Nothing like that."

Fuck, is she telling me no one has ever sucked her pussy? Well, I'll rectify that again before I leave. I smile at her. Her hands start to caress my body, I watch mainly because I don't feel it.

She shuffles back slightly onto my knees and then grabs my cock. I watch exactly what she does. He's standing at full attention, rock hard. She puts two hands around him, the first hand is at the base and she starts squeezing and pumping. The second hand is at the top, and she starts squeezing, I can see the pressure she's putting on him. I smile at her when she looks at me. She then bends down and starts to lick my cock like a popsicle. She plays with the head and swirls around the hole with her tongue. I can see pre-cum seeping out each time her tongue leaves the head. This is the only time I feel anything and it feels fucking fantastic.

I start to gyrate, lifting my ass off the floor. "Put him in your fucking mouth and suck now," I demand, she doesn't hesitate.

She scoots down my legs to my shins and leans right over him, inserting him deep into her throat. Fuck me. That feels fucking amazing. I feel like I want to burst. I want to explode but I want more, I want it to last. I push up more and more. She starts to gag, but I want her to feel it right there, deep down her throat. She's playing with my balls with one of her hands, she's squeezing as she's gagging. I don't want her to stop. I hold the top of her head down hard, I thrust up harder and harder, until I explode down her throat. I keep going. More and more. Thrusting harder and harder. She's squeezed my balls so hard I'm surprised they haven't burst, but I don't fucking care. I don't want to stop. I have more cum than ever. Has it been that long since my last release? Just then Primrose appears in my head and I stop. I let go of this bitch's head, and I stop thrusting. I pull my cock from her mouth. What the fuck.

She collapses on me, shit, I don't know if she's breathing. Did I fucking kill her with my cock? Fuck, I need to get inside her. She better not be dead. Why the fuck did Primrose suddenly appear in my mind? I haven't laid eyes on her for all these years, but now I know what she looks like as an adult from the picture I saw, and she suddenly appears out of nowhere. I want inside this bitch now. I shove her to the floor. She doesn't make a noise but I see her chest rising. Good, she isn't dead, but she doesn't open her eyes. I climb on top of her, spreading her legs with my knees. She doesn't move. I don't care. I still have more in me, I need this. I lift her legs, place them on each of my shoulders, and I line my cock up, right at her hole and I thrust as hard as I can inside. Her eyes fly open and she looks right at me. I start to pull out right to the edge so just the tip is inside and I thrust with all I have again. She smiles at me, breathing heavy and licking her lips. The whore is enjoying this, she likes it rough. I repeat the process of pulling almost out then slamming back in trying to get deeper and deeper each time. I'm watching her licking her lips at each thrust, she grabs my nipples and starts to play with them, pinching them hard. I feel it, but it's not pain, it's not that she's hurting me I don't think, it's just sensations running through my body.

I'm so hard, but when I look down at her, I can only see Primrose. The face from the cell, the one with the blemish in her eye. It's her I see here, I want her so bad.

She screams out, "More, more, harder, faster."

I thrust, getting angrier and angrier at each thrust, the fact that it's not Primrose here with me, telling me more. I'm thrusting so hard and so deep that she's moved up the floor and is now squashed with her head against a chair. I lift her ass to give me more room to keep slamming in, I'm almost there, so I keep at it, harder and harder, with my balls slapping against her ass. I have my arms wrapped around her legs giving me leverage and spreading them farther apart so I can get deeper. That's it, just one… more…

"Ahhhhhhhhhhhhh," I scream out as I come inside her over and over. I'm balls deep inside and shuddering with my release, I keep going jutting inside her. I stop with just a few more hip thrusts to empty me. I let go of her legs and they fall to the floor like dead weights. I never make a noise when I come. It must be because I'm thinking I'm fucking Primrose.

She doesn't move. I never noticed she hadn't moved. I can see her head at a funny angle and her eyes are just looking up to the ceiling but they look glazed over. She isn't smiling or making any noises. She was really into it, wanting it harder. Now she isn't doing anything. Did she come already? I have no idea, I wasn't paying any attention to her, I was too focused on Primrose. I lean forward and pinch a nipple but there's nothing. I watch her chest, it's not moving. Fuck, she isn't breathing. I scramble to her face and stare down into it. Nothing, her eyes are lifeless. I killed her, but how? Death by cum, fuck, what happened?

I get up and grab my jeans and tee and put them on quickly. All the while watching her, just to see if she moves. What a fucking waste of death that was. I didn't even inflict pain on her. I'm so angry with myself. I walk back to her and pull her by the legs forward so she's away from the chair. I don't know what the fuck happened. I stand over her looking at her body. For an older woman, she's not bad, I also found I loved the bush she had going on. I bend down and lift her head. It's then I know what happened. With all the thrusting, I've somehow broken her neck against the chair.

Well, fuck me. Now what? I need to think. I've watched a lot of TV shows while being laid up with my ankle, one called *Criminal Minds*, I found out a lot from that show. I know there will be what is called DNA from me in this place. I need to think about what I touched. There's the glass on the table, then the couch but nothing else. But my cum is inside her, I didn't use a condom. Shit, I need to buy some of those. They also stop women from getting pregnant and me getting diseases. I must remember them.

I sit on the couch trying to remember back to first coming to the house. I didn't touch anything outside, wait, the glass outside she dropped it and it smashed. There's only one thing to do here, I saw it on *Criminal Minds* that burning the body is the best thing to do to get rid of the evidence. I'll burn her and this place so there won't be anything left. No one knows I was here. There isn't anyone around for miles, she told me herself. That's what I'll do, then leave, get back to my motel as quickly as I can, and hide if I see any cars on the road.

I go to the kitchen, trying not to touch anything. I grab a towel, I use it to open the drawers to find something to start a fire. This might take a while. There's an oven, I turn the burner knobs on and press the little button and there it is, fire. I look around and see the bottle of what must be the whiskey. I pour some onto the table, then I grab some newspaper and put it to the flame, I then put the burning paper onto the table and it ignites immediately. The whiskey just explodes. I take the bottle before the fire gets to it and I go and pour it over her body. I run back to the kitchen and grab some more newspapers to light up. As quickly as I can, I run into the room and throw the burning paper onto her body. It ignites immediately. I stand and watch as all her hair burns and her flesh starts to bubble with the heat. I see it spread to the floor and before I know it, the couch starts to catch fire. It doesn't take much before the room is alight. I watch the flesh bubble away until I know I have to leave before I get burned.

I'm standing at the front, on the dirt road, and I'm watching the fire spread rapidly throughout the whole house. By the time anyone sees it, if anyone does, it will be burned to the ground. I need to head back to the motel and get cleaned up, I must stink of smoke. Well, my ankle hasn't given way on me so far so it must be okay. I start to jog once I reach the main road. I get a bit quicker, starting a sprint, just then I see headlights coming toward me, I duck into the bushes along the road's edge, lying flat on my belly, hoping no one sees me. I wait until it passes, then check around and start to jog on the road again.

It doesn't take too long before I'm approaching the bar we were at earlier, which means my motel is not far now. I stop jogging and just walk at a nice steady pace with my hands in my pockets. I don't want anyone to see me running and think I'm running from something. Once I'm past the bar, it's fine, there are a few more people around and it's not unusual for anyone to see me walking to and from the bar. I still keep my head down and get to the motel as fast as I can. Once inside, I strip and head for the bathroom holding my clothes. I run the bathtub and get the soap and try to wash my jeans and tee. Once I've done that, I hang them up to dry. I look in the mirror, my face looks like I got sunburned, fuck, and it's dirty from the smoke. I don't want Poppy to come around and ask questions. I jump in the shower and scrub myself from top to bottom, hoping I can get rid of the smell of smoke.

I'm just wrapping the towel around my waist when I hear a knock on the door. I look through the peephole and it's Poppy standing there. Fuck, she's supposed to be working. I don't want her to come in while I'm in just a towel, she might try something. I know how hard I am to resist. I'm big-headed as well. I move to quickly get a clean pair of jeans and white tee like I had on earlier. This is my usual attire anyway. I crumple the bed a bit to make it look like I was lying on top. I put the TV on but muted and I move to open the door.

"Hey Pops, thought you were working?"

She smiles at me and holds up a bag of food. "Hey, I had a break and thought I would drop by and bring you something to eat. I felt bad the way we left things earlier." She looks a bit sheepish as she hands me the food.

She does know I can get around now, doesn't she?

"Thanks, come in." I open the door wider, making her duck under my arm to enter. She sits at the small table and I sit opposite her.

"You had a hot shower again?" she says, pointing to my face. It must be red still from the fire.

Shit, I hope I didn't get so close that it blisters up. "Yeah, came back from the bar and needed a shower. Just got out now as you knocked. You know I like it hot."

She nods at me and smiles.

"Yeah, I'm surprised you can stand it that hot and that it doesn't scorch you. By the looks of your face, I would say you had it hotter, I hope you don't get blisters from burning yourself."

She looks at me funny, then stands up and leans over the table.

"Shit, Nick, the side of your face looks like it's blistering. You need to stop with the roasting yourself in the shower." She reaches out to touch the side of my face, I pull back from her before she touches me. She looks wounded by that move.

Fuck, why are women so complicated? At least she only thinks it's the shower.

"Sorry, that was just instinct in case it hurt."

Bullshit, I wouldn't even feel her touch on my face, but she doesn't know that.

She sits back down and smiles at me, I smile back. She starts pulling the food out of the bag. "Do you have any water?"

I nod and get up to get a couple of bottles of water for us.

We eat and just make small talk. She apologizes for her reaction earlier and I just accept it for what it is. She said she understood how I could come to that conclusion as there aren't many jobs where you work the streets at night.

"Well, time for me to head back. Is there anything you need?"

I shake my head no. "Okay. I'll pop by with breakfast if that's okay?"

Shit, it's getting too much, all this. I know I have to keep it up to try to find out where Primrose is, but it's getting harder. I can't stand Poppy coming around. I know she wants more, and I don't want to go near her.

I'm starting to loathe her.

"Actually, Pops, I'm going into work early tomorrow. Old man Johnson said he had a couple of cars that need looking at, I said I would be there early."

She looks a bit wounded by that but I don't care. I need to somehow start to talk about Primrose, to try and find out more. She smiles at me and heads to the door.

"Okay, Nick, maybe we can catch up after you finish work, and before I start. Shall we meet in the bar?"

"Yeah, let's do that. Thanks for the food, Pops. See you tomorrow." She hesitates at the door, opens it and leaves without saying another word.

I sigh with relief. Thank god she's gone.

Fourteen

Blaine

I'VE BEEN WORKING AT THE LOCAL GARAGE FOR A COUPLE OF WEEKS now. I do all sorts of things from tinkering under the hood of cars to cleaning them or just changing the oil and helping to pump the gas for customers. I also got a job in the bar, can you believe I fucking work in the place? It's just in the evenings making sure the place is clean, wiping down the tables and stocking the shelves. I don't serve anyone which is fine by me. I'm no good at math and money. I needed the additional work, the money from the garage just about pays for the motel I'm staying in. It's costing me a lot to stay here and get info on Primrose when I have a perfectly good home I could be living in.

Working at the bar means I also don't have to spend too much time with Poppy, but just enough. I haven't been able to talk to her about Primrose yet. I don't want her getting suspicious, I have never mentioned her since she came back. I heard rumors about a fire a few weeks back, the remains of a woman who lived at the house were found, but she was burned to a crisp. No one has ever come looking or asking questions, it's a good ten miles or so away from here. I listened to people saying no one really knew the woman, just that she lived on her own, they reckon she must have started the fire to kill herself, a suicide, from being lonely. The one good thing about being in the bar is I get to listen to what's going on.

Don comes into the bar more than I realized. He comes in with different guys, I think they are just friends but now and then he's a little intimate with some of them, but not all. I think he's a man whore. I've sat with him a couple of times getting to know him a little more. He had that picture of Primrose so I figured he may know more info. He's just come into the bar on his own. He does this when he's waiting for Tilda and Poppy. They don't work every night, in fact, it varies all the time.

I have a break, so I take a Coke over to him. That's his drink when he's going to work.

"Hey Don, how you doing? You waiting for the girls to arrive?" I place the drink in front of him and take the chair opposite. He has a crush on me, I see the way he looks at me all the time, but I also know he wouldn't try anything because he wouldn't want to upset Poppy, or get knocked on his ass by me. He has his cell on the table in front of him. "Hey Don, you know I don't have a cell, right? If I wanted one, how do I go about doing that? I've never had one, I don't have the first idea how to get one."

He smiles at me.

"You're a bit of an enigma, Nick, I must say, in this day, I don't know many people that don't have a cell, except some of the homeless we help, but even most of them have one."

I just shrug at him. "It's not something I grew up around. I lived with my mama and she never had one."

"If you have some money, I can pick one up for you. What do you want one for? Just calls or to go on the internet?" I must look bewildered. "Guess I must be speaking another language to you, judging from your expression." He laughs and I just laugh with him.

We talk for a little while, he agrees to pick me up a cell, nothing too fancy, but he will set me up on it and show me everything I need to know. The main thing I need to know is where and how he got that picture of Primrose on his cell. As long as I can do the same thing then I will be set.

I start back at work just before Poppy comes in. She comes to see me like she normally does. If I get this cell, maybe I won't need to keep up this pretense with her. Every day gets harder. She blows hot and cold all the time. I never know where I am with her. Maybe most of that is my fault. Maybe because I don't let her get all touchy with me and I definitely don't get touchy with her. I still let her put an arm around my waist, sometimes, as she has just now to say hi to me. I don't remove it and smile down at her. How can I start to despise someone that's identical to the one person in this world I want more than anything? It just doesn't make sense to me. Surely I would want to be with her if I couldn't have Primrose? But maybe Primrose is just like her and I might despise her as well. I really need to find her and see for myself.

I watch as they all leave for work. I really need a release. I haven't had one since that crispy chick a few weeks back. I have so many whores coming on to me in here it's unreal. Do they all just see me as a piece of meat? Maybe that's another reason Poppy gets so uptight, watching all these women flirt with me. I have them stuffing paper into my jeans pockets with their cell numbers, or they scribble on a napkin or coaster and pass it to me. They all just end up in the garbage. If I want a release, it needs to be far away from here.

I'm thinking of taking off for a few days. Moving on to another town and getting what I can there. Maybe I might stay away if I can find where Primrose is. Maybe move near her and make my move. Get rid of Poppy, pretend I never knew her. Maybe take Poppy to my place and see her in pain. The pain I crave. The pain she feels would be all I need until I find Primrose. I need to hatch a plan. I'll wait to see what Don does for me with a cell, see if he can teach me how to use it and get that picture of Primrose. I know it's going to be hard with me not being able to read, but I have learned a lot more recently. I've been trying to teach myself.

It's been a few days since I've seen Don, he's just come into the bar with a smile on his face. "Hey Nick, you get a break soon? I have something for you," he says, holding up a bag.

"Yeah, be with you in a few, Don, can I get you a drink? You working later?"

He nods. Twenty minutes later, I sit down with him and he's got a box on the table which I'm guessing is my cell.

"Let me know what I owe you for it and I can give you some now and the rest next time I see you, if that's okay?"

He takes it out of the box, turns it on and starts to do things on it. I just sit watching, not having a clue what he's doing. He asks me questions about my email address and what preferences I have for a screensaver. I just look at him blankly, not having a clue what he's talking about.

He shakes his head and carries on doing what he's doing. He takes some paper and a pen from his bag he always carries around and starts putting things on the paper. He passes it to me, I take the paper but have no idea what it says. I know the numbers now, I can read to ten and count to twenty but nothing else. He explains that the top is my cell number, if I want him or Poppy to have it then they put it in their cell, then they can call me. He shows me by putting my number in his cell and then he calls my cell. He then takes mine and does something, then calls it again. This time instead of numbers appearing he tells me that's his name, that way I know it's him calling me. He shows me how to answer the call by clicking on the green circle or click on the red if I don't want to answer it. He then shows me how to call his cell. It's like fucking magic, but so complicated.

He's going through a few things and tells me he's set me up on Google to give me an email address. He has to explain what that is and what it's used for, I have no idea. He then shows me he has set up something called Facebook. I remember that name from when he showed me the picture of Primrose. Fuck, my heart is racing.

"So is this the place where you found that picture of Primrose?"

He nods yes.

"Here look, I put in her name Primrose Tomlinson, it brings up anyone with that name and I know that's her profile picture, I click this and here are her details." He shows me and there she is on my fucking cell, I can look at her all fucking day now.

I just realized I never even knew what her full name was either. "How do I get it so I can look anytime?" I don't want the cell to turn off then me not be able to find her again. He shows me.

"Don, I know it's weird but can you write her name on this paper for me please and Poppy's and yours." I look away then back to him, I see him look at me quizzically. "I can't read, Don. Please don't tell anyone. I've never told anyone before. If you've got the words written down then I can copy them."

"Hey, I'm sorry, Nick, I had no idea. I promise I won't tell anyone. Listen, I teach an English class at the local community center to immigrants to learn English. I'm more than happy for you to come along to the classes and learn. I won't charge for it, Nick, we're friends. If you're willing, I will help you anytime I can."

Wow, he'd actually do that for me? I'm taken aback. I smile.

"Thanks Don, I just thought you would laugh at me and call me a retard. My mama used to call me a retard all the time."

He looks at me pitifully. "Never, Nick, I would never laugh at anyone who couldn't read or write."

I like Don, he's the first person I feel I can call a friend. I don't know how long it will last.

Poppy and Tilda came in a little later, Don had finished showing me stuff on the cell. He said just the basics for now because too much info and I would just get lost, I agreed with him, I'm already lost. I was walking around clearing the tables when Poppy came over to me. We talked a little but she could see I was working, I didn't make it easy on her. I don't think I need her. I think with this cell and Don's help, I may be able to find Primrose without Poppy.

Once they left for work, it wasn't long before I finished. I'd had some women come on to me, yet again, one even took my cell from my back pocket, put her number in it asking me to call her. I wanted to take her out back, give her a good fucking, and squeeze her throat until her eyes were popping. Then I would let her breathe and make her tell me what she was thinking. How did it feel, the life being slowly squeezed from her body? I would then break her fingers, one by one, and listen to her scream at each snap. I need to move on for a while and then maybe come back. It's starting to fester inside me, it's all I can think about. That crispy whore was great for the fuck, but a waste of fucking time not being able to ask her how it felt to burn. If I don't leave for a week or so, then I fear I will do something stupid right here.

Back at the motel, I start to pace. I start to pull on my hair without realizing I've done it until I see a clump in my hand. I feel like a caged animal. I feel trapped. If I feel like this now, how will I feel if Primrose would have me? How would I cope after going so long and not being able to witness the pain? I decide to pack up my stuff from the motel and leave for a week. I need to get away, even if it's to head back home for the week.

I stop by the bar, I know it's late, but Terry who owns it lives there. I tell him I have to leave just for the week, that I will be back. He's cool about it. Tells me not to worry, that I can still work there if I decide to come back to Reedley, I never knew what this town was called before. There's that at least. I just feel so wound up, like I will snap at any moment, which is why I need to leave, to clear my head and feed my needs. I'll come back. I just need to think and plan what to do next. I just need to breathe.

I start the walk home which is stupid because it's nighttime. Maybe I'll get lucky as I did with the crispy whore. Find a lonely woman in the middle of nowhere, just waiting to have my cock in her. Who knows. It's going to take me a couple of days to get home if that's where I want to go. I just at this moment need to get far away from here and find a new town to stay for a few days. Get exactly what I need and leave. Maybe I can hitch a ride to somewhere farther away.

I've been walking for a long time. It's so dark with no street lighting anywhere. I'm in the middle of nowhere. I hear lots of noises from the undergrowth, and in the trees as I pass what looks like a large wooded area. Not the safest place to be wandering around late at night. It's one of the reasons I'm sticking to the road and not wandering off. There have been a few trucks passing me, but nothing more. None have stopped, but then would you stop to pick some stranger up in the middle of nowhere at night? I wouldn't unless it was a whore on her own.

I've been walking for hours, I'm sure of it. It's still dark, I've passed so many wooded areas, then fields that go on and on. I've spotted farmhouses in the distance but not taken the chance to wander to any of them. It must be getting close to sunrise. I need some sleep, I know that much. My ankle must be okay, it hasn't given on me at all. I see a building coming into view up ahead, looking toward the left of me, I can just make out on the horizon the night sky getting lighter. I've been walking all night. I passed through two towns but thought they were too close to where I had been staying, I wanted to keep going farther. I don't have a clue where I am, if this is a town coming up then I will find the motel and crash for the day. Then come evening I'll scope the place and see what's going on.

I needed that sleep. I stopped at the next motel I found and got a room. Looking out I see it's getting dark, I must have slept all day. I shower then head out, I need food. I stop at a diner and eat a huge steak and eggs. I head down the road to see if there is a bar nearby. That's the best place to see what's what. In a bar, I order a beer and sit in a booth so I can see everything. I watch people come and go, I've decided no matter where you are, you will always find whores in these places. It doesn't change from one bar to the next. This bar, like the last one, is on the very edge of the town, set back from the road. Only this one is set farther back with a dirt track leading to the parking lot out front. It's more run-down than the one I work at. It stinks inside of piss.

I don't know if I can sit here for long, it reminds me of Mama too much. I've watched as the whores mooching around have noticed me and eyed me up, I don't smile at them, my stare alone should frighten them off, but it does the opposite. I've had a few of them come to sit in front of me and smile, asking me questions, but I never engage with any of them, unless one catches my eye. Just like the one that just sat at the bar on her own. She's in short shorts and a very small top. It's off the shoulder and then tied just under her tits showing all her middle section. I'm looking at her and just then she turns and spots me. Gotcha.

She comes over to me. "Hi," she says all shy and timid.

Like fuck, she's shy dressed like that. I don't look at her, instead, I just twirl the glass in my hand, which is now almost empty.

"You wanna talk?" she asks.

Talk, like fuck I do and she knows it. I know her type.

"Nope, just fuck. Meet me out back in ten, I just need to finish my drink."

I watch as she sashays out of the bar, trying to make it look like she has a big ass when she doesn't. She's tiny, but she'll do. I watch her leave and I sit there sipping the rest of my beer, making her wait. I saw the look she gave me. I know she wants me. She's on her own, she didn't speak to anyone that I saw before we spoke and she certainly didn't speak to anyone as she left. Fucking whore.

I make my way out of the bar, keeping my head down, not making eye contact with anyone. I've made her wait long enough, but I wanted to leave a gap between us leaving, just so no one saw us leave together. I have plans for her. It's dark out when I exit, there's a small veranda to the bar with very dim lights. I look both ways then spot her leaning against the wall at the far end. I could only just make her out in the dim light. There isn't anyone else around, thank fuck for that. I head toward her and walk straight past her down the steps and head around the back of the bar. I have no idea what's out back, but I'm hoping to God it's just nothing but beer kegs with a wooded or bushed area to the back.

There are no cameras that I can see as I head around and I hear her following behind me.

"Hey, hold up, wait for me, will ya? Don't you wanna fuck?"

I stop and turn to see her trying to catch up to me. I sneer at her as she approaches, it's so dark and I'm so much taller than her, she probably can't see my face clearly, like I said, she's tiny.

"How old are you?" I ask because I want to make sure she's legal. I know it's not gonna be pretty, but for my sanity, I will not do anyone underage. That repulses me. Ha, me being repulsed when I do what I do, but yeah underage is a hard no-go for me.

"I'm twenty-two, why?"

She looks younger than that. "Just wanna make sure you're legal for what I'm gonna do to ya."

She lifts her face and I see a big smile on it. I turn and walk around the back, I scan the area, looking at what there is, making sure there are no cameras anywhere. She walks up behind me, puts her arms around my waist and lowers a hand to my groin. Well, shit, she really does wanna just fuck. I stop her before she can grab my cock. I set the pace, not her.

"You here alone?" I ask, I just want to make sure.

"Yeah, why? Do you want me to call a friend to join us? Is that what you like?"

I do, but no, I just want to make sure there is no one inside waiting for her.

I turn and stalk her until her back is against the wall of the bar. I undo my jeans and pull out my cock, she licks her lips and seems to know exactly what I want, she lowers herself to a squatting position in front of me and takes my cock into her mouth. I throw my head back as she does her thing. She's experienced, you can always tell. I grab her head and slam in as hard as I can over and over. She takes it all, it doesn't bother her, I'm being rough, maybe she has the same tolerance to pain as I have? Could it be?

I'm coming in no time and shooting it down her throat. God, I needed this. But with that thirst satisfied, now I want to see the pain. See if she does feel it. I pull her up by the hair to test it.

"Ow, you fucker, why'd you do that? You nearly pulled my hair out."

Yes, she feels pain, good. I still want to fuck her.

"Come with me, I need that fuck now." I start to walk toward the trees at the very back of the bar.

"Hey, wait, why are we going there?"

I sneer to myself. "Don't want anyone to come running when they hear you scream. You'll be screaming loud when my cock is rammed into you."

"Oh, okay," is all she says.

I walk through the first line of trees, keeping my eyes peeled for anything moving, I know this could be dangerous. I hear her following behind me.

"Ouch, ow, how much farther? This undergrowth is attacking my legs."

That's not all that will be attacking her. We've gone quite far into the wooded area, I see a fallen tree and I stop. She catches up to me. I turn to her and grab her arm.

"Ouch, you're hurting me, don't squeeze so hard."

I don't say anything. I pull her over to the fallen tree and move her in front of me, I bend her over the tree, face-first, with her ass in the air. I feel up her inner thigh to her pussy, she gasps as I stroke her. I rip the panties from her and spread her legs. I undo my jeans, releasing my cock I line up and slam straight into her. She screams, I pause then do it again, over and over.

She's loving it, she keeps pushing back onto my cock as I thrust in deeper and deeper. I love these feelings, the only feelings I ever feel. I'm not far from blowing my load, she screams out with her release, panting and screaming, that sends me over the edge and I blow my load into her, pushing and pushing. I reach around to her front and find her clit and I squeeze and squeeze trying to wring her out. She screams out more, this is a pained scream, not an ecstasy scream. I twist and pull, I'm still inside her but I'm not hard anymore, I slide out and turn her around to face me. She has her back bent over the tree, looking up at me.

I can just about see her face. I grab her tits and squeeze.

"Ow, stop fucking hurting me. Let me go now. We fucked, that's it."

I sneer at her again and squint. I lean down, still squeezing her tits and I whisper in her ear, "Tell me, is this hurting or are you turned on by it?" I pinch her nipples hard.

"Get off me, you fucker, that hurts. I want to leave now."

Like hell she is. She tries to grab my fingers to get me to stop. I grab her hand and I bend her fingers right back until I hear them all snap. She screams a bloodcurdling scream. As much as I want to hear her scream, I put my other hand over her mouth to muffle the sound.

"Be quiet, you whore. We don't want anyone to come and see what a good time I'm having."

I laugh at that, as her eyes that are now glistening from her tears widen with horror. I take the other hand and one by one, I bend the fingers back until they snap. The jolt from the snapping in my hand makes me smile. The horror on her face makes me smile harder. I take my hand from her mouth.

"Ssshh," I say as I put my face right in hers, I lick her tears as they roll down her face. "Now, tell me exactly what you are feeling. Tell me what the pain was like as each finger snapped, does it still hurt or only when I do this?" I whisper as I play with the floppy broken fingers.

She screams out, and I put my mouth over hers to swallow the sound, and to see if I can feel her pain from the scream. She tries to shove me off her with her body, then she tries to push my mouth from hers with her tongue. I catch her tongue with my teeth and I bite hard. I enjoy the metallic taste of her blood, just like with Primrose's pappy. I feel her vibrating body underneath me, she's crying hysterically, and her body is shaking with shock.

I pull back and ask, "Tell me, I need to know what the pain is like."

She can't speak, her mouth is full of blood that's oozing down her cheeks and her eyes are shut.

"Open your fucking eyes and tell me how it feels."

She opens them and shakes her head no. I slap her face, hard, making her cheek slam against the tree trunk and blood comes sputtering out of her mouth.

"I can't talk, hurts so much," she says, but she's talking funny.

I turn her face to mine by grabbing it on either side of her mouth. "Open your mouth and stick your tongue out."

She does and I can see I bit off some of her tongue. I thought I only bit it and drew blood, but no, some of her tongue is missing. Nice. She spits at me but luckily misses. Now I have blood splatter on my white tee. Great.

I lay flat on her, crushing her body to the tree trunk, my full weight on her slight frame pressing down hard. I want to see her eyes bulge from the pressure of me on her chest, squeezing all the air from her lungs. I see her eyes go bloodshot and I put a hand on her throat and squeeze. She's nearly at the passing out stage. Then suddenly I hear a loud snap, I wonder what it is at first, looking around us, then I look down and she looks funny. It's her back, I snapped her fucking back over the tree trunk with my weight. Fuck. I get off her body and look at the angle it's at, really bent over, her head is practically touching the ground on the other side.

I walk around to where her head is and look down. She's still alive, I crouch down next to her head and try to lift it by the hair. She's barely breathing. I see tears flowing out the sides of her eyes, her eyes are open wide, staring at nothing, they look lifeless. I bend over her.

"Can you speak? Can you feel anything? I want to know if you feel any pain at all?"

She doesn't move, not even her lips.

"Blink once if you understand what I'm saying."

Nothing, but she's still alive, just.

"Fucking blink if you hear me." I stand up in a rage.

She blinks, very slightly.

"Good, now can you feel the pain. Blink once for yes and twice for no."

I stand above her, but bend to get close to her face, I see a slight flicker of her eyes, that's a blink? Yes, she feels the pain. No, that's another slight blink. Fuck, she can't feel the pain. What a fucking waste of my time again. What is it with a lot of these whores? Some of them die too quickly.

"FUCK," I shout out and without realizing it, I bring my foot down on her head, really fucking hard. I hear her neck snap, her head is at a funny angle from the rest of her broken body.

I sit on the tree trunk next to her lifeless body. I look at her, watching her chest to see if it rises at all. I know it won't, I know she's dead. Now what? At home, it's easy. I just bury them or leave the body for the bears and mountain lions to eat. Here though, someone might find her, and I don't have anything to dig a hole to put her in and it would take too long. The last one was fine because the fire took her, this one though, they will find the evidence of a sexual encounter and get DNA. Even though they don't have my DNA to match it to, I don't want it on their records. If I burn her, it may attract the attention of people from the bar and I don't know how close we are to anything else.

Maybe if I just leave her, something will come along and feed off her before she is found. I think that's all I can do. Leave her and sneak away from here as best I can. Find my way back to the motel and leave this place. I pick her up and walk a little farther into the trees, it gets denser there. Her body is so small and light, she's just like a rag doll in my hands. I find a big tree with its roots sticking out of the ground and I place her in between the roots, I gather leaves and branches and cover her body so she's not easy to spot, only an animal would smell her.

I walk through the trees leaving her body there and head in the direction of where I think the motel is. I don't want to go near the bar again. I don't want anyone to see me emerge from the trees. As the trees and bushes thin out, I cautiously leave and head to the road and try to find my bearings and figure out where the motel is. As it happens, it isn't that far. I keep my head down, putting my Starter cap on so I can hide under the bill, I get into my room as fast as I can. I didn't notice anyone around.

I lie on my bed after my shower, thinking. I know what I want to do, I pick up my cell and I do as Don showed me to get on that face thing, I take out the piece of paper and I put in the letters from the paper which Don said are Primrose's, I stare at her on the cell, he showed me where to go to look at any pictures she has on there, I look through them. I'm going to go back as though everything is normal. I've waited this long, it won't harm anything to wait a little longer. I'll go to the classes Don teaches. I'll learn to read and write and he said he would help me when he is free as well, that way I will learn quicker. I'm not going to engage much with Poppy, I don't want her thinking there is something between us. I'm going to keep my distance from her. She won't like it, but I don't give a fuck what she likes, and to be honest, if I carried on as we were, I would end up killing her. I'm going to leave at first light, so I need to try to get some sleep and hope no one stumbles across that whore in the woods.

Blaine

I couldn't sleep much. As soon as I saw it was getting light out, I got dressed and left. I had a long walk back to Reedley where I've been staying. I didn't even know what the place was called, until Don told me. I've been to so many towns and never known the names of them, I may not be able to read or write but I have a fantastic sense of direction. It's dark by the time I get back to the motel in Reedley and check-in for a couple of weeks. I get cleaned up then go grab some food from one of the places up the road. I'm not going into the bar tonight, I need to try to get a good night's sleep. I'll call Don and ask when the classes are, or when he has some free time. I'm quite excited to finally learn how to read and write, instead of feeling like a fucking retard all the time. It gets so hard not knowing the simple stuff.

The sun is shining through the crack in the curtains, I must not have closed them completely last night. After the food, I must have just passed out. I needed the sleep. I shower, then go grab some food before I head to the garage to see if old man Johnson has any work for me there today. I did say I may be away for a week, but it's only been a few days. On my way, I call Don and hope I haven't woken him.

"Hey Don, it's Nick."

"Yes, Nick, I know it's you."

How the fuck does he know? I pull the cell away from my ear to look at it. I hear him speaking.

"You there, Nick?"

"Yes, how the fuck did you know it was me?"

He laughs. "Because your name comes up on my cell when you call. Remember I showed you? We put my name next to my number and I did the same on my cell. Here, let me hang up and call you back."

With that, he's gone. I look at my cell again. It rings in my hand and I see a name which is Don's. He showed me his name written down. I press the green button to speak.

"Yeah, I see your name, now I get it. Hope I haven't woken you up? Not sure if you were working last night."

"I was working and only got in about ten minutes ago so you didn't wake me. What's up?"

Oh yeah, I was forgetting. "I'm back and was wondering when we could start with the classes, or you helping me to read and write. Just when you can, but I would appreciate your help. You haven't told the others, have you?"

"No, you asked me not to. I haven't said anything. Okay, classes are every Wednesday and Friday at three in the afternoon, for an hour. I know you're working two jobs, so they may not fit in with your schedule. If not, we can do an hour each morning if you like. I could bring books and stuff to you first thing after work and before you go to work. Does that help?"

"Yeah that would be great, but won't you be too tired after working all night?"

"It's fine. I will just go straight to bed when I get home instead of puttering around like I normally do."

I worked at the bar as usual and kept on at the garage but started an hour later than normal. Old man Johnson who owns the place said I can come and go as I please. He likes having the company and some muscle around the place to help shift tires and stuff. It worked out great. Don came to the motel in the mornings after his night shifts, which was about five mornings a week. That was six weeks ago and I can now read and write simple words. Not perfect, I still have a ways to go but I'm getting there. Thanks to Don, I can make out signs on the roads, and items on the menus and the bar messages they post daily, also I'm now a whiz on Facebook. The only downside to the last eight weeks has been Poppy. When I first got back, she was clingy, wanting to come to see me all the time, and coming into the bar a lot. At first, I just let her think something was going to happen but then two weeks in, I had to tell her we were just friends. Let's just say it didn't go down well.

I'd had enough and thought it best not to string her along. The fact she was starting to fuck with my head made it worse. I imagined all the ways I could torture her and make her feel pain, I was starting to despise her. I had told her not to come to the motel in the mornings, but I didn't tell her it was because Don was coming, I still didn't want anyone to know I couldn't read or write. She thought it odd as she had always come after work, but she did as I asked until one morning she arrived with Don. I looked at Don and raised my eyebrow and he just slightly shrugged at me.

"Hey Nick, I saw Don was heading here this morning, so I thought I would tag along."

I scowled at her and walked into the room and sat on the bed. Don, thank god, kept the books in his bag and I moved the books I had under my pillow before she saw them.

"I told you not to come here in the mornings, Poppy. I have to leave for work soon."

She glared at me. "Well, what's he doing coming here then?"

Don thinking fast pulled out a magazine he had in his bag. "I was just dropping this off for Nick. It's got that article in it I was telling you about, Nick. Here, read for yourself." He passed me the magazine.

"Great, thanks, Don." I looked at him and nodded slightly to the door, asking him to leave. I think he got the message. He left right away, leaving Poppy standing there looking at me.

"What's going on, Nick? You've been acting strangely for a couple of weeks now."

I rubbed my hands over my face, playing with my beard, thinking it's now or never. "Look, Poppy, I'm not sure where you think this is going—"

"Where what's going?" she interrupted me.

I sighed and got up off the bed and stood in front of her. "This, me and you. There is no me and you, Poppy. You're a nice girl and a good friend, but that's all it will ever be between us, friends. I don't do relationships, Poppy. Not yet anyway."

She put her hands on her hips, scowling at me. "What's that supposed to mean? Not yet? You going to screw someone or are you already doing tha...?" She stops and squints at me. "Fuck, it's Don, isn't it? You're gay, aren't you? How the hell did I not see it before? That's why he was here. Has he been here every morning?"

I moved to the side and grabbed a bottle of water and took a swig. I turned to face her. "Fuck, Poppy, no I'm not gay. I'm not seeing anyone, as I said, I don't do relationships. Look, thank you for everything you've done for me, but it's not going any further. We're friends, Poppy, that's it."

The next thing I knew, she slapped me across my face. It jerked my head slightly so it must have been hard. I just didn't feel a thing. "Fuck's sake, Poppy, what was that for, you stupid bitch?" Wrong thing to say when you want to remain friends.

"You've been stringing me along all this time, you asshole. I thought it was going somewhere. So you don't do relationships, so what? You just screw around? I've seen all the whores in the bar passing you numbers and coming on to you. Is that what you do at the end of the night, screw one of them?"

"Look, I haven't screwed anyone in a long time if you must know. I like you Poppy, but as a friend, nothing more. You've been getting clingy, and I don't do clingy. Can we stay friends, please?"

She eyed me skeptically. "Why was Don here? I know he's been here a few mornings, Nick. That's why I insisted on coming with him this morning. What's going on with you two?"

Fuck, she thought we were screwing. Time to tell her the truth. I didn't think she would ridicule me.

"He's been coming every morning, Poppy." I held up my hand to stop her as she was going to start again. "It's not what you think. Look, fuck, I can't read or write, okay? My mama kept me home, away from school and never showed me much at all. Fuck, I hate telling anyone. Anyway, Don got me the cell and was showing me how to use it and I had to tell him, he teaches English to immigrants and offered to help me. That's it, nothing seedy going on. I just want to concentrate on learning as well as working two jobs. I just want to be friends." I put on a sad face, I watched her soften.

"I'm sorry, Nick, for being a bitch and jumping to conclusions. I understand completely. Look, yes, let's stay friends and maybe one day, who knows? If you need any extra help learning, I can help."

That's a positive spin. I'm getting used to the fact not everyone thinks I'm a retard, and they don't laugh at me.

After that, I've only seen her at the bar. I didn't get any extra help from her, Don has been a great teacher. He's been so patient with me, even when I've had a fucking hissy fit like a girl, because something wouldn't stick. As he said, it's not because I'm thick, but because I'm older, and it takes a little more time to stick once you're older, but when you get it, then it's there for good. He's become like a brother to me. I'm so grateful for all his help.

I've been stalking Primrose on Facebook, just waiting for her to put something new on there. She doesn't post much at all. Don has just left, I'm on my way to the garage when I look at Facebook and her page, and oh fuck, she posted a new picture. She looks gorgeous, I can't stop staring at it. I think she's put 'so glad to be back home in my own bed'. The fact I could read that amazes me and makes me smile. I'm not a smiley person normally, but anyone watching me now would think I was a lunatic smiling to myself. I'm on the biggest high at the moment. I was starting to get agitated again, wanting to feel and the only way I can feel is fucking. Now that I've seen this, I can wait. I don't give a fuck.

I've spent the last few weeks learning from Don, working both jobs and stalking her on Facebook. The Facebook thing is becoming an obsession. Every day as soon as I wake up, I look to see if there is anything new on Primrose's page, then again throughout the day and nighttime. There hasn't been anything since that one. I'm good at reading, albeit slowly but it's there and I can count. I've just woken up and like always I look at Facebook, and like always, I get angry because there is nothing. I shower knowing Don will be here any moment. There's a knock at the door and when I open it, I see Poppy standing there.

"'Morning Nick, I just stopped by to tell you Don can't make it, he got held up with the police, he asked me to let you know."

She could have just called me. She has my number.

"Oh, okay. Thanks, Poppy, I hope he's okay and it's nothing serious."

"Not for him, no, just one of the girls got beaten badly and he found her, so he's been with her at the station. All part of what we do. If you want, I thought I could help you this morning." She looks a little sheepish as she holds up a bag of food. "Breakfast?" she asks timidly.

If I'm smart, I could use this to my advantage. I open the door for her to enter under my arm and smile at her. What's with the fucking smiling all the time?

We sit and have some food, making small talk.

"Hey Nick, have you learned about money with Don yet? I know he's been showing you lots of things. I could help you."

She opens her wallet and pulls out some bills and coins. I haven't touched on the money too much with Don, but I know some of the basic stuff now. She goes through the bills and coins with me, it helps me understand them all, which is a big help. We finish up and I pick up my cell to check the time.

"I have to go soon, Pops, old man Johnson wants me at the garage. Thanks for your help though, it's been a great help."

"I liked helping you, Nick. Anytime Don can't make it I could step in. I'm pretty good at this stuff although not as good as Primrose."

Bingo, time to jump on that. "Have you heard from her? She was away last time you went to see her. Is she back yet?"

She looks to the water bottle in her hand and plays with the label on it.

"We don't talk, Nick. Haven't for many years, since we were young. I want to fix that with her. I've learned a lot lately, and I want to try to have a relationship with her. The problem is she works away a lot, and she doesn't live near here."

I take a swig of my water and don't say anything. I don't want her to think I'm after anything.

"The thing is, she came home a few weeks ago, and when I spoke to Aunt Cassy the other day she said Primrose was there. I'm thinking of going to Aunt Cassy's and visiting Prim, and try to fix things."

"Does Primrose live near your aunt Cassy?"

She nods. "Yes, they live close by. Prim lives in our childhood house where we lived with our parents. She bought my share from me, so she now owns it. It's not far from Aunt Cassy's house, it's like a ten-minute walk, if that."

My heart is beating, I'm finally getting some info but I don't want to ruin it.

"They live in Piedmont, Oakland, not far from San Francisco, it's about a three-hour drive from here. I'm going to go over the weekend, maybe stay there for a little while, but I'll be back, depends on how it goes."

Shit, I wonder if I can come up with a way of following her or going with her.

"Nick, you okay?"

"Huh, yeah, just thinking." Fuck. I need a plan. "How far is it from San Francisco?"

She smiles.

"Not too far, only about twenty minutes. Have you ever been to San Fran? I used to go to the city a lot when I was younger."

I shake my head. "No, I've never been. I think this is the closest I've ever been. I've always wanted to visit, but then again, I would love to visit a lot of places. I need to save and get a car, I can drive, but I don't have a license so that would be the first thing to do. Then I will travel around. At the moment, I travel on foot or hitch. I've always done that, which is why I never get that far."

She looks a little sad, I smile. "Not like your sister, huh? She seems to travel the world. I could only dream of doing that. I'll settle for traveling the states."

She's thinking, then her smile widens suddenly.

"Hey, why don't you come with me? I could drop you off in San Fran if you want to visit the city. Another place on your list."

Fuck, how can this be so easy? I smile at her.

"You would keep me company, we're friends, Nick. You could come with me and either come to my aunt Cassy's or I could drop you in the city. Road trip, what do you say?"

Fucking hell, she's like putty in my hand. I play it all cool and let her make all the suggestions, that way it's all her idea when it all goes wrong. Genius.

"I don't want to impose on you, Poppy. If you're going to go and sort things out with your sister, the last thing I want is to get in the way." Play it cool.

She smiles. "Honestly, you would be doing me a favor. Having someone else there on my side if I need it. Anyway, you said you met Prim years ago? It would be good for her to see you, don't you think?"

I can't believe she's this easy.

I nod. "Yes, but only if it's okay. I would love to see San Francisco. Maybe you could show me around?"

She beams at me. How can this be that easy? I've waited months for this, telling her we can only be friends and nothing more and she suddenly says come with her to meet her sister.

"Tell me the details, when you're planning to leave, and I will let old man Johnson and Terry at the bar know I won't be around for a few days. I need to get to the garage now though. Thank you for your help with the money today, Pops, you have no idea how helpful that was for me. Now I won't feel so stupid going into the café or store where I just hold out the money for them to take what is needed."

I lean down and kiss her on the cheek. I see her blush. Is she really into me like this? She was a firecracker when we first met, now she seems like a different timid person. I can't put my finger on the change in her. This is where my trust issues come full force, I don't trust her. This isn't like her to be this nice and forthcoming, but to be honest, I'll take it. I don't give a fuck what she's thinking or planning as long as I get to finally see Primrose.

Poppy should be here any minute to pick me up for our trip to San Francisco, the last few days have dragged so much, I didn't learn much when Don came in the mornings. I told him we were going, but he already knew from Poppy. He thought it was strange I was going with her. I think he suspects there's an ulterior motive to taking me to San Fran, but I didn't ask him. I didn't want to make him suspicious as well. I just played on going to San Fran as somewhere I've always wanted to go. I didn't even mention Primrose and neither did he. It's going to be a long three-hour drive in the car with Poppy. Let's see what it brings.

The drive wasn't bad at all. We talked about nothing in particular. She did tell me more about herself growing up, how she never got along with Primrose, and how she went off the rails and caused so much trouble and heartache for her aunt Cassy and uncle Trevor. She does love them and going back hurts her, but she didn't say why. I let her talk mostly, I just told her a tiny bit about me, I never like to give too much away. I only told her it was just me and Mama and I never went to school, that Mama was supposed to home school me, but she never did. We did stop off at a truck stop just for a coffee and pee break, so it took a little longer than she said it would.

We've just passed the sign saying Welcome to Oakland, the population was too high a number for me. "I've always wondered what the signs were, for each town you enter, now I can read them, it's like I have a new life. Why do they put the population on them? Surely the population changes constantly with people coming and going, deaths and births, so they can't be true figures." I'm looking out my side window and I hear her laugh.

"I'm glad you're seeing things differently now you can read. The population is usually changed annually if they can be bothered. Each year there's something called a census and everyone is supposed to complete it. Not everyone does. This gives the city the figures they need for population and everything else, but they are never accurate. I mean, how can everyone fill in this form if the government doesn't know about them? That's what I always say."

I smile at her. "Is this where you grew up?"

"Yes, we're not far from Piedmont now. Nearly home and I'm nervous."

"Does your aunt know you're coming and that you have a guest?"

"She does, and she knows we are friends so we will have separate rooms. No need to worry. In fact, she will probably put you in the guest house out back by the pool."

Fuck, they have another house? They must be loaded. We drive in silence the rest of the way. We turn into a drive and just ahead is a huge house, I must be gawking with my mouth hanging open.

"Nick, you can close your mouth now." Poppy laughs at me as she stops the car.

She climbs out and I follow behind her. We climb up some steps to a porch that is huge and has a lot of chairs either side as you look. She doesn't ring a bell or anything, she just walks straight in.

"Aunt Cassy, we're here!"

I just follow behind like a little puppy. I feel out of place in here already. My cabin back home is as big as this hallway alone. Just then two young girls come bounding down the staircase, just as who I presume is Aunt Cassy comes barreling in from a doorway we are heading to. She grabs Poppy and hugs her, just as the two girls come and they join in.

"Poppy, we've missed you. I wish you would come back and live near us." These must be her cousins, Trix and Pix she called them. They are identical and must be about fourteen or fifteen.

Standing here watching, they all look a lot like each other, all of them standing together, you can tell they are all related. I feel a bit awkward, so I turn and look around.

"You must be Nick? Hi, I'm Cassy and this is Trixie and Pixie. Trevor's at work and will be home later. Come through to the kitchen, I've been baking and made some sandwiches. You're not a vegetarian, are you? I never thought to ask." She hasn't stopped talking yet and hasn't given me a chance to answer before she's linking my arm with hers and walking me into another room. This house is huge, I've never been in something like this before. It's a little intimidating.

"You okay, Nick?" It's Poppy, I think she sees the startled look on my face.

"Yes, sorry, hi Cassy and no, I'm not vegetarian. Hi girls," I say, turning to look at the twins following us. They both giggle and don't say a word.

"Hormonal teenagers, Nick," Aunt Cassy says. "You sit here and I'll get the food from the fridge. What would you like to drink, Nick?"

"Water if you have it please or juice, I don't mind." The girls sit on either side of me, they both turn to face me and just stare.

"Girls, leave poor Nick alone. You'll frighten him off if you stare like that." Aunt Cassy comes to the rescue.

We sit eating and drinking and the girls start asking questions about Poppy and me, Poppy answers the questions, then when we've finished she shows me to the guest house, which is still bigger than my cabin. I don't have much in the way of clothes to unpack, just jeans and white tees, the usual. I told Poppy to go and spend time with her aunt and cousins and I would come in later on. I was going to go out for a walk and explore a little which is exactly what I'm doing now. It's a lovely area they live in, all the houses are huge.

I find the local main street that is full of bars, cafes, little shops, it's nice here. There are an awful lot of people around which makes me feel a little uncomfortable. I stop at a bar for a beer. I watch the people coming and going. This is so far from the beaten-down bars I'm used to. This is so clean, and the people here are all nicely dressed. Certainly not full of the whores I'm used to seeing. It's like a whole new world. I only ever stop at the small towns usually in the hills where there aren't many people around, just a motel, a bar, and a café or diner, with a couple of shops and a garage. That's usually it.

I get my cell out and go on Facebook. I look at Primrose for a while, she still hasn't posted anything. I look at Poppy's profile, she's put on there she's going on a road trip with a friend, and a picture of her in the car and the back of my head as I look out of the window. When the fuck did she take that? Good fucking thing it wasn't my face. I don't want pictures of me on Facebook.

I walk back to their house and head straight to the guest house. I come to a stop as I see Poppy sitting by the pool. It's not exactly hot out now as the sun's going down.

"Hey, you okay?" I ask as I get a little closer.

She has on shades and a floppy sun hat which is odd. She doesn't speak, maybe she's sleeping.

"I'm just gonna change and I'll be right out."

Still nothing. I move quietly to the guest house, I shower and change. I head outside and Poppy's gone. I must have woken her when I shut my door. I head to the back door that leads through the mud room to the kitchen. I stop as I see all the females standing in the kitchen talking all at once. Whoa, what the hell is going on here? They're shouting, each raising their voice higher than the other, but they're laughing, it's just so loud. All except Poppy who still has on the hat but I can't see the shades as she has her back to me. Just then Poppy walks into view shouting she's sorry, then stops when she sees me.

Oh fuck, if that's Poppy there, then that's not Poppy in the hat. I'm standing frozen as I realize who it is standing there in the hat. She hasn't turned around, but I know it's her. Why hasn't she turned around? She must have heard me coming in and out by the pool. Poppy walks over to me.

"Sorry you walked in on this. Come take a seat."

I ignore her and I turn back around and leave the way I came in. I'm not ready to come face to face with Primrose just yet. I can't believe I spoke to her and didn't realize it was her and not Poppy.

I'm sitting in the guest house trying to think about what to do when there is a knock on the door. Fuck, what if it's her coming to see Poppy's friend. I never thought I would freak out like I'm doing right now.

"Nick, are you in there?"

It's Poppy. I hope she's alone. I open the door slowly, making sure it's just her.

"Hey, you okay? You bolted out of there so fast."

"Yeah, sorry, I was just shocked at all the noise and I needed the bathroom." Bullshit.

"You can come back in now. The twins have gone out to their friends and Prim has just left. Aunt Cassy has made some supper for us, then I'm going to go to Prim's to talk to her without all the others joining in. It got a bit mental. You could come with me if you want and say hi to Prim?"

Uh no, I would rather do that with just the two of us, but I'm not sure how likely an opportunity like that's going to be. If only I'd known that was her by the pool. Fuck, that would have been the perfect chance.

I finish my food, I don't speak other than when I first went to the main house. Trevor was there and I was introduced to him. He seems like a nice man. I feel sorry for him with all these shouting women around. I guess I'm not used to it. After we finish eating, I go into their den with him, we have a beer while Cassy and Poppy clean up. He wants to know more about me, rightly so. Not much to tell, so I just tell him I travel around, working where I can and that I've always wanted to see San Francisco. I don't realize Poppy is standing there until she speaks.

"We can go into the city tomorrow if you like, Nick. I can show you the sights. We can take the ferry to Alcatraz and I can drive you up and down the streets. They are wild. We can grab lunch at the pier, oh and Lombard Street, you gotta see that."

She's all excited and I have no idea what she's talking about, but I play along. I don't go with her to Prim's, instead I tell her I'm gonna go for a walk and then have an early night so I'll be ready for our sightseeing day tomorrow.

She leaves and I leave not long after her. I didn't realize she was walking to Primrose's until I see her at the end of the road. Shit, I start to run so I don't lose sight of her. I want to know where Primrose lives. I see her as I turn the corner and start to follow. I stay as close to the tree line as I can, in case she turns around. She's quite a ways in front of me so she won't hear me. She turns down another road and I jog to catch up and sneak a peek before rounding the corner. She's just ahead now, so I wait a minute to let her get farther ahead, then follow again. This goes on for a few roads until I see her entering a house. Fuck. I don't know which house it was. She was too far ahead. I cautiously move forward, but I cross to the other side of the street, and I watch each window of each house I pass, staying close to the trees. Thank fuck for tree-lined streets. Good old suburbia. I know it's one of these four houses, but I don't know which one. I stay hidden until I see someone walking a dog, I decide to move away. I don't want to look suspicious. Well, I know the whereabouts of where she lives, it's just pinpointing the right house.

I head back and settle in bed. I think about her lying on the lounge chair just outside. Thinking how close I was to her. I start to get aroused thinking about her and before I know what's happening I'm rubbing one out and shooting a load into my hand. Fuck, I needed that. I go to sleep thinking about her. A knock at the door startles me awake. I pick up my cell to see it's almost eight in the morning. I haven't slept that soundly in forever.

"Nick, breakfast is nearly ready. Are you up, Nick?"

I throw the covers back and pull on my jeans, my cock is rock hard so I hide behind the door as I open it slightly.

"Sorry Poppy, I slept like a log last night. Give me ten minutes to take a shower and I'll be out."

She smiles at me but there's something about the look on her face. I stroke and play with my cock in the shower and explode yet again to the image of Primrose in that hat, only this time I have her in the skimpiest barely-there white string bikini and she has the shades pulled down and she's licking her lips winking, at me. I explode and I'm panting so hard, my cock just doesn't want to stop.

We have breakfast and head into the city.

We've had a great day so far, she's shown me a lot of the tourist sights. We are about to go and have something to eat at Pier 39, which apparently is very famous for the seals and the food markets.

"I'm just going to slip to the bathroom, Nick. I'll come and find you."

I wander around looking at the stalls and the little shops when I feel a presence. I thought it was Poppy coming back, but when I turn around, Primrose is standing right in the middle of the pier, it's her. I know she's identical to Poppy, but I know the difference. Don't ask me how, but even from this distance, I know it's her. She suddenly notices me and stares right into my eyes as I stare right back into hers. I start to move closer to her, she doesn't move and we never break eye contact, not even when people walk between us. She's just standing there, mesmerized. The closer I get, I see the brightness in her eyes. They shine brighter than Poppy's, and I see it. The little blemish that I saw all those years ago. I stop dead in front of her. She still hasn't moved or said anything. Neither have I.

"Is it you? After all these years of wondering if I would ever see you again, and here you are. I don't fucking believe it. I think it's a trick. Has Poppy done this as a trick?"

She doesn't speak, but now instead of staring at my eyes, she's staring at my mouth as I speak. I reach up and move a piece of her blonde hair behind her ear. Like I did all those years ago.

"It's you, the boy with the greenest eyes and the messiest black hair," she whispers. She reaches out and strokes my cheek as if checking to see if I'm real. I can't believe she's here and we're alone. Well, for the time being at least. Suddenly she slaps my face. It must be hard because my head turns with the force. What the fuck. Not how I expected this to go. I rub my cheek, just to make her think it hurt.

"What the fuck was that for? Not exactly the welcome I had pictured all these years."

She's watching my mouth again as I speak. She leans into my ear. "You killed my parents. You caused the accident. I have never forgotten. I still picture you in my mind," she says, probably thinking she's whispering so no one else can hear, but it's louder than she realizes and someone does hear.

I turn at the gasp and see Poppy holding her hand over her mouth and looking at me and Primrose. She suddenly moves her hands and she's smiling, but it's an evil, wicked smile.

"Well, that happened quicker than I anticipated." She sneers at us.

I knew it. This is exactly what she was playing at. She wanted to know. She said the same thing to me, the boy with the greenest eyes. She knew I existed, but didn't know in what capacity I knew Primrose.

Primrose is walking away. Poppy comes up to me and gets right in my face.

"I knew it, I knew you had something to do with my parents' death. I just needed you to see her. I needed the answers from you both, I just never thought it would happen so quickly. What did you do, Nick? Is that even your real name? I want to know exactly what you did to kill my parents. If you don't tell me, then I will call the police."

Fuck, fuck, fuck. Do I run after Primrose? I can't let her go, not now, I've wanted this for far too long. Do I tell Poppy the truth or do I take Poppy and do away with her? Fuck, I need to think fast. Deny it.

"Poppy, I didn't do anything. I was a kid. How the fuck could I do anything to two adults?"

She squints her eyes at me. "I don't fucking believe you. She said it, I was close enough to hear her and read her lips. That's what we do in our family."

I have no idea what the fuck she's talking about. "Look, let's get Primrose, maybe she can tell you what she's talking about." I walk off in the direction Primrose was going, but I don't see her. I frantically run around trying to spot her, I hear Poppy running after me.

"Nick, stop, I know where she'll be."

I stop dead and turn to face her. People are stepping around us and watching us. I wish they would all just fuck off.

"Let me speak to her, Pops. I need to speak to her first, alone if that's okay?" I can see the fury on her face as she squints at me.

"She'll be heading to the ice cream parlor, farther down Beach Street that way." She points.

"I'm coming with you, Nick. I want to know what part you played in my parents' death. I've known all these years the boy with the greenest eyes had something to do with it, I just don't know what. She's never told anyone, always protected you."

I turn and walk fast the way she pointed. I see her ahead and I shout at her, she doesn't turn around. I hear Poppy laugh and look back to glare at her. She's grinning at me. I ignore her and rush to catch up to Primrose. I reach her and I grab her arm. She swings around suddenly, startled and wondering who grabbed her. I let go of her and hold up my hands to show her that I mean her no harm, I didn't mean anything by it.

"Hey, can we talk, Primrose? Please?"

She watches my mouth again and she huffs out, then nods her head.

Just then Poppy catches up to us. "Hey sis, surprise." They scowl at each other.

"You knew who he was? You knew it was him?" Primrose says to Poppy.

Poppy just shrugs.

"I had an idea when he told me he knew me. He called me Primrose, and then I saw his eyes. Not many people have eyes like that and know you. I just put two and two together and came up with six."

Primrose looks at me. "Yes, let's talk. Alone," she says, looking at Poppy. She speaks a lot different than Poppy does, it's quite nasally, I wonder if she has a cold.

Poppy holds her hands up. "Okay, I get it. I'll go grab something to eat. I'll come back here in a while. Don't leave this place." She points to the ice cream shop. I just need a strong black coffee or a beer. Either will do.

Primrose and I walk into the shop and sit down at a table in the back. A waiter comes over and I order a black coffee and Primrose goes for a soda float, whatever the fuck that is. We sit in silence for a while, just staring into each other's eyes. Anyone would think we were some love-struck teenagers. I can't believe I'm sitting here with her, the girl I've dreamed of for all these years.

"So, how have you been, Primrose?"

She doesn't speak, she just glares at me.

"I've never in all these years stopped thinking about you. Wondering if you were alive, married with kids or even living in the US. I've never stopped, Primrose. I've fallen asleep so many times with your eyes in my mind."

I look down just as the waiter comes back with our order. I look at her drink. It's a soda in a tall glass with ice cream on top of it. The soda's making the ice cream all frothy. She spoons some into her mouth then drinks some of the soda through a straw.

"I can't believe you're here," she says but doesn't look at me.

"After all these years. Like you, I've thought about you so much. One minute I hate you because I remember you standing in the road causing the accident, but then the next minute, I'm thankful because you saved my life."

I can only just make out what she's saying to me. She looks up into my eyes and I see the light in hers has dulled, and she has tears dripping down her face. I get the napkin and dab at her cheeks. She lets me.

"I'm sorry, Primrose. If I could change it, I would in a heartbeat." Lie number one. I fucking loved it, watching her papa die like that. He was the first human I watched die. She looks away from me.

"I'm so conflicted right now. I don't even know your name." Do I tell her the truth or stick to Nick?

"It's Nick." Lie number two.

I hold out my hand. "Nice to meet you, Primrose. Can we start over without you round housing me again?"

She doesn't smile when she looks from my mouth to my eyes. "I'm sorry I hit you. I don't know why I did that."

Well, in all honesty, she had good reason to. I did kill her parents.

I want her more than anything. I feel it, that connection we had back then, I feel it stronger sitting here with her. She's the most beautiful woman I've ever laid eyes on. She's also the only woman I would protect with my life. I don't want to hurt her, not like the others and especially Poppy. I could even quite happily do away with Poppy right now. That reminds me she'll be back soon. I take a sip of my coffee just watching Primrose. She's uncomfortable sitting here with me. I don't want her to be like that around me. I want to put her at ease. I'm going to tell lie number three, and this will be the final lie but the most important one. One I will have to stick to for as long as she's in my life and I hope that will be a long time unless I crash and burn right here.

"Hey, I don't blame you. I need to tell you what happened that day if you'll let me. I need to try and explain."

She's looking down, playing with the spoon for her soda. She doesn't answer me.

"Primrose?" I say, but she still doesn't answer.

She looks up and must see the quizzical look on my face. "Sorry, did you say something?"

She must be far away in her head to have not heard me. I repeat what I said and she nods at me to continue.

I lie, I hate it but I've thought about it for so long. I always thought, if by some miracle, I did run into her again then I would tell her I was running after my dog Toby, and that he ran across the road and that I didn't hear the car until it was too late and I just froze when it nearly hit me. It was an accident and one I've regretted ever since, and that the only thing that stops me from feeling so guilty about her parents' death, is that I saved her life. Just to rub it in. That's the story I made up and will stick to for her and for Poppy when she finds out. I just hope Primrose never saw me standing there with a smile on my face just waiting for the car to swerve, or that she doesn't remember what I was saying to her papa. I remember it all like it was yesterday.

She looks at me with a sorrowful look on her face. I see the tears falling and reach across and swipe them with my thumb. She doesn't flinch, she leans into my touch. Dare I think it? I think she likes me. I smile at her and she looks down. I gently lift her chin with my finger and look deep into her eyes.

"I am so sorry for that day, Primrose, it will haunt me for the rest of my life. It was a terrible accident. The only thing I'm grateful for is that I saved you, Primrose, that you got out unharmed. I watched as they saw to you, just to make sure you were safe."

Her eyes widen. "You watched? You waited to make sure? I didn't know where you had gone. I was looking for any sign of you. I didn't know if you were hurt, from the blast. You just pushed me up and made sure I was safe."

It's getting harder to understand her the more upset she's getting. I find I'm trying to read her lips like she does mine, but I can't read lips. She picks up her napkin and blows her nose. She suddenly gets up.

Shit, is she leaving?

"I just need to use the bathroom." She must have seen the worry on my face.

I sit and wait for her to return. She's been gone for a while now and I'm getting a little worried. Just then Poppy sits in the seat opposite me. Fuck, I can do without her. I want to be alone with Primrose and sort this out.

"What?" I snap at her. I didn't want to see her.

"Well, that's nice. Where's Prim? Did you scare her off already? Now are you gonna tell me what the hell is going on?"

I glare at her. "Nope," is all I say.

Just then Primrose arrives and sits next to Poppy. Poppy turns to her and taps her arm.

"You okay?" she asks her, making the sign for okay with her hand.

Primrose nods yes to her.

"You look upset. What did he do?" she then asks, using her hands to talk and making a sad face.

What is it with her? "I didn't do anything," I snap.

She glares at me.

"He's right. He didn't do anything, I was just upset. Seeing Nick has brought back so many memories." She looks at me as she says this.

"Will you tell me what's going on?"

Primrose and I both say 'no' at the same time. She glares at us. This is the real Poppy coming out, this is the Poppy I first met. She stands up.

"Well screw you both then," she says, looking at Primrose.

"If you don't tell me, you can deal with him and Aunt Cassy. I know he had something to do with their deaths, Prim, I've always known it, and those creepy fucking pictures you keep drawing of him, well it's not right. You're as sick as he is, but I'm telling you now, you both need to explain to me and Aunt Cassy, or I will be calling the police."

What the fuck. I stand up, my chair falling backward, I want to take her and make her suffer so bad.

"Just wait a fucking minute, Poppy. You have no idea how or when we met. You have no idea this has anything to do with you, so I don't know where you get off threatening us with the police. We haven't done anything wrong, we met once a long time ago and that is none of your fucking business."

I'm losing it big time, I can feel myself getting agitated with her standing here. No way is she calling the police. I look to Primrose who is looking between us both. She grabs Poppy's hand, making her look at her.

"There is nothing to tell. It was a long time ago. You have it all wrong, Pops, as usual. You just jump in without thinking. Please, can you just leave us to talk? I will drop Nick back at Aunt Cassy's later."

I can see the hostility coming from Poppy, Primrose is the complete opposite of her and is calm. What a difference between them, even though they are identical. It's kind of freaky seeing them both together but to me, they are as different as the deep sea and the sun. One shines bright while the other is deep and mysterious and dangerous. Well, she's met her match with me.

"Don't bother dropping him off. You can have him." With that, she storms out of the shop, leaving Primrose staring at her departing back.

Thank fuck for that. I pick my chair up and sit down. I watch Primrose still standing there looking at the door, still conflicted, trying to decide if she should run after Poppy or stay with me? She looks at me, then sits back down.

I smile at her. "You know, you two are as different as could be. Thank god for that."

She's sizing me up wondering if she should ask me something.

"What do you want to know, Primrose?"

She fiddles with her napkin again, then looks me straight in the eye. "That was a lot of jealousy from Poppy, I know her well enough to see it. Have you and she had a thing going on? Have you slept with her?" She blushes as she asks me, but she doesn't look away.

I smile to myself then shake my head no. "We have never done anything. She wanted to, believe me, she tried hard enough, but I couldn't."

"Why couldn't you? Are you married or with someone?"

I shake my head no again. "I don't have anyone, never been married and never had a girlfriend longer than a few weeks. As to why I couldn't, that's easy. She wasn't you."

She takes a sharp intake of breath, shocked at what I just said, she blushes more then looks down at her napkin, before taking hold of her glass and drinking some of the soda through the straw, avoiding eye contact.

"I meant it, Primrose, what I said."

She doesn't acknowledge me again, then I think back to her talking to Poppy and how they both used their hands to speak as well as spoken words, and then how she doesn't seem to hear me when I speak.

"Primrose, I love you, I always have."

Nothing. Holy fuck, she's deaf. I didn't know that. It explains her tone when she speaks and how she's always watching my lips. I rub my hands over my face and stroke my beard, I look up to the ceiling. It explains why she didn't speak all those years ago, except I remember her shouting Pappy and Mama, so I didn't think anything of it, that means she didn't hear me, she couldn't hear anything I was saying to her pappy, she couldn't hear his screams. I sigh with relief. I look back to her and she's now looking at me. Probably thinks I'm crazy, I have a smile on my face.

"You okay?" she asks.

I nod yes, I'm so fucking happy right now. I can see the look of concern on her face.

"I was just saying to you, but you were miles away, that I meant what I said. No one has ever been you. Don't get me wrong, I've been with women, but could never stay with anyone. I could only ever think of you. When times were bad with my mama, I only had to close my eyes and think of your eyes to get me through it. I hoped that I would one day find you. When Poppy helped me when I fell and hurt my ankle, I thought she was you, I couldn't believe it, only it wasn't you, if you know what I mean. I knew after a little while it wasn't you, but she played along when I called her Primrose, letting me think it was you. I knew she wasn't you because I remember your eyes so clearly, and you have this tiny little blemish in your left eye. After seeing you both together just now, anyone would be a fool to not be able to tell you apart. You are so much more gentle and caring, where she is like a bull in a china shop as they say, and she doesn't really give a shit about anyone but herself. But then the job she does says differently. I don't know."

I see a smile emerge on her face.

"I have never forgotten you. I always blamed you for their death, but in the back of my mind, I knew you couldn't have done it on purpose because you saved my life. I remember you being with Pappy a while, but I couldn't see what you were doing. I've played it over and over in my mind. I remember when you dragged me out of the car, you made me run up the hill, and I was wondering why you didn't try to save them. Is that what you were doing with Pappy? Were you trying to save him? What about Mama? You didn't go near her."

Understandably, she needs answers and I'm the only one that can give them to her. I take a deep breath, this is technically still just lie number three. "It was too late for your mama, she was already gone. I didn't know you were in there at first, or I would have gotten you out straight away. I was trying to help your pappy, yes, but I knew he only had minutes to live. Even as young as I was, I could see the injuries on him and he couldn't breathe. I'm going into too much detail but there is no way anyone could get to him and save him."

"But you came to see me, then went back to him? Why didn't you try to get me out then?"

I sigh and rub my face again. "I checked to make sure you were okay. Then I went back to try to get his seatbelt off him, but it was cut too deep into him, he was barely alive Primrose. I didn't know the car was going to blow up but I smelt the gas and saw a spark, I knew in that moment he was not going to make it and I just had to get you out. That's why I made you run up the embankment so you wouldn't get hurt. Did you get hurt, Primrose? From the explosion?"

She nods yes.

"I ended up with a cut on my head, I had a bad break on one of my legs. It took a while for that to heal. I don't remember how it happened, I think the blast had something to do with it, but it could have been far worse if you hadn't dragged me farther away. What about you? Did you have any injuries? I looked for you but you weren't around."

I think back to that day, and how I crawled home. "Yes, I had metal and glass lodged in my arm from the blast, and I too broke my leg. I was laid up for six weeks. It drove me crazy." I smile,

letting her know it's all good now.

"We both ended up the same then, with broken legs. It drove me crazy too. I thought about you a lot. I couldn't grasp why you would be standing in the middle of the road, and you didn't run, but now I understand. Poppy knows you were involved somehow with the accident, but I never told anyone about you."

"How does Poppy know then?"

She looks away from me then takes a sip of her soda before looking at me. "I used to draw you all the time. I drew pictures of you standing next to the exploding car, Poppy found them, she asked me who you were and what you had to do with the accident. I wouldn't tell her, I just said I had made you up."

She never told anyone about me? I was worried for so long thinking the police would be coming for me, that she would have told them and described me. I thought she would have told them I caused the accident, but she didn't. She protected me.

"Did you never tell Cassy about me?"

She shakes her head. "No one. I didn't want to get you into any trouble. Maybe now you've explained it to me, I should have told them. Now I know you didn't do it on purpose. With you running into Poppy and thinking it was me, she put it together. The boy with the greenest eyes and messiest black hair. That's what I used to say when I was sketching you. That I made you up. I still can't believe you're here, sitting with me. I started to think I did make you up, that you were an hallucination, all part of being in shock from the accident. The mind can play funny tricks on you when you're in shock."

I smile at her and she smiles back. Sitting here talking to her it's hard to believe she is deaf. She hasn't told me yet, but then why would she? This is only the first time we have ever talked.

We sit for nearly two hours talking. She tells me about her job and her travels and all the countries she's visited. I'm actually in awe of her right now. She has a disability and it hasn't stopped her from doing anything. She's traveled the world. It makes me feel like the retard Mama said I was. I haven't done anything to be proud of. Nothing I can say I've accomplished, unless you throw in killing whores, oh and my mama. It's now that I realize I'm no good for her. As much as I want her, she would be better off not knowing me. She's far too good for me. I need to leave. How could I bring her down to my level? I need to do what's best for her. I think it would be better if I left, collected my things from Cassy's and then just headed back home.

Don has helped me so much, I'll just call him and tell him thanks for everything. He's the first real friend I've ever had. I rub my hand over my face and play with my beard, Here goes.

"Primrose, it's been amazing seeing you after all this time." She's watching me closely. "I know we have this connection, because of what happened, and I have never stopped thinking about you for all these years, but…" I grab her hand and stroke the back with my thumb, she watches me, I reach over and lift her chin to look at me. "I'm going to get going now. I'll stop in at Cassy's and pick my things up, then I'm going to head home. I have some cash so I should be able to get a bus to the nearest town."

It's so fucking hard, she's looking at me with a creased brow, like I just slapped her in the face. I start to get up and her eyes follow my mouth the whole time, probably waiting for an explanation for my sudden departure. "Please don't look at me like that. Poppy is pissed at me anyway, so it's best all-around if I go."

She stands up quickly, she knocks the chair over this time. "Wait," she shouts a bit too loudly, but she wouldn't know that. I turn to look at her.

"Let me drive you to Aunt Cassy's, you don't know the way."

That's true, I have no idea of the address or how to get there. "Okay." I nod and smile.

We walk out onto the main street, I follow her to where she's parked. We don't speak, she's walking in front of me, she wouldn't hear anything I had to say. We're silent back in the car, it would be useless trying to say anything while she's driving.

Once we arrive back at Cassy's, I head straight for the guest house to collect my things. The door suddenly opens with a bang, I turn and see Poppy standing there, hands on hips, scowling at me.

"Prim said you're leaving."

Fuck, I could do without her dramatics.

"Yes Poppy, I'm heading home, and when I say home, back to where I live."

She doesn't move, just stands, scowling at me, I turn and continue gathering my stuff. I don't have a lot, it doesn't take long. I turn to leave but she's still in the doorway, blocking my exit.

"I want to know what you had to do with the death of my parents."

And here we go again.

"Nothing. Now, will you move so I can leave please?"

She doesn't move, just scowls at me.

"I know you were there, Nick. I saw the drawings Prim did of you standing by the car. Tell me what happened."

I move toward her, standing tall, towering above her and trying to look very intimidating. It works, she cowers slightly. I'm standing close, looking down at her.

"Speak to Prim, not me. I have no idea what you're talking about."

She tries to stand tall. I have my bag flung over one shoulder, holding it by the straps and my free hand will be moving her by the neck if she doesn't step aside.

"Like fuck you don't. I know you had something to do with it. You need to tell me before I go to the police."

No one threatens me. I grab her by the throat, not too hard. She's so slight it's easy to get my hand around it. I move her to the side and bend right into her face so she can almost touch my lips.

"Don't threaten me, Poppy, or you'll regret it. Go to the police if you want, but there's nothing to prove." With that, I leave the guest house and head around to the front of the main house. When I get there, Primrose is waiting for me.

"Let me at least take you to the bus station in town."

She still wants to help me. She is completely different from Poppy. I nod but don't speak. Cassy comes out onto the porch.

"Thank you for putting me up, Cassy," I say, nodding my head. She waves and smiles at me. I climb into the car and we head to the bus station. Like earlier, we don't speak. She pulls up and I turn to her. "Thank you for bringing me, you saved me a lot of time."

She looks sad and nods. "Will I see you again, Nick? Do you have a cell? Maybe we could keep in touch, you know, if you want to?"

How can I say no? Of course, I want to, I just don't know if it's a good idea or not. I take out my cell and pass it to her so she can put in her number.

"Would you mind if I messaged you?" she asks timidly.

I shake my head no. "I would like that, Primrose."

I smile and she smiles back. I lean over and kiss her cheek. She looks shocked, I have no fucking clue why I thought I had to do that, it just felt like instinct. I wish I could kiss her lips. I get out of the car and grab my bag from the back seat. I lean in before shutting the door.

"Thank you," I say with a smile and then I leave.

Sixteen

Primrose

I WALK INTO AUNT CASSY'S AND I SEE POPPY STANDING IN THE kitchen full of smiles when she sees me. She never smiles at me. We haven't seen each other for such a long time, I have no idea why she wanted to see me now.

"Hi," I mouth and sign, she signs back to me, "Hi."

She comes over and hugs me. I freeze, not knowing how to react to this. I can't remember the last time she hugged me. What is she after now? Or is she on drugs again? I look to Aunt Cassy, I see the huge smile on her face, why isn't she surprised at this show of affection from Poppy? I hesitantly put my arms around her to hug her back, almost expecting her to pull away and laugh in my face. I don't trust her. She hugs me tighter when she feels me hugging her. We stand there like this for a few minutes.

I'm the one to break away. "Nice to see you, Poppy. How have you been?" She smiles at me.

"Great, and better now you're here. I came to see you all. I've missed everyone."

Aunt Cassy makes some coffee, we all sit around the island talking. We just talk about random things, they ask me about my travels. I love them all so much, we all sign to each other, we all learned how to sign, it was something Aunt Cassy made Poppy and I do, then the twins were taught from an early age, so I have never had a problem communicating with any of them. It just gets hard with so many conversations going at once.

I lost my hearing when I was five. I had a stuffed teddy that Pappy won from a fairground we visited. The stitching came undone one day, and I pulled out all the little polystyrene filling and started playing with the polystyrene pieces pretending they were teeth when Poppy came up with the idea of seeing how many I could put up my nose and in my ears. I stuffed them so far into my ears that I had to be taken to the hospital and have them removed, I damaged my inner ear by doing this and they couldn't save my hearing. That's why I still have a voice.

People that are deaf from birth don't usually have a voice, that's because they have never heard the spoken word. I know I don't sound the same as a hearing person, that's because I have no idea of my volume, or how I sound, but Poppy told me so many times over the years that I sounded like a retard who couldn't speak. I stopped speaking for a long time because of her taunts. She has no idea what she put me through while growing up. I don't hold it against her and I've never blamed her for losing my hearing, I came to terms with it a long time ago, I will never hate her. I love her.

After a while the girls go upstairs to get ready to go out, I go out for some fresh air and sit by the pool. I put on my shades and hat, even though the sun will start to set soon. I must have closed my eyes for a few minutes and fallen asleep when Trixie comes out and nudges me. We head back inside and all of us are in the kitchen again laughing and having a big discussion about singers. Trixie is crazy about Billie Eilish and Pixie is crazy about Ariana Grande. Poppy ran to her room to get something. We're all laughing. It must be getting louder and louder in here the more excited the girls get.

Poppy enters the kitchen and I read her saying, "Sorry you walked in on this. Come take a seat."

She's looking past me. I frown, confused at what she's saying. I turn but there's no one there.

"Who are you telling to take a seat?" I ask but she doesn't answer me, she's now engaged in the best singer debate.

The twins go out and I decide to go home, telling everyone I will see them tomorrow. Just as I get home Poppy messages me to say she's coming to see me in about an hour. I have no idea what this is all about, or why she is being like this. I get so suspicious of Poppy because she never does anything without a reason for it. She would never just think to visit me, so why now? What's she up to? I messaged her back telling her to leave the car and we can have some wine.

About an hour later she arrives, she hugs me again as she comes in. We head to the kitchen where I get the wine and glasses out and some potato chips, then we sit in the den.

"You know, I got nervous about coming back here, Prim. I haven't been in this house since we were young, as you know."

She looks sad. I hadn't thought about this being her first time in our house. It looks so different now, I had it remodeled a couple of years back and the entire house has been redecorated.

"I'm sorry, Pops. I never thought about it. I'm just so used to living here, I forgot you've not been here since we were kids. It's completely different, do you want me to give you a tour or would that creep you out?"

She looks sad still and her eyes well up.

"I would like that, Prim. Thank you, it might make me feel different about being here."

I show her all around the house and we laugh about some of the antics we got up to when we lived here with Mama and Pappy, back when we were a normal family, doing normal family things, the last time I remember us being real sisters.

We had a good talk and drank a lot of wine. I made her get an Uber to collect her and take her back to Aunt Cassy's. I did tell her she could stay here but she said she didn't feel right staying. I told her how much I've missed her, and I hope we can do this again soon, and try to make it a regular thing. Before she left, she told me she was taking a friend sightseeing tomorrow and it would be nice if I could join them. I told her I had some work to get finished in the morning but I would meet her at Pier 39. I would text her and let her know when I was on my way.

I finished my work and messaged to tell Prim I was on my way. She didn't say who the friend was, I didn't even know she had brought anyone with her. Why didn't she introduce us at the house and why didn't anyone tell me she had a friend staying? Why is she being all mysterious about it? This is where the trust issues come in. I thought last night had gone well, even after she left and told me about a friend, I honestly didn't think anything of it. Maybe it was the wine. But this morning, I couldn't stop questioning why she hadn't told me, or even brought the friend with her last night. I've been thinking about it all the way there.

I park my car and head for the pier. I text to say I am two minutes away. I reach the pier and stand looking around for Poppy. I can't see her anywhere. I turn and turn, suddenly I feel eyes on me and I find the source. I stare in disbelief, it's him. Oh my goodness, it has to be him. I pictured him grown up all these years but never did I picture this giant of a man. It definitely is the boy with the greenest eyes and messiest black hair. The boy is a full-grown man and he's beautiful, I could just die on the spot. I'm mesmerized by him. We stand staring at each other, then he starts toward me and I don't know what to do. I can't breathe the closer he gets, I have all these mixed-up feelings, I just keep staring at those eyes. I fell in love with those eyes all those years ago and I've never stopped thinking about them. The closer he gets, the more I have to tilt my head back to look into his face. His beautiful bearded face.

He stops in front of me. I have to break eye contact as I watch his mouth move. My brain isn't quite computing what he's saying, I must say it out loud, "The boy with the greenest eyes and messiest black hair," because I see the recognition on his face. I'm feeling all kinds of things with him standing here, I'm so overwhelmed right now, he moves a piece of my hair behind my ear, just like he did all those years ago, I suddenly reach out and stroke his cheek, I just have the urge to make sure he's real. My brain is having a hard time, my heart is nearly popping out of my chest with just one touch, but my head is well, in a different place, it's thinking back to the accident, I suddenly hate him for causing it, without thinking I slap him hard across the face.

I have never been violent, and I have no idea why I just did that. I've shocked myself. My hand is stinging from the slap, it was that hard. He doesn't react. I get closer to him and stand on my tiptoes so I am near his ear, I whisper, telling him he killed them. He turns and looks behind him and I see Poppy standing close by with her hands over her mouth. When she moves them she's smiling, an evil smile. I look to him but only see the back of his head, I look to Poppy and she's sneering at us both.

She planned this, I know she did. This is her friend, the one she was so insistent that I meet. How did she know it was him? How has this happened? That she brought him here for me to meet, and by the way she's looking at us, I can see she thinks she has accomplished something. She always wanted to know who he was, and why I was obsessed with drawing and painting him, she always said he had something to do with our parents' death. I can't handle this or her schemes. I turn and walk away from them both. I walk without knowing where I'm walking to. My head is in turmoil.

Maybe they're together, and she's done all this on purpose. This is why she's been so friendly. I knew it was too good to be true, I knew she was up to something, she'll never change. I'll never trust her. I said I couldn't hate her, but she's running very close to that in my heart. I don't understand why she is so cruel to me all the time, even now as adults. I'm finished with her.

I'm still walking, not realizing where I'm heading until I look up and I'm standing in front of the ice cream parlor pappy used to bring us to, whenever we visited the pier to watch the sea lions. It was my favorite thing to do as a little girl. He would do this a lot, I used to laugh at the seals just sunbathing on the little wooden docks and making silly noises before I lost my hearing. When I lost my hearing, I missed the noise they made so much, but I could imagine them making them in my head. When I used to be sad, Pappy used to bring us to this ice cream parlor to cheer me up. We were never allowed soda, that was one of Mama's rules but he used to break the rule and gave us the best of both worlds when we were here. A soda float, it was my favorite, and I used to try to drink all the froth the ice cream made in the soda before it got messy and spilled out all over the table. It was Poppy's and my secret we kept from Mama.

Just then someone grabs my arm, I turn suddenly ready to hit whoever is touching me. It's him, he stands back with his hands up. Great, he followed me and now he wants to talk. Poppy catches up to him and smiles a sarcastic smile at me.

"Hey sis, surprise."

The bitch. I ask her if she knew who he was and she shrugs, telling me she had an idea, mainly because of his eyes. I tell him, yes, let's talk alone, while looking at Poppy. I don't want her in on the conversation we are going to have. I won't tell her anything about that day, no matter what she thinks. Poppy leaves, saying she'll be back in a while. We head into the shop, sit at a table at the back and order. I get my favorite soda float.

We stare at each other for a while, then start talking. He explains it all to me and I feel awful. We admit to thinking about each other all these years and I have butterflies in my tummy. To think, he has always thought about me, that it wasn't just one-sided. We talk for a while, I get upset and decide I need a break, I head to the bathroom. I stand looking at the mirror with tears streaming down my face. Why do I keep crying? I splash my face with cold water and pat it dry. I don't know what to think. All this time I thought he was standing in the road on purpose, causing the accident. Now he tells me he froze. It was an accident, either way, someone would have ended up dead. If Pappy had hit him, he would have died, and we more than likely still would have crashed. It's no use trying to second guess. At the end of the day, he saved my life.

I know we suffered a great loss, I've never stopped thinking about them, but it's him I think about more and more. I became obsessed with him, the boy with the greenest eyes. As I got older I thought I loved him, but I didn't know him, and I also hated him, but now I know it was an accident, and he saved my life. I sat looking at him across the table and I realized I've fallen head over heels for him. I mean, who wouldn't. He's tall, mean and broody, and when he took his jacket off and only had on a white tee, I couldn't stop taking sneaky glances at his muscles, the sleeves were tight on his biceps and his arms were covered with tattoos. He fascinates me. I can forgive him for the accident, I think it was a case of us being in the wrong place at the wrong time. It was one of those things.

Now I've met him and he's explained it all and says he hasn't stopped thinking about me, my heart skips a beat. Just thinking about it, I have all these butterflies in my tummy. I've never had these feelings before. Am I feeling like this because of the fantasy of a knight in shining armor saving my life, I know that's a syndrome, I've read about it. I'm so conflicted, I don't know if the feelings are real or just that he saved the damsel in distress. I need to spend more time with him, get to know him, the man he is. See if that changes these feelings, he could be horrible and we may not have anything in common, but at this moment in time, I doubt it will change anything. I've been in this bathroom for a while, now I need to use it instead of staring at myself in the mirror.

I head back to my seat and find Poppy sitting there. Great, and judging by the look on her face, she's pissed. I sit next to her, she has the nerve to ask if I'm okay. She started to get angry wanting to know things, Nick and I both shot her down and she stormed out. She threatened us with the police, what for? There is nothing to tell. She's always had it in for me and now Nick will be on her radar unless he's already been there. I had to ask him if he and Poppy had anything between them, she was very jealous when she left. If they had a thing, well there is no way I want anything to do with him. Surely that would make the butterflies go away, but they don't, they flutter harder and my heart beats faster waiting for his reply. Thank god nothing ever happened, or so he says. My trust issues are terrible.

We sit and continue to talk for a long time, talking about my work and travels mostly. I sensed him getting a little agitated, he was looking away and getting restless, then he suddenly decides enough is enough and he wants to leave. Not just the shop, but leave here for good and head back home. What did I say? We were getting along great. Why the sudden change? He was just telling me how he has never stopped thinking about me. I suppose now he's seen me as an adult and probably realized I'm deaf, because of Poppy signing with me and the sound of my voice, he's realized this isn't what he wants. He can't handle a disabled person. He's not that type of guy. I'm used to it, so screw him, if he's that shallow I'll be better off not knowing him. At least I got the answers I needed. It's just even with these thoughts, the butterflies will not leave.

We drive to Aunt Cassy's, we haven't spoken since leaving the ice cream parlor. I head into the house while he goes and gets his stuff. Poppy's inside with Aunt Cassy.

"Hey," I say as I enter the kitchen.

"Oh hey sweetie, how was your afternoon with Nick? Poppy has been telling me you two are old friends of a sort, but I have no idea what she means." She looks to Poppy who is sitting there all smug.

"You gonna tell her or shall I, princess?" she mouths to me, making the sign for princess.

I scowl at her. "There's nothing to tell. We met once a long time ago and that's it. Anyway, he's getting his stuff together, he's leaving, heading home."

"What?" Poppy says, shooting off her seat and leaving us alone as she heads out the back of the house.

"What's this all about, Primrose?" Aunt Cassy touches my arm so I know she's talking to me.

"It's nothing, I think she has a thing for Nick and is jealous because we know each other. Well, we met once before."

She takes a sip of her coffee. "Do you want to tell me how you know him? Poppy seems to want you to tell me."

I shake my head no. I see him out of the back window walking toward the front of the house. I head to the front to meet him.

I offered to drive him to the bus terminal. When he was saying goodbye to me, he was sad. He leaned over and kissed my cheek. It sent sparks through my body, and tingles all over me, the damn butterflies were trying out for the Butterfly Olympics in my tummy. I'm so sad he's going and we didn't get to spend more time together. I really wanted to find out about his life and what he's been doing. We say goodbye and I watch as he disappears into the bus terminal. I drive back, but I go home instead of going back to Aunt Cassy's, I don't want to see Poppy. She did this on purpose. I'm not sorry she did. Now that I know who he is as an adult, I am definitely not disappointed. But this is typical Poppy, she's all smoke and mirrors, hides the real reason she does something until it becomes apparent.

All the way home, I kept thinking about him and his smile. He didn't smile when we were kids, I remember he was so intense, but given the situation, I don't blame him. I'm thankful he told me my parents didn't suffer, which put me at ease. The not knowing if Mama was alive or not used to haunt me. I used to see her turning to me as we were about to crash. The look of panic in her face, but the look of love from a mama who only wanted her daughter to be safe.

I go into my attic and dig out all the paintings I did of Nick. I look at them all closely and I'm amazed at how I got him almost spot on. I set up my easel and get out all my paints and I start to paint him as he is now. I paint his features as I remember them sitting at the table. I give him a little cocky smile surrounded by his beard, the greenest eyes which have never changed, and still with the messy black hair, which I now realize is messy because it's curly. He's still fresh in my mind and I want to get that down in paint. Not that I think I will ever forget him.

I stay in the attic for the rest of the day and into the night. I get carried away and I just keep painting him. If he ever saw my collection, he would think I was creepy. When I'm too tired to continue, I head down to the kitchen. I haven't eaten anything all day. The house is completely dark with me being upstairs, and just as I'm about to turn the light on in the living room at the front of the house, I see a figure standing outside across the street. I don't turn the light on as I move around the edge of the room out of sight of the window. I peek through the side of the blind to look. I noticed on the clock it was past two in the morning, so why would someone be standing outside? It scares me as I try to see who it is. I can't make out the figure, it's a male, he's tall, and he has his hands in his front pockets. I squint trying to see if I know him, he turns and walks a few steps one way, then he turns back, walks past my house and a few more steps the other way. I watch as he does this a few times. Is he scoping out the houses? I need to call the police. I close the blinds. I need to find my purse and get my cell.

I find my cell and see I have a few missed calls. I don't recognize the number. Why would anyone I know call me anyway? There are a couple of text messages from two hours ago. I open the messages, it only shows the phone number of the caller but I read them:

12:13 Primrose its nick i am outside not sure wich house you are at I could not nock

12:55 i am still here hope you are not in bed yet if not please look out so I see you

01:46 still here i will wait till i see you i cold not leve i need to see you

I look at the time on my cell and it's 2:34 a.m. Oh my god is that him out there now? He would be freezing if it is, it's freezing at night. I'm too scared to open the door, in case it's not him. I text back.

02:35 Nick, I will turn the light on. If you're still there come to the door.

I turn the light on and head to the door, I look through the peephole. He's there, it's him, I breathe out with a sigh of relief. I see his teeth, he's smiling. My heart is racing, the damn butterflies are back. I can't believe he's here. I unlock the door and open it slowly, he's standing on the step with his bag slung over his shoulder.

"Hi, I'm sorry, Primrose, I couldn't do it, I couldn't leave you. I thought me going was for the best, for you, but I couldn't do it. I walked here but I didn't know which house was yours so I just waited, hoping to see you. I felt sure you would have been in bed by now, but I was just going to wait until the morning as long as no one called the cops on me."

I laugh, I can't help it, I find this all too funny. He looks at me, scowling at me, laughing, still standing on the step.

"I'm sorry, I can't help it. I didn't have my cell on me. I was working and didn't even realize what time it was. I only came down to get something to eat, I haven't eaten today."

He smiles and it melts me. I open the door to invite him in. Am I mad? I mean, I don't know him, do I? He could be a serial killer for all I know. I know we have a connection, and I do believe in my heart, he wouldn't intentionally hurt me. I hope my heart is right because my head is screaming at me for letting him in.

I shut the door and he follows me into the kitchen. He drops his bag by the island, I open the fridge and pull out some eggs, cheese, and ham. I was just going to make an omelet. "Would you like an omelet, Nick?"

The look on his face tells me everything. He nods yes. I set about making omelets for us both and put a pot of coffee on, we sit at the island to eat. Neither of us speaks. We just eat, looking at each other. He seems comfortable with not speaking. Maybe he's a bit of a loner, like me. Although we talked for a few hours today, he didn't tell me anything about himself. He just sat listening to me, oh god was I just blowing hot and cold? Is that why he wanted to leave? I was nervous, but I felt relaxed in his company. Now I don't want to speak. I don't want to chase him away.

He finishes his omelet way before I do, in fact, he ate his like he hadn't eaten in a while.

"Would you like another one?" I ask, pointing to his empty dish. I still have half of mine left, to be honest, I've had enough so I push my dish toward him. "Here, you finish this, I've had enough."

He smiles and takes my plate. "Are you sure? You didn't eat much."

I nod. "Yeah, it's too late for me really, and too much. I need to get to bed." Oh god, now he's going to think that was an invitation. "Have you got anywhere to stay, Nick?"

He shakes his head as he takes the last mouthful of food. "No, I didn't want to go back to Cassy's. The last thing I want is to run into Poppy. I just needed to see you."

I blush and look away shyly. I twirl my cup of coffee around in my hands, not looking at him. He touches my fingers gently to get my attention. He must have been speaking to me. "I'm sorry, did you say something? I was deep in thought."

He looks me right in the eyes. "I know, Primrose, I know you're deaf, I may not be the smartest man, but I worked it out."

I look away. I feel ashamed and embarrassed. I get up and take the dishes over to the dishwasher to load. He's behind me, I can feel him. He places his hands on my upper arms gently. He doesn't want to startle me. I feel him breathe into my hair as he puts his chin on the top of my head. I can see our reflection in the window. He smiles and turns me around to face him.

"Please don't hide from me. I don't care if you can't hear me as long as you see me. You looked embarrassed when I said I knew. Never, ever, be embarrassed by it. I grew up with just my mama who was supposed to homeschool me. You can probably tell from my text messages, I'm not the brightest person."

He turns away from me now, it's his turn to be embarrassed. I step around him and stand right in front of him. "Hey, look at me. I don't care if you're smart or not. It's not your fault if you didn't have the support when you were younger. How have you managed to read and write now?"

He rubs his face and goes and sits back at the island. I follow him and sit opposite so I can see his mouth. He tells me all about Poppy and her friends Don and Tilda. He tells me about their work which shocks me. I never thought Poppy would ever care for people. She has never shown compassion for anyone. He tells me Don has been teaching him and if it wasn't for Don, he wouldn't even have a cell, never mind be able to read or write. I tell him why I can speak and how I lost my hearing. We laugh at each other, we are a pair together.

"Hey look, as long as you're not a serial killer, you can stay here. I have a spare room if that's okay with you."

I see a look of panic on his face as I say this. Maybe he thinks I'm being forward or maybe he wants to sleep in my bed. I have no idea what he's thinking. I stare into his eyes. There's fear in his eyes. Why is he scared? What did I say?

"Are you okay, Nick?"

He doesn't answer right away then he nods. "Yeah, sorry, I thought you would kick me out with not knowing me. The spare room would be great, thank you, if you're sure. I would even sleep in the basement if you have one." We laugh.

"You saved my life once Nick, I doubt you would take it after saving it," I say as I get up and head for the stairs. I turn to see if he's following me.

Seventeen

Primrose

IT'S LATE BY THE TIME I GET NICK SETTLED IN THE SPARE ROOM. I needed to put clean bedding on. It has its own bathroom so we shouldn't get into any awkward situations in the morning. I do trust him, I think, but I still lock my bedroom door and put a chair up under the door handle. Luckily I don't have to go into the office this week, everything I need to get done I can do from home, I don't have any trips coming up either for a while. Don't get me wrong, I love to travel, but I love being home also.

It took me a while to fall asleep last night. I kept watching the door handle to see if it turned. I eventually must have given up. The front door light that I have in my bedroom wakes me up. It flashes continuously and it's the flashing that wakes me. I dive out of bed to see if I can see who's at the door. I only peep through a slit in the blinds, I see Poppy standing on the sidewalk looking up at my window. Shit. I pull back so she can't see me. If I ignore her, hopefully, she'll go away. The last thing I want is a confrontation with her, and I doubt Nick wants to see her or let her know he stayed here. Oh Nick, I completely forgot about him. Shit, he might go and open the door.

I move the chair and unlock my door. I'm in my PJs when I open the door and see Nick standing there, near the top of the stairs, in just his jeans, that are not fastened. I can't help but look him up and down, he's like some kind of god standing there. I lick my lips, unintentionally, I look at his abs and pecs and the tattoos he has on his body. He crosses his arms over his chest, I look at his face.

He's smiling so hard. "Like what you see?" he asks me and I go as red as a tomato.

"Don't go down, Poppy's at the door. If we just stay quiet, maybe she'll go."

He nods and unfolds his arms.

"She's been hammering on the door for about twenty minutes. Why, I have no idea. She knows you won't hear her. How did you know she was there?"

I point to the flashing light above him. "I have them in all the rooms. When someone presses the doorbell, they flash continuously until I press the button to stop them. I didn't want to press the button, because she would know I've deactivated it. I also have a camera on my cell and get notifications of anyone at the door, usually when I'm out."

We stand there for a while.

"I'm going to go grab a shower. If we're ignoring her, I might as well get ready. Is there any way she can get inside? Does she have a spare key?"

I shake my head no and then I see the look of horror on his face as he looks down the stairs. He quickly jumps to the side out of sight, I watch him say, "Poppy just came in."

I frown, how the hell did she get in? Then I remember Aunt Cassy has a spare key, she must have taken that one. I doubt Aunt Cassy would have given it to her. I changed all the locks when I moved in and gave Aunt Cassy the key, she keeps an eye on the place when I'm gone for long periods of time. He dives into the spare bedroom and shuts the door.

I open it and I mouth without sound, "Stay in here until she's gone, lock the door."

He nods at me. He must have understood what I mouthed.

I head down the stairs, she isn't in the hallway, I head to the kitchen and I jump out of my skin when I see her. "What the hell, Poppy? What are you doing here? How did you get in?"

She turns toward me with a smile on her face. "Oh hi, Prim. I got the key from Aunt Cassy." She just shrugs and opens the fridge, I don't believe Aunt Cassy would give her the key.

"What do you want, Poppy?" I ask her again.

She doesn't turn to me, so I march over and pull her so she swings around and faces me.

I sign, "What do you want?"

She signs back, "Breakfast and a chat."

I don't want her in my house. When she mentions breakfast, I look at the clock to see what time it is. It's nine-twenty, I never sleep this late, but then I don't usually stay up until after three in the morning.

"No Poppy. I don't want to talk, and I don't want you here for breakfast. If you want to talk, I'll meet you later on, after I've showered and finished my work. I worked late last night and haven't had much sleep, and I can do without your interrogations right now. So if you don't mind, give me back the key, and leave."

She actually looks stunned that I just told her to leave. I mean it, I vowed yesterday, I would not take any more crap from her. All these years, I've stood by when she's been around and let her get away with treating me bad, all because I felt sorry for her. Why the hell I felt sorry for her, I don't know, but I did. It should have been the other way around, I was the one in the accident, I was the one that saw Mama and Pappy die, I was the one that got injured, and have suffered from my leg ever since. I'm sick of being nice to her just so she doesn't lash out at me, and she still lashes out anyway.

She stands, staring at me. "Poppy, I'm tired and I need a shower, please leave."

She doesn't move, instead, she pulls the key from her pocket and places it on the island.

"I'll text you later, Poppy. We can meet up for something to eat if you still want to?"

She doesn't say a word, she turns and starts to head out toward the front door. She stops and turns around, she looks up the stairs. Shit, has she heard Nick moving around? I scowl at her. She just shrugs, then goes out the front door without saying a word. I sigh and rub my head. I then put the security chain on the door, that way even with a key, no one could just walk in.

I head up the stairs and knock on Nick's door. He might be in the shower so he may not hear me. I wait a few seconds, nothing, I head back to my room. I shut the door but don't lock it and start to take off my PJs, ready to get in the shower. As I turn, I see Nick standing there in my doorway, leaning against the doorjamb with his arms folded over his naked chest, and one leg crossed in front of the other. I scream and grab my PJs trying to cover up. He smiles and puts his hand over his eyes, too late, he saw me naked.

"What the hell are you doing, Nick?" I shout while covering up my nudity.

I see him laugh, watching his shoulders move up and down. I move to my bathroom and get in the shower and hope he's gone by the time I get out. I left my bathroom door slightly ajar like I always do and just trust he doesn't peep in. I think secretly, I want him to. I shouted at him for being at my bedroom door, but in all honesty, I was excited he was there and not even trying to be a gentleman.

I head down to the kitchen after drying my hair, Nick is sitting at the island looking out the back doors, nursing a cup of coffee. He hears me entering and turns with a big smile on his face. I try to play it cool, I look away with a scowl on my face. I pour some coffee into my cup and turn only to bump into Nick, I spill some of my coffee, just missing him.

"Shit," I say as I put the cup back down, then get a cloth to clean up the mess. He's still standing there in just jeans and nothing else. "Oh Nick, I'm so sorry, did I burn you?" I ask, wiping coffee from his bare feet.

I look up his body slowly, I see his jeans open and what a sight. I think I'm going to pass out. Being this close, I can see the trail of hair from his navel disappearing down into his jeans. I lick my lips unintentionally and I continue up his body until I get to his smiling face, I have no idea if he said anything, my brain was engaged in its own little fantasy. He's folded his huge arms over his huge chest again.

"Did it burn?" I ask him.

He just shakes his head no. I make sure his feet are clean, and oh my, what huge feet he has, then I clean up the coffee on the floor, all the while trying to compose myself, getting ready to face him.

I stand up slowly, closing my eyes so he doesn't get the pleasure of ridiculing me, because I'm melting at his physique. I stand there, not saying anything, and not wanting to open my eyes, I don't want to see what he says to me. Suddenly I feel his lips very softly kiss my cheek. They linger there, for what feels like forever, and I feel myself lean into him. I think I go as red as a tomato, yet again, and I slowly open my eyes. His face is level with mine and I gasp.

"Did you like what you saw, Primrose? I know I certainly did."

Oh my god, he's referring to seeing me naked. I need to move away from him. He's doing all kinds of funny things to my body, just by being this close. I turn and pick up my coffee, I didn't spill that much, and I walk around him and put the coffee on the island.

"Do you want some breakfast? I have eggs, I could make another omelet, or I could fix you some bacon, toast, and eggs. Any preference?" I don't turn to look at him.

He's right behind me again, just like he was last night. He puts his hands on my upper arms and leans down and kisses the base of my neck, then he moves slightly to my shoulder. The top I have on is loose and hangs off one shoulder. He starts to pepper kisses along it. I feel goosebumps from his gentle touch, I lean my head back onto his shoulder and expose my neck to him. He peppers kisses back from my shoulder to my neck and under my ear. I grip the granite on the island, I feel like melting, the tingles all through my body make me shudder, I feel him smile on my neck. I can't do this with him. I don't know him, I'm not one of those who sleeps with someone on a first date, and we haven't even had a date.

I pull away, as much as I can, because he has me almost pinned to the island. I step sideways out of his reach and look at him. He turns and leans against the side of the island and he crosses one arm across his torso and plays with his beard with the other hand, and he's smiling at me. I scowl, what is he doing to me?

"What do you want to eat?"

"You."

I stare at him, wide-eyed, then look away, I feel so embarrassed, yet it's so hot all at the same time. I feel like melting at his feet. I go to the fridge and take out bacon and eggs and set about making them with some toast. I pour us a glass of orange juice each and lay it all on the island. He watches me the entire time.

We sit opposite each other, eating in silence, it's slightly awkward because he doesn't take his eyes off me and I'm obviously doing the same. I feel quite brazen with him sitting there staring at me, I eat my scrambled eggs provocatively, placing the fork into my open mouth slowly, then lick the fork and lick my lips. I have no idea what I'm doing, or why I'm even doing it, but the look on his face makes me feel powerful. He leans across the table, taking a small piece of bacon from my plate, he shamelessly puts it to my mouth and plays with it on my lips. My mouth opens and he slides the bacon in and out of my mouth slowly, I try to catch it with my teeth, but keep missing. This is flirting tenfold. I laugh as he places it inside my mouth, but his finger slides in with the bacon, and I shamelessly suck his finger, then lick it as he withdraws it.

I see his eyes narrow into slits, and he wriggles on his stool a little, I bet he groans as well. Maybe he's a little uncomfortable there. I smile a smug smile to myself. We finish our breakfast. Well, he finishes my breakfast because I can't eat anymore. My tummy is in knots and those damn butterflies are back in training. I get up to clear away the dishes. As I'm at the dishwasher bent over loading it up, he comes up behind me and presses himself into my ass and holds on to my hips. Oh my god, what is he doing, the thing is I don't move away, I let him do this to me. I let him stand there rubbing himself on my ass. I would never in a million years let anyone I just met do anything like he is doing.

I only have on a skirt and top, I just threw them on, I call them my house clothes, I wouldn't be seen dead in them outside. The skirt isn't so short that when I bend over you can see everything, but it isn't long either, it's just above my knees when I stand up.

I feel one of his hands move from my hip and gently he strokes around to my ass. I feel it lower more, and he starts to hitch up my skirt with his fingers, very gently and very slowly. I'm still bent over the dishwasher, but I start to get a bit panicky inside. There is no way I'm having sex with him. As gorgeous as he is, it's not happening. I'm not that type of girl. Is this the only reason he came back? I stand up, putting a stop to his wandering hand.

He turns me in his arms to face him and pulls me into his chest. He bends his head and starts to kiss under my ear, down my neck, and along my collarbone. I tilt my head up to give him better access, I'm not sure how long I can do this before I give in. I want him so bad. I put my hands on his sides, his jeans are still undone and are hanging off his hips. I could push them down no problem, but then that gives him the green light. I play with the waistband of his jeans, I brush my knuckles along his hip-bones and on his sides. He smiles on my neck. I feel him breathe in, as though he's ticklish. I get brave, I use my fingertips to stroke his sides, to his navel and then braver still, I play with the trail of hair that dips into his jeans but don't go too far.

He pulls away from me and looks down into my face. "Are you okay with this?" he asks me.

I smile and nod yes at him. That little nod was all he needed. He's on my mouth prying my lips open with his tongue. I feel him groan. Oh god, I'm like jelly shaking in his arms. He kisses me with such passion, his tongue dueling with mine, he presses his body farther into mine, I feel how hard his cock is on my tummy, he starts to move in circles, his hands wander down to my hips as he pulls me to him, as much as he can. He keeps his hands on my hips, he slowly edges them upward but under my top.

I breathe in sharply, from the first touch taking in a deep breath, he strokes my sides with featherlight touches, mirroring what I was doing to him. I'm ticklish, I start to squirm a little in his arms which makes him smile, while still devouring my mouth. He touches me more, enjoying how responsive I am to him. I feel goosebumps all over my body, my head tingles from his touches. I start panting into his mouth. I need to tell him to stop before we go too far. I don't want him thinking I'm an easy lay, or him getting all worked up. His hands start moving upward to my breasts. I push on his chest to stop him from going any further. He carries on, I push firmer, making my point. He breaks the kiss, stops moving his hands, and looks at me with a slight frown for an answer.

I hang my head, he tilts it up toward his face and gently kisses my lips.

"It's okay, baby, we don't have to do anything you don't want. I'm just really struggling with keeping my distance from you. I want you so fucking much, but I've waited for so long, there's no way I'm going to screw it up by jumping in there and being impatient."

I have tears forming in my eyes, he bends his neck and licks the stray ones falling from my eyes. "I'm sorry, Nick."

He tilts my head to his face again. "Don't be sorry. Primrose, I just can't explain right now how I'm feeling. I thought it would just pass, that once I saw you, I would realize all these years of being infatuated with you would just disappear, and that would be that. I didn't think the connection would still be there, let alone be so strong. I still can't believe my luck, that we've met and that you're not married or with anyone."

I feel ecstatic inside. "Me too, Nick. I thought it was just infatuation, you know, from you saving my life, but it's not, at least I don't think it is. I want you, Nick, oh god do I want you, but I'm not the type of girl who jumps into bed with a man the minute I meet him. That's not me, Nick. I'm sorry."

I hang my head again, not wanting to see the disappointment on his face. I feel his breath on the top of my head as though he just spoke to me, I look up to his face. "Did you just say something?"

He shakes his head no and leans down to kiss me. He then picks me up and I wrap my legs around his waist. I can't help it, I do want him, so much. He sets me on the island and stands between my legs with them still wrapped around his waist.

"I want you so bad, Primrose," he says then kisses my collarbone again.

I sigh, I want him too. I play with his messy hair while he kisses, sucks, and licks my neck, he lowers his head toward my breasts and through my top, he bites my nipple gently. It sends electric shots through my body, I instinctively throw my head back and lean my hands back on the island jutting my chest out toward him. I watch as he takes his hand and gently strokes from my neck down the middle of my breasts, then with both hands, he takes a breast in each and starts to squeeze, rub, and gently pinch my nipples. I start panting, watching him, and I nod to let him know it's okay.

With the nod, he gently lifts my top up and off over my head. I reach for his pecs and I start to play with both his nipples, I feel him shudder from my touch, I see the lust all over his face. He bends down, as he lifts my bra up over my breasts, he takes a nipple between his teeth and starts to circle it with his tongue. With his other hand, he plays with the other one. I lean back again with my hands on the island behind me and I let him play. He licks up and down from my navel to my neck stopping on the way to bite my nipples gently. I lean forward so I can stroke his hair, and pull his head farther into my breast, the one that is currently in his mouth. I start to gyrate a little against his body, My skirt has risen right up with my legs being wrapped around his waist, and I know my panties must be soaking wet rubbing against his body.

He breaks our connection and looks at me. "We don't have to have sex, but can I taste you?" he asks.

I shiver at the thought. Only one boyfriend has ever gone down on me before. I wasn't that thrilled about it, but I trust Nick to be gentle with me. I nod and smile sheepishly, I know he sees the apprehension on my face.

"I promise that you will enjoy every minute of it." He smiles that cocky smile at me and I melt.

He gently lifts my ass off the island as he pulls my panties down, he pulls away so he can take them off my legs completely. I feel exposed as he stands there looking at me and I close my legs. He smiles and shakes his head no. He moves closer to me and gently opens my legs, so he can get between them again.

He leans forward and kisses my navel, my breast, and then my mouth. He deepens the kiss with such passion, using his tongue. While he's doing this, his hand wanders up my leg, up my inner thigh, stroking me gently until he reaches my core. He plays a little with his fingers around my lips down there, before spreading me open and inserting a finger very gently inside. He sighs into my mouth, I shudder as he moves his finger in and out, slowly and ever so gently. In and out, over and over, and every so often stroking my nub. I'm now sitting up and he has one arm around me supporting me while the other is working below. I'm shuddering and shaking. It's been a long time since I slept with anyone, but I've never felt as aroused as I feel right now.

I have both my arms around his neck, holding him tight to my chest. He's starting to build up speed in and out, round and round, in and out. He mimics his finger with his tongue on my nipple. He inserts another finger stretching me wider, he's getting faster and faster and I start gyrating on his hand. I reach down and grab his hand, trying to pull it farther into me. I feel like a whore, but I feel so liberated, trying to take charge. That's it, I get faster and faster as does his hand in and out, round and round and he hits it. That one spot he hits just right, I freeze in his arms. I whisper don't stop as his fingers are so far inside, circling the spot. I'm almost there, frozen, not wanting to move in case he loses the spot and that's it, one, two, three more strokes and I scream out with the biggest orgasm I think I've ever had. I can feel the wetness down there and I'm squeezing his head so hard into my chest.

Before I know what's happening, he's pulled away and is on his knees in front of me. He's just the right height as he pulls my hips forward and spreads my legs wide. He puts each of my feet on the stools on either side of him and he dives straight in, licking and licking all the juices coming from me. I'm still coming down from my orgasm, still spasming. When I look down at him licking me, I find this to be the most erotic thing I've ever encountered. I'm at the edge of the island, he's licked me dry and now he's put a leg over each of his shoulders and is nuzzled right into my core. I feel dirty, cheap, but oh god, it's so good. He puts his tongue inside me and starts to swirl it around and around in and out, lapping and sucking as he does. He latches on to my clit and starts sucking and sucking then he has a finger back inside me. He's pumping in and out, I can't believe I'm being so receptive to him after just having an amazing orgasm.

I start to feel myself going again. He removes his finger and inserts his tongue. He grabs hold of both my legs, wrapping his arms around them from underneath and pulling me farther onto his face. His tongue is relentless. He doesn't stop and the next thing I know, I'm screaming and wriggling in his grip. I try to edge backward, it's too much, but it's not enough, all at the same time. He keeps a firm grip on my legs and he laps away at the juices flowing out of me. My head is buzzing as is my entire body. I have never ever had anything like this. But now I'm coming down from my high, I realize Nick has let go of me and I'm lying back on the island with my arm resting over my eyes. I don't want to look, I feel ashamed and embarrassed, I feel like a slut. I don't know him, but I know in my heart I'm in love with him, I have been since the first time I saw him.

I suddenly feel something cold and wet at my core, I jump at the touch. I move my arm and lift my head up and see Nick standing there with a cloth. He's actually cleaning me, down below. Oh god, I put my head back on the island and my arm back across my eyes. I feel tears flowing down the sides of my face, why am I crying? I've just had two fucking fantastic orgasms with the most beautiful man I've ever met, and I'm crying. I don't get it. I feel so emotional. Is it because I feel ashamed? He grabs my arms and pulls me up gently, I'm sitting up with him standing between my legs again. I hang my head, putting my chin on my chest. Oh, look at me, I look like a whore sitting here, my bra tight above my breasts, my skirt around my waist and I smell of sex even though we haven't actually had sex.

I put my face in my hands and cry. He gently lifts my chin.

"Hey, what's this for? Didn't you enjoy that?" He looks really worried and who can blame him, with a half-naked crying woman sitting in front of him.

I nod my head to say I enjoyed it. He wipes away my tears with his thumbs as he holds both sides of my head. He looks me in the eyes and then kisses the tip of my nose before moving on to my mouth. I feel terrible, I'm all snotty and I must look a mess. I break away and rest my forehead on his chest. He wraps his arms around me and kisses the top of my head. I open my eyes and I can see right down his torso to his rock hard cock sticking out of the top of his unfastened jeans. I cry more. He gave me two amazing orgasms and what did he get in return? Nothing. I'm now a blubbering mess, he just holds me for a while until I've calmed down.

He lifts my head again.

"Now are you going to tell me what you're thinking? The female brain baffles me, I'm afraid. For you to be sobbing after that, makes panic set in. I've never had a woman cry like that before after I've given her orgasms."

Great, just what I need to hear. And here come the tears again. I push him away and I edge off the island and run up the stairs into my room, I throw myself onto my bed, not before slamming my bedroom door. This now makes me feel even worse because now he must think I'm this stupid, crazy-ass woman. How do I explain? Just 'hey Nick, yeah I loved it but now I feel like a whore and thanks for telling me about your previous conquests, just what I want to hear when I feel like shit, oh and by the way what did you get out of any of that? I never even touched your cock'.

I have my head buried in my pillow when I feel the bed dip beside me. He climbs on gently so as not to startle me, he just holds me. He's spooning me, and now I'm dead.

"I'm really sorry, Nick. I don't know what came over me. I've never acted like this before. You must think I'm a nut job." I'm not facing him so I have no idea what he's saying, I feel his breath on my neck as he speaks, I feel the vibrations from his chest through my back from his voice. I don't turn around, I'm scared to think about what he just said.

We must have both fallen asleep on the bed cuddling. I wake up and I'm facing Nick, who is still asleep. I think him breathing on my face woke me. I hadn't realized I had turned around. I have no idea what time it is. I don't want to move and disturb him. I watch him sleep, I look at his chest and I can see his tattoos a lot clearer. I start to examine them and it's only through being this close I notice scars hidden in them. I feel them gently, trying not to disturb him. I also notice he has scars on his face, all faded but still slightly visible. I feel his back gently, lifting my arm over his and he has scars there too. I wonder how he got all these scars? His eyes open, the greenest eyes I have ever seen, they mesmerize me, especially being this close, he smiles at me and I melt. I snuggle up closer to him, into his chest and he wraps his arms tightly around me. We lay like this for a little while, I tilt my head back to look at his beautiful face.

"Hey, did you have a good sleep?"

He nods. "The best, I never sleep in the day, even when I've been awake all night, but I was so at peace with you in my arms. So relaxed."

My heart melts more. I love this man. I know nothing about him, but I can categorically say I'm in love with him. I have never felt anything this strong for anyone before.

"Please forgive me for acting like a crazy-ass woman before. I really have no idea why I was sobbing, I can only put it down to hormones and what you brought out of me. I felt bad because I didn't want you to think I was easy or a whore, then I felt bad because well, I didn't touch you, so you got nothing out of that and…"

He stops me from rambling on by kissing me. The kiss soon deepens and before I know it, I'm sliding down his body to his still unfastened jeans and I'm putting my hand inside and grabbing his rock hard cock. I try to pull his jeans down, so he lifts his ass to help me. I then bend down and I lick his cock, I try to keep my eyes on his face so I can see his reaction, he has one arm over his eyes and the other hand is wrapped around the iron bed frame above his head.

I scoot lower so I can watch him. I put his cock in my mouth and swirl my tongue around the head. It's huge, I use my hand at the base, then put what I can deep inside. I suck and suck, swirling my tongue then licking the head. There is cum seeping out and he now has hold of the iron bed frame above his head with both hands. He has his eyes screwed shut, I can see his chest rising, getting faster and faster which spurs me on more. His face looks anguished, as thought he's fighting with himself. I bob up and down while trying to watch him. He's panting hard and he's thrusting up into my mouth. I pump with my hand and grab his balls with the other one.

His hand suddenly rests on the top of my head, his grip gets a little tighter the more I pump, suck and lick. Then, with one thrust up, he explodes deep into my throat. I feel like I want to gag, but I hold it back. I need to give him this, to be honest, the few times I've done this previously, they've never been like this. He's so gentle with me all the time, making me feel like a breakable doll, he doesn't lose it, I actually love the taste of him. He has a unique smell and taste, I find it turns me on more and makes me want him more. He's thrusting his hips up, still holding my head, but gently, his cum is never-ending. Some drips out the sides of my mouth, there is that much, I swallow as much as I can.

He settles back on the bed and he stills. I lick him clean. I sit back on my knees and watch him. He has his arm over his eyes again, but he has a huge smile on his face. He removes his arm and looks at me.

"Come here, you."

I crawl up his body and lie flat on top of him. He takes my mouth and kisses me with so much passion. I stay on top of him for a little while, with the side of my head on his chest. I know he says something because it vibrates through my head.

I look at him and ask, "What did you say?"

He smiles and I'm sure he goes a little red, he looks embarrassed. "Erm, I just said that was fucking amazing baby."

He's lying and I know it, I can tell from the look on his face.

"Shall we get cleaned up? Not that I mind staying like this all day, but you said you were going to meet Poppy. I would much rather spend the day in bed with you."

I slap his chest and look over to the clock. It's two in the afternoon. Ooops.

We get up and rather than shower together, he jumps in his and I jump in mine. I think if we had a shower together, I wouldn't be leaving the house at all today, not that I would mind. Poppy can take a hike for all I care. In fact, I'm going to message her and tell her I'm still working, can we meet tomorrow. I would rather spend the day getting to know Nick.

We do just that. The rest of the day we talk, a lot. I find out about how he was brought up. I ask about the scars, he pretends he doesn't hear me and changes the subject. That gets my mind racing. I tell him some of the places I've visited, he says it would be a dream to go traveling. Well, let's see how things go. I cook us dinner and we cuddle on the couch, talking for the rest of the evening.

Eighteen

Primrose

H E SLEPT IN MY BED LAST NIGHT. WE DIDN'T HAVE SEX, BUT we got very close to it a couple of times throughout the night. I have never had as many orgasms in one day as I did yesterday, and to say I'm feeling it today is an understatement. I can say one thing, we both seem to be addicted to tasting each other.

I've had to leave him in the house on his own, while I go to meet Poppy for lunch, I hope it doesn't end up like the last time where she threw a glass of water all over me. I'm late this time. Nick didn't want me to leave, I rush into the restaurant. I see Poppy sitting there, but she's with Aunt Cassy, great. I thought she was going to grill me about Nick, when we were younger, I still think that, but in front of Aunt Cassy because I can't lie to her.

"Hi," I say and sign to them both. I sit down and the waiter comes over to fill my water glass and ask if I want a drink. I'm driving, so water is just fine. "Have you been here long? Sorry, I got engrossed in my work."

Aunt Cassy smiles at me while Poppy ignores me. "You working on anything good right now?" Aunt Cassy asks me.

"Yes, it's a big project in the UK. I'll be going there in a few months to meet up with the developers to go through my drawings and designs with them. If they accept it all, then it will be huge, not just for the company but for me also."

"That would be great for your career."

We chat for a little while about work, but Poppy's bored. She has no interest in my work and she makes a show of it. I know she only wants to know about Nick and right on cue, "Have you heard anything from Nick?"

I take a sip of my water, pretending I didn't see her talk, and divert my eyes. She taps my arm so I have to look at her.

"Have you heard anything from Nick?"

I just shake my head no, not wanting to get into this with her. She squints her eyes at me, she knows I'm lying. Aunt Cassy can sense Poppy is up to something, she changes the subject, telling us the antics of the twins.

We eat our meal and continue with the small talk. Poppy finally opens up, telling us all about her work at night, helping young girls that are either on the streets or on drugs. I see the tears start to well in Aunt Cassy's eyes.

"Oh Poppy, that is wonderful. I always knew you were compassionate, and helping others like that, I'm so proud of you."

Poppy actually seems to melt a little at hearing that from Aunt Cassy. Maybe if I can just finish, tell them I have to leave to get back to work, then I can escape the inquisition I know is brewing. I want to get back to Nick. I miss him already. God, I sound like a love-struck teenager, I actually feel like one. I must be sitting there smiling to myself, in a world of my own, when I get a nudge by a foot under the table. I look up at both of them.

"Huh."

Poppy rolls her eyes at me. "I asked you again, have you heard from Nick? It was a bit weird him taking off like that. What happened?"

Aunt Cassy's looking at me and waiting for me to answer.

"Nothing happened, we talked, and he said he had to go home. Just like that."

"How did you and he meet? He seemed like a nice man, although a little bit guarded, which I suppose is understandable being with a bunch of new people."

I look at Aunt Cassy. "We just met many years ago when we were young. I only met him once and have never seen him since." In my head I'm chanting, 'please Poppy drop it.' I give her a stern look.

She grins at me. "Tell Aunt Cassy about your paintings of him. This boy, now man, with the greenest eyes." She leans forward on the table, resting her head on her hands and smiling at me. Aunt Cassy looks at me.

"There's nothing to tell. I remembered him as a young boy from the time we met. I imagined what he would be like grown up, so I painted a few pictures of him." I sign most of this to her.

I look to Poppy and glare at her, she scoffs, I see it. I push back on my chair. "I need to get going, I have a lot of work to do for the UK project, I also have the office Face-Timing me soon for a meeting, I don't want to miss that."

I look at Poppy. "When are you leaving?" Aunt Cassy stands up to give me a hug and a kiss and Poppy glares at me.

"I should be heading back tomorrow."

Great, the sooner the better, I hate myself for thinking that.

"If you want, I could drop by tonight, we could have a chat and some wine before I leave tomorrow. Who knows when I'll be back."

I glare at her, what's she playing at? I know she has an ulterior motive.

"I had someone contact me from Vegas asking if I would like to go and work for them. They have a facility for young girls that need help, getting them off the streets and finding them homes, helping to get them clean. It's really well paid, I said I would go there and check it out before making the move. I know it's not that far but it's far enough."

Aunt Cassy praises Poppy again and I can see she's happy about this but I don't want her coming to my place tonight.

I go around to her side and I hug her and give her a kiss on the cheek. "I would have loved that, Poppy, but I really need to work on this project. I'm a little behind on it as it is, who knows how long this meeting will go on. I'm so proud of you Pops, I love you." I do, no matter what she does and how she treats me, I love her. But I don't like her.

I say goodbye and head back home. I get butterflies as I pull up outside my house. I'm excited to see Nick. I stopped at the market and got some fresh fish for dinner tonight, and some wine. I walk into the kitchen expecting to see him, but he's not there. I walk into the den and nothing. Maybe he's gone out. I stand in the hallway.

"Nick, are you home?" I shout, waiting for him to appear. But nothing. That's odd.

I go up the stairs and knock on his bedroom door in case he's asleep, nothing. I go into my room to get changed, expecting to find him in my bed, nothing. I change then head back to the kitchen to start preparing dinner, I happen to look out of the back doors and I spot him out on the deck in just some shorts, doing some kind of workout routine. I watch him for a few minutes, just standing and admiring the view.

He's one hell of a man, I've never met anyone like him before. He's had a hard life, by all accounts, but he's such a caring person. I slide open the floor to ceiling, bi-folding doors which I had installed so I could let the outside in.

"Hey," he says, looking at me out of breath, just as he falls to the ground over and over, doing burpees. He's all sweaty, guess he's been at it for a while.

I grab a glass of water for him and an orange juice for me. I sit crossed legged on the chair and watch him do his routine. He fascinates me in more ways than one. He finishes, then comes over and sits with me, taking the water and finishing it in one gulp.

"Do you need some more water?" I ask and he shakes his head no.

He lays his head back, catching his breath and getting some of the sun's rays before it sets. I sit and I look at his body from top to bottom. I know he has a lot of scars on his torso, which he doesn't want to talk about, but now I can see his legs in the light, they are full of scars. I look to his face and he's watching me looking at his legs.

"And that's why I'm always in fucking jeans." He looks at me a little hurt.

"I didn't mean to stare, Nick. I'm sorry, I didn't mean anything by it. I just noticed the scars and wonder what your story is with all of them. That's all, I'm curious and want to know about you, I wasn't judging you."

He gets up, grabs the towel from the railing on the deck and wipes his face, neck, body, and head. He leaves the towel draped around his neck then heads into the house. I don't know if he said anything as he turned his back. A couple of times he's spoken to me without looking at me, I think he forgets I have to be watching him speak. I leave him alone and drink my orange juice before heading in to do dinner. I lied to Poppy and Aunt Cassy. I don't have a call to the office today but I do tomorrow and I do really need to get some work done.

I'm at the sink prepping the salad and vegetables when he comes up behind and presses himself against my back. He puts his arms around me and splays his fingers on my tummy. I lean my head back and smile.

"Hmm. I could get used to this," I say and turn in his arms to face him. "I'm sorry about earlier, Nick. I didn't mean to stare, but who can blame me? I mean, look at you." I reach up and kiss his lips gently.

He reciprocates and before I know what's happening, he has me lifted onto the counter next to the sink and has me half naked while he goes down on me. I most definitely could get used to this.

We eat dinner but don't talk about his scars. Our conversation flows freely, but we never get back to his childhood or the accident. I think as far as he's concerned, we talked about that yesterday and cleared it all up. We have a cozy night in front of the TV, watching one of the older *Fast & Furious* films, he says he's never seen any of them. He managed to watch a few films while he was laid up with his bad ankle when Poppy was looking after him. I didn't know Poppy actually looked after him.

"You didn't tell me she took care of you." I feel a little hurt. Now I'm beginning to wonder if they did have a thing. There is no way I would ever sleep with anyone that had been with Poppy first.

He looks at me quizzically. "Didn't Poppy tell you she looked after me?"

I shake my head. He just shrugs. I actually get annoyed. "Hold on, don't just ignore this, Nick. HOW, did Poppy look after you exactly?"

He looks at me, annoyed. "What's got you all riled up? She just looked after me, no big deal, in fact, if it wasn't for her, I would probably have starved and stunk to high heaven."

Oh my god, did she wash him, naked? I get up, I can't take this. He's so nonchalant about it like it's no big deal when it is a big deal, a very big deal to me. Maybe this won't work. Maybe it's just the hero syndrome thing.

I'm sitting in the kitchen nursing my glass of wine and reading some work papers. I see him enter out of the corner of my eye. He takes his glass to the sink then he sits next to me at the island. I don't look at him or speak, I just ignore him and continue reading. He taps my arm, I look but don't speak.

"What's wrong? I thought you wanted to cuddle on the couch?"

Uh, I did until he dropped that bombshell. He's so blasé about things, I guess that's men in general.

"Hey, talk to me?"

I turn away from him, take a sip of wine, but I don't look at him when I say, "I need to know the truth. Did anything ever happen between you and Poppy? Did she bathe you? Did she see you naked?"

I can see him out of the corner of my eye, sighing. He turns my chin toward him and tries to kiss me, I pull away. I see a flash of anger in his eyes, it's only a flash before he looks at me and laughs. What the hell. I don't think this is funny. I get up and walk over to the sink. I don't look at him as I walk out of the kitchen and up the stairs to my room. I shut the door behind me and head into my bathroom to get ready for bed.

As I come out of the bathroom, he's sitting there on my bed in just his unfastened jeans. He looks up at me as I stop in the doorway.

"Are we friends? I don't understand why you're so pissed with me."

Men, they have no clue, they have no filters, and they definitely don't see things the way we see them.

"I asked you questions and asked you to be truthful and you didn't answer. Silence says a thousand words, Nick."

"It's Blaine."

I look at him confused. "What's Blaine?"

He looks at me and hesitates. He rubs his hands over his face and then lays back on the bed.

I can see his mouth moving but I'm not sure what he's saying from this angle. I knock his leg with my foot and he lifts his head to look at me.

"I don't know what you're saying."

He realizes I couldn't see his mouth. "Sorry, I forget sometimes."

"Well, what did you say?" You can tell I'm getting angry because I'm signing as well to him, even though he doesn't read sign language.

"My name is Blaine, Primrose. Not Nick. It's Blaine."

I don't understand, I frown.

"I never give my real name out to anyone I don't know. When I first met Poppy and realized it wasn't you, even though she pretended to be you, I told her my name was Nick and it just stuck."

Oh, okay. I suppose I understand not giving your real name, kind of.

"I want you to call me by my real name. Only you." He looks sheepishly at me as though I'm going to kick him out for lying or something.

"Okay Blaine, so now answer my other questions."

He looks me dead in the eyes. "Like I told you before. Nothing has ever happened between Poppy and me, she has never seen me naked. It was Don who used to help me in and out of the shower. She wanted something to happen, and she tried a couple of times to kiss me, but I never let her. The only reason I stuck around was in the hope I eventually got to see you one day, once I realized she was your twin. It was all for you, Primrose."

I don't know what to say. He's really opening up to me. I should trust what he says. I move over to him, he sits back up. I stand in between his legs and hold his head to my tummy, he wraps his arms around me. I stroke his hair and play with the curls.

"I'm sorry, Blaine, that feels weird now, calling you that. I'm sorry for questioning you, but if anything happened between you and Poppy, then that would be it for us. I could never be with someone Poppy had been with. I hope you understand. I know she's my sister, and I love her, but I really don't like her. She was horrible to me our whole life, well, since our parents died anyway. She's always blamed me for it."

He looks up into my face. "How, it wasn't your fault. How could she blame you? You were injured, you lost your parents too."

I tell him how she always blamed me because I never told her who the boy with the greenest eyes was, and she always suspected he had something to do with the accident. He nuzzles into my tummy and I feel him sighing. We stay like that for a while.

"I need to go and make sure everything is locked up and turn all the lights out if you're coming to bed now."

"I'll do it." He's out the door before I can say anything.

———

I wake up with him between my legs, he pops his head up when he realizes I'm awake.

"Good morning, beautiful, just having some breakfast," he says, winking at me.

We did this a lot last night, I can't get enough of him either. I still don't want to actually have sex with him just yet. Well, that's a lie, of course, I want to, but I just want to wait a little while longer, we get very close to it though. I want to find out what his plans are. Another conversation I need to broach.

In the kitchen he's attempting to make some eggs for us, I laugh because he's never done it before so I teach him how to do it. I get us some muesli with yogurt and berries and we have some eggs and bacon. He pulls his face at the muesli and yogurt. I laughed at the face he pulled, he's like a little boy and I find it adorable. He's never had anything like this before and says he won't have it again. I love the camaraderie we have so soon.

"Ni... sorry, Blaine, what are your plans? I mean, are you planning on sticking around for a bit, or do you have to get back? Just I—"

"Do you want me to leave?" he interrupts me.

"Oh god no, I just, well, I have to work and as much as I want to spend all day every day with you, I'm falling behind on my project. I have this week off to work at home, then I'm back in the office next week. Poppy leaves today, she's heading back and then she's going to Vegas, something about seeing if she wants to work there, she got a job offer."

He looks at me quizzically.

"Well, if she's leaving today then I could go out for a walk, and let you work without any distractions unless you want a distraction, that is?" He wiggles his eyebrows and winks at me, he's incorrigible.

I love it when he's playful.

"Do you think you will stick around?"

He sighs and takes a sip of his coffee. "If you want me to, then I'm more than happy to stick around, but if you want me out of your hair, then I can leave."

Okay, not what I was expecting.

"What do you want to do? It's not just about me."

He looks me in the eyes. "I would love to stay, but I need to find a job if I do. Not sure if there are any garages around here, but I can try the bars."

I smile the biggest smile. He wants to stay.

"I'll also need to find a cheap motel."

That makes me choke on the coffee I just drank. I'm coughing and he gets up to rub my back. He kisses my shoulder. "Why do you need a motel?"

He turns me on the stool, opens my legs and stands between them. He takes my face in his hands and looks at me seriously. "There is no way I'm depending on you. If I was to stay here, then I would need to pay my way, and looking at this place, it would cost me more than staying in a motel. I don't take handouts from anyone, baby. I never have and I never will. It's just the way I am." He shrugs.

I have to think about this carefully, if I approach it wrong, I could see him leaving. "Okay, you find a job and I don't mean today, then you pay me rent to stay here. It will be the same as a motel…"

"No, it won't, Primrose, look at this place, it must cost you a fortune each month. I know you're successful but I could never afford this. The mortgage payments alone would be more than a cheap motel."

I don't grin or try to be patronizing. "Blaine, it's only the monthly household expenses I have to pay. This was my parents' house, it was left to me and Poppy and I bought her out, there are no monthly payments to be made. Please stay. I couldn't bear thinking of you in a motel. Even if you want your own space, the room you are in now can be yours."

He thinks about it then kisses the tip of my nose and my forehead and he nods. "Okay, but I will find a job."

Great, glad that's settled.

He heads out to look around and get his bearings and see if he can find a job. Looking like he does, he would have no trouble getting work in a bar. He's gone out to give me time to work, which I need to do desperately. I'm in my office when the light goes off letting me know someone's at the door. I gave Blaine a key, so I know it's not him. I look at the time and it's just after three. I head to the door and look through the peephole. Oh shit, what's she doing here? I thought she would have left already. Good thing Blaine's out though. I quickly look around to see if there's anything of his laying around. The light is still flashing. I press the deactivate button as I open the door. I put on a fake smile, I really do not want her crap today.

"Hey Poppy, I thought you were heading back today."

She scowls at me and barges past me.

"Yes, come on in why don't you," I say sarcastically as I close the door.

I follow her into the kitchen where she stands and looks around. What the hell is she doing. "What's up with you, Pops?"

She turns around and glares at me. She's angry and she starts to sign, "He's been here all this time. You lied to me and Aunt Cassy. Why would you do that? What aren't you telling us, Prim? Why all the secrets?"

I roll my eyes at her and lean against the counter. "Because it's none of your business, Poppy. I don't have to tell you anything."

She walks up and gets right in my face. "You're hiding something, you've lied to us all, ever since you killed Mama and Pappy. You're a lying bitch, Prim, and I want to get to the bottom of it. Why would you hide him? I suppose you're fucking him now. Wanted him all to yourself, that's why you lied to us. I saw him earlier walking down the street. I followed him and saw him go into a couple of bars. I followed him into one and heard him asking for a job. He's staying here. I fucking brought him here and now he's fucking staying so he can fuck you." She's screaming into my face.

I have tears rolling down my cheeks, she's so vile with so much venom coming from her body language and her face is all red and distorted. I'm so angry with her. How dare she. "Get out, Poppy. I don't have to answer to you, or anyone. I'm a grown woman and who I screw is none of your business."

Suddenly she lashes out at me and slaps my cheek. She slaps it so hard my head jolts to the side and I bang it on the cupboard next to me. I'm shocked, I turn my head slowly toward her, rubbing my now stinging cheek.

"What the hell was that for? Get out, NOW," I scream at her and point my hand toward the door.

"I knew you would screw him, you fucking whore. He would have been mine if it wasn't for you. I nearly had him. Did he tell you how he wanted to fuck me, did he tell you how he sucked my tits and almost stuck his cock in me? He would have, had we not been interrupted. You fucking whore, how dare you take him from me. I was going to go back and work it out with him." She's raging. "I couldn't believe it when you said he was going. I hate you, Primrose, I hate you with a passion. You're no fucking sister of mine. You killed our parents, that was all on you. I bet you were having a temper tantrum in the car, distracting them and that's how they crashed. Poor invalid Primrose, the deaf one. You took all their attention from me and then you fucking killed them. It's all your fault. Everything."

She's spitting this right in my face. Suddenly she moves back slightly and grabs my hair, then I see it, her fist comes flying toward my face. I can't move, she has my hair pulled that tight. She punches me in the nose and my head jolts back and bangs hard against the cupboard behind me. She does it again and again, then she slams my head into the cupboard on purpose, over and over again.

I feel like I'm floating, my body feels so light. I try to open my eyes but they don't want to open. I can see light through the slits of them. What's going on? The lights are moving. I'm floating past them. I try to wiggle my legs, I'm not walking, that's for sure. I want to lift my head, but it's against something hard. Then I'm going down, oh god, I'm falling. I start to panic and try to move to stop myself from falling but I'm being held. I remember Poppy. She was here. Oh god, has she got hold of me now? What's she going to do? I remember her hitting me, I remember her vile words to me. I start to panic.

I'm being laid down gently onto something soft. I open my eyes to slits. I'm in my bedroom. I look up into the most beautiful face and the greenest, but saddest eyes. It's him, Blaine. He was carrying me to my bed. Oh god, I bet I look horrendous. I don't know what happened after she was slamming my head into the cupboard. I don't know if she carried on hitting me or she just left.

"Baby, can you see me?"

I watch his mouth as he speaks. "Yes. Is she gone?"

"Who baby? Who did this?"

"Poppy." I can just make out the murderous look on his face.

"Fuckin attac you? Your own fucki sister did thi? Leav ng you dead kitche floor? I'll fucking her." He's going mad, I only see some of what he's saying through the slits in my eyes, but he's putting the covers over my face so I miss a lot.

I remember what Poppy said about him and her. I don't know who to believe. He's gone somewhere, I turn my head to the window. That hurt, it's dark outside. How long was I unconscious? How badly did she hurt me? I can't breathe through my nose, my eyes must be swollen, and my mouth hurts, not to mention the bad headache I have. Just moving my head hurts. I try to lift a hand to my face but I'm stopped by a hand, I feel a cold cloth on my head. He very gently wipes at my face. I flinch because it hurts. I turn my head to look at him.

"Is it very painful, baby? Tell me what the pain's like?"

I try to frown at such an odd question, but my brow hurts. Then I suddenly have a flashback to the accident. I remember reading his lips, he was asking what the pain's like. I never remembered that before until just now. I remember he leaned over my pappy to see me and he was still in my sight when he said that to my pappy. I never thought anything of it and certainly didn't remember it until right now.

"Why did you ask my pappy to tell you what the pain was like back in the car?" I see his expression change from anger and compassion to fear.

"Shh, don't think about that now. Just tell me where it hurts."

He's still wiping at my face, being very gentle and trying not to hurt me. He pressed slightly harder when I asked him that question. Could it be he lied to me about the accident? Did he cause it like I always thought? If he did and he lied, what else has he lied about? Did he and Poppy get intimate? Did he lie to me about that too?

"Leave me alone, Blaine. Leave my room, please. In fact, you can call Aunt Cassy for me."

He looks shocked and annoyed that I'm telling him to leave. My head is thumping so bad, I really don't know what to think or believe anymore. I turn my head back to the window so I can't see his face. That way if he speaks, I don't know what he's saying.

I must have fallen asleep as I feel the bed dip. I panic and bolt upright. My head is banging so hard and now that I've moved my body, the pain is excruciating and I struggle to breathe.

"Shhh, hey it's me, Prim. Oh god love, what happened to you? Nick called to say there had been an accident and that you needed me here. I was out with Uncle Trevor, it took me a while to drive back. Nick told me not to panic, that you were alright, but that you needed me. Who did this, Prim? Did he do this to you? I thought he left? What's he doing here? I think I need to call the police."

I grab her hand to stop her leaving. It's then I see Blaine standing at the door. He heard everything. He looks so sad and dejected as he hangs his head. He leaves us, closing the door behind him.

I turn to Aunt Cassy.

"He didn't do anything. It was Poppy. She came by today, she saw Blaine was still here. She went into a rage saying the vilest things, she lashed out at me a few times. She must have knocked me unconscious, ow, my ribs hurt." I lift my top up, Aunt Cassy breathes in sharply, she has a look of horror on her face.

"Oh Prim, you're black and blue. Did she do all this?"

"I don't know, she must have kicked me when I was unconscious. Blaine found me and carried me up here, I told him to call you."

She has her hands cupped around her mouth. "I can't believe she would do this to you. She's your sister. All this because Nick stayed? Who's Blaine?"

"Can you call Nick in for me and I can tell you both at the same time."

I introduce Nick to Aunt Cassy as Blaine. I explain about his name. I tell her we are slightly more than just friends. I tell them both everything Poppy said to me. Blaine is horrified. He assures me it's all lies and he wouldn't lie to me. That he and Poppy had never been intimate. I believe him. I know how manipulative she can be and how she lies.

"Sweetie, I think I need to take you to the hospital to be checked out."

I shake my head and wince doing so. "No hospitals, you know I hate those places."

"Have you had any painkillers for your head and ribs?"

Blaine tells her he has them now, he grabs the water and tablets and makes me take them.

"If you have a concussion then you need to be woken up every hour, is Blaine staying here with you?"

He answers yes and says he will make sure I wake up every hour. He sits on the other side of the bed and cradles me very gently to him. Aunt Cassy seems pleased I have someone to look after me.

"If you need anything, you let me know, okay? That means both of you." She kisses the top of my head gently then leaves.

Blaine goes with her. I feel him get back on the bed beside me and he takes me in his arms again to cradle me. I fall asleep on him. He wakes me constantly. I get angry, but he's only doing what Aunt Cassy told him. He gets me more water and painkillers. I just want to sleep. He stays with me constantly, never letting me sleep for too long and making sure I'm okay. He washes me down and gets me clean PJs. He's an expert at looking after me, which makes me wonder if he had to do this with his mama.

It's been a week now, I'm okay. I've been able to finish my project, finally, although with the concussion, I couldn't even look at the computer screen the first few days. Blaine has looked after me, making sure I had food, water, tablets, in fact, anything I needed. He can't cook, bless him, but he tried his best. I've been so grateful for everything he's done, I was glad to get back into the kitchen after a few days though. It's then he told me about the mess, he said Poppy had smashed glasses and dishes. He cleaned it all up. I still need to find out about the pain question from him, it's been playing on my mind a lot, about why he asked my pappy the same thing.

I've been in the office today for the first time. I only went in for a few hours, it's all I could manage with what I suspect are broken ribs. I got an Uber as I still can't drive, I'm in one now, on my way home and texting Blaine to let him know I'm nearly there. I walk into the house and I see his bag by the door. I look up and he's standing in the kitchen entrance with both hands in his front jeans pockets.

"What's this?" I ask, I must look shocked.

He comes over to me and pulls me into his chest, hugging me gently. I pull back and look up at his face.

"Why are you leaving? You said you were staying. You were going to get a job, now you're leaving, why?"

He smiles at me but it's not a real smile, it doesn't reach his eyes. I really thought we had a connection. Is this because he doesn't want all this commotion, me being injured and him having to look after me, or is it being tied down? He did say he's never had a girlfriend for longer than a few weeks. Maybe this is it, maybe he feels we're at an end and it's time to move on. He's been used to coming and going as he's pleased all these years. Maybe he now feels restricted. I'm still searching his face.

He breathes out. "Primrose, I need to go. I have some things to take care of back home and then I'll come back to you."

Is he just saying this so I don't make a scene? I search his face to see if he's lying to me. I can't honestly tell. I step out of his hold and walk past him into the kitchen. I need a glass of wine, I don't care if I'm on painkillers.

He waits until I notice him in the kitchen before he moves up behind me, stroking down both my arms, he tries to turn me but I don't let him. I feel stubborn. He's leaving and I know he's not coming back, I can sense it. Maybe it's true about Poppy, and he's going back for her.

"Where are you going, Blaine?" I turn and look up into his face.

He breathes out. "I've got to go back to Reedley."

My eyes widen, that's where he was before, it's where Poppy is. "Are you going back to Poppy?"

Now his eyes widen. "What? No. Why would you say that? I've told you there was never anything between us, we were just friends. You don't believe me, do you?"

I do, but it just keeps coming back to Poppy. "I do believe you, Blaine." I have to reassure him, but at this moment I don't feel much like making him feel good.

I feel the pain because he's leaving me. How have I become so attached to him? What will happen when I have to go to the UK for a while? Now it's making me think, do I want to go? I walk away from him with my glass of wine. I sit on the stool still facing him in case he speaks. He doesn't say anything, he just walks up to me slowly, takes my glass and puts it on the island behind me, and lifts me from my seat. He widens his legs to get to my level and wraps his arms around me, linking his hands behind my back so I can't go anywhere.

"I can see you're upset, baby. I'm upset I have to go. I need to tie up the loose ends there, and then I will be back. I promise you. I don't know when because I then need to go home and shut that place up. I'm hoping for good. If I never went back there again, it would be a blessing. Do you believe me when I say I will be back? I've waited all these fucking years to find you, do you honestly think I could just walk away from you now?"

He leans in and kisses me gently on the lips. He's being very gentle with me because of my ribs. We haven't done anything intimate since the attack. I was in too much pain. He just slept in my bed with me every night holding me close. At this moment, and in fear of never seeing him again, I want him. I want to make love to him, to feel what it's like.

I rest my head on his chest and I whisper, "I love you, Blaine."

He heard me. Shit, I didn't think he would hear that. He freezes, almost stops breathing for a minute. I don't move. I feel embarrassed. He moves and kisses the top of my head. I feel him speak with the breath on my head, and the rumble in his chest, but I can't see him, so I have no idea what he's saying. Probably what a stupid person I am. I don't say anything. I look up at him and I kiss him. I try to deepen the kiss and start to feel his torso, I start to undo his jeans. He stops me. I look at him.

"No baby, I have to leave. Believe me, I would not hesitate if I knew you were up to it, but you're not. I can see the pain you're in now, I will not add to that. I will never hurt you."

I look down and I feel the tears in my eyes. He lifts my chin up.

"Please don't cry, Prim. Please believe me when I say it's you I want. We will just have to wait until I'm back and then there will be no stopping us." He smiles at me, but again it doesn't reach his eyes.

I watch as he leaves the kitchen, I decide to follow slowly. I watch him pick up his bag and he just stands there. He's talking, I can see him moving, but I don't know what he's saying. Why does he keep forgetting to let me see his face so I know what he's saying? Maybe it's a goodbye for good. He's rubbing his hand over his face and through his hair. He turns and looks at me, I can see his pain.

"Bye baby, see you soon. I'll text you when I get there, okay?"

I just nod and watch as he slings his bag over his shoulder and disappears out the door. I have my back to the wall. I slide down and sit on the floor crying. I don't care that my ribs hurt. He's gone, I don't know if I will see him again. After all these years of waiting for him, and I just let him walk out.

I have a pity party for one, just me and a bottle of wine. I end up in the attic surrounded by all the pictures of him, including the new ones I've managed to finish. I cry myself to sleep surrounded by him, wondering if I will ever see him again.

Nineteen

Blaine

THE LAST WEEK OR SO HAS BEEN A WHIRLWIND, TO SAY THE least. I've had more confrontations than ever. I've had to explain myself when I've never had to do that since my mama was alive, and to top it all off, I want to kill that fucking bitch Poppy for what she did to Primrose. When I walked in and saw her lying knocked out on the kitchen floor, the place was a mess, smashed glass and pots all over, I went into a full-blown panic. I almost blacked out. I went into a rage and added to the destruction in the kitchen, kicking the stools over, swiping things off the countertops and onto the floor. I didn't know what to do. She looked dead. I ran to her, thinking she was dead. I screamed out and took her slowly into my arms. Her face was a mess, it looked like she had been in a boxing match and lost. She was breathing, thank fuck, but I nearly went mad myself when I saw her.

I carried her up to her bedroom, she started to come around. I placed her on the bed very slowly and gently, she started talking. When she told me it was Poppy that had done this to her, well, let's just say I knew Poppy's end was near. I wanted to leave right then and go kill the bitch. I did my best to hold it all in. When I went into the bathroom to get the damp cloth to wipe her face, I screamed at the top of my lungs that I was going to kill the bitch. I vowed I would pay her back and make her suffer. I knew Prim couldn't hear me having the meltdown. I took a minute, then calmly went back and looked after my Primrose, my angel.

When Cassy arrived, I told her what had happened, she couldn't believe it. She didn't believe me, I saw the way she looked at my cut hands. But when Primrose told her, she had no choice but to believe her. Cassy was so angry that Poppy could do this to her own sister. When we left the room, she asked me outright if I was playing them both. Had I been with Poppy and now fancied trying the other twin. I told her no way. Poppy wanted that, but I wouldn't entertain it because I wanted to one day find Primrose. She looked at me skeptically, I think she believed me. I don't blame them at all, none of them know me or who I am. I just appeared and swooped in on Primrose. For all they know, I did have a thing with Poppy and this is now her revenge. She certainly made it seem like that by telling Primrose I had sucked her tits and almost fucked her. I wouldn't touch her if you paid me except to inflict pain on her. I vowed to myself that night I would get her back. I would make her disappear for good. I would make her suffer and feel the pain they feel.

I've had the best time being with Primrose, apart from the attack. Even being able to look after her like I did, I loved it. It brought back so many memories of my mama, I never thought I would be able to look after another person in my life. Well, I just proved to myself I can do it. Especially for someone I love. I do love her. I've never had feelings for anyone like I do for Primrose. I want to protect her so fucking much, I think I'd give my life to do it. I've told her so many times I love her, but never to her face, always to her head or back or even walking away from her. I'm too much of a pussy to say it to her face. When she told me she loved me, I wanted to tell her the same. I can't describe what I felt in that moment, it was the best thing anyone has ever said to me. When I left her a few hours ago, I stood in the hallway with my back to her, I told her I would be back, I told her how much it breaks my heart seeing her hurt, and that I loved her with everything I am, that I could never leave her and the only thing I regretted at that moment was not having made love to her. I don't want to fuck her, I want to make love to Primrose. I also promised I would tell her about my past and my condition when I returned. Obviously, she had no idea what I said.

I've been on this fucking bus for so long, all I want to do is get there and find Poppy. Primrose told me she was going to go to Vegas for some job thing. If she hasn't gone yet, that would give me an excellent excuse to get rid of her. If she decides to go to Vegas, I can get rid of her before she goes, then everyone will just think she's there and no one will be any the wiser, hopefully for a few years. In that time, I can build a new life with Primrose and who knows, maybe we can move away somewhere, move to the east coast, or Canada, or even Europe.

I finally get back to the motel in Reedley, the first time I've ever been able to read the fucking sign saying Welcome to Reedley. It's late, I picked up some food and headed right here so I can get some rest. I'll find Poppy tomorrow. I need to think about this. Do I want Don and Tilda to know I'm back? I'll call the bar and old man Johnson at the garage and tell them I won't be back in town and to thank them for the jobs. If I stay low key, but message Poppy and ask her to meet me, then I can take it from there. I can play her, reel her in. I just don't want to give her a chance to tell the others I'm back. The fewer people that know, the better for me. In fact, I'll call her and tell her I'm home, that it didn't work out with Primrose because I could only think of her, that I realized it's her I want. I'll find out about Vegas then take it from there.

I messaged Primrose last night and told her I had arrived safely. She wanted to FaceTime me but to be honest, it would kill me seeing her face and how sad she would be. Reading her short text, it sounded a bit off. I need to lay low on all aspects. If Poppy worked last night, then she should be getting home pretty soon. I take my shower and get dressed, then I call Poppy. No answer. Fuck, is she just ignoring me? I try again and still nothing. I lay on the bed and think about what to do. Just then the cell rings in my hand. It says Poppy, I answer.

"Hi Pops."

Silence.

"Poppy, you there? I just wanted to hear you." I put on my best seductive voice, if I fucking have one.

"That's not what you want, Nick."

Gotcha.

"Poppy, it is. Are you at home or are you working still?"

Nothing.

"Come on, Pops, it's me. I made a fucking mistake, Okay. There, I admit it. I've missed you." I hear her sigh.

"Yeah right, Nick. You have your precious princess Primrose now."

"No, I don't, I left. I couldn't cope with her after she got attacked. Did you hear about that? It was fucking bad, Pops. Anyway, she was just so clingy. I hated it and I realized it was you I wanted all this time. I just had some creepy infatuation for her, once I was there it just disappeared. I missed you, Pops."

Like a fucking hole in the head I did. Reel her in.

"I don't believe you, Nick. Where are you?"

She doesn't even mention the attack? Bitch.

"Back at the motel, come over and see me if you want, for a chat. Let's clear the air."

"You seriously telling me you left the princess and came back here for me? I don't believe you, you're full of bullshit."

I need to work at this.

"Call Primrose or Cassy. They'll tell you." I need her to think Primrose hasn't told us she attacked her.

"Yeah right, like either of them will talk to me ever again."

I sigh, letting her know I'm getting frustrated.

"What do you mean? Why won't they speak to you?"

"Seriously Nick, you telling me Primrose hasn't said anything?"

"Said anything about what, Pops? You're confusing me, you know it doesn't take much."

"Nothing, it doesn't matter. I haven't been to work. I left yesterday. I'm moving to Vegas, Nick. I thought Primrose would have told you."

"Vegas, wow, when? And no, she never mentioned it. She got attacked, Poppy, did you know? She was badly beaten, she doesn't know who did it. She was unconscious and couldn't remember anything, she's been a whiny bitch ever since. I had enough. You know me, Pops, I can't take that kind of shit. I reckon whoever attacked her did me a huge fucking favor."

I hear a small giggle from her.

"What's so fucking funny? It was bad, Pops. I wish you hadn't left, then you could have looked after her. As it was, Cassy was working so it was left to me. I hated it. It reminded me of caring for my fat fucking mama, who I hated."

"You're terrible, Nick. What do you want, really? I have lots of packing to do. I leave tomorrow, I have a new job starting next week and I need to find someplace to stay in Vegas, I'm leaving in the morning. I'll book into a hotel when I get there, then I have a few days to look for a new place to live."

"It sounds great, Pops. I wish I was going to Vegas. Yet another place I would love to visit one day. Guess you need money to stay there though."

She doesn't speak. Oh no, what now.

"Pops, you there?"

"Why don't you…"

Go on, say it.

"What, Pops? Why don't I what?"

She sighs. "Come with me? I can pick you up on the way in the morning. Come with me, Nick. We could start over in Vegas. Start a new life together, just you and me. Who knows, they have the Little White Chapel there, eh."

WHAT? Fucking no way on this earth would I marry her. Is she off her rocker? But she just gave me the in I need. She can pick me up.

"You know what, Pops?"

"What?"

"That sounds like the best fucking idea yet. I've got nothing here, no ties. Fucking ace, Pops, road trip again."

I hear her squeal. "Tell you what, Nick. I'll finish packing up here, I said goodbye to Don and Tilda yesterday, then I'll come over and pick you up and we can head off today. Check into a hotel on the way, have a little fun, if you know what I mean, then hit up Vegas tomorrow. I love Vegas, Nick, so much to do and so many opportunities there. How does that sound?" She's all giddy, big difference to when she first called.

I've got her hook, line, and sinker.

"Sounds perfect, Pops. Call me when you're leaving and I'll check out of the motel and wait for you. See you soon, Pops." I hang up and lie there, smiling up at the ceiling. That means I have to hang around here for the rest of the day. I don't want to chance going out and anyone seeing me around.

Then when she picks me up, she's all mine.

I hung around bored stupid. I hate being cooped up anywhere. I flicked through the TV channels and then went on Facebook to see if Primrose or Poppy had put anything on there. I didn't think Primrose would and thankfully nothing from Poppy about Vegas. It's a good thing she only posts now and then and doesn't tell the whole world her business from day to day. I get a message from Poppy, she'll be here in ten minutes. Great, I grab my bag and go check out. Just as I finish, she pulls up and I jump straight into the car.

"Hey," I say, she acts shy. "Hi Nick, you sure about this? I was surprised when you called."

I lean over and kiss her on the cheek. "Of course I'm sure. Thank you for giving me this opportunity. I missed you, Pops."

She blushes. She's like putty in my hand. We head out and luckily it's in the direction for my home.

"Hey Pops, do you mind if we take a detour first?"

She looks over to me with a frown. "Detour to where? Is it on the way?"

"Kind of. We're heading in that direction, but we will need to go a longer way to Vegas. I just need to head home and make sure everything there is boarded up. I won't be going back for a long time. Better to be safe than sorry. Don't want the bears getting in there and wrecking the place, even if it is a shithole."

I see the look of pity on her face and I fucking hate that. I never want pity from anyone.

"Yeah, sure, we're just winging it anyway. We'll get to Vegas when we get there. Tell me which way to go."

I direct her straight to my cabin. I'm turned slightly in her direction, I want to see the look on her face when she sees where I live. I'm not looking to the front, we're on the dirt road and I know exactly what's at the end. I see the exact moment she notices my home. I see the look go from panic to horror to pity. I. Fucking. Hate. Pity, I could scream at her. I turn back to the front just as she pulls up outside.

"You live here, Nick? Is this where you grew up?"

I don't look at her, I try to see what she sees. After being in Cassy's house and Primrose's house, I see this differently myself now. It's bad. It's a rickety old shed, no water, no electricity. How the fuck have I survived all these years here?

"Yep, home sweet home. You coming in?" I ask, opening the door and grabbing my bag from the back seat. I saunter over to the cabin, shed, whatever the fuck you want to call it. It's just some wood that's seen better days, nailed together. I pull the key out of my pocket and open the door. I turn to look at Poppy, she's still sitting in the car, the fuck?

I don't plan on coming back here and to be honest, standing here in the kitchen, living area, I think it should just be burned to the ground. It's not worth a cent, why keep it when it's just full of bad memories. I do alright out there wandering around, but now I've found Primrose, that's where I want to be. That's where my heart wants to be. I'm not sure if anyone knows this place even exists, if it's even legal. I couldn't tell you if I owned the land it's on or not. I know my mama said it was her mama's, but who knows. What if they just knocked this up anywhere, not giving a fuck who owned the land? Who would know around these parts?

I hear her car door slam shut and hear the gravel as she walks up to the door. I'm standing with my bag still slung over my shoulder, just looking around. There isn't anything I want from this place. Just my clothes. I head to my room, it's tiny. There's the rickety old bed I built for Mama, I don't even fit into it and haven't since I was fourteen. My legs hang off the end. When I'm in it, I have to curl up, bringing my knees into my chest. There's one threadbare gray blanket on the bed and one pillow. They've been with me since we first came to live here. In the corner of my room is where my clothes are. I don't have many here, from the looks of what is left, the rats have been in here. I usually have everything I need in my bag.

I hear Poppy come up behind me, I turn to look at her and she has that pity all over her fucking face again.

"Is this your room, Nick?"

I just nod slightly.

"Where did your mama stay when you were growing up? There are only three rooms here."

I look away from her. "She stayed on the couch out there or when she wanted the bed, she just locked me outside. I used to wonder around out there most of the nights she did that. I found hiding places to keep me safe from the bears and mountain lions. I used to catch a lot of wildlife in my traps out there. I had to constantly search for food for her. I know this place so well. Do you want to see? It'll probably be the last time I ever come back here."

She nods hesitantly. She turns and stands looking into the other tiny little room.

"That's the bathroom. Just a bucket and a bowl."

She looks above and turns around. "You don't have lights?"

I scoff at her. "We don't have fuckin-tricity out here or running water. I used to have to fetch the water from the creek which is a good twenty-minute walk from here. Then I had to collect firewood so we could boil the water, making it safe enough to drink. We managed. She looked after me the best she could after my papa left us, for a time anyway."

"I'm so sorry you lived like this, Nick."

I turn on her. "Don't be so fucking patronizing. Not everyone grows up with money, you know? You think you had it bad, losing your parents, you don't know how lucky you are. I had to fucking look after my fat bitch of a mama. She got so fat she couldn't even move off the couch. I had to wash her daily, trying to turn her and wash in the folds of fat. I did that for years until I let the rats feed on her. She belittled me my whole life, blaming me for Papa leaving her, telling me day in and day out what a fucking retard I was. That I was a freak of nature, telling me I was the Devil's son, that there was something wrong with me, making me believe I was bad."

She recoils from my venom and clasps her hands over her mouth in horror. I see tears welling in her eyes. "I had no idea."

Why would she? Why would anyone? I didn't exist to anyone.

"Don't fucking pity me, Poppy. It is what it is. It's made me who I am today, a fucking survivor." I move past her and head out the front, it's the only entrance to the place. I grab my hunting knife that's next to the door as I pass it. I walk past her car and throw my bag on the ground next to it and continue walking. I never covered the traps, and who knows what's rotting in there now. I hear her follow me.

"Nick, wait up, please. I didn't mean to offend you."

I slow my pace slightly, I hear her clambering behind me then oomph, I turn to look, she's flat on her ass. I sneer at her and turn to continue toward the traps.

"You could have helped me up, you ass."

"You'll be fine," I shout back to her.

It's overgrown out here without me cutting it all back, or flattening the ground. I stumble on a fallen branch but manage to stop myself from falling flat on my face by grabbing at a tree. The last thing I want is another broken bone or sprained ankle. I hear her laugh, I turn to see her with a smirk on her face.

"Good catch, serves you right for not helping me."

I smile at her. "Not far now. I set the traps away from the cabin so the animals didn't come too close to the cabin. I used to catch all sorts out here. I dug so many holes for animals to fall into. Make sure you only walk where I walk. Some of the holes are covered to look like the ground."

"Did you actually kill them all and then chop them up to eat?"

"Yep."

"Eww, that's so gross."

Ha, if only she knew. "It's called survival, Poppy."

I come to the first of the open traps and peer down. There, lying on the ground is a deer. I watch it closely and see it's still breathing, only just. It must be starving or injured, which is why it's lying down. I'll come back and kill it in a bit after I've checked out the other traps.

"Nick, Nick, it's still alive, we need to help it. Nick?" she shouts after me. "How can you just leave it to suffer like that? It's only a baby. NICK."

I stop and turn around. "Poppy, will you be quiet, please, if you shout you will startle anything that is out here." I watch her looking into the hole.

"You poor baby, we'll help you."

Like fuck, we will. I move on toward the other trap.

"Nick, please help me get it out. We can't leave it to suffer like that."

I stop and rub my hand over my face, rubbing my now overgrown beard. I walk back, jump in the hole, lift the deer's head, and slit its throat.

Poppy, who has moved around the hole to the other side to get a clearer view, screams and starts backing up.

"Poppy, please be quiet. What if a bear suddenly appears now while I'm down here? You will be a goner for sure."

She looks at me, disgusted. "How could you do that, Nick? I thought we were going to help it? You don't need it for food."

She has no idea.

"Poppy, it was nearly dead. If we had gotten it out, it couldn't go anywhere and would just die a slow death. It wouldn't have survived. We have to be cruel to be kind."

She's still backing away with her hands over her mouth. I think she's going to puke, for fuck's sake.

I'm about to climb out of the hole when I hear her scream, again. I look to where she was, she's not there anymore. I have foot holes in the sides of the traps for me to get out of. There are only a couple because I'm tall and can then lift myself out. I get out of the hole, she's gone. I see one of my other traps which is now uncovered. Shit, she fell in. Maybe I'll just leave her there for a bit, check on the other traps. She isn't making a noise. I'll leave her. I go about checking all the others. Some smaller animals had gotten stuck and another adult deer who was dead and being eaten by rats. The fucking rats get everywhere. I hear Poppy shout. I've wandered much farther away from her, so I know she's shouting loud. I uncover the remaining traps I have. I don't have time to fill them in so I will just leave them, at least they are more visible to animals now. I head back to where I can hear Poppy, I stand at the top looking down into the hole.

"Nick, where were you? Help me, I hurt my back and my leg when I fell. I think I knocked myself out. We'll have to stay here for the night until I know it's safe to drive."

I smile on the inside. She knocked herself out, payback for knocking Primrose out, you bitch. This is just what I want, not that we were going anywhere anyway. At least she's not. This will be her final resting place, once I've finished with her.

I jump down into the hole and I try to get her to stand up but she really has hurt herself. She fell backward, straight onto her back. I try to lift her but she screams out. "Poppy, stop with the fucking screaming will you. You're going to attract more wildlife, then we'll both be screwed. Now, tell me where it hurts so I can help you."

She has tears running down her face and she's biting her tongue. I know she wants to lay into me, but I'm her only hope of getting out of here. I press the base of her spine.

"Fucking hell, Nick, that fucking hurts."

Bingo.

"Don't shout," I scold her. "So when I press here, that hurts," I say, pressing it again and she screws her mouth shut trying not to scream but glaring at me. I love it.

"Tell me, what's the pain like, Poppy." I smirk.

"Tell me what it feels like when I press, don't shout or scream, talk to me." I press again only slightly higher up, she jolts forward and goes to scream, I put my hand over her mouth. "Quiet, don't make a sound. Shhh, I can hear something. Can you hear that noise?" She goes rigid in my hold and listens. There's nothing there, I made it up so she doesn't scream again. "Tell me what you feel Poppy, when I press, describe the pain for me, I'm trying to help, I need to understand what you've done." I press again and she jolts slightly and glares at me.

"Why do you keep pressing when it fucking hurts, you sick fuck," she whispers to me. I slap her across the head, hard. She almost falls back again, but I have hold of her.

"If you want me to get you out of here, tell me what you feel. I need you to describe the pain to me," I grit out and spit in her face.

"It's like you taking that fucking knife and jamming it into my spine." She glares at me.

"That doesn't help, I wouldn't know what that felt like. Tell me if you were having a hardcore fuck, how does the pain you feel now compare to how that feels? Pretend you're on your hands and knees and I'm ramming your ass so hard with my cock, just jamming it in there as far and as tight as I can go. Would that pain feel anything like the pain you feel now?"

She's looking at me like I'm crazy. She's not far from the truth. I just need someone to tell me what pain is like. The only thing I ever feel is sensual when I'm fucking. I want to know if the pain feels anything like that. She smiles at me.

"Is that what you want to do to me, Nick. I like it rough, fast, and hard. Are you man enough for that?"

She's as sick as I am. Maybe we're meant for each other. For her to be able to do that to her own sister, yeah she's sick. Maybe I've met my match in Poppy. Maybe it is her I should be with.

"If you rammed your cock into my ass, yes, the first time would hurt, but then after that, it would be fucking amazing. The pain I feel now would be similar to that first time. I've had that done to me before, I cried then with the pain. Now are you going to help me out of here so we can go try it?" She smiles at me and licks her lips.

I let go of her and she falls to the ground on her ass. She scrunches her eyes shut but doesn't make any noise.

"I need to go and get the rope so I can pull you out from the top. That's how I get the deer and bears out, only they're usually dead when I do that. Can you stand?"

She tries to get up using her fingers in the dirt of the walls. She manages to get up on her own, she didn't cry out once, but I watched her grimace. I use the two-foot holes and then jump out. I head to the cabin to get the rope but I take my time. I pull out my cell, shit no service here, but then what did I expect. If Primrose tries to text, she'll think I'm ignoring her and no doubt start to go into a panic. I fucking miss her.

I hate being here with Poppy, not because of her looks, but because her personality is nothing compared to Primrose's. This one has a lot of evil in her. I reach her car and think about her cell. I get it out of the car and switch it off. I watched the crime programs when I was laid up with my ankle. I remember they can trace you by your cell. I never knew anything about cells, so I don't even know if the other whores who are buried out here had them. Tough shit really, I threw everything they owned in the grave with them. I doubt they could be found underground. Once hers has turned off completely, I try to twist it to break it, but it's proving difficult. I get the shovel and smash it to bits.

I grab the rope and saunter back, thinking of my next plan. We've been hostile to each other since arriving here, maybe that's what she likes. She could sense it in me all along. She said she'd like me to ram her with my cock, hard. Not that I'm going to touch her. Not in that way anyway. I look down at her in the hole. She's leaning against the side, arms crossed over her chest pushing her tits up, waiting for me. She hasn't heard me approach, I watch her for a few seconds.

"Hey, here, if I throw this down, put it around under your arms and then use those two-foot holes to help. so I can then pull you up trying not to hurt your back. It's the only way to get you out, I'm afraid."

She's startled hearing my voice, she pushes off the wall, she seems okay. I think she was just a bit shook up, and yes, hurt her back but not that bad. I throw the rope and she ties the loop around her body, then does as I told her. I manage to grab her hand and then pull her right up out of the hole, it was easy, she doesn't weigh anything near a deer or bear.

"Thank you, Nick, you were gone for ages, I thought you were going to leave me there."

I shrug. "Nope, just couldn't find the rope."

We walk back to the cabin slowly.

"Were there any other animals in your traps?"

"Just a dead deer being eaten by the rats, and a few small animals, the rabbits can burrow out of there themselves. I don't have anything here to eat. With us staying the night, I'll go back for the baby deer before the rats get it. You up for a bit of deer?"

She screws up her nose. "Please don't let me see you slice and dice it. I can eat it once it's cooked, but the other just grosses me out."

I laugh. "What do you think happens to all the cows for steak or pigs for pork? They don't just die on their own and jump into the flames. They have to be killed and prepped for human consumption."

"I know, but you don't think about that when you're eating them."

She seems to be walking okay, she wasn't that badly hurt in the fall. She was lucky she didn't break anything. It's at least ten feet deep in that particular hole, it's a long way to fall.

Upon entering the cabin, she looks around. "Where do you sit?" Ah yeah, I burned the couch after Mama died, it was not fit to be used.

"On the floor."

She looks around, I'm not sure what she's looking for.

"Have you seen my purse? Oh, maybe I left it in the car." She goes outside, I follow her. I hope she doesn't look for her cell. She gets her purse and pulls out some tissues. "I need to pee, I don't think you have any toilet paper in there."

I shake my head and then head off to get the deer.

I'm chopping away at the deer on my butcher's block of wood at the side of the cabin, putting the meat we need for tonight and maybe tomorrow in a bowl of cold water I fetched from the creek. Just to clean it. I then light a fire and start to cook the deer. We eat the meat, or venison, as she tells me it would be called in a restaurant, and she's shocked me. She's taken to the cabin and the way to eat the food better than I thought she would. Her back seems to be okay, she's not moaned about it hurting, she winces now and then.

"Nick?"

I don't look at her as I continue chewing my meat. "What?"

She's turned toward me. "Are you ever going to tell me how you met Primrose all those years ago?"

I wish she would fucking drop this already. I shake my head. "Nope, that's for her to tell. Although she's closed up a bit from the attack." I watch her and she hangs her head. I wonder if she will admit to the attack.

"Was she badly hurt? I feel so terrible."

I look her in the eye. "Why do you feel terrible?"

She looks at me, I can see the turmoil. Should she admit it or lie. "Just because I had no idea, I did feel something weird inside me but didn't know what it was, I also didn't get to see her before I left."

Bullshit.

"Yes she was bad, think she had broken ribs but she refused to go to the hospital. Said she hated them. She was black and blue and her face was all swollen, like a fucking balloon. Whoever did it, really did a number on her. Left her for dead. The funny thing is though, it had to be personal because nothing was taken and there was no sign of a break-in, she knew her attacker."

I watch her face as I say this. I see the guilt written all over it, and she can't look at me. I've had enough of all this shit. I just want to get this over with and then I can get back to Primrose.

"So, you gonna fuck me or what?"

I nearly choke on my last piece of meat. I cough and take a swig of the water from the water bottle we had in the car.

"Fucking hell, Poppy, are you that desperate? Can't you fucking wait until I've finished eating?"

She doesn't care, she just shrugs. "I just want your cock rammed into me, ever since you asked me about it in the hole, I want you in all my holes."

She's a fucking whore. There is no way I will touch her. I smile. "God girl, am I that irresistible?"

She nods and licks her lips. She starts to crawl toward me on all fours. Fuck.

"NO," I say sternly and she stops. "Go into my room and wait on the bed. I'm gonna take my time with you, I want to play. You up for that?"

She nods, closes her eyes and licks her lips. She stands up and walks right up to me, pressing her thighs into my face. My forehead pressed against her pussy. I scream inside for her to move, but I have to play it cool.

"You sure you're up for it, Pops, 'cause I want to give it to you good and hard, I'm gonna tie you up, tell me if you don't want to play and we don't go any further."

She starts to rub herself on my face. I cringe, closing my eyes.

"Yes Nick, I'm up for anything you're willing to give me."

"My room, now," I growl at her.

I get some loose rope and take it into my room. Fucking hell, she's naked on my shitty bed, just waiting for me. I saunter over to her, taking off my tee. I watch her eyes go wide as she takes in my physique. This is all she will get the pleasure of seeing, I hate that she's seeing this much. I straddle her on the bed, I take one hand at a time tying each one to the headboard. It's a rickety old wooden thing, I don't think it would stand me fucking anyone on it. I hope the headboard doesn't break from her trying to get free once I start the torture.

"Ow, Nick, that's tight. You're going to cut off my circulation if you're not careful."

I just smile at her.

I want to tie her ankles up as well, just so she can't kick at me. I take each one and tie them tight to the end of the bedposts. I stand there looking at her naked and tied up. She disgusts me. She thinks I want her, she's trying to look sultry, pouting and licking her lips, it's not working. All I can see is Primrose lifeless on the floor, thinking she was dead. It's then I pull out my hunting knife from my back pocket, her eyes go as wide as saucers when she notices what I have in my hand.

"Nick, what's that for?"

I just smile at her. "You'll see." I place the knife on the floor and I move to the corner of the room and pull out a pair of dirty old jeans, just in case there's a lot of blood, then I can get rid of these. "I'll be right back." I don't want her to see me naked, I change into them in the tiny bathroom leaving my clean ones there ready to put on when I'm finished with her.

I walk back into my bedroom, she's watching me. I pick up the knife and I climb on top of her but facing her feet. I take the knife and I gently, without cutting her, start to run the tip down her shins to her feet. I repeat this on both legs for a few strokes.

"Oh, Nick, that tickles." She tries to wriggle.

"Keep as still as you can, Pops, or I'll end up cutting you." I repeat the actions a few times until she relaxes, then with the point of the blade, I start to make little stabbing motions.

"Careful Nick, that's nice but hurts as well."

"Shhhh."

I continue doing this and then move the blade to the soles of her feet. I start at the heel putting the point there and I press in, she flinches. I then move the blade up to her toes slicing her sole open. I repeat this on the other foot. She has no idea I've sliced, she thinks the blade has just stroked like I did on her shins. They're not deep cuts, but enough if she was to stand on her feet it would hurt. I lean over and watch as the blood pools out of the cuts then starts to drip down onto the bed. I smile to myself.

"Nick, come on, enough with the pain thing. Fuck me already."

I climb off her and stand, looking down into her face. "Patience," I say in a whisper, leaning down next to her ear. I then straddle her again, but facing her this time so she can see me. I move up so my crotch is practically on her face, teasing her, but so I can lean over and do the same thing on her arms and hands. I kneel up and she tries to bite my cock, he's not even hard. The stupid bitch hasn't even realized I'm not aroused. I take the point and I run it up and down her forearms as I did on her shins. She starts to squirm.

"Nick, come on. Why don't you get your cock out and I could be sucking while you're doing this."

I ignore her, she wiggles her arms again. "Poppy, you will end up cut if you keep doing that."

She stops moving. "Nick, this is boring. It's not even turning me on. Just give me your cock, will you?"

I ignore her and continue with the knife. I get to her palms, which I open up. I start tapping with the point, hard enough that it leaves indents on her palms.

"Ow, Nick. I don't like this, please stop."

I continue, she's moving her hands and the headboard starts creaking. I really hope it doesn't give way, it's old and too much movement, I think it would break. With her wriggling, the knife sticks in her palm,

"OUCH!" she shouts, she felt that.

The tip is still in, so I drag it down toward the rope at her wrists so it cuts from her palm to the end of her hand.

"What the fuck, Nick, you're cutting me for real."

She starts thrusting up with her body. I sit back down on her chest, flattening her tits. I'm too big for her to throw off. I can still lean over her head and do the same with the other hand.

I watch as the blood comes oozing out of the cuts, these are much deeper than on her feet. A lot of blood is running down and soaking into the ropes.

"What does that feel like, Poppy? Can you feel it, can you feel the blood coming out?"

She's trying to buck me off, but she's only wearing herself out. She screams so loud I punch her in the mouth to shut her up.

"I can't stand the fucking noise, you stupid bitch. Just answer my questions. How does it feel, try and describe the pain to me. Can you feel it now, or is it going numb?"

She stops moving, her lip is split and blood is coming out of it, she licks her lips and tastes the blood. I want a taste.

I lean into her face. "I wonder if your blood tastes the same as your pappy's?" I see the moment she realizes what I just said, I lick her lip just for a taste. "Yep, just the same metallic taste." Her eyes are wide, I grin down at her.

"You were there?"

I smile and nod.

"I knew you had something to do with it. Why has that bitch protected you all this time?"

I sit up and play with the tip of the knife above her face. I shrug. "Because we love each other."

She's trying to process everything I'm saying. I can see the confusion on her face. I stab her cheek with the point of the knife.

"Now are you going to tell me what the pain feels like? So many before you could never tell me. You see, I can't feel pain. In fact, I can't feel anything apart from when I'm fucking and have an orgasm, now that, I do feel." I smile.

I take the point and move it to her mouth. I put it at the very edge of her open mouth and I start to pull toward her cheek. I see the skin ripping as I pull it up, she tries to scream. I stop. "Tell me what it feels like and I might stop." I can see the blood on the new cut seeping out and running into her mouth.

"You tell me what you did to my parents, I'll tell you what it feels like."

I take the blade and do the same on the other side of her mouth. Now she looks like she has a permanent smile. "Nope, it doesn't work like that. I can just continue cutting until you start telling me. I need you to be descriptive."

She attempts to lick the sides of her mouth where the cuts are, she flinches, it must hurt. They are only little cuts, nothing bad.

"It stings, but the adrenaline is stopping it from being unbearable. The adrenaline is a high, similar to an orgasm, it's euphoric, it kind of stimulates your insides, like getting your cock sucked. Do you feel that?"

I smile. "Ah yes, very much so. It's one of the first times I ever felt anything. Usually, when someone touches, say my hand or arm, I don't feel it. I can cut myself and not even know, I've done that so many times. I've always been fascinated with pain, and how it feels. I asked your pappy to describe it when he was taking his last breaths, he couldn't. All the others after him have said it's hard to describe unless you've felt anything like it. I haven't, you see."

She closes her eyes, she's crying, I can see the tears seeping out of the corners of them. I take the tip of the knife and lift her eyelid with it.

"Look at me. Do you know the pain you caused your sister? She's the love of my life and always has been. You hurting her makes me so fucking mad, like crazy fucking mad. Do you hear me, Poppy? Ever since that day, I've known she was different. I knew then I loved her, somehow at only ten years old, I knew. It's a good thing she's deaf. I didn't know that back then, but if she wasn't, well, she would have heard me asking your pappy how the pain felt. Your mama was already dead by the way, from the crash, just so you know. I told Primrose that, she was relieved your mama didn't suffer." I still have her eyelid held by the knife, she's stiff trying not to move.

"Anyway, you're going to be my last one. I'm going to have a life with Primrose. You will just disappear." I can see she's in shock.

"How many before me?" she manages to breathe out.

I just shrug. "A few, I didn't keep count. I'll introduce you to them when I bury you with some of them."

I raise myself off her and move down to her feet. I take her little toe and I slice it right off.

She screams out, a bloodcurdling scream. She starts to buck on the bed.

"You fucking sick fucking son of a bitch. That fucking hurts."

"Now that's what I want to hear. It's music to my fucking ears." She's crying hard. I then walk around to her and place her toe on her chest. I then start playing with a nipple with the tip of the knife. She tries to buck, she's moving her hands and the headboard is about to break by the sounds of it.

"Keep still, you continue moving like that and I'm likely to slice your nipple off, or stab you."

She stills again.

"Can you describe how this feels?"

I take the nipple with one hand and start to stab it with the knife. I accidentally, well maybe not accidentally, slice into the nipple. It's still attached, just. She screams another bloodcurdling scream.

"You deserve this and more if I'm honest. You've put Primrose through hell her entire life. Feeling sorry for yourself and taking it all out on her. You left her for dead." I lean into her face. "She told me you attacked her. You left her heartbroken. Her own fucking sister leaving her for dead. When you hurt her, you hurt me, so to speak. There is no us, Poppy, there never will be. I only stayed close to you in hopes of meeting Primrose after all these years. I was fascinated with her back then. She was in this horrific car accident and she never even got a scratch on her. How could that be? We were meant to be, her and I, there is something so special about her."

She's crying and has her eyes shut, I get right into her face.

"Boo!" I shout, she opens her eyes. "Are you listening to me? I hope you are."

She nods slightly. "She had cuts and a broken leg. She was hurt in the accident."

I shake my head. "Actually you're wrong. She never had a scratch on her from the accident. The cuts were when I got her free, the car was on its roof, you see, so she landed on her head when I released the seatbelt. Then the car was about to explode, I had to drag her away from it. I saved her life. The blast got us both. We both ended up with a broken leg and cuts from it. So you see, we are destined to be together. It was meant to be."

She looks confused. "You saved her life, but not my pappy's?"

"No, he was practically dead when I got to the car, he was just taking his last breaths. It was no use. In fact, he took his last breath as I was looking at Primrose. It made me so mad I missed it, but then looking at her soothed me. I had to get her out. There was nothing that could be done for the others."

She opens her eyes and looks right into mine. "All this time I blamed her, I said it was all her fault they died, now you're telling me they were dead anyway. How did the accident happen? Did you see how it happened?"

I nod my head and smile. "I did it. If you're still in the land of the living when I come back, I'll finish the story for you."

With that, I move away and out of the room. I need to leave her there for a while, she'll be weaker when I get back, hopefully, from the blood loss. I need to get rid of her car. I can't use it, Primrose or Cassy would know, and I don't have a license. As I'm not coming back here, one of my traps would be big enough to roll it into, I'll just cover it a bit with the mound of dirt out there.

Standing outside the cabin for some fresh air, I think about getting back to Primrose. I might as well get this over with now, then I can get on the road. I miss her so fucking much. I think I feel sorrow because I miss her, I feel like my heart has this aching, it's weird because I don't feel any pain just like a yearning, I think. Dare I even dream of a life with Primrose? All these years I've waited for her, now she loves me as much as I love her. What are the fucking chances of that? My life up to meeting her again was just an existence, can I even have a better life? Am I worthy of a better life? The things I've done, I'm not so sure. What I do know is that I would never hurt her. I couldn't, no matter what.

I sit on the wooden log and think about Primrose. I know she was hurt when I left, but I had to do this. I was going out of my mind with anger at the fact that Poppy had left her for dead when I'd only just found her. It was festering in me, and I needed to leave. I was going to explode on who knows who. I couldn't have Poppy coming back and starting this shit all over again. She had pure hate for Primrose, all based on jealousy. If I get rid of her once and for all, Primrose will be okay. She won't have to worry and she won't have to mourn another loss, unless the body is found of course. I need to just finish Poppy, she's not giving me any answers to my questions about pain apart from what I've been told before. She's suffered now. Time to just finish this.

Twenty

Blaine

I SIT ON THE FLOOR WITH MY BACK TO THE BED READY TO TELL HER how I did it. She might as well know, she'll be dead soon enough. I hear the bed moving and her trying to wiggle free.

"Stop moving, Pops, and I'll tell you how I did it."

She doesn't, the next thing I know I'm face-planting on the floor. What the fuck. I turn around and see she broke the headboard, with the wood from it she knocked me over the head, with some force I might add, and here I was thinking she'd be getting weaker by now. I didn't feel a thing but then I wouldn't.

I start to get up, trying to avoid her attempts at swinging the piece of wood in my direction. She's still tied by her feet so she isn't going anywhere. She tries to lash out at me over and over with the wood, but she misses me apart from the one time she got me in the side with it. I manage to take the wood out of her grasp, I punch her in the face again, a few times, and I tie her hands together.

"Aww Pops, I was going to tell you the story. I guess now it doesn't matter. You can go to hell knowing your sister is innocent. She never did anything wrong that day and you've blamed her all your pathetic life. How you think she could have had anything to do with it, I don't know, but it was all on me."

She screams, "Go to hell yourself, you sick fuck."

I laugh right in her face, she spits in mine. I wipe the drool away, it's saliva mixed with blood. I take the piece of wood and I hit her over the head with it again and again. I watch her body jerking as she starts to lose consciousness. I watch the blood from her mouth and nose dripping down her face. I take the knife and I stab her in the stomach. Her body is twitching but I've had enough of this now. Time to bury her.

I drive her car to the edge of my biggest hole, it took me fucking hours upon hours to dig this hole, it's the one with the dead deer and all the rats. I park right at the edge then get out and push it over. It lands on its front, upright. I could still bury it like this, the hole is big enough but I prefer it to be flat on the bottom. I sit on the edge and I push it with my feet, it rocks at first, it's probably the deer stopping it. I get up and find a tree branch, one that's thick and long, I push the car over using that as a lever. The car falls on its roof, I'll come back and cover this up after I've put her in with the others.

I take the shovel and start to dig where the others are buried. It's the one burial site with them all on top of each other, with Mama on the bottom. There should be enough room to put Poppy in. It doesn't take me long to reach the last body. I feel funny, the sun's blaring down on me, it's never bothered me before, my vision keeps blurring. Maybe I'm dehydrated. I'll get some water from that bottle we had earlier when I get her body.

Picking her up and carrying her to the burial site isn't difficult, but I nearly stumble a few times. She's not heavy. She's not dead either, I can see her chest rising and she looks a mess. Her face looks as bad as Primrose's did after she left her for dead. It's swelling up and her forehead has a lot of nasty cuts. I put the toe in her mouth, I hope she chokes on it if she wakes up, but then the dirt will do that. I wrap her in the cover that was on the bed, it was covered in her blood anyway. I throw her into the hole. She lands face down on the last decaying body.

I start to cover her with all the dirt. It's quite a shallow grave for her. Good thing she's the last one. With any luck, a bear or something will sniff her out, dig her up and eat her, but then that would expose the grave. I don't give a shit really, no one knew we lived here. I head to where the car is and I just throw some dirt into the hole and then I throw on lots of tree branches and debris I find lying around the place. I even grab my bed and throw that in. It just looks like a dumping ground and if any animal falls in they should be able to climb out easy enough. All the time I'm doing this, I feel like closing my eyes, I feel tired, I feel like I might keel over at any point. I don't know what's wrong with me, I've never been like this before. Even with the sun beating down on me, I've always been okay with it.

I get more water from the creek to boil. I'll have some of that and a wash before I set off, back on the road to Primrose. I'll head to the nearest town where I can get on a bus to San Francisco, then head to Primrose's from there.

While washing, I noticed blood on my hands. I assume it's from carrying Poppy. I look all over my body. It's then I see a small hole in my side. How the fuck I got that, I don't know. It's small but constantly bleeding. That's why the jeans I wore had a lot of blood on them, which I just thought was from Poppy. I also felt a cut at the back of my head while washing it and again some blood, but I think that one has stopped bleeding. I patch the small hole on my side as best I can with a needle and thread. I used to watch Mama doing this all the time, I've had to do it countless times myself since. I then stick a bandage over it. Hopefully, that will stop it.

It's late and dark, certainly not ideal to be walking to a town this late on these roads in the hills with no streetlights or paths, and lots of wildlife around here. I'm still very tired, I fall at one point. What the fuck, I must have tripped on a rock. I look at my hands to make sure there's no blood, they seem okay from what I can tell. I feel like I've been walking for hours. But when I look at my cell, it's only been just under two hours. Fuck, I'm never gonna get anywhere at this rate. I feel like I'm walking slowly and sometimes it feels like I'm dragging my feet. I think I may get a room at the first motel I come across and have a rest. I can get a bus later on.

Three hours later, I come across a small town with a motel. I get a room and I just throw myself on the bed. I hear knocking, who the fuck is knocking at my door at this time? I slowly open my eyes and the sun is shining brightly through the window. Fuck, I didn't shut the curtains. There's a knock again. I get off the bed, I stumble, I feel off-balance but I manage to get to the door. It's one of the cleaners.

"Sorry, I'm sleeping. Been a long night. No need to clean. I'll be leaving later today."

She just looks at me like I'm talking a different language. I shoo her away with my hands. Maybe she's foreign and doesn't understand me. I put my hands to the side of my head and show her sleeping. She shrugs and leaves. I slam the door shut, take a piss then flop back down on the bed.

There's another knock, for fuck's sake I told her to leave. Another knock, I open my eyes and realize the room is in complete darkness. Fuck, I need to get going. I get to the door and there's a man standing there.

"Yeah?" I say.

"You were supposed to leave earlier. You need to pay for a night's stay, you only paid for a few hours."

I pull out some money from my jeans pocket and hand him some bills. He just takes it, doesn't even look. I shut the door and sit on the bed. I put my head in my hands. I don't know what the fuck is wrong with me. I just want to sleep. I check the wound on my side. It's bled through the bandage but I think it's okay, it doesn't look like a lot of blood. Just a bit more sleep and I'll get the next bus to where ever the fuck it takes me as long as it's in the same direction as Primrose.

I wake up needing to piss again. I pry my eyes open and the fucking sun is shining right in at me again. What the fuck. I think I must have slept for a day. I check my cell for the time and it's eleven-thirty in the morning. I take a leak and jump in the shower. Everything is taking me so long to do. I wonder if I have some kind of bug. I've never had a sickness in my life, there's a first time for everything I suppose. My main focus is just getting to Primrose. I remember giving a guy at the door money. I look in the pocket of the jeans I just took off and all my money's gone. Fucking thief, he stole all my money. Luckily, I have more in my bag. But it's the last of what I have. I hope it's enough for the bus. I head out and see the guy standing at the office door.

"Hey you, how much did you take off me?"

He shrugs. "Just what you gave me, man. Covered your stay and a tip. You handed it to me. I wasn't gonna argue. You seemed to be out of it though. Must have been some rocking weed you took there. If you have any more, I'd be willing to pay good money."

What the fuck is he talking about? "I don't do drugs, I was just tired."

He scoffs and snorts then turns away from me, I hear him say, "Yeah right, selfish prick."

If I didn't feel this tired, I'd knock him the fuck out.

"Where's the bus for outta town?" I ask him to point me in the direction. I head off that way.

I'm on a bus to who knows where. I asked the driver to let me off as close to San Fran as he was going. He said he would holla at my stop. I get dropped off at some town somewhere, I have no idea where. I ask them where to get the bus to Piedmont, Oakland at the ticket office. I remembered where Primrose lived, luckily, he took the last of my money and gave me a ticket right to Piedmont. Thank fuck for that. I asked this driver to do the same and let me know when we got there. I would work out the way to Primrose's from there. I slept the whole time on the last bus and no doubt will on this one.

I've been traveling all day. I've also slept most of that time. I still have no idea why, and why I keep stumbling. People seem to be giving me a wide berth. I think I'm heading in the right direction, I seem to remember some of these bars, yes it is.

Some guy asks me for a light. "I don't fucking smoke." What did I just say? It sounded nothing like what I thought I said. He looks at me weird. I sneer at him, warning him off from giving me any shit. I continue past him.

"Hey dude, you might wanna ease off the drinking and drugs for a bit. Look at you, you can't even walk straight, never mind slurring, you dumb ass."

I try to turn to look at him and the next thing I know I'm on my ass on the sidewalk. I hear him laughing at me, the fucking ass wipe. I get up but it takes a lot of effort. I look to see what made me fall, I don't see anything. I continue down the street, each step seems to take me forever. I look down at my feet and focus on putting one in front of the other. It's like my boots are made of lead, they feel really heavy. I keep bumping into people, who then just curse me.

I somehow manage to make it to Primrose's street, it's taken me so long to get here. I focus on getting to her house. I head up the steps but have to bend over using my hands to climb them, I knock on the door. I wait. I sit on my ass with my back against the door and I wait. I knock again, banging my head behind me, and I wait. She's not fucking home and I shouldn't have done that with my head. Now I'm having trouble seeing at all. Shit. Where is she? I then start to laugh to myself. I'm banging on the door at a deaf woman's house. No wonder she's not answering. I guess I'll just stay here and wait until she opens the door.

"Blaine, Blaine, hey, Blaine, look at me. Can you hear me, Blaine?"

Wait, it's her, she's here but I can't open my eyes. I want to look at her, why can't I open my fucking eyes so I can see my angel.

"Blaine, what's wrong? Have you taken anything? Blaine."

I try to open them again. I tell her no but I'm not sure I spoke the word or if I just thought it. I can hear her clearly, I want to see her. I want to see my Primrose so badly.

"Blaine, oh god, Blaine, you're bleeding. What happened?"

Bleeding, why would I be bleeding? No one's done anything to me that I know of. I didn't do anything that I know of. Oh, wait, I fell a few times, maybe it's something to do with that.

I feel myself moving, I try to open my eyes. Someone opens one of my eyes and shines a light in it, then the other. *He's going to crash, we need him on the bus ASAP, looks like he's hemorrhaging, blood in the eyes.* I'm being moved a lot but I have no idea why. I can hear things going on, but I keep drifting in and out.

"Blaine, oh baby, can you hear me? Blaine, it's Primrose, you came back to me, baby."

I know I came back, that's what kept me going, getting back to you. I feel like I'm talking to her, but I'm not sure she's seeing me.

"Blaine, please come back to me. I love you, Blaine. I can't lose you now."

I'm not going anywhere, what the fuck is she talking about? I didn't wait for nearly twenty fucking years for her to then throw it away. I try to open my eyes. All I can hear is beeping all the fucking time and it's driving me insane. I have no idea what's going on. I'm on the move again.

Twenty-One

Primrose

I'VE BEEN MOVING AT A SNAIL'S PACE EVER SINCE SHE ATTACKED me. Then Blaine running off as he did, I just wanted to hide away from the world. I didn't leave the house for a couple of days. Just sat wallowing in self-pity and sketching Blaine. I haven't been into work since she attacked me, they know what happened, but today I thought to hell with it, I'm not letting her or him ruin my life. I just have to hope he finds his way back to me as he promised, but I don't know him, not really, having the most amazing orgasms of my life does not mean I know him. My feelings for him are the strongest I've ever had. I truly love him. It's a deeply embedded love I must have harbored all these years. How could I know that, from being seven? Whatever it is, it's breaking my heart that I don't know if he will return or not.

I went into work today, the first time out, it was hard, everyone asking how I was. I haven't told anyone it was my sister that attacked me. I feel ashamed and embarrassed. It was a long day, I didn't drive as I still don't feel right, my ribs are still healing. I took the bus there and I'm just on my way home now. I get off at the top of the high street and go into the mini-mart to get some bits for home. I can't carry too much, again the ribs hurt.

I'm just approaching my house and getting my keys out when I look up, I can't believe he's here. He's sitting on my top step, resting against the door. He looks terrible, so pale. He looks like he's slumped, rather than just resting. His eyes are closed. He hasn't heard me approach. God, any-one could have approached him. He doesn't have his bag with him either, that's strange. I rush up the steps and dropping my bag of groceries, I kneel in front of him.

"Blaine, Blaine," I say, stroking his face. He's cold. I feel his forehead and it's the same. It's getting cool out here now. "Blaine, Blaine, hey, Blaine, look at me. Can you hear me, Blaine?" Nothing, he's not responding to me at all. I feel his wrist, he has a pulse, but it's weak. I feel his chest, he's breathing, although it's a bit ragged. "Blaine, what's wrong? Have you taken anything? Blaine." It looks like he's trying to say something, I see his mouth moving slightly, it looks like he's saying *my angel* but he's barely moving his lips enough for me to read. I search his body and there's blood under his jacket on his white tee. "Blaine, oh god, Blaine, you're bleeding. What happened?"

I get my cell out of my pocket and text 911. This is a new service I read about for the deaf, but it only works in certain areas. I never looked into it enough, I never thought I would need it. I watch my cell and nothing happens. I have no choice, I need to call them.

I dial 911, I wait a few seconds then say, "Hello, I'm deaf, I cannot hear you, I need an ambulance, it's urgent." I give them my address very slowly, then I hang up.

There isn't anything else I can do at this point. I sit beside him and I pull him onto my lap, I stroke his head and his face. I watch him very carefully, terrified in case he stops breathing. If he was intoxicated, he would still be semi-awake, but he's unconscious.

"Please don't leave me, baby. You came back to me. You can't leave me now. Help is coming. I love you, baby." I lean down and kiss his cold head. He's freezing. I try to keep him warm by carefully cuddling him. Before I know it, I see paramedics running up the steps toward us.

"Did you call 911. ma'am?" One of them bends to my level so I can read his lips.

"Yes, I'm deaf, please help him, I don't know what's wrong with him. I found him here when I came home from work."

One of the paramedics very gently removes Blaine from my hold and lays him down in front of me and tries to examine him, the other crouches in front of me.

"Do you know him?"

"Yes, he's my friend. Blaine."

"Okay, we're going to take good care of him."

I watch the other paramedic very carefully for any telltale signs on his face. I spot the concern as soon as he looks into Blaine's eyes. He turns to the other paramedic and tells him they need to move him quickly. He's hemorrhaging. My eyes fly open, I look to the one crouched in front of me.

"Do you want to come with us in the ambulance to the hospital? You will need to provide his details once we get there. Does he have insurance?"

I have no idea but I would say no. "No, I don't think he does, but it doesn't matter where you take him, I can cover the costs, just take him to the best hospital, please."

He nods at me and they both get Blaine onto a gurney and into the ambulance with me in tow.

It's not long and we're at the Kaiser Foundation Hospital. I hate this place so much. This is where I spent a lot of time after the accident. That doesn't matter now. Blaine matters. I let them take him inside and follow close behind. I'm stopped at the doors to the emergency room by a nurse. She must have been calling me and ended up grabbing my arm to stop me from going through the doors. I swing around to her, I must look annoyed.

"Sorry, I said you can't go in there. It's for patients who need emergency care only."

"I'm deaf." It's all I need to sign. I see the usual look of sympathy, the one I get from everyone I tell.

She takes me over to the administration desk and I have to give her details about Blaine. There's nothing I can tell her except his first name. I don't even know his last name, his date of birth or anything. I tell her we've only been friends for a couple of weeks, just getting to know each other. I have to tell her what I know about finding him. I give her my credit card to pay for anything that needs paying for. I tell her I don't care what it costs. I don't, just as long as they bring him back to me.

I'm shown to a family room where I have to wait for any information. I send a text to Aunt Cassy and let her know where I am and what's happened. She arrives sometime later with Uncle Trevor. There's nothing I can tell them. I'm waiting for any information. It's taking so long. Uncle Trevor goes to get something to eat and some coffee for us. I can't eat anything, not yet. I need to know what's going on. Just then a doctor comes into the room. Everyone in the waiting room looks at him, he looks at his clipboard, I watch his mouth, just waiting.

"Ms. Tomlinson," he says.

I shoot up from my seat immediately. I rush over to him. He turns his back and starts to walk out. I look confused, I turn to Aunt Cassy frowning, she signs to me to follow him and I turn quickly but he's back in the door facing me this time.

"Sorry, he says to my face, I didn't realize." He saw Aunt Cassy sign to me. I follow him to another room. I don't like this.

"Ms. Tomlinson, it's not good news."

Oh my god. "He's dead, isn't he?"

I bury my head in my hands not waiting for the doctor to speak, I cry. I feel him gently tug on my wrist for me to remove my hands.

He's shaking his head. "No, Ms. Tomlinson, but he is critical. It appears Blaine has been hit on the back of the head, or he fell and banged his head, hard. There is a deep cut, but that isn't the problem. The problem is he has a bleed on the brain from the head injury. We've had to operate to try to relieve the pressure from the bleed. Do you know how he sustained the injury?"

I have my hands over my mouth and tears are streaming down my face. "I don't know. I found him at home like that. He's been away for a few days."

He looks at me sympathetically. "He's in ICU, we need to monitor him, he's classed as critical care and needs someone with him at all times. With any bleed on the brain, it can be life-threatening, even if he recovers, there's a chance of being brain-damaged. It depends on how hard he was hit. Looking at it, we would say it was very hard. Once we completely stop the bleed and the pressure subsides, we will know more. There is also a wound on his side which looks infected. We're treating this with antibiotics to try to clear up the infection. It looks like a puncture hole, but it's quite deep and someone had actually tried to suture it up, but not very well. If you would like, I can take you to his room."

I get up and nod. I can't walk fast enough to get there. I just need to see him and see he's okay.

I follow the doctor into his room and see him lying there with tubes and monitors everywhere. He's laying still, his head is bandaged up and in some kind of brace. I cry when I approach his bed. I put my hand under his, not being able to hold it with the cannula at the top. Oh god, he looks terrible.

The doctor taps my shoulder to speak to me. "Don't be afraid of all the tubes and monitors, Ms. Tomlinson. The next seventy-two hours will be critical. This is Nurse Cook, she and Nurse Hilton will be monitoring him at all times. You're welcome to sit with him, but only one visitor allowed, please. They say it does a patient good if someone sits and talks to them."

I nod at him and the nurse sitting in the corner behind a table. I didn't even notice her when I walked in. The doctor goes over to her and looks at the charts and monitors. I watch Blaine.

"Blaine, baby, it's me, Primrose. Please don't leave me. I love you, Blaine," I whisper in his ear.

I told Aunt Cassy and Uncle Trevor what was going on and told them to leave, there was no use in them hanging around for me. I wanted to stay with Blaine until they kicked me out. Nurse Cook has been amazing, she had coffee and sandwiches brought in for me so I could stay sitting by Blaine's side. I sat talking to him until I fell asleep on the chair next to him with my hand under his. I feel someone shake me and startle awake. It's chaos when I open my eyes, I have to think where I am for a second then someone is trying to lift me under my arm. I see a nurse.

"You have to leave, Ms. Tomlinson."

I look around and the room is full of people attending to Blaine. "What's happening?" I ask.

"We need to rush him back to the operating room. Please wait in the family room and someone will come and speak to you soon."

I nod, I'm in a daze, watching the commotion as they wheel Blaine out of the room. I head to the family room on autopilot, then I just sit there trying to process this whole thing. I look at my cell and it's three-forty a.m. I curl up on a chair and wait.

I must have just closed my eyes when I suddenly feel a hand on my shoulder. I startle awake, it's a different doctor than the one I saw earlier.

"Are you Ms. Tomlinson?" she asks.

I nod, I must look startled. She places her hand on my mine.

" It's okay," she says, with a slightly pitying look on her face that I don't like. "As you know, we had to rush Blaine back to the operating room. The bleed hadn't stopped and was putting more pressure on his brain. The surgery has taken some time but we are confident we have now stopped the bleed." I sigh out with relief. "He's still critical, and still needs monitoring non-stop, but he's back in his room. You can see him if you like but only for a few minutes. I'm sorry, we need to keep the room free, just in case there's another bleed. You can come back later this evening. I can give you a mobile number you can text for updates today if that helps."

I don't want to leave, I want to stay here so I can be near him. "Okay," I say reluctantly.

We head back to his room and he looks just how he did when I was with him earlier. I don't even know what time it is. I look at my cell and it's 9:33 a.m. He must have been in the operating room for a good while, at least a few hours.

I stand by his side again and lean down to his ear. "Blaine, baby. You can do this. You're strong, you can come back to me, baby. I'll be right here waiting for you." I kiss his cheek, and linger there for a few seconds longer, with my tears falling onto his face. I gently wipe them away. "I love you, baby."

At home, I go out of my mind. I try to do some work, but it's no use. Instead, I sketch Blaine. It's the one thing that has always grounded me, all these years. I sketch him lying in his hospital bed with his head bandaged. My Blaine. I hope he comes back to me. I try to get some sleep but find it difficult. I just can't wait to get back to the hospital.

When I enter his room, he's just the same as when I left him this morning. Nurse Cook says there is no change. They induced a coma to let his body heal. They'll try in a few days to bring him out of it if there are no more complications. I stay by his bedside each day, only returning home in the evenings. Each day they say 'we'll give it another day before trying to bring him out of the coma.' Each day I go in and pray this will be the day. Work has been amazing, they have let me have as long as I need off and will just delay any projects they need me to take on.

It's been nearly four weeks, Blaine has been in a coma all this time. The bleed stopped thankfully, but they wanted to give him the extra time, especially with fighting the infection he has on his side. I've been talking to him every day, telling him about all the places I've visited, and read books to him. Aunt Cassy and Uncle Trevor have been to sit with him a few times, even though they hardly know him, but they know how much he means to me. I told Aunt Cassy I'm in love with him. She was a little concerned because I don't know anything about him, or where he's come from, but I told her I don't care. You can't help who you fall in love with. She hugged me.

Today they're going to bring him out of his coma and do some tests to see if his brain responds. Aunt Cassy has just arrived, I think to give me some moral support. I'm so scared for him. We sit beside him as they do what has to be done, early indications showed there was some brain activity which is why they decided to bring him out of it today. I stand up and hold his hand, talking to him the whole time.

He's out of the coma, his eyes flutter. Nurse Cook smiles and nods at me, that's a good sign. He doesn't open his eyes. The doctor bends down and talks to him, he says something. I see his lips move, they look confused but I could tell what he said.

"Aunt Cassy, he just said my name, he said Prim." I cry, the doctor smiles.

"That's a good sign, Ms. Tomlinson. If he said your name, he remembers you." I sigh with relief. "It doesn't mean he's out of the woods. He could have memory loss or still have problems with his brain."

I stay for the rest of the day. He doesn't wake up but they said that was normal. I don't want to leave but I have to. I'm not a relation, I'm not allowed to stay over.

It's been a few days and he hasn't woken up fully yet. I keep panicking about it thinking there is something wrong, they assure me he will wake up in his own time. He's been fluttering his eyelids as though dreaming and he's moved his fingers. At one point, while I was sitting with him, his arm flew out nearly ripping the drip from his arm that has been keeping him hydrated, it made me jump.

I'm on my way to see him but it's later than normal, there was an accident which closed the roads and I've been stuck in traffic for what feels like hours. Finally, I arrive and I'm walking into the ICU past the nurse's station when I see one say to the other, "She changed quickly" as she then looks at me and smiles. I found it a bit odd, but maybe she wasn't talking about me in particular. I walk into Blaine's room and smile at Nurse Cook sitting in her corner.

She looks a little puzzled and says, "That was quick."

I frown at her, looking confused, she just motions to my body. I look to Blaine in the bed and forget about the nurse. I lean over him, kiss him like usual. I linger a little longer than normal, so relieved to see him. I pull back to look at his face and his eyes are open. He's looking straight at me. I smile the biggest smile ever.

"Hey handsome, how are you feeling?" I can't help the tears falling, I'm relieved. I see a puzzled look on his face. Oh shit, he doesn't remember me. He hasn't said anything since the day they brought him out of his coma. I'm ecstatic inside that his eyes are open but now I feel fear creeping in. I look over to Nurse Cook, she notices and comes to stand beside me.

"Hey Blaine, do you know who I am?"

He looks at me as if trying really hard to remember, then looks to Nurse Cook. He searches my eyes, I see it as soon as he recognizes me.

"My angel, Primrose," he whispers, he sounds hoarse. I can't help the beam on my face as I pour him some water, putting the straw to his mouth to see if he can sip it. He sips.

"Oh Blaine, my baby. You've scared the life out of me. Do you remember what happened?"

He sips again then looks at me. "No, where am I?"

"You're in the hospital, baby."

He closes his eyes as if trying to remember but he goes back to sleep. I turn and smile at Nurse Cook as she checks his vitals.

"Did you hear him? He spoke to me."

She looks at me and nods, smiling.

He drifts in and out of sleep all afternoon. He doesn't speak, except to say my name, but then sleeps again. The doctors came in to do more tests. They're pleased with his progress which makes me happy. I don't want to go, I don't want him to wake and realize I'm not there again, but I have to go. They said they will be moving him out of ICU tomorrow, which is great news. Once he wakes more and we see if he has his memory and all other sensors are checked, they said they will be able to start physical therapy to get him mobile again. I cry on the way home, I'm so relieved. I told them he would be staying with me when he's released so there is no problem with him being looked after.

I spend the next few days talking to him. He stays awake for longer periods now. He doesn't have much memory, but the doctor said not to worry, he could get it back at any time but to be prepared that it may never come back. The fact he remembered me is a blessing, but he has, on the odd occasion, called me Poppy in a panic when he's woken up suddenly. Only once he realized it was me by searching my eyes did he relax. I find that a little odd, but don't question him. His brain could be playing all kinds of tricks on him.

It doesn't take long, in fact only two weeks, and he's ready to be discharged. The doctor came to see me while I was with Blaine before the discharge, he said he wanted to speak to us both. He asked for Blaine's permission to speak about his health in front of me, he agreed.

"Blaine, as you know when we have been doing tests on you some of the results were, let's say, very puzzling to us. You told us you haven't been in any pain and you haven't needed any painkillers. Can I have your permission to try something on you?"

Blaine looks to me worriedly.

"It's up to you, Blaine, you don't have to. If you would rather I leave, then I can."

"No, stay, baby. I need you here. Okay, doc, what is it you want to try."

The doctor goes to the end of Blaine's bed and he gets out a little tool that looks like a pen and does something to his foot with the pen. Blaine doesn't flinch. He then comes up to Blaine and takes his arm and he runs the pen up his arm. Blaine again doesn't flinch. I can see the mark on his arm where the pen was.

"Did you feel anything I just did, Blaine?"

He shakes his head no, but then hangs his head as though in shame.

"I didn't think you would. I'm going to try something else." He takes out a little gadget that has a needle on it and he pricks Blaine's finger. Nothing, no reaction at all.

"Doc, I don't feel anything. I never have, I remember that much. Ever since I was a little boy, I have never felt pain. I'm a retard, doc. My mama always used to tell me I wasn't normal, that I was a freak of nature."

I have tears in my eyes from what he just confessed. I look to the doctor who is shaking his head.

"Blaine, I can assure you that you are not mentally disabled or a freak of nature, just because you don't feel pain. You have a rare condition called Congenital Insensitivity to Pain or CIP for short."

I look confused, as does Blaine.

"You mean there's an actual name for what I have? That it's an actual medical condition?"

The doctor nods at him, I see tears in Blaine's eyes. They start to run down his cheeks.

"After twenty-seven fucking years, I find out it's a medical condition. It's not that I'm not normal, or a freak. She told me I was the Devil's child. If only she took me to the doctors back then, I would have known." He hangs his head and breaks down.

"Look, Blaine, I have only ever come across this twice before you, which is how I recognized it in you. I can see you have multiple scars and you've had multiple broken bones. We did X-rays which showed a lot of deformed joints, you have a few fractures on you now. This is probably from you falling down recently. I recognized the signs immediately. There are a lot of doctors out there that wouldn't know about this condition. You're the oldest case I've seen, and you're an incredibly fit man, which is maybe why you are this age now."

I look concerned, as does Blaine.

"A lot of people with this condition don't survive into their twenties, Blaine. Not because it kills you, but because from being young they end up so deformed and have no idea about danger because they don't know what pain is, they end up hurting and even killing themselves by accident."

Oh, well thank god Blaine isn't in the majority then. I see the look on Blaine's face.

"I think I remember from an early age, I knew the signs. I knew when my mama would hit me I didn't feel anything, I used to laugh because she got so frustrated. Or if I fell and broke a leg or arm or cut myself. We became experts at fixing me, because I didn't feel pain, she could just put my bones back in place and splint them. Or she would sew up any cuts. I also kept myself physically fit from doing work for my mama."

"It's good you remember all that Blaine. It shows you haven't lost all your memory."

He nods at the doc. "I try to remember events but I struggle. I can't seem to remember actual things that happened. It's all jumbled up."

The doctor tells him that's normal. It may come back.

I'm relieved we know about his condition now, it's something I can watch for if he gets hurt. It also explains all the scars on his body hidden under his tattoos. He was always embarrassed and wouldn't talk to me about them.

I think we will be fine, I think we were meant to be, we are two not normal people in a not normal world. Whatever normal is, I don't think anyone knows, I don't think normal exists.

Epilogue

Blaine

You have no idea how fucking relieved I am, I have a medical condition, it's not just me being a freak. All my life I thought I was strange, a freak, as Mama used to say, when all along it's been a rare condition. If I'd have known from being young, I don't think I would have been so fascinated by pain, wondering all these years why I couldn't feel anything when everyone else could. Apparently, it affects my nervous system which is why I don't feel anything, and having sex is completely different because it has nothing to do with the nerves in my body. Primrose read up on the condition. I'm glad she was there when I found out. They released me that day and we headed home, yes home, to her house which is where I now live and have done so for over twelve months.

I don't have all my memory back. Well, at least as far as Primrose or anyone else is concerned, but I remember every-fucking-thing. I remember it was Poppy that hit me over the head with the wood, it had to be that which caused the brain bleed, that fucking bitch. It's a good thing she's dead and buried or I'd have to do that now, although I vowed I wouldn't hurt anyone again.

I kept having flashbacks to being in the hospital, hearing Poppy. One time I opened my eyes and it was her standing over me, sneering at me. But she looked okay. Her hair was down and hanging over her face. To be honest, I wasn't sure if it was Poppy or Primrose. I couldn't focus on her eyes or much of anything. But to be looking at me the way she was, that I could see, with such hate, I thought it had to be her, even though I knew she was dead and buried. I closed my eyes quickly. It was my brain play-ing tricks on me, it had to be, but I swear I heard her whisper in my ear 'payback will be a bitch' that she would get her revenge. I opened my eyes and Primrose was standing there looking down at me with such hope and admiration on her face, she started to cry. According to her, that was the first time I had opened my eyes. I was confused and must have looked it, but I swear to this day, it was Poppy standing there the first time I opened my eyes. I put it down to my brain injury and her being the last person I remember seeing.

My rehabilitation was slow, a lot to do with me telling the thera-pists to fuck off because no one ever told me what to do, not since my mama died. One refused to work with me unless I changed my attitude. Primrose had to come to those sessions with me to make sure I kept my cool. None of what I had to do hurt, obviously, but my brain wasn't tell-ing my legs and arms to move how they should. I was told it would get better. It has but I still struggle, sometimes, even now with coordination. Especially when I'm making love to Primrose, everything goes out of the window then. We get in such a mess at times, we laugh.

She brings such joy to my otherwise very dark existence. I love her more than I've loved anything in my life. God help anyone that wrongs her, they have me to deal with. Cassy, comes around to see us a lot, she's great. I sometimes regret ever causing this family the heartache I did all those years ago. But I think everything happens for a reason, if I hadn't have done what I did then, my life would either be over by now or I would be in a very dark place, because I wouldn't have ever met Primrose. She's my fucking angel, my light in this dark world, she's also my fiancée. Yeah that's right, me who would never even dream of getting married. We were making love, nice and slow, one morning and we were staring into each other's eyes as we did. I love taking it slow with her.

I looked at her. "Baby, I'm going to marry you."

She stilled, right in the middle of it and she cried. I had no idea what was wrong. "Blaine, I love you and I would love to marry you."

That was it, we bought a ring and we're going to get married. We ha-ven't planned anything yet. Oh and the nice slow lovemaking we were in the middle off, well, that turned into a heated, rampant session. She loves the dirty side too.

No one has ever mentioned Poppy. I think they're all glad she isn't around and Primrose vowed never to mention her or let anyone talk about her again after the attack. She will never forgive Poppy for leaving her for dead. I just keep the secret that Poppy is rotting in hell.

I'm at a class with Primrose. I'm learning to sign, so we can talk to each other that way also. She taught me how to read and write properly and she showed me how to use a laptop and the internet. Wow, the fucking internet is sorcery, so much of everything at your fingertips. What a world we live in. I confessed about stalking her on Facebook, both of us deleted our accounts, we didn't need it. Having each other is enough. We're just finishing class and are on our way out, heading to a little café to get something to eat. We do this after each class, we sit outside and watch the world go by.

I get a funny feeling as we walk to our café, Primrose's arm linked with mine, I've had it a few times just lately. It's hard to describe, it's like there is always someone there, as if I'm being watched. I always look around whenever I get the feeling, I never see anything or anyone unusual. This time I look around and see the back of a figure just disappearing out of view as they turn down another street. I stop and turn in that direction.

"Hey Blaine, what is it?"

I turn back to Primrose and shrug. "Nothing, I just had a feeling and thought I saw someone."

We get to the café. I sit at the table outside, facing the window of the café, while Primrose goes in and gets us some coffee. I watch her through the window and I think to myself how fucking lucky I am, how the fuck did I turn my life around from what it was? I suddenly notice a figure reflected in the glass. A small figure that looks too fucking familiar to me, because through that window I can see Primrose, and by her side, the reflection is the image of her, except the clothes are different. How the fuck can it be her? I stand and turn quickly, I look to the sidewalk across the street. Is this my brain playing tricks on me?

She's standing there. What the fuck. She sneers at me. That fucking bitch. I go to make a dash for her. A bus cuts me off from crossing the street, blaring its horn at me. I jump back, luckily it misses me. I wait for it to pass which is only seconds. Once it moves, I start to run over, dodging the cars as I go. She's gone. I look up and down the street and there's nothing. Not a sign of her or a figure anywhere. How the fuck could she disappear that quick? I know it was her. I'm positive she was standing there. It has to be my mind playing tricks on me. She's dead. She couldn't have been standing there watching us. It's not possible. I stand with my back to the café, confused, I rub my hand over my head to the scar on my scalp.

"Blaine, Blaine, what are you doing over there?"

I turn to look at Primrose across the street. She's standing by the table holding a tray with our coffee. She looks concerned. Suddenly I see her, the fucking bitch. She's walking up to Primrose. My eyes go wide as Primrose starts to put the tray on the table.

"Primrose, get out of the way. Primrose," I scream at her.

It's no use, she isn't looking at me to see what I'm saying.

Poppy looks out of place, she's in a hoodie with the hood up, sunglasses covering her eyes, and jeans even though it's hot as hell out today. I'm running back in their direction to get to Primrose, trying to dodge the cars again, but it's too late. I watch as Primrose goes down, knocking her head on the table as she does and blood spewing from her mouth. Poppy has run off down the street.

I'm crouched down on the ground next to Primrose. I see blood, so much blood, she's not moving, I look to see if she's breathing. People are starting to gather, I hear sirens. I suddenly look up. I feel her there. I spot her right away standing farther down the street. She's too far away for me to see her face. I want to run to her. I want to kill that fucking bitch right where she stands. The urge to run is strong but there is no way on this earth I will leave Primrose, my angel.

Fuck, I scream in my head. I look down to Prim, then I look back up to that psycho bitch Poppy, and I watch her hands move as she signs to me,

"Revenge will be sweet."

The End

Reviews

I really hope that you enjoyed this story. Reviews are lovely! Honestly, they are! And they also help other people to make an informed decision before buying this book.

I would really appreciate it if you took a few seconds to do just that. Thank you!

Amazon

Goodreads

BookBub

Lynda Throsby Xx

Books by
LYNDA THROSBY

Catfish
A dark, gritty, romantic thriller (this book contains graphic scenes)
for 18+ only

The Best Day Of My Life
A sweet, single dad of twins romance.

Chef
A semi-dark romantic thriller.

A Christmas Wish
A sweet fairytale novella set around Christmas time

More about Lynda

Lynda lives in Cheshire in the UK with her husband Peter and cat Bailey also with two grown-up daughters and has a twelve-year-old granddaughter and a ten-month-old granddaughter

She runs a successful financial business with her husband.

As a young teenager, Lynda used to read horror books with a love for everything Stephen King and James Herbert. She has always wanted to write and even wrote horror stories at age thirteen.

A little later she started reading Jackie Collins and Jilly Cooper and has always had a love of books. This then exploded with Twilight and Fifty Shades of Grey. Oh, and the introduction of e-readers.

In her spare time, she has a season ticket for Manchester City Football Club and goes to all the home games. She loves going to concerts and the theatre. She goes to the cinema at least once a week. When the weather is nice, you can see her gliding down the road on her Harley Davidson 1200T motorbike. Travelling is also high on the agenda, and her dream is to visit every state in the USA.

Acknowledgments

I wouldn't have done this without the help and support I got from friends and family.

First to my husband, who made time for me to write by running our business and the continued support he gives me, encouraging me to carry on.

Stuart Reardon my second bestie again for being on my cover, and for the cover images.

Thank you to ellie from My Brother's Editor—for editing and formatting my words, you have no idea what your words meant during this process.

Thank you to Rosa from My Brother's Editor for proofreading my words, such a huge help.

My family and friends who read the books and give me feedback.

Sybil Wilson from Pop Kitty for the amazing cover as usual.

Thank you to everyone who supports me and reads my words.

Printed in Great Britain
by Amazon